UNEARTHED

JC RYAN

BOOKS

By JC Ryan

Rex Dalton K9 Thrillers

The Fulcrum

The Power of Three

Unchained

Sideswiped

The Inca Con

The French Girl

Duty of Care

Donna Teresa

Under the Pope's Windows

The Shanghai Strain

The Delphi Technique

Holes in the Wall

The Abyss

Unearthed

Remorseless

The Message

If you can read this, thank a teacher.

—Harry S. Truman

*Dedicated to my high school English teacher, Mr. Herman Steyn.
The Japanese say, "Better than a thousand days of diligent study is
one day with a great teacher." It was only many years after school that
I realized what a great teacher you were and what a hard time you
must have had to teach me.
Someone once said, "Teaching is the greatest act of optimism."
Mr. Steyn, I can only thank you for your optimism and hope that you
will enjoy this book more than you did my English essays forty-seven
years ago.*

Vinci Books

vinci-books.com

Published by Vinci Books Ltd in 2025

1

Author's Note

I was born and bred in Namibia, so I don't apologize if I come across as biased—Namibia is an amazing country.

The bits and pieces of background information about Namibia the reader will encounter throughout the story do not tell everything there is to know about the country. Admittedly, a narration of Namibia's history can never be complete without recounting the conflicts and wars and accompanying atrocities, checkering the country's history from its earliest days. I only mentioned those in passing merely because more details would not have contributed much to the story.

Major characters

Rex Dalton: Former black operations specialist working for CRC. Married to Catia née Romano, former Mossad mission support specialist.

Digger: A black Dutch Shepherd. Former military dog. Rex and Catia's companion.

Josh Farley: Black operations specialist working for CRC. Married to Marissa, black operations specialist working for CRC. Friends of Rex, Catia, and Digger.

John Brandt: CEO of CRC (Crisis Response Consultancy), a private military contractor specializing in black operations on behalf of their clients such as the CIA and other US security agencies.

Christelle Brandt née Proll: Former deputy director of the DGSE, the French equivalent of the American CIA. Married to John Brandt.

Greg Wade: Team leader of CRC's small but highly skilled group of IT specialists engaged to Rehka Gyan, an IT expert from India.

Howard Lawrence: Director of the CIA.

Martin Richardson: Deputy director in charge of CIA operations.

Justus Aruseb: President of Namibia.

Erwin Krige: Fourth generation German-Namibian, a geologist with four small mining operations in Namibia, married to Mieke, nature photographer and painter. They love the Namib Desert, where they live a nomadic lifestyle.

Thea Naudé: The daughter of Erwin and Mieke, a geologist like her father and owner of a lapidary business. Married to Pieter Naudé, a farmer. They live on the Krige family farm, Eldorado, in the Khomas Hochland Mountains west of Windhoek, the capital of Namibia.

General Quan Zhelan: A former general in the People's Liberation Army (PLA), now a billionaire and CEO of Sino-Africa Development Corporation pursuing commercial opportunities of Africa's natural resources—mostly in the illegal wildlife trade.

Tian Chao: Works at the Chinese embassy in Windhoek. Posing as a junior attaché of trade and commerce but is an MSS agent and PLA officer. His real boss, the man he fears, is General Quan Zhelan.

Andreas Nakanyala: Tian Chao's enforcer. An egotistical maniac who fancies himself as the commander of a mercenary force.

Jackson Kaura: The Namibian Minister of Natural Resources and Energy.

Simon Nuusiku: The Commissioner of Mining in charge of the Mines Directorate at the Ministry of Natural Resources and Energy. The nephew of Jackson Kaura.

About Unearthed

A geologist makes an astounding discovery—the world's biggest deposit of rare-earth elements—in the remote Republic of Namibia on the west coast of Southern Africa.

But China controls ninety-seven percent of the planet's rare-earths and uses it to hold the world's electronics industry at ransom. If they discover this new find, they will go to war to maintain their monopoly.

The CIA sends a team of black ops specialists under the command of Rex Dalton, accompanied by Digger, his special forces dog, to ensure China doesn't get their hands on the mine.

Though Rex and the team try to keep the discovery a secret, it's too late to keep the Chinese from finding out. Soon, Rex and Digger are in a race against time to keep the USA and China from starting World War III and destroying the small, fledgling nation of Namibia in the process.

Prologue

The sun was setting after another perfect day on Eldorado, the Krige family farm in the Khomas Hochland Mountains west of Windhoek, the capital of Namibia. A tiny smile was playing on Thea Naudé's beautiful face as she hummed along with the tunes of *Jonathan Livingston Seagull*. Neil Diamond was her parents' favorite singer of all time.

Thea inherited her love of rocks from her dad, Erwin Krige. From her mother, Mieke, she got her stunning looks and creative talent. She had a four-year bachelor's degree in geology from Stellenbosch University in South Africa and a three-year diploma in jewelry design from the Ruth Prowse School of Art in Cape Town. She was twenty-five when she finished her studies and returned to Namibia in 2015. Like her parents, she couldn't live in a city; she settled on the family farm and started a lapidary business. In 2018, she married her college sweetheart, the young neighboring farmer Pieter Naudé, and they'd decided to live on Eldorado. Pieter was two years older than her. His parents and only sibling had died in a tragic motor accident two years before. After they got married, they turned Eldorado and Pieter's farm into one big game farm.

Part of Thea's gemstone operation was a small laboratory equipped with leading technology using scanning electron microscopy and X-ray techniques with which she could perform thousands of analyzes per minute.

The reason for the smile was the machines had confirmed that her dad's instincts and basic field tests were spot-on—as they always were—when he quoted a slightly adapted version of Mark Twain's immortal words in a mimicked Texas drawl, "There's silver in them thar hills."

It was a significant discovery. Not one that would crash the price of silver on the world market, but enough for a small mining operation to turn a nice profit for five to ten years. Her dad had four small mining operations, producing semi-precious gemstones, copper, African blue sodalite, and marble in various locations in the Namib Desert. It had made him a rich man and provided work for more than a hundred and twenty people. This silver mine would double that income.

But she knew all too well how often prospectors would look for one mineral and stumble across something totally different and more valuable. Or, as she was about to find out, more perilous.

She stopped humming, blinked a few times, and shook her head. "Impossible," she whispered. The smile was gone. She added a few more conditions to the report generator and ran the query again.

A few seconds later, she stared at the report. "It can't be. There's something wrong with the software. Or the scanner. This means I'll have to run all the tests again."

But before she did, she retrieved two bags of old samples from another site from the storeroom, conducted a few tests, and compared the results with the original reports generated six months ago. "A hundred percent match. Absolutely nothing wrong with the scanner or the software."

She went to the farmhouse, found her husband in front of the TV, and dragged him to the lab. On the way, Pieter told her their dogs, Tom and Jerry, probably knew more about geology than he did.

"I don't need another geologist. I need someone to check my sanity."

Pieter had a degree in agriculture; he knew about animals and plants, and biology, and genetics, and book-keeping, and such. Geology? Not so much. He listened carefully as she stepped him through the tests she had conducted and the results they produced. He found no fault in her logic or procedures. And the equipment was functioning correctly—she'd already proved that.

It was approaching ten p.m. when Pieter pronounced, "It's with great confidence that I can say, very much to my relief, you haven't lost your sanity."

"But Pieter, this goes against everything that I've ever learned about rare-earth elements."

"Why? Did you not expect to find any in the samples? I understand the name rare-earth is a misnomer; they're not really scarce. Or am I mistaken?"

"Yes, the rare in the name is because rare-earth elements, REEs, although ubiquitous, are extremely difficult and expensive to extract. I expected to see REEs in the samples because we often associate them with igneous rocks derived from carbonate-rich magmas, in other words, volcanic rocks like these. But this... this..."

"What?"

"There are seventeen rare-earth elements—some of them are available in quantities as common as chromium, nickel, tungsten, and lead. Even the scarcest of them, thulium and lutetium, are nearly two hundred times more common than gold. But we rarely find REEs in economically exploitable concentrations. China has a world monopoly and produces about ninety percent of all REEs on earth. Well... up till now... it seems."

"What does *that* mean?"

"These samples contain all seventeen rare-earths and in concentrations of a magnitude I've never seen, read, heard, or even dreamed possible."

"So, why do you look like one who saw a ghost? Is this not exciting news?"

"Pieter, REEs are to the electronics industry what oil is to the automotive industry."

"And China would stop at nothing to protect their monopoly?"

"Exactly."

"We need to talk to your dad."

"Absolutely. I'll let him and Mom know we'll be over for breakfast."

Chapter One

TAKE ME TO NAMIBIA—MY SOUL NEEDS TO BREATHE

Erongo Mountains, near Karibib, Namibia

From Eldorado to the Krige campsite in the Erongo mountains was about a ninety-minute drive. Erwin and Mieke were having their first cup of coffee, savoring the sunrise, when Kaiser stood and looked down the two-tracked dirt road. The characteristic ridge of hair on his back, running in the opposite direction from the rest of his coat, stood on end.

Once known as the African Lion Hound, the pedigreed Rhodesian Ridgeback was more native to southern Africa than Erwin was. Kaiser could trace his forebears back to the hunting and guarding dogs of the Khoekhoen or Khoikhoi people, a.k.a. the Hottentots, the traditional nomadic pastoralist indigenous population roaming southwestern Africa for over two thousand years. Ridgebacks have even, dignified temperaments, devotion, and affection for their masters but are reserved with strangers.

Erwin's great-grandfather arrived in Namibia in 1885, a

year after the German chancellor Otto von Bismarck established Deutsch-Südwestafrika (German South West Africa) as the first German colony. Over the years, small numbers of Germans immigrated to 'the only German colony suitable for colonization by Europeans.' Among them were traders, diamond miners, colonial officials, and soldiers known in Germany as *Schutztruppe*. In 1885, Heinrich Krige, Erwin's great grandfather, arrived as one of a contingent of *Schutztruppe*.

Heinrich Krige served in the wars with the indigenous Nama and Herero tribes. His grandfather, Karsten Krige, took part in the First World War when Germany lost all its colonies. Namibia was placed under the administration of South Africa. During World War Two, as a preventative measure, the South African government interned both Erwin's father and grandfather to keep them from joining the Nazis.

During the *Grensoorlog* (Border War), Namibia's War of Independence (1966 to 1989), his father served in the Kommandos, a general term used for special police and military forces in German, Dutch, and Afrikaans speaking countries. Erwin served in the same war as an infantryman for two years after finishing school in 1974 as part of his compulsory military service.

"Don't worry, Kaiser," said Erwin, scratching the dog's back. "It's Thea and Pieter."

Erwin was a sixty-five-year-old tall, sinewy, suntanned man with silver-gray hair and a face reminiscent of his rugged surroundings. His easygoing manner concealed an inner strength.

Erwin was about ten years old when he met his first love —rocks. It hit him in the heart like Cupid's arrow as he watched his father slice a geode (hollow rock). The light fell on the cluster of six-sided purple crystals inside the hollow for the first time in five million years. Amethyst. The crystals which ancient Greeks and Egyptians believed helped the wearers to control evil thoughts, kept them sober, warded off guilty and fearful feelings, and protected them from witchcraft.

He was in love. He scoured the hills and mountains on Eldorado and further afield in search of more rocks. Before long, he had his own basic lapidary equipment and started cutting, polishing, and engraving gemstones. In his quest for more knowledge about rocks, he enrolled for a four-year bachelor's degree in geology at Stellenbosch University near Cape Town, South Africa, in 1977, after completing his military service.

When he graduated cum laude at the end of 1980, he had learned enough to know how little he knew. Not only about rocks, but also about life and the people with whom he shared the planet. That was his answer to one of his professors, who asked him about his plans for the future, hoping he could steer the brilliant student to enroll for a doctorate.

The elderly scholar had nodded thoughtfully. "That, Mr. Krige, is the beginning of wisdom."

That was also when he realized he possessed what the Germans call the wanderlust—the yearning for far-off places, the opposite of homesickness.

He sold part of his gem collection, packed his rucksack, and flew to Auckland, New Zealand. Those were the days when he could buy one US dollar with seventy-five South African cents.

For nearly seven years, in search of the meaning of life and that far-off place, he worked on dairy farms in New Zealand, sheep stations, fruit farms, and mines in Australia's

Outback. He taught English to Taiwanese, Chinese, and Japanese. He waited tables, worked on cattle, alpaca, fruit, and wheat farms across the USA, Canada, and Europe, and drove heavy trucks in Alaska. He worked in gold mines, coal mines, copper mines, and salt mines, and he traveled through South America, Europe, and the Middle East.

On September 1, 1987, the first day of spring in the southern hemisphere, he got another visit from the Roman god of love, Cupid, on Italy's Amalfi Coast. Her name was Mieke Opperman; she was almost as tall as he was. She had dark hair and deep brown eyes. She was more beautiful, colorful, and vibrant than any precious or semi-precious stone he had ever laid eyes on. Like him, she had been born and bred in Namibia. She was six years his junior, a nature photographer and painter on her OE (Overseas Experience) *au pairing* in Germany, France, and Italy to still *her* wanderlust. But above all, they were of a kindred spirit. Three months later, they were married.

And then, about a month after their wedding, while trying to make a new year's resolution on the first day of January 1988, a little over seven years after leaving Stellenbosch University, he discovered the far-off place he had been looking for. It was the country of his birth all along. He just had to see all the other places in the world to realize it.

"Take me to Namibia; my soul needs to breathe," he said to Mieke.

She had thrown her arms around his neck and whispered, "I thought you'd never ask."

Erwin's parents were still living on the farm when he and Mieke returned. Erwin loved the farm, but not farming. He and Mieke got a Mining Claims license, bought a Toyota Landcruiser and a caravan, and headed for the

Spitzkoppe in the Namib Desert, 150 kilometers east from Swakopmund.

The license is available only to Namibian citizens for small-scale mining. It is valid for an initial three-year period and multiple two-year extensions, provided the claim is being developed. They could hold a maximum of ten claims at a time.

Although Erwin grew up as a Christian, it was more out of tradition than belief. The deep-seated belief in God came on June 4, 1989. It happened in a single instant when he held the tiny, rumple-faced, dark-haired bundle of life in his callused hands for the first time. Tears were welling in his eyes when he said, "Let's call her Thea, the Greek word for a gift from God."

Erwin Krige often proclaimed himself to be one of the richest men on earth. His wealth had nothing to do with the number of digits in his bank balance, although that would definitely have placed him in the well-to-do bracket in any country. His wealth came from discovering the secret of eternal contentment—love of God, love of his wife and daughter, and doing what he loved in the country that he loved.

He found humanity's perpetual quest for proof of the existence of God amusing. "You'll find the answer in Namibia," he would've told them if they asked.

Chapter Two

WHERE TO FIND THE 'UNFIND' BUTTON

Erongo Mountains, Namibia

The camp was on the bank of a dry riverbed. The large mobile home stood under a massive two-hundred-year-old *kameeldoring* tree, often translated into English as camel thorn, giraffe thorn, or Acacia erioloba—the scientific name no one ever used. The hardy, drought-resistant, and frost-resistant trees the Namibians sing about in their *'Südwester-lied'* can grow up to twenty meters tall and live for up to 240 years.

Erwin and Mieke were happy and excited to see their children. And, of course, Kaiser was ecstatic to have his pack together again.

After they'd loaded their plates with food, filled their mugs with coffee, and Erwin had said grace, Mieke had an almost imperceptible smile on her face. "Now then, my dear, why don't you tell us the exciting news?"

Thea immediately sensed what that brief smile was about. "Aww, Mom, if only it was about that."

"About what?" Erwin asked.

"A grandchild, Dad."

"Oh... So, you're not..."

Thea was shaking her head, and her dad stopped talking. It was obvious her parents had been hoping the reason for the visit was to tell them a grandchild was on the way.

"Thea, your mother and I decided last night; you're old enough now to be let in on the secret—it's not really the stork that delivers babies, you've got to—"

"Dad!"

Pieter was laughing so much he almost choked on his food. When he finally recovered from the coughing fit, he turned to Thea. "I told you the storks are on strike. We've got to make alternative arrangements."

When the jocularity subsided, Thea changed the subject. "So, Dad, any last-minute adjustments to your estimate before I give you the report?"

"Oh, you've completed the tests? That was quick." He took a long, contemplative sip of his coffee and said, "I stand by my estimate."

"One day, you'll have to teach me how you do it, Dad. You were spot-on." She handed him the first report containing only the data about the silver deposit.

Erwin donned his reading glasses and studied the report while the rest continued talking and eating. When he finished, he poured more coffee and said, "I guess I need to fill out the paperwork to get a claim registered. But where's the rest of the report?"

She handed it to him. He studied it for a few minutes, stared at her for a long while, opened his mouth to say something, and closed it again. Eventually, he whispered, "Is this for real?"

"Yes, Dad. And I checked the equipment against old

samples. It's functioning correctly. I did the tests on your samples twice; the results are the same. You've struck the motherlode of rare-earth elements."

Erwin was shaking his head slowly as he tried to come to grips with the enormity of the discovery—and the implications.

"I did a bit of research last night. The total worldwide reserves of REEs are about hundred and twenty million metric tons," said Thea. "On average, one hundred and fifty tons of mineral-bearing rock produce one ton of REEs. So, how much rock is in that mountain of yours?" She opened an Excel spreadsheet on her laptop while talking.

"Five billion cubic meters at three metric tons per cubic meter."

She entered the figures. "That's fifteen billion tons of mineral-bearing rock, which should produce one hundred million tons of REEs. That's in terms of known world standards. However, in your mountain, the concentration is two to three times more than the richest deposits anywhere in the world."

"So, we're looking at between two and three hundred million tons?" said Erwin.

Thea nodded. "More than double the current world reserves—"

Erwin closed his eyes.

"At sixteen hundred US dollars per ton, we're looking at—"

"A three hundred-billion-dollar mountain," said Erwin as he leaned back in his chair and whistled softly.

"Namibia's GDP is a little over twelve billion US per year," said Pieter. "This mountain can support the entire country for twenty-odd years. Thea told me the global consumption is around two hundred and forty thousand metric tons per year. In other words, you can supply the entire planet with REEs for the next hundred years or more."

"China will go to war over this," said Erwin. "They've been holding the world hostage with their monopoly on REEs and will do anything to protect and maintain their strategic advantage. Especially so with the trade war going on. And, of course, the rising animosity against them as more and more people suspect COVID-19 came from the Wuhan Institute of Virology."

Thea added, "China controls the price and availability of rare-earths. About ten years ago, the prices on the world market spiked dramatically when they cut their exports of REEs. That sparked a boom for rare-earth mining projects worldwide. But as soon as mines started production, China dropped the prices, making those mines unprofitable. A few years ago, they also eliminated export tariffs for rare-earths, leading to a further drop in prices."

"So, they're using REEs as a weapon in the trade war and doing their damnedest to keep everyone else out of the market?" said Mieke.

"Exactly," said Erwin.

"But how do they produce the stuff profitably? It seems no one else can do it," said Pieter.

"Well, they care little about profitability," said Erwin. "It's about strategic value. Instead of exporting the raw REEs to other countries, they built them into their electronics and other products that require them. Thus, they've got control of the world's electronics market. A few years ago, one of their ministers summed it up accurately when he said, 'The Middle East has oil; we have rare-earths.'"

"There's a scary thought," said Mieke.

"Absolutely," said Thea.

"Further to your question about profitability," Erwin continued, "because REEs appear in very low concentrations in nature, it takes a lot of labor and environment-unfriendly processes to collect the stuff. Mining, refining, and recycling REEs have nasty environmental consequences, such as low-level radioactivity in tailings where thorium and uranium are present in the ores. And don't forget the other uglies such as deforestation and contamination of land and water.

"And, as we all know, China will not get nominated for a Nobel prize for its environmental protection efforts anytime soon. It's a lot cheaper for them to not bother about the environment, as their competitors do.

"Last but not least; their labor practices, which, to put it mildly, are horrendous, and that's why their labor costs are considerably less than any of their competitors."

"Let me see if I understand this correctly," said Mieke. "If someone other than China gets control of this mountain, China's domination of the world electronics market could end?"

Thea nodded. "You've got it, Mom."

Pieter spoke softly and measuredly. "That means China has everything to lose if they don't get their hands on this mountain, but the rest of the world also has everything to lose if they do."

"Yep, that's about the size of it," said Erwin. "They'll go to war over it. It's a kind of damned if you do, damned if you don't, situation. Isn't it?"

Mieke had a wry smile on her face. "Erwin, what are the chances that you could put all those samples back where you found them—'unfind' them—you know, like the undo command on a computer?"

Everyone was chuckling. "I suppose I can try, my dear, but then you'll have to show me where to find the 'unfind' button."

"It should be right next to the 'unremember' and 'unsee' buttons."

Chapter Three

LET'S DO IT

Erongo Mountains, Namibia

The gravity of the situation had dawned on them. Four ordinary citizens of a small, isolated, desert country, which few people on the planet even knew existed, were besieged by an ominous premonition that they were about to unleash an international firestorm.

Undoubtedly, the discovery was of such strategic importance, the government would cancel Erwin's license and nationalize the mine if they were to learn about it. The problem was, Namibia didn't have the expertise or the money to extract and refine the REEs on the scale required. They'd have to rely on external investment and expertise, such as China's. And in that, they were unanimous—China must not get its hands on that mountain.

Erwin and Mieke were rich. Pieter and Thea were not struggling financially, either. Still, none of them were influential in any circles in Namibia or anywhere else. Notwithstanding, they understood the country and its people and its politics. They were patriots but not blind to the shortcomings of the land of their birth. Therefore, painfully aware of the pervasive corruption in government circles and the inordinate influence of Chinese politicians and investors in the hallways of power in Namibia, they decided it was prudent not to reveal anything to anyone in government—not yet.

As they discussed their options, they concluded that only one country on earth could handle this—the only country with the means to keep China in check—America.

"I'd imagine that the Americans will jump at the chance to turn the tables on China," said Pieter.

"I'm sure they will," said Erwin. "But we have little time. It's a condition of my license that I must file quarterly reports about my mining activities. I filed one when I started prospecting and one a week or two ago, stating that I am still busy prospecting. The next report is due in twelve weeks. So that's the time we have to get the Americans involved."

"Who in America can we talk to?" asked Pieter.

"Why not start with their ambassador in Windhoek?" asked Mieke.

"Good idea," said Erwin. "But I guess it won't be as easy as turning up at the embassy and telling them we'd like a private word with the ambassador?"

"Hang on," said Thea. "What about that American couple from Texas—Bill and Cheri Armstrong? They were our first customers on Eldorado after we turned it into a game farm and have been returning every year since. He's a senator. He should be able to get us in front of the ambassador, don't you think?"

"That can work," said Pieter. "Congress is in session. He

should be in Washington. Six hours behind us... eight-thirty in the morning their time. Want me to call him?"

"Let's do it," said Erwin.

Pieter took his mobile phone out, found Bill Armstrong's number on his contact list, and dialed. Thus, they started a chain of events that would land their beloved country in the middle of a dogfight between America and China.

Chapter Four

THE HALLMARKS OF A CIA OPERATIONAL MATTER

*Windhoek, Namibia | Washington, D.C., USA |
Langley, Virginia, USA*

Senator Armstrong knew Pieter well enough to recognize he
was serious and must have a good reason he couldn't give
any details over the phone. He had no hesitation in calling
Ambassador Megan Edwards right away.

Ambassador Edwards knew Senator Armstrong well—
he was on the Senate Committee on Foreign Relations who
appointed her in this position. Senator Armstrong used
words and phrases such as trustworthy, salt of the earth, say
what they mean, and mean what they say. He ended with,
"Pieter told me it's of a sensitive and critical nature, I
believe him. I'd appreciate it very much if you'd listen to
Thea and her dad." Ambassador Edwards was happy to
oblige.

Two days later, Erwin and Thea were escorted into
Ambassador Edwards's office at 14 Lossen Street, Windhoek. She welcomed them, offered them something to

drink, and then listened to Erwin's brief explanation. She was no expert on REEs, but she understood enough about its strategic importance to realize the ramifications of Erwin's discovery for Namibia, the USA, and the rest of the world.

Edwards was also well aware of the December 2017 executive order signed by the President of the United States. It stated, *"I, therefore, determine that our nation's undue reliance on critical minerals, in processed or unprocessed form, from foreign adversaries constitutes an unusual and extraordinary threat, which has its source in substantial part outside the United States, to the national security, foreign policy, and economy of the United States. I hereby declare a national emergency to deal with that threat."*

They published a list of thirty-five critical minerals, which the US military, national infrastructure, and economy depended on. The president stressed that America couldn't produce those minerals in processed form in the quantities required.

About REEs, the president said, *"The US imports eighty percent of its rare-earth elements directly from China, with portions of the remainder indirectly sourced from China through other countries. China used aggressive economic practices to strategically flood the global market for rare-earth elements and displace its competitors. Since gaining this advantage, China has exploited its position in the rare-earth elements market by coercing industries that rely on these elements to locate their facilities, intellectual property, and technology in China. For instance, multiple companies were forced to add factory capacity in China after it suspended exports of processed rare-earth elements to Japan in 2010, threatening that country's industrial and defense sectors and disrupting rare-earth elements prices worldwide."*

Ambassador Edwards told Erwin and Thea she'd immediately report to her boss, the Secretary of State, and keep them posted.

Within minutes after they'd left, Edwards was in the embassy's SCIF talking to the Secretary of State over a secured satellite link. A SCIF (Sensitive Compartmented Information Facility) is a secured room where secret meetings can be conducted.

Within an hour after the call with Ambassador Edwards, the Director of the CIA, Howard Lawrence, walked into the office of the Secretary of State in Washington, D.C.

The position of CIA Director had been for many years, and still was, a political appointment by the president. Director Howard Lawrence came from old money, born and raised in Boston, a Yale graduate with a baccalaureate in ancient history. He spoke three languages besides English. And his family contributed generously to the presidential campaigns of their party. Before being appointed as Director of the CIA, he had held ambassadorial positions in Italy, France, Israel, and the UK.

Howard Lawrence understood a lot more about America's REEs dilemma than Ambassador Edwards or the Secretary of State.

Back in his office at Langley, Lawrence summoned Martin Richardson, his deputy director in charge of CIA operations. Richardson was sixty-three. The CIA had recruited him out of the United States Army Special Forces, colloquially known as the Green Berets, in 1986 at age twenty-eight, five years before the official end of the Cold War in 1991. During Richardson's tenure at the CIA, he had seen the Soviet Union dissolved, the rise of Islamic radicalism, and the rapidly emerging threat from the People's Republic of China (PRC).

Richardson and Lawrence had a good working relationship. One of Lawrence's many outstanding traits was his understanding of his own strengths and weaknesses. Right from the outset, he made it clear to his deputy directors that he was the PR person of the CIA and expected them to do the spy stuff. Although he wanted to know what was going on in his department, he always deferred to his deputy directors to lead the way in operational matters.

Erwin Krige's discovery had the hallmarks of a CIA operational matter.

Chapter Five

THEY'RE THE REAL THING

Langley, Virginia, USA | Windhoek, Namibia

Three days after the meeting with Ambassador Edwards in Windhoek, 175 bags, half of Erwin's original samples, were packed into crates and trucked to Hosea Kutako International Airport, Namibia's main international airport, east of the city. The containers were loaded into a private jet's cargo hold, a Bombardier Global 8000, heading across the Atlantic to Washington, D.C. The plane, capable of traveling 7,900 nautical miles at a cruise speed of Mach 0.85, would cover the 6,420 nautical miles in a little over eleven and a half hours.

The jet was one of the CIA's fleet of 'private' jets stationed all over the world, registered in dummy corporations of which the ownership was so obfuscated it would take a lifetime to unravel.

Two days after taking delivery of the samples, Howard Lawrence and Martin Richardson were in a meeting room at CIA headquarters listening to Dr. Liam Collins of the

United States Geological Survey and the president's senior advisor on strategic minerals. He played a leading role in the formulation of the executive order of December 2017.

Lawrence asked him to report his findings. "Director, the problem is whoever you're planning to hoodwink with this will not fall for it unless they're monumentally stupid."

"Why, what's the problem?"

"Sir, the concentration of REEs is way too high. Not even a first-year geology student would believe those results. At the Mountain Pass mine in California, we have REEs-bearing rock—unfortunately, not enough of it, but what we have are the highest concentrations on earth. The samples you gave me have concentrations two to three times higher than what we're getting at Mountain Pass."

"Okay. What if we did not tamper with those samples?"

Collins was shaking his head. "Nothing is impossible, Director, but I'd be hard-pressed to believe there are rocks on God's earth that are as rich in REEs as those samples."

"Says the man who has tested every rock on God's earth," retorted Richardson.

Collins grinned, a little embarrassed, and raised his hands in surrender. "I know there are always results that defy all logic and trends—outliers, but..." He shrugged. "Okay, let's assume it's true. I hope and pray the deposit is big, and it's in America or a friendly country."

"What if this source has fifteen billion tons of REE-bearing rock?" said Richardson.

Collins drew a sharp breath. "Fifteen billion tons!"

Richardson nodded.

"That will produce between two hundred and three hundred million tons of REEs. That's more than double the current known reserves on the entire planet."

Richardson leaned forward. "So, we could tell the

Chinese to shove their REEs, and while we're at it, just to make sure they get the message, show them the middle finger as well?"

Collins chuckled. "Yes, sir, exactly like that."

Lawrence said, "Doctor, as of this moment, you're assigned to Deputy Director Richardson's operations team as scientific advisor. A geologist living in Namibia collected those samples. We have no reason to believe the man is up to devilry, but we need to be sure. So, there's your first job; question him, fly over there, if necessary, find out if this is real or not."

Collins nodded slowly. "I'd suggest we start with a meeting with this guy, primarily to validate his collection methods."

The next morning at nine a.m. in Langley, three p.m. in Namibia, Martin Richardson introduced himself and Dr. Collins as employees of the United States Geological Survey to Erwin and Thea over the secured video link in the US embassy SCIF in Windhoek.

Collins cross-examined them about their qualifications, experience, and methods to collect and analyze the samples. Richardson, the spymaster, watched the two in Windhoek closely, trying to find the slightest signs of deceit. There were none.

Within half an hour, Collins scribbled on his notepad for Richardson, who sat right next to him. "They're the real thing. We couldn't do it better ourselves."

Thus, Namibia's rare-earth mountain had just become an official CIA operation.

White House, Washington, D.C., USA

The president listened quietly as Director Lawrence delivered his report. "Howard, I need no convincing; that mountain can upend the status quo. China must not get its hands on it. Even if it produces a quarter of the REEs you mentioned, we *must* acquire it. Not only in *our* national interest but also for our NATO allies."

"That's what we have in mind, Mr. President."

"Admittedly, my administration, and others before me, stood by idly while China made inroads into Africa. This is our wake-up call," said the president. "Let me know who and what you need. And if anyone is even remotely unwilling to cooperate, let me know. Whatever it takes, Howard, but China cannot get it."

"Thank you, Mr. President. Presuming your approval, we already started on a plan."

"Good. Keep me posted."

Chapter Six

OPERATION SIERRA

CIA headquarters, Langley, Virginia, USA

A computer usually generates the codenames, but humans can create one now and then. For this operation, Martin Richardson had the honor. "Sierra," he said without hesitation. "I always wanted to name an operation, Sierra. Besides, it also means mountain."

"What's the story about the mountain?" asked John Brandt.

"Ever heard of a country called Namibia?"

"Of course, I have. Contrary to you, I tried to stay awake during my geography classes in grade school. During the Cold War, Namibia also came to our attention because the Russians and Chinese stuck their noses into the border war. Did I pass the IQ test?"

John and Martin were old friends and seldom let an opportunity pass to needle each other. All in good spirits, of course. Howard was used to their antics; it didn't bother him. In fact, he enjoyed their humor. Sometimes, it made the stress of his job a little more bearable.

John stood at six-foot-two in his socks. A handsome man with gray hair and hazel eyes, stately comportment, and in excellent shape for someone of seventy-odd years. He was a veteran of the Cold War who left the CIA in 1995. Six years later, in 2001, after the 9/11 attacks, the CIA came knocking on his door, begging him to establish Crisis Response Consultancy (CRC), a private military contractor specializing in black operations on behalf of the CIA and other US security agencies.

About six months ago, Martin had persuaded John to return to the CIA temporarily to run Operation Peregrine. It was a Cold War-like strategy aimed at containing China's expansionist ideals and preventing an all-out war, which, if it eventuated, would undoubtedly see the use of nuclear weapons.

John had handed in his resignation after the last mission against China, which ended in a big win for the USA only a few weeks before. He told Howard and Martin, "Mission accomplished. I'm now officially too old for this stuff. With Ollie Campbell at the helm, Peregrine is in excellent hands. So Christelle and I are going back to the Ranch."

Christelle, a former deputy director of the DGSE, the French equivalent of the American CIA, had worked with John on a few joint missions in their younger days during the Cold War. There was a romantic spark between them back then, but the Atlantic Ocean and work had put an end to it. More than thirty years after their last joint mission, they caught up again. The old flame was rekindled, and two months after Christelle's retirement, she and John got married. Shortly after they'd launched Operation Peregrine, the president had given special permission for Christelle to join the team.

John had a week to go before his notice period ended. Howard and Martin had accepted his resignation, but now they wanted to retract it.

"Well, Martin and I changed our minds," said Howard. "We want you to stay for a little longer to run Operation Sierra."

"You must be desperate if your only choice is a crazy seventy-four-year-old has-been from the Cold War."

Martin grinned. "True; you are crazy, old, and past your best-by date. But you have Chinese experience, and we need Rex Dalton and his team to go to Namibia to collect information."

"Ahh, okay. Why didn't you say so in the beginning? I accept, but only if I can run the operation from the Ranch. Christelle and I have had enough of the city," said John.

"Agreed," said Martin and Howard in chorus.

The Ranch, as they called it, was a twenty-thousand-acre property in Yavapai County, in the western part of Arizona, and had been in the Brandt family for four generations. John had turned it from a cattle farm into CRC's headquarters and training facility. It was a secluded place, pristine and beautiful. The air was clean, the spring water fresh, and the climate perfect. With arrays of solar panels, a few wind generators, and banks of Tesla batteries, the Ranch was self-sufficient in electricity. The homestead comprised three beautifully remodeled homes and two barns converted into offices, a mission control center called the Ops Center, a communications center called the Cyber Room, and a lecture room. There were also three helipads and a landing strip long enough for most small jets to take off and land, including CRC's Dassault Falcon 2000 DX private jet.

"Now, tell me about Operation Sierra."

For the next hour, Howard and Martin told him everything they knew about REEs and the situation in Namibia.

When they finished the discussions, John said, "I suggest we set up a full-day workshop for tomorrow. I'll make sure Rex and company are there. You can arrange with Dr. Collins to brief us about rare-earth elements. We'll also need an analyst to educate us about Namibia. In the meantime, it would be good if you could task a satellite to have a closer look at that mountain and surrounding areas."

Martin nodded. "Will do. See you at nine."

Chapter Seven

HIS MOST VENERATED OPERATORS

CIA headquarters, Langley, Virginia, USA

By 8:00 a.m., John, Christelle, and Cupcake were in the Peregrine ops room having their first coffee of the day while waiting for the Daltons to arrive. Cupcake was a nine-month-old, short-haired, brindle-colored Dutch Shepherd. She was a gift to them from Rex and Catia when John got out of the hospital after brain surgery seven months ago.

John had asked Rex and Catia to come an hour early so that he could give them an overview of the operation before the workshop started. He was pensive as he sipped his espresso—thinking about Rex, Catia, and Digger, his most venerated operators.

A terrorist attack on a Spanish railway station in 2004 killed Rex's parents and two younger siblings. The peaceful young man who'd looked forward to a career in the US Foreign Service was emotionally damaged in that attack. He'd transformed into a brooding, angry man who'd joined the Marines to avenge his losses. John pulled some strings to get Delta Force to take Rex out of the Marines and train him as a Special Forces operator. At the end of his Delta Force training, John recruited him into his black ops outfit, CRC. There they trained him to become one of the world's most lethal assassins—a capacity in which he rained terror, destruction, and death on the enemies of the US for years.

Rex was a polyglot. John had lost count of how many languages he spoke—seven? It could be more. Rex had an almost supernatural ability to learn new languages. A mysterious quirk was he adopted the accents of his language instructors. The only language he spoke with a strange accent was Hebrew, because Catia spoke it with an Italian accent.

When John agreed to run Operation Peregrine for the CIA, it was on condition that Rex would take over as CEO of CRC. Although Rex didn't like the administrative side of things, he did a brilliant job as CEO. John hoped Rex would continue in the role but knew it would be an uphill battle to get him to agree.

Rex met Catia, an Italian Jew, in 2010 when she provided him with part of his European tradecraft training. At the end of Rex's training in Rome, he and Catia, although they didn't say so, knew much more than a tutor-student relationship had developed between them. They got married in May 2016.

Catia was an only child. Terrorists had also killed her parents. A lone assassin, working for the Jihad Council, the military wing of Hezbollah, poisoned them while on holiday in the Caribbean. The official version was they drowned while on a boat trip. It had happened in 2005, the year after Rex's family was killed. Mossad recruited and trained her as a mission support specialist—a *sayan*—the Hebrew word for helper.

John's thoughts had turned to Digger when Cupcake started wagging her tail and looked at the door in anticipation.

"I think Cupcake is telling us the Daltons are here," said Christelle.

Whenever Rex and Catia were out in public, Digger had a "Service Dog" sticker attached to his harness. But the big black Dutch Shepherd wasn't a service dog. It was a ruse Rex had used ever since inheriting the dog from his friend, Trevor Madigan, a former SAS operative from Australia who'd been killed in an ambush in Afghanistan. Digger, an Australian military dog, had been his companion since Trevor asked Rex to take care of him with his dying breath. Rex, mortally scared of dogs ever since one had attacked him when he was a small child, had agreed.

Rex and Digger had a strained relationship while Trevor was still alive. That was mainly because of Rex's fear of dogs, which he told no one about, but Digger sensed it and badgered him about it.

But Rex was a man of his word; he and Digger worked through their issues, and they'd become inseparable mates. Digger had acknowledged him as his alpha in their pack and accepted Catia from the moment he met her. Digger was Rex's best man; he brought their wedding rings in on a dainty white satin cushion balanced on his nose.

Rex never learned to give Digger proper commands, like military dog handlers do. But working as a team on many missions over the years, they had developed a unique communications system between them. Some of Rex's colleagues thought the two spoke some kind of "language" only they understood. The reality was Rex had learned to be very attentive to Digger's behavior at all times.

Cupcake was right; a minute later, Rex, Catia, and

Digger walked into the ops room. Rex was an inch short of six feet, with penetrating dark eyes, black hair, tan skin, the physique of a gymnast, and a stern-looking facial expression. Not movie-star attractive, but certainly a very handsome specimen.

At five-foot-nine, Catia was tall for a woman. She had shoulder-length waves of stunning auburn hair and a scattering of light freckles across her nose, attested to the natural red in her hair. A near-constant dazzling smile lit up her face—she was breathtakingly beautiful. Rex would tell anyone who wanted to listen that her eyes were the color of the Mediterranean, blue at times and aquamarine at others; they changed with her mood and what she wore.

After the greetings, while Rex and Catia were preparing their espressos, Digger stood close by, looking at them, wagging his tail, and licking his lips. Obviously telling them, "Hey, don't forget about me."

Catia laughed, ruffled his ears, and took out a few pieces of beef jerky she always kept in a plastic bag, stuffed it into a kong, and gave it to Digger. It earned her a big, friendly dog-smile.

The kong was an odd-shaped toy, part cylinder, part cone, with indentations that made it look like a hard-plastic snowman. A hole ran through it from top to bottom, which could be stuffed with delicacies such as jerky, peanut butter, and other treats. It was always a joy to see Digger and Cupcake losing all dog-dignity going into a frenzy when they saw their kongs.

Chapter Eight

THE ATTENTION OF CHINA'S MINISTRY OF STATE SECURITY

CIA headquarters, Langley, Virginia, USA

By nine a.m., Martin, John, Christelle, Cupcake, Rex, Catia, Digger, and Dr. Collins were in the ops room. The Namibia specialist would join them later; she had no need to know all the details of the operation.

Martin welcomed everyone and asked Collins to brief them about REEs.

"Rare-earth elements are essential in manufacturing everyday high-technology consumer products and advanced military weapons systems and hardware," Collins started.

"Rare-earth batteries have a greater energy density, better discharge characteristics, and fewer environmental problems upon disposal than any other type of battery. High-strength rare-earth magnets made it possible for components in audio and video equipment, computers, vehicles, communication systems, and military gear to be miniaturized.

"REEs are critical in laser- and precision-guided missile

technology. They're widely used in control systems, disk drive motors installed in aircraft and tanks, satellite communications, and radar and sonar systems. For example, each F-35 Lightning II aircraft requires 920 pounds of rare-earth materials."

"I get the impression our military will be all but useless if they don't have access to this stuff?" said John.

"You're right," said Martin. "That's why we need access to reliable sources; it's key to our national security."

"The thing is," continued Collins, "in the search for clean and renewable energy, as oil, coal, and gas are being sidelined, the demand for REEs is proliferating. Think of wind turbines, lithium batteries, electric vehicles, and such. The market is exploding. Demand will soon exceed supply by forty thousand tons per year. We're in desperate need of alternative sources."

"And until we can get alternative sources, the Chinese Communist Party remains in control of the world's rare-earth market, right?" said John.

"Right," said Collins.

"What a comforting thought," mumbled Christelle sarcastically.

"Doesn't the US produce some REEs of its own?" Catia asked.

"We do," said Collins. "But only a fraction of what we need. The sad part of the story is, until the late 1990s, we held the global monopoly and met domestic demand. But dwindling interest in REEs by the US scientific community, more stringent environmental regulations, and higher labor costs caused us to lose that hegemony. China stepped in and filled the void. Now they supply over ninety-five percent of rare-earth elements to the world and control all but a few mining and processing operations."

"So, we were fast asleep at the wheel?" said John.

"Uh-huh," Collins grunted.

"So here we are," said Martin. "The stage is set for a high-tech arms race between us and China. But we're unable to get enough REEs to build weapons. And if the situation was reversed, would we sell REEs to China knowing full-well they'll use them to build weapons to destroy us?"

"But it's not all sunshine and roses for China," said Collins. "They have to cope with illegal mining, international condemnation about their unsavory labor practices, and enormous pressure to change their extraction methods which are destroying the environment. They're desperate to get other sources and paranoid about protecting their monopoly.

"They have been scouring several African countries for high-grade, high-volume deposits of REEs. These countries include Namibia, South Africa, Kenya, Madagascar, Malawi, Mozambique, Tanzania, Zambia, and Burundi.

"Over the last five years, most of those countries have all but drowned themselves in extraordinary amounts of international debt, which they're unable to repay."

"Let me guess," said Rex, "China is those countries' largest creditor, right?"

"Right," said Collins. "Sixteen percent of the world's direct investment into Africa comes from China. The United States and France contribute about eight percent each."

"And of course, the more the financial situation of those countries deteriorates, the more susceptible they become to China's charms," said Catia.

"Yep," said Martin. "Unlike the US and other countries, China doesn't care much about good governance. As long as they hold some of the country's national assets as collateral, they'll dish out the money. For example, a few years ago, when they helped Zambia out of a financial jam, they took a copper mine as collateral. It could just as well have been a rare-earth mine."

"This find in Namibia will drive them berserk," said John.

"Absolutely," said Rex. "The moment they find out, which is only a matter of time, we'll find ourselves in a major scrap with them."

They would have been alarmed to know that Erwin Krige had already come to the attention of the MSS, China's Ministry of State Security, one of the most brutal intelligence organizations in the world.

Chapter Nine

PLA INCORPORATED

Beijing, China

The 75-year-old Quan Zhelan was reading the monthly reports from his managers in Africa in his opulent study. He owned the magnificent house, surrounded by sprawling gardens, in Chaoyang Park, the wealthiest neighborhood in Beijing. The business venture entrusted to him fifteen years ago was now a multibillion-dollar conglomerate of international companies with disguised registrations, obfuscated shareholding, and ambiguous mission statements. Not to mention highly questionable business practices.

To become rich in China, one had to be a devoted member of the Chinese Communist Party (CCP). That Quan was. A good track record, serious palm-greasing, and incessant bootlicking were also required. He did all of that and finally ticked all the boxes to be a billionaire. The CCP had only ninety-one million members, about 6.5 percent out of the population of 1.4 billion. In 2019, China had 4.4 million millionaires and 621 billionaires. In 2020, amid the

COVID-19 pandemic, China minted 257 new billionaires —five per week on average—taking the total to 878.

In the USA, with a population a quarter the size of China, there were 20.27 million millionaires and 788 billionaires by the end of 2020.

Quan believed in no deity. He learned early in life that all power came from the Party—the Chinese Communist Party. The Party was your life—it took care of you from the cradle to the grave. The Party made you what you were. And in return, like all divinities, expected zealous loyalty. If Quan had a religion, this was it.

His grandfather was a senior officer in Mao Tse Tung's Red Army, the predecessor to the People's Liberation Army (PLA). He was with Mao on the Long March. An eight-thousand-mile strategic retreat by the Red Army of the Communist Party of China to evade the Kuomintang (Chinese Nationalist Party) Army. Only ten percent of those who started the arduous march completed it. The Long March was the beginning of Mao Tse Tung's ascension to power. It sealed the personal prestige of Mao and his supporters as the new leaders of the CCP. They were heroes and appointed to leadership positions and assured of a well-heeled future—they and their offspring.

Quan's grandfather was a Party man and a revered general in the PLA. His father was a Party man and member of the Politburo, the principal policymaking committee of the CCP.

Quan was born into privilege, grew up in Beijing, went to the best schools in China and the prestigious Heidelberg University in Germany. Here he mixed with and befriended the children of other privileged CCP members, party officials, and senior officers. Finishing his studies, he returned to China to become an officer in the PLA, as the CCP had preordained it for him, a child of the privileged class.

The Party's economic policies had lifted China from obscurity to the second most powerful economy in the world in three decades. China's total GDP had grown from a paltry $90 billion in current dollar value in 1980 to over $12 trillion in 2020. The west was smiling; China was on the way to democracy, a new player in the international market. To them, China was the answer to many of their own economic problems caused by expensive labor and over-bearing labor unions. The world had never seen such immense economic growth in such a short time.

The west believed the liberal fiscal policies were proof that China was well and truly on the way to becoming a capitalist state. They were wrong; the Party's only intent was to gain foreign capital, technology, and other resources to modernize China and *strengthen* the Communist Party. Mao's communism didn't exist anymore—it had morphed into socialism with a Chinese flavor—the euphemism for economic policies appearing to be capitalistic and free market-orientated. In reality, it is a totalitarian, top-down structure with rigid rules and social restrictions.

The PLA is the military wing of the Party. The PLA brought the Party to power; it is their job to *keep* them in power. Under the doctrine of "*the Party commands the gun*," the PLA is under the absolute civilian control of the Commu-nist Party.

However, in the 1980s, when China embarked on its economic development program, it shrunk its military and diverted the funds to the economy. As a result, the PLA found itself cash-strapped, unable to modernize and keep up with the armies of other countries. The solution was to generate their own funds. As a result, by the mid-1990s, the PLA had extensive commercial enterprise holdings.

As the PLA became more and more successful in their business endeavors and less dependent on government funding, the Party leaders got more than a little nervous. Worried that the PLA's loyalty to the Party might be relegated to second place, the Party leadership set out to divest the PLA from its non-military business interests. By 2000, the Party leaders announced they had completed the separation of the PLA from its commercial interests. Outsiders were surprised that it happened with so little resistance. But very few people knew it went so smoothly because the transition was a ruse. Although not officially part of the PLA anymore, retired PLA officers now managed these enterprises. No wonder they referred to it as PLA Incorporated.

Quan retired from the PLA as a two-star general at age 60 and was installed by the Party as CEO of the upstart multinational business venture, Sino-Africa Development Corporation, to pursue commercial opportunities of Africa's natural resources.

The algorithm flagged his name

Windhoek, Namibia

Dr. Liam Collins was right when he said China was desperate to get other sources of REEs and paranoid about protecting their monopoly.

Tian Chao worked for the Ministry of State Security (MSS), China's intelligence, security, and secret police agency, responsible for counterintelligence, foreign intelligence, and political security. They have been described as one of the most secretive and brutal intelligence organizations in the world.

Tian received his military training as a Special Forces operator in the PLA's Special Operations Forces unit. There he came to the attention of General Quan Zhelan.

Tian's job was to find natural resources business opportunities in southern Africa for Quan Zhelan's Sino-Africa Development Corporation. He had to keep his eyes and ears open for any news, rumors, gossip, speculation, even conspiracy theories about oil, gas, and rare-earth deposits. Other natural resources as well, but those three were top priority. He had to collect all the information in any manner necessary. Therefore, from time to time, he had to use heavy-handed tactics to abduct, assassinate, bribe, threaten, and bully.

But it was not Tian's informants who brought Krige to his attention; it was the MSS's computer algorithms. Tian was a non-declared, meaning he was posing as an innocuous junior attaché of trade and commerce working in the Chinese embassy at 28 Hebenstreit Street, Ludwigsdorf, Windhoek. In fact, he was an MSS agent and PLA officer. On paper, for administrative purposes, Tian reported to the MSS chief of station in Windhoek, but his real boss, the man he feared, was Quan Zhelan.

During his four years in Windhoek, he'd built up a vast network of informants and collaborators across the country, including police, ex-police, military, ex-military, mercenaries, criminals, government officials, and politicians. Even a few pastors from various denominations.

With the MSS's sophisticated electronic surveillance systems and global human intelligence-gathering capabilities, keeping tabs on mining activities across the globe, even the small mines, was a breeze for them. One of their methods, which worked well, was to bribe or blackmail officials in charge of issuing prospecting and mining licenses. But if that didn't work, they would simply hack into their computer systems to access the data they needed. Or they'd get rough with their targets. Thus, they maintained a database of almost every prospector and concession holder in virtually every country they monitored.

That's how Erwin Krige's name came to be in their mining database. But Krige never warranted more than a passing interest from Tian. Krige was a small-time miner of gemstones, copper, African blue sodalite, and marble. His quarterly reports filed with Namibia's Ministry of Natural Resources and Energy were thorough, honest, and utterly boring.

When it comes to electronic espionage employing sophisticated computer hacking techniques, surveillance cameras, and facial recognition systems, the Chinese MSS is the most prolific in the world. Case in point, one of their secret surveillance cameras outside the American embassy in Windhoek captured Erwin's and Thea's faces when they visited the first time and every time after. The system passed the images on to the facial recognition team in Beijing. They found a match for Erwin's face among the photos in the mining database within the hour.

The computer could not tell them who the woman accompanying Krige was because there was no matching image in their databases. At that stage, the algorithm didn't flag Krige's name; a single visit to the embassy was not out of the ordinary. But when they visited the embassy for the third time, the algorithm flagged his name and alerted Tian.

Chapter Ten

ABOUT NAMIBIA

CIA headquarters, Langley, Virginia, USA

While the attendees helped themselves to lunch, Martin called Jodie Reynolds, the specialist on Namibia, to join them. She arrived a few minutes later. Jodie was about five-foot-six, in her early forties, with strawberry-blonde hair, a little overweight, yet attractive and friendly.

Martin did the introductions and asked her to take over. She had a Google map up on the big screen, zoomed in on southern Africa, showing Namibia on the southwest coast of Africa. The Atlantic Ocean forms its western border. It shares land borders with Zambia and Angola to the north, Botswana to the east, and South Africa to the south and east.

"It's the world's thirty-fourth largest country," said Jodie. "Roughly three times the size of the UK, two-and-a-half times the size of Germany, twice the size of California, and twenty percent bigger than Texas."

"Anyone here who has been to Namibia?"

Everyone was shaking their heads.

"It's on my bucket list," said Rex. He had double major undergraduate degrees in history and linguistics, an MA in political science, and a keen interest in history.

"Care to tell us what you know about the country?" said Jodie.

Rex shrugged. "I've read a bit about it, and it seems it's one of those places one has to experience in person to appreciate. But if my memory serves me correctly, the country's name is derived from the eighty-million-year-old Namib Desert, the oldest desert on the planet. Namib means vast place. It was a former German colony, later governed by South Africa. They had a long war on the border with Angola until they became independent about thirty years ago. I also know of a few Hollywood block-busters that were filmed in the Namib Desert. Oh, and a few years ago, the media all but crucified Donald Trump for mispronouncing the name. Twice. In public."

Jodie smiled and nodded. "I had the most amazing three months of my life when touring through Namibia after I finished college. It's a vast place, as the name suggests. It's dry, sparsely populated, and poor, yet it's the most amazing place I've ever been to."

She handed each of the attendees a neatly bound folder.

"Your folders contain an extract from the CIA's World Factbook. Inside, you'll find information about the demographics, geography, communications, government, economy, and military of 267 US-recognized countries, dependencies, and other areas in the world, including Namibia.

"If you want to, I can give you a quick overview of some interesting stuff?"

"Go for it," said John. "One can never have too much information."

"They found ample evidence to prove human presence as far back as twenty-five thousand BC. Rock paintings dating back to around two thousand BC are not uncommon.

"In more recent times, though, between 1486 and 1497, Portuguese seafarers searching for a sea route to India were the first Europeans to see the west coast of Namibia."

She had a slideshow of photos through which she flipped while telling them about the five-hundred-million-year-old Fish River Canyon in the country's south, the world's second-largest canyon after the Grand Canyon.

And a unique desert plant, the Welwitschia mirabilis.

And the sixty-six-ton iron meteorite, Hoba, discovered in 1920 on a farm in the Otjozondjupa Region of Namibia, the largest single meteorite ever found.

While flipping through wildlife images, she told them that Namibia takes conservation seriously—the first country in Africa to incorporate the protection of the environment into its constitution. A little over 43% of the country is protected, making it the country with the largest percentage of conservation areas globally. The Etosha National Park is one of the world's greatest game reserves and conservation areas.

"Want to see the fastest land animal on the planet? The cheetah. Namibia is home to the world's largest population of free-roaming cheetahs."

She had some spectacular photos of the world's tallest sand dunes in the Namib Desert. "The Atlantic Ocean along the west coast is too cold for people to go surfing. So instead, they go dune boarding or dune surfing. Believe me, it's an exhilarating experience."

She also told them Namibia was a stable multi-party parliamentary democracy and a member-state of the United Nations (UN). Agriculture, tourism, and mining—gem diamonds, uranium, gold, silver, and base metals—formed the basis of its economy.

Although fewer than three percent of the population speaks it as a home language, they instituted English as the sole official language in 1990, when Namibia became independent. German and Afrikaans were official languages before that.

Jodie wore a big smile as she ended with a word of caution. "When in Namibia, neither should thou drink and drive, nor should thou drink and walk—drivers and pedestrians alike can be breathalyzed."

For the next part of her presentation, she handed out another folder containing information about China's activities in Africa, including Namibia, and gave them a summary.

China's relationship with Namibia went back to the early 1960s when they started supporting SWAPO (South-West Africa People's Organization) during the Border war, which eventually led to independence.

The two countries established diplomatic relations on March 22, 1990, one day after founding the Republic of Namibia. However, while the governments of Namibia and China refer to the bilateral relations between them as an "all-weather friendship," the citizenry perceives China's engagement with a lot less enthusiasm. Ranging from reserved to outright suspicion and rejection.

No one really knows how many Chinese are in Namibia; estimates range from 7,000 to 100,000, even 130,000. The issue is, Namibia is a poor country with limited job opportunities. The Chinese, however many there are, are not helping to create new opportunities—they bring in more Chinese to do the work. Rumors abound that China sends prisoners to do hard labor on their projects in African countries.

"There are about one million Chinese in Africa and over ten thousand Chinese-owned corporations," said Jodie.

Martin was nodding.

"The question of what the Chinese corporations are doing in Africa is highly controversial," Jodie continued. "Many believe the answer is simple—to exploit the people and take their resources. The same as the European colonists did during colonial times, except under the Chinese, it's worse. Some say they're slowly but surely turning Africa into a Chinese-controlled continent. Squeezing Africa for everything it has. Catching fish by draining the pond, so to speak.

"Those are not only the views of regular citizens," she continued. "Several African politicians have the same opinion, such as Michael Sata, President of Zambia. In a paper presented to Harvard University in 2007, he stated, *'European colonial exploitation in comparison to Chinese exploitation appears benign because even though the commercial exploitation was just as bad, the colonial agents also invested in social and economic infrastructure services. Chinese investment, on the other hand, is focused on taking out of Africa as much as can be taken out, without any regard to the welfare of the local people.'*

Jodie's next folder contained information about corruption in Namibia.

"While it's true that Namibia has less corruption than other countries in the region, media headlines accusing government officials and politicians of corruption suggest it happens regularly. One of the most prominent corruption cases is the Fishrot scandal," she said. "It's alleged the Icelandic company, Samherji, paid hundreds of millions of Namibian dollars to high-ranking politicians and officials to obtain the country's coveted fishing quota.

"An American-based organization, Trading Economics, keeps accurate corruption information about one hundred and ninety-five countries. The Corruption Perceptions Index (CPI), as they call it, ranks countries and territories based on how corrupt their public sectors are perceived to be. There on the screen are the rankings of those countries."

The least corrupt countries, at the number one spot, were Denmark and New Zealand. Namibia's CPI was 57.

"As a matter of interest," she said, "the USA is at number twenty-five."

Syria was at the bottom at number 179. Namibia's neighbor to the east, Botswana, had a CPI of 35. South Africa, their southern neighbor, was at 69, and their northern neighbors, Zambia and Angola, at 117 and 142, respectively.

"Bribes and irregular payments are often exchanged in return for licenses and public contracts. One in ten firms indicated they expect to give gifts to secure government contracts. They perceived favoritism to affect officials' decisions when awarding contracts. In particular, the granting of licenses for mining and fishing.

"The report makes special mention of the concern about the influx of Chinese businesses. Here's what the report says: *'Chinese frequently do not have to adhere to the same legal provisions as local companies due to alleged corruption and favoritism. Poorly conceived regulations combined with a ballooning public procurement sector led to many instances of procurement fraud.'"*

Jodie concluded her presentation. "And keep in mind, China owns sixty-nine-point-nine, call it seventy percent, of Namibia's external long-term loans."

"In other words, China has Namibia in their pockets," said Rex.

"Yep," said Jodie.

Chapter Eleven

FIRST IMPRESSIONS

Enroute to Namibia

The morning after the workshop in Langley, Rex and his team: Catia, Digger, Josh, and Marissa Farley, boarded a Lufthansa commercial flight for the thirty-three-hour trek from Dulles International Airport in D.C. via Frankfurt to Windhoek. Fortunately, they were traveling in first class. The Daltons and Farleys were best friends.

John Brandt regarded Josh Farley to be nearly as good a special operator as Rex. Standing two inches over six feet, Josh was a pleasant-faced, All-American type with blond hair. He looked slightly older than he was. Rex had trained Josh in hand-to-hand combat and street craft, and, in Rex's words, he was "one tough, lean, mean bastard." Between the two of them, they had more than just a few war stories to tell and the battle scars to show for it—they trusted one another without reservation. Josh was the team's eternal prankster and joker.

Marissa and Josh were married. She looked younger

than she was, making it appear as if she and Josh were of the same age. John described Marissa as the best of CRC's handful of female agents. She was beautiful. Shoulder-length, raven hair and azure eyes suggested French heritage, and her forty-something years gave her an alluring mantle of maturity. She was almost ten years older than Josh, but one would have to see her birth certificate to know that. She was an expert social media analyst and spy and could give good account of herself in a fight. She also spoke two languages besides English—Arabic and French. The latter she had spoken along with English since her childhood, thanks to her French father.

Howard had briefed Ambassador Edwards about Rex and the team's visit, and she had briefed Erwin and Thea. Edwards didn't know, so she couldn't tell them that the visitors were covert ops specialists, nor that they were contracting to the CIA. She did, however, tell them their guests were crisis response consultants on a fact-finding mission. Thea immediately reserved two of the chalets on Eldorado for them. It was the beginning of September, the beginning of the mating season. The farm was closed to hunters and tourists for the next three months.

The team was traveling on tourist visas valid for ninety days. Their passports showed their real names, but they would operate under the legends of stinking-rich New Yorkers. John called them four tree-huggers with more money than brains on a game and bird watching excursion while looking for business opportunities in Namibia's gemstone market.

Digger was in his usual service dog disguise, and that was *his* legend. Rex had the paperwork from doctors and vets to back his story up that he would suffer irreparable psychological damage if the big black dog was not with him at all times. That included traveling in the passenger compartment of public transport with Rex, including planes.

Hosea Kutako International Airport, Namibia

Digger was asleep while the four of them looked out the windows as the plane approached for landing. They had internet available on both flights and lots of time to read up and watch YouTube videos about Namibia to get more information than what was available in Jodie Reynolds's information packs. They were, therefore, not too surprised by the landscape and vegetation they were looking at from above.

"Some of it reminds me of parts of Arizona," said Josh.

"Yeah," said Rex, "and out there to the mountains, it looks a little like Austin, Texas."

By the time the plane had taxied to the one and only terminal at Hosea Kutako International Airport, they had agreed that this was the smallest international airport anyone of them had ever been to. It did not surprise them to learn that the airport often experienced congestion, leading to frustrations among travelers and airport staff alike as they tried to process over one million people per year. Apparently, plans were afoot to expand the facilities.

The airport was built in 1965 and named J.G. Strijdom Airport after one of South Africa's former prime ministers. The name remained in use until 1990 when Namibia became independent, and the name changed to Hosea Kutako, in honor of the former leader of the indigenous Herero people.

Rex, the eternal history student, was the first on the team to come across the information about one of the darkest chapters of Namibian history—the Herero and Nama Genocide. At the United States Holocaust Memorial Museum on the National Mall in Washington, D.C., a bibliography of the genocide is kept. It makes for some sad and disturbing reading.

The genocide, the first of the twentieth century, happened between 1904-1907 when German Schutztruppe was responsible for the deaths of approximately 80,000 of the indigenous Herero and Nama people.

For nearly 114 years, Germany had remained unrepentant about the atrocities of that conflict, refusing to even acknowledge that it took place—let alone make amends. Eventually, on Friday, May 28, 2021, Germany would apologize for its role in the slaughter and undertook to fund projects worth over one billion euros as reparations.

Windhoek, Namibia

The airport and passport control staff were welcoming and helpful. There was no congestion today. The team and their luggage received only cursory inspection before being waved through to the arrivals hall.

Any scrutiny of their luggage would have revealed camping equipment, powerful binoculars, top-of-the-range cameras, various lenses, and other wildlife watchers' paraphernalia. All of it confirmed their claims of being ecotourists and nature lovers. The four mini surveillance helicopters were disassembled, and the components spread among their luggage along with the parts of Digger's tactical harness. They also had an array of other spy gadgets in their luggage, all of it disassembled or disguised and highly unlikely to be recognized as such by anyone without the necessary training. Other than multi-utility Swiss army knives, they had no weapons.

But none of the border control staff was interested in searching the luggage of a group of rich Americans with a dog on a wildlife expedition. They were waved through with big, welcoming smiles and an "enjoy your stay in Namibia."

Pieter and Thea Naudé were waiting for them in the arrival hall. They discarded the formalities during the introductions and greetings. Digger was also made to feel welcome when he sat down and extended his right paw for shakes, as usual.

The ten-seater Toyota Quantum minibus had more than enough room for them. Pieter was the driver, and Thea, in the front passenger seat, the guide. She told them that Windhoek was in the country's central highlands about forty-five kilometers (twenty-eight miles) west of the airport. Eldorado, their farm, was another fifty kilometers (thirty-one miles) west of the city.

Thea stopped Pieter just when he was about to start the engine. She turned to their guests. "Anyone not interested in a cold beer?"

"Never!" they shouted in unison, as if they'd been rehearsing it all the way from the US. Even Digger let out an excited yelp.

Thea retrieved five cans of ice-cold Windhoek Lager from the icebox in the back, handed it to them, and opened one for herself. Pieter got a can of grapetiser, sparkling red grape juice.

While they all took a swig of their beer, Thea explained it was a natural beer, brewed according to the German *Rein-*

heitsgebot, literally meaning "purity commandment." The German Purity Law of 1516 dictated that only certified organic ingredients had to be used in the beer.

All beer aficionados knew it; America's mass-market beers were underwhelming, and that was putting it nicely. One sip of the Windhoek Lager and they all smacked their lips and proclaimed it to be exquisite.

Next, she took out two brown paper bags and gave them to Catia and Marissa. "*Biltong* and *droëwors*," she said.

Seeing the blank stares, she explained, "*Biltong* is something akin to your jerky. *Droëwors* is the Afrikaans word for dried sausage. Some people say it's an acquired taste. So don't worry, we won't be offended if you don't like it."

They tasted the *biltong* and *droëwors*—hesitant at first—but not for long. Thea explained how it was made from game meat or beef and dried by hanging in a cool, dry place—never dried with heat like jerky.

Marissa was the first to realize that nowhere in the process was the meat ever cooked. "So, this stuff is raw dried meat?"

"Y-e-s," Thea said cautiously. "Is that a problem? Apologies, I should've—"

"Don't worry," said Marissa. "I'm already hooked."

"This stuff is addictive," said Josh. "Especially in combination with the beer."

Rex and Catia apparently felt the same; they just kept chewing and nodded in agreement. Digger was too busy begging for more to make any comments.

About twenty minutes later, they got their first glimpse of Windhoek. Thea told them that there were two theories about how the city got its name. Some said it simply derived from the Afrikaans words *wind* and *hoek* (wind and corner). But others said Captain Jonker Afrikaner, a Nama leader, named Windhoek after the Winterhoek Mountains around Tulbagh in South Africa, where his ancestors had lived. The latter theory was probably because the first known mention of Windhoek was in a letter by Jonker Afrikaner dated 12 August 1844.

Windhoek was the social, economic, political, and cultural center of the country. Nearly every Namibian national enterprise, governmental body, educational, and cultural institution had headquarters in the city.

The team's first impressions were that the city was much more modern than they'd expected. The German heritage was immediately noticeable in the architecture of the older buildings, such as the 1890s *Alte Feste* (Old Fortress), a former military headquarters on a hilltop. And the sandstone *Christuskirche* (Christ Church), initially known as the Church of Peace, officially dedicated in October 1910, after the wars between the Germans, Herero, and Nama.

They drove by the Independence Memorial Museum dedicated to the anti-colonial resistance and liberation struggle of Namibia. A North Korean organization had designed and built the museum. The Sam Nujoma Statue flanks the museum (Sam Nujoma was Namibia's first president) and the Genocide Statue (honoring those who died during the Herero and Nama Genocide).

The population of Windhoek numbered 431,000 in 2020, of which two-thirds lived in Katutura, a township north of the city center. It was another of the dark chapters in the country's history. The authorities established Katutura under the apartheid laws of South Africa, which governed the country from 1915 until 1990. The black people who were forcefully moved there named it Katutura, a Herero word meaning *'Where people don't want to live.'* The people protested and started boycotting municipal services when they were told to move. Things got out of hand, and on 10 December 1959, the police opened fire on the protesters, killing eleven and wounding forty-four others.

December 10 is Human Rights Day in Namibia.

On a much more cheerful note, when they drove past the Hage Geingob Stadium, named after the current President of Namibia, Pieter told them that rugby was a popular sport in Namibia. The national team was called the Welwitschias, and they had played in every Rugby World Cup since 1999 but had yet to win one of their world cup games.

After the drive through the city, they headed west to Eldorado with the promise to return for a more extensive tour on another day. As they reached the outskirts of Windhoek, Thea told them that Windhoek was the first city in the world to recycle wastewater and turn it into potable (drinkable) water.

"They've been doing it since 1968," she laughed at the mixed looks of disbelief and disgust on the faces of her guests. "I'm serious."

"It's true," added Pieter. "T2T, Toilet-to-Tap, we call it." No one saw the slight grin on his face.

"Yuck!" shouted Marissa and Catia.

"As long as they're not using it in the beer, I don't care," said Josh. "I'll survive on the beer until I can get normal water."

"Well, Josh, why do you think I don't drink the beer?" Pieter sounded serious.

Thea was giggling when she held her hand up before Josh could reply. "Pieter's just pulling your leg, Josh. It's not like that. It's actually cleaner than any wastewater treatment plant can ever produce. In places like Australia, California, Texas, Singapore, South Africa, Kuwait, Belgium, and the

United Kingdom, they're also reusing treated wastewater for drinking water. Oh, and don't worry, Josh, they use only distilled water in the beer."

Windhoek, Namibia

Mid-afternoon, about the same time the Naudés and their guests were leaving the city, Tian Chao returned to his office after a string of meetings. He checked his email and saw the alert from the MSS's tracking database.

He logged into the system and studied the data and the images. What was the reason for Krige's affair with the US embassy? It could be a lot of things, none of them to do with his mining activities. But Tian knew he would work as a peasant on a pig farm in China's backwater for the rest of his life if it turned out this had something to do with mining, and he hadn't investigated it.

Tian checked the Chief of Station's calendar online, found a fifteen-minute slot early the following morning, and booked it.

He knew the chief had an asset inside the US embassy. But he didn't know who it was, nor in which department the asset worked.

Chapter Twelve

A GUIDED TOUR TO ELDORADO

Khomas Hochland Mountains, Namibia

It was as if they were on a guided tour in a game park as Pieter drove along the gravel road, passing by farms on the way west to Eldorado. He had to slow down or frequently stop as his passengers saw yet another wild animal they'd never seen in real life or even on TV. The warthogs, zebras, ostriches, oryx, kudu, eland, even a few rhinos were obviously used to humans; they didn't even raise their heads when the minibus passed.

About halfway to the farm, going around a curve in the road, was a colossal *kameeldoring* tree beside the road. About one-third of the top of it was covered by what was clearly a nest, the likes of which they'd never seen.

"So far, I have seen no flying dinosaurs," said Josh. "But what else can build a nest like that?"

Pieter was shaking with laughter. He had heard many theories from people who saw those nests for the first time.

But the flying dinosaur hypothesis was a first. He stopped next to the tree.

Everyone got out, and Thea told them. "No dinosaurs, Josh, but two to three hundred or more small birds. *Versamelvoëls* we call them in Afrikaans, Sociable Weavers in English. As you can see, they're about the same size as the weaver birds of North America. You will find them all over the dry parts of southern Africa except in the Namib Desert."

"Amazing," said Catia as she took photos with her cellphone. "It's like a weaver condo block."

"Indeed," said Thea. "Their claim to fame is that they build the largest tree nests of any bird in the world. Some of these nests are over a hundred years old, meaning many generations of the same family lived there. And the nest can weigh more than a thousand kilograms."

"Incredible!" said Marissa.

"And what about other birds? Don't they harass them?" asked Rex.

"They protect their nests by lining the entry with broken grass stems facing forward toward the opening. So, no predator bigger than a social weaver can go in, although snakes can, and if they do, they can cause havoc, as you can imagine."

A few minutes later, they were back on the road.

They had a good chuckle when a troop of baboons ran across the road, and Pieter said they were distant relatives. To which Thea quickly added, "But only from Pieter's side of the family."

Pieter had the Americans screaming with laughter when he told them, "People sometimes call a troop of baboons a congress or parliament of baboons."

Marissa wanted to know about the origins of the farm's name, Eldorado.

Thea explained. "The name Eldorado originated in South America when sixteenth-century Spanish explorers heard fables about a tribe high in the Andes mountains in what is now Colombia. The legend was that the king of this tribe would often cover his body with gold dust and then jump into a nearby lake to wash it off. Thus, they called the city, which they would never find, El Dorado, Spanish for 'gilded one.'"

Rex and company didn't expect to arrive at a place where they'd find a king covered in gold jumping into a lake. Notwithstanding, the place they arrived at was spectacular. Words such as serene, breathtaking, and tranquil scarcely did it justice. The landscapes and glimpses of animals at the riverfront below were scenes they wouldn't easily forget.

A long time ago, an old Brit who'd lived in Kenya for more than three decades told Rex, "Once the dust of Africa gets into your blood, she won't let go. You'll always yearn for her." Standing there, unmoving, quietly taking in the panorama, something stirred deep inside him. He couldn't explain what it was, but now he understood what that old Englishman was talking about.

There were twelve beautifully designed stone chalets under thatched roofs, surrounded by rock faces and large shade trees, on the hills next to the river, giving the occupants uninterrupted views over the river and beyond. Each chalet was equipped with a kitchen, bbq facilities, en suite bathrooms, air conditioning, minibar, and TV.

The Daltons' and Farleys' chalets were about twenty meters apart. Although the fridges and shelves were stocked with food, they would have their meals with their hosts at the farmhouse, about half a kilometer away from the chalets.

They quickly unpacked their stuff, showered, dressed, and then gathered at the Daltons' chalet before heading over to the farmstead. Rex wanted to hear everyone's opinion of the Naudés. The four of them were trained in the art of analyzing people's body language and micro-expressions. It was one of the essential skills of their trade. On more than just a few occasions, the ability to quickly detect deceit in people had kept them alive.

"Any reservations about our hosts?" Rex asked.

"They're honest, God-fearing, patriotic, and whatever other accolades we can bestow on them," said Marissa. "No reservations."

"What Marissa said," added Josh.

"Great. That's precisely how Catia and I feel. Digger is also thrilled with them."

When Trevor Madigan was still alive, he told Rex dogs are the best lie detectors and judges of character on the planet. "Dogs can smell our emotions, all of them," Trevor told Rex. "When humans lie, their body chemistry changes; dogs can smell it. The same when we're sad, excited, nervous, etcetera."

Rex was skeptical, but over the years, he had learned that Trevor was right. Digger was a much better lie detector than any human or machine.

"Okay," said Josh, "Let's check out this *bry* thing they talked about."

Chapter Thirteen

BARBECUE VS. BRAAI

Khomas Hochland Mountains, Namibia

The farmstead comprised the main house and several outbuildings, including Thea's lab and jewelry workshop, staff quarters, sheds, and storage spaces, all with thatched roofs over stone walls. All of it sourced from the farm.

. As they approached the house, two dogs started barking. The next moment, two big, vicious-looking Rottweilers stormed around the corner of the house and stopped about ten paces away, snarling and growling.

Rex and his party stopped in their tracks. Digger's hair stood on end. He growled softly and took a few steps forward, placing himself between his pack and the threat. Rex held onto his leash. "Easy, buddy. We're on their turf. They've got reason to be worried."

Though Digger was a trained military dog and a ferocious fighter, two grown Rottweilers would rip him apart. But there would be no fight. The Rottweilers only acted to protect their pack; the barking and growling were their versions of a friendly but serious warning.

"Tom! Jerry! Stop it! Sit!" That was Pieter. "C'mon, you two. Behave yourselves; they're our guests." The dogs stopped barking and sat down, flipping their eyes anxiously between Pieter and the strangers.

Rex and Pieter introduced the dogs to each other and assured them that everyone had nothing but friendly intentions. It took a little while for the three canines to sniff each other from head to toe and front to back and start wagging their tails. That was the confirmation that the new friendship had been sealed, and Rex could remove Digger's leash.

"Tom and Jerry? Like the cartoon characters?" Rex was amused.

Pieter laughed. "Thea's crazy about that little mouse and his cat; she's got every one of their escapades recorded. I'm worried she might want to name our children after them as well."

Pieter got a playful punch in the arm from his wife. "Ouch!"

Thea steered them to the massive, thatched-roof building that was at least a hundred and fifty square meters, if not more. It was an outdoor dining room, bar, and entertainment area with an enormous fireplace on one side, a bar with a stone counter and marble top, a detached kitchen at the back, and an open-air deck. Standing at the deck rails, looking down at the river, they saw kudu, oryx, zebra, and eland at the waterhole, only fifty meters away.

"Do you hunt them?" asked Catia.

Pieter nodded. "Yes, for our own consumption and from time to time, when the herds become overpopulated, we have to thin them out. But mostly, we sell them at game auctions. We never hunt within three kilometers of the waterholes. The animals know the waterholes are safe for them; that's why they come here."

The wall covered in memorabilia behind the bar counter caught their attention when they went back into the dining area a few minutes later. Ballcaps, hats, warthog tusks, mounted antelope horns, and some stunning nature photos and paintings, the latter signed by MO.

"Who's the artist?" asked Catia.

"My mother, Mieke," said Thea. "Her maiden name was Opperman."

"Stunning."

A cloth embroidered with what looked like the words of a poem or a song caught Rex's attention. He took a few steps closer and saw it was in German. The heading read, *"Das Südwesterlied."*

Thea saw him reading it. "Do you understand German?"

"Yes, my mother was German."

"So is my dad. It's often called the unofficial anthem of the Germans in Namibia. But, over the years, it became popular among most Namibians of European descent."

"Rex, let's hear how good your German is," said Marissa. "What does it say?"

Rex smiled and started reading and translating.

Hart wie Kameldornholz ist unser Land.

Hard as the wood of the camel thorn tree is our land.

Und trocken sind seine Riviere.

And dry are its rivers.

Die Klippen, sie sind von der Sonne verbrannt.

The rocks are scorched by the sun.

Und scheu sind im Busch die Tiere.

And the animals are hiding in the bush.

Refrain:

Und sollte man uns fragen:
And if someone asked us:
Was hält euch denn hier fest?
What is keeping you here?
Wir könnten nur sagen:
We could only say:
Wir lieben Südwest!
We love Southwest!

Rex continued and translated all the verses and got a thunderous round of applause when he finished.

Thea smiled. *"Ich bin beeindruckt, Herr Dalton. Die beste Übersetzung, die ich je von einem Englischsprecher gehört habe."*

"Vielen Dank, Frau Naudé."

"English, please!" shouted Josh.

Rex grinned. "She said you remind her of Pieter's family. You know, those politicians we saw running across the road earlier today."

Thea laughed and held up her hand. "I think Rex's German has taken a turn for the worse. I said I was impressed. It was the best translation I've ever heard from an English speaker."

"Thanks, Thea. With friends like Rex Dalton, I don't need enemies," said Josh through the laughing.

"The words are exceptional," said Catia. "I'd like to hear the song."

"Pieter, Thea, how about it?" asked Marissa.

Thea laughed. "We'll ruin it. Let me rather play it over the Hi-Fi for you." She switched the Hi-Fi on, connected her cellphone via Bluetooth, and selected the song from a playlist.

Rex immediately recognized the melody of the German *panzerlied* from the classic war movie, *The Battle of the Bulge.*

The beat was striking. They were all humming along by the second verse. By the third, all six were singing along.

Digger had a look on his face that could've meant *I'm happy that my pack is so cheerful.* Tom and Jerry were nowhere to be seen.

Soon after, they were all seated in comfortable camping chairs in a semicircle facing the *kameeldoring* wood fire Pieter had started. They were sipping Windhoek Lager, munching on *biltong* and *droëwors*, and talking about Namibia.

Josh couldn't contain his curiosity anymore. "Now, please tell us, what is this *bry* thing you've been talking about?"

Pieter smiled and took a long swig of his beer first. "We spell it b-r-a-a-i. Some people will tell you it's merely the Afrikaans word for barbecue; in my opinion, they're uninformed. But instead of giving you all the reasons I think they don't know what they're talking about, why don't we return to your question when we're done here tonight, and you can give me your verdict?"

"Deal," said Josh.

And as the evening progressed, they kept score of the differences.

Three hours later, Pieter said, "Okay, let's hear the jury's verdict. Is a barbecue the same as a *braai*?"

Josh said, "Your honor, let me be succinct; calling this a barbecue is tantamount to blasphemy."

Rex chimed in, "And so say all of us, your honor." Catia and Marissa applauded. Digger couldn't make his opinion known because he had fallen asleep when he couldn't eat anymore—two hours ago.

It started when Pieter lit the wood fire. There is just no comparison between lighting a wood fire after stacking the wood in just the right way and pushing a button on a gas barbecue after removing the plastic cover.

Then came the eland steaks and *boerewors* and *braaibrood* grilled over it. For starters, none of them had even heard of eland T-Bone steaks, let alone *boerewors* and *braaibrood*.

Boerewors, directly translated, was farmer's sausage. But the Afrikaans word had been adopted by all languages and cultures in Namibia and South Africa, even as far afield as Australia and New Zealand. Everywhere those delicacies could be found, it went by the name *boerewors*. Various recipes existed; some families had secret ingredients, but usually, it was made from pure beef or lamb, pork, and spices. The latter gave it a unique but exquisite and unforgettable taste.

But *boerewors* tasted good even if barbecued on gas or in a pan on the stove, Thea told them.

Braaibrood, directly translated, would be barbecued bread or toasted sandwich. But once they tasted what difference a wood fire made to a sandwich made with cheese, tomato, and onion, they agreed that a toasted sandwich was definitely not the same as *braaibrood*.

There were no differences between the salads served at a *braai* and a barbecue. The *melktert* directly translated as milk tart (almost but not quite the same as custard pie) and maroela liqueur with their coffee were all a first for the Americans but were not unique to a *braai*.

So, they concluded, it was not so much the uniqueness of the food and the exquisite taste coming from the wood fire; it was the combination of the food, the atmosphere, the companionship, the conversations, the humor, and... well... it was most definitely not the same thing as a barbecue.

They concluded that the English language would be

enriched by including the words *biltong, droëwors, braai, boere-wors*, and *braaibrood*.

As they walked back to their chalets shortly before midnight, Catia started humming the Südwesterlied, and soon the rest of them joined in.

The next morning, they were all up at sunrise, drinking coffee and watching the animals at the waterhole. Pieter and Thea arrived shortly after to pick them up to visit the Kriges at their camp in the Erongo Mountains near Karibib.

Thus far, they had not talked about Erwin Krige's discovery or the team's mission—that was the purpose of today's visit.

Chapter Fourteen

THE MSS CHIEF OF STATION

Windhoek, Namibia

About an hour after they'd left Eldorado, Tian arrived at the office of Zhong Yang, the MSS's chief of station in Windhoek.

Zhong was a declared, meaning he didn't work undercover like Tian did. Therefore, Zhong could interact openly with his counterparts at the Namibia Central Intelligence Service and officials of various government departments and foreign embassies in Namibia. If a declared agent got caught in the act of espionage, they would lose diplomatic immunity, be proclaimed persona non grata, and get kicked out of the country. A non-declared caught spying would be arrested and put in jail, in some countries executed.

"Sir, this might be nothing," Tian started after Zhong had asked him to take a seat, "but until we've checked it, we can't be sure." He explained that Erwin Krige was on the MSS's mining watch list and the alert he'd received about

Krige's and an unknown woman's recent spate of visits to the US embassy.

The chief listened, started shaking his head, then stopped and said, "A wild goose chase if you ask me. But just in case there's something to it, leave it with me. I'll see what I can find out."

Tian was happy with that; it was precisely what he hoped Zhong would say. The ball was in the chief's court.

Tian's information was only half-right; Zhong had an asset inside the US embassy, but he didn't have direct access to the asset. He had to go through a third party, his asset in the Canadian consulate, codenamed Snowmouse, real name, Sara Bishop. She had been working for the MSS for the past three years.

Zhong's predecessor recruited her. So he didn't know all the details, and he didn't care; Bishop did good work. She was not a spy in the sense that she stole her country's secrets and handed them over to the Chinese. She had never given Zhong any sensitive information about Canada, and he didn't expect her to do so. Her job was to recruit and handle informants on behalf of Zhong because he couldn't do it himself lest he got caught and deported. It was a win-win arrangement; Zhong avoided the risk of being compromised, and Bishop earned obscene amounts of money on the side.

Zhong and Bishop took great care never to be seen in each other's company. In the old days, before the internet and mobile phones, they would've used dead letter boxes, also known as dead drops. These days, chat applications similar to Skype, WhatsApp, Messenger, and such, were used. Except that the app they were using was secured with end-to-end encryption operating over an impenetrable virtual private network (VPN).

Five minutes after Tian had left Zhong's office, Sara Bishop received her instructions and went to work on it immediately.

Her text message to James Blake at the US embassy read: "Hey stranger, how about lunch today or tomorrow? You pick the place. I'll pick up the tab."

Ten minutes later, Blake replied: "Great. 12:30 today. Joe's Beerhouse, 160 Nelson Mandela Ave."

She replied with a thumbs-up and smiley-face emoticons.

Under the *kameeldoring* tree

Erongo Mountains, Namibia

As they approached the campsite, Rex said to Digger, "Listen, buddy, we're about to meet new people. I want you to be on your best behavior, okay?"

Digger made no reply. His tongue was lolling out and his lips drawn back at the corners—the canine version of a smile. As if to say, "When have I ever embarrassed you?"

"Yeah, I know, but there's always a first time for everything."

Digger yapped once.

"No need to take that tone with me," replied Rex.

Pieter had slowed the minibus down to a near-crawl. Thea had turned in the front seat, staring at Rex and Digger. Pieter's eyes flipped between the rearview mirror and Thea, trying to figure out if Rex was joking or if he and Digger really had a conversation.

Digger whined softly.

"Okay. Sorry. I won't insult you again," said Rex.

Digger licked Rex in the face once and whined softly again. As if to say, "Apology accepted. Don't worry about it; I know how to behave." But it could've been that he was just excited.

"Okay, now one more thing," said Rex. "There's a gentleman there by the name of Kaiser. Be nice to him. It's his home and his pack, so don't make him nervous, okay?"

Digger yelped.

"Thanks, buddy. I knew you'd understand."

Josh saw the gobsmacked looks on Pieter's and Thea's faces. He laughed. "Don't mind them; they talk to each other. Digger thinks he's human, and Rex thinks he's a dog or something like that. Nobody knows how they do it, but they understand each other. You'll see, when we get there, Kaiser and Digger will be like old friends."

Pieter and Thea smiled, highly skeptical. But their doubts disappeared when they got to the campsite and saw it was as if Kaiser were expecting his old friend Digger. Precisely how Josh said it would be. There was no growling or raised hair, only friendly sniffing and tails wagging excitedly, the canine version of a hug and a "Welcome. I've heard so much about you; it's a pleasure to meet you. Nice place you've got here."

Following the dogs' greetings were the human greetings and introductions. And, as the day before at the airport, formalities were ditched right away.

A breakfast of freshly baked pot bread, bacon, eggs, and *boerewors*—a meat lover's banquet otherwise known as a vegetarian's nightmare—awaited them on arrival.

When Josh saw the food, he whispered to Rex, "If the bad guys don't kill us, the cholesterol will."

Rex suppressed the urge to laugh out loud.

Two hours later, the breakfast a pleasant memory, they were in camping chairs in the shade of the two-century-old *kameeldoring* tree with mugs of coffee in hand. Mieke was doing the rounds with a plate stacked with what she called *koeksisters*. It looked like a plaited doughnut, deep-fried and soaked in syrup, and it was cold. It was the sweetest, most delicious confectionery any of the Americans had ever tasted. They couldn't stop until the plate was empty.

By now, Rex and the team were sure that Erwin and Mieke were all those nice things Marissa said about Pieter and Thea—honest, God-fearing, patriotic, and all that. Good people. Trustworthy.

It was time to talk about the reason for their visit to Namibia. Rex typed something on his satellite phone and showed the message on the screen one by one to Erwin, Mieke, Pieter, and Thea. It read: "We would like to talk about the REEs. But are worried about security. Please switch off your phones and remove the batteries."

Understandably, the atmosphere had turned from jovial to sober as they nodded and did as requested.

"Apologies," Rex started. "We're a little paranoid about security."

They assured Rex it was no problem.

"Before we delve into the details," Rex continued, "would you mind telling us what made you decide to contact us? And what are your expectations?"

Rex was recording everything on his satellite phone without their knowledge. He felt like a criminal, but for now, that's how it had to be. Rex's and the others' phones, which they kept out of sight, were CIA-designed encrypted satellite phones—the most secured phones on the planet. In

Langley, John, Christelle, Martin, and Dr. Collins listened to every word.

"Well, the four of us had a long conversation after Thea analyzed the samples," said Erwin. "We know REEs are the oil of the electronics industry. But, unfortunately, as we all know, there are limited quantities, and ninety-plus percent of what's available is in the hands of the Chinese Communist Party. So, this deposit can end their siege, but only if they're prevented from getting to it.

"We believe America is the only country that can stop China from getting it. They'll be able to break their stronghold on REEs, and we hope, obstruct any attempt by China to make Namibia its first African colony."

Rex liked Erwin's no-nonsense, straight-talking manner. He nodded slowly. "Okay, next question. What are your expectations in terms of compensation?"

"Money, you mean?"

"Yes."

Erwin looked taken aback. He raised his right hand and made a circle with his thumb and forefinger. "Nothing. Zilch. This is not about money, Rex; this is about saving our country and its people from the claws of communism. If America doesn't step in here, we might as well start learning Mandarin."

"We agree with you; America is the only country that can stand up to China," said Rex. "And I'm sure you've figured it out; we wouldn't be here if America was not interested in this discovery of yours."

"That's a relief," said Pieter. Thea and her parents nodded in agreement.

"Okay, let's talk about security first. Who on your side knows about this?" asked Rex.

"The four of us and the US ambassador," said Thea.

"What about your workers?" asked Josh.

"My workers helped me collect the samples, and my foreman transported them to the farm. But I have not shown them the test results," said Erwin. "They know we were looking for silver, but I haven't even told *them* we've found a sizable deposit of it."

"The farmworkers only helped me unload the samples and put them in the storeroom. I conducted the tests on my own," said Thea. "So, we're okay on that side too."

"What about your computers?" asked Marissa. "Have you stored any of this information on your computers, and are those computers connected to the internet?"

She didn't have to explain the omnipresent risk of hackers and electronic espionage. One had to have lived under a rock in the Namib Desert for the past two decades to be unaware of it.

"Mieke and I have one laptop. I have stored nothing about this on it," said Erwin. "We switch the laptop off when we don't use it."

"Have you done any REEs research on it?"

"Damn, I didn't think of that—my searches can be tracked. I did quite a bit of Googling since getting the test results."

Marissa turned her gaze to Thea.

"I'm afraid my situation is much worse than Dad's. I've stored the test results on my laptop and on the lab computer. I always switch the lab computer off when not in use. But I've also done extensive online research about REEs on my laptop. We have a permanent internet connection on the farm, so Pieter and my laptops are always on and always connected. However, I brought my laptop along today."

"Okay, for now, until we can conduct a comprehensive

forensics audit on all your computers, don't switch them on," said Marissa.

"You know," said Mieke, "you read and hear about these computer hackers and all the trouble they cause all the time but never spare a moment to think you could be a victim yourself. It's like death and illness; it only happens to other people."

"And believe me, Mieke," said Catia, "the Chinese are the world's foremost cybercriminals. They've got government-sponsored hacker battalions doing nothing but breaking through firewalls and encryptions into computers, stealing intellectual property, sensitive military data, and personal data. They're causing hundreds of billions of dollars of damages to enterprises, governments, and individuals every year."

"Let's hope and pray they haven't been into our computers already," said Pieter.

"Oh, and don't forget the same goes for your mobile phones," said Josh. "That's why Rex asked you to switch them off."

"Have you stored any of this information on your phones or used them for research?" asked Marissa. She got confirmation they hadn't.

"My understanding is," said Pieter, "some governments can, and do, track calls and even record conversations. Is that correct?"

Catia nodded. "Yep. It's called SIGINT, the acronym for signals intelligence. That's what the NSA does in America and the world over. Their equivalent in the UK is the GCHQ. Most countries have similar agencies, and those who don't have their own outsource it to friendly countries with the capabilities to do it."

"Such as China?" asked Erwin.

"Right," said Catia. "I'm not sure if your government is doing it, but I'll be surprised if they're not."

"So, should we assume, at the very least, the Chinese could see that we've been in touch with Senator Bill Armstrong of Texas and the US embassy in Windhoek?" asked Erwin.

"Absolutely," said Josh. "Have you mentioned REEs during any of those conversations?"

Pieter and Erwin took a few seconds to recall the conversations, then confirmed no mention of REEs were made or even alluded to.

"One more thing, as if we haven't scared you enough already," said Marissa. "They can hack into your phones and install software that enables them to follow your movements. They can also listen to all your conversations whether you're on a call or talking to someone face-to-face."

The four were staring at Marissa, slack-jawed.

"Can you check if our phones were compromised?" asked Thea.

"Yes," said Marissa. "Catia and I will check your phones and computers and make them safe."

"How many times have you been to the embassy?" asked Rex.

"Four times in ten days," said Thea. "Why?"

"I'm pretty sure the Chinese are watching who's coming and going at the embassy. Four times in ten days would've garnered some interest from them."

"How would they be able to do that?" Pieter sounded incredulous.

"Secret cameras watching the embassy, or hacking into the embassy's security cameras, or satellite images, or a combination of all three," said Josh.

"How the hell... sorry, how are they able to know who we are?" asked Erwin, clearly perturbed.

"China has the most comprehensive camera surveillance system on the planet, one CCTV camera for every four people in China. They have the most sophisticated facial recognition, artificial intelligence, and digital technologies to augment their vast network of monitoring systems. Eight of the top ten most surveilled cities in the world are in China. They track one-point-four billion people with their facial recognition every day. Believe me, they know how to do it—they're experts."

The Namibians were staring at Josh in stunned silence.

"I was wondering how we're going to keep this away from the Chinese," said Erwin. "With all that technology available to them, it seems there's little we can do to stop them from finding out."

"We could use a bit of deception," said Rex.

"How?" Erwin verbalized the question on everyone's mind.

"Let me answer your question with a question. How much time and money is required to get everything set up to start mining the silver?"

"Ah, I see where you're heading. The paperwork will take half a day or so to complete. Then the approval should take four to six weeks if I don't pay any bribes. I never do, and hopefully, I won't have to start now," said Erwin.

Rex nodded. "Let's do things by the book—as far as possible."

"The mining equipment we need is readily available in Namibia and South Africa. We can get that delivered onsite within a week or two from placing the orders. I'd estimate the cost of the equipment to be no more than half a million US dollars."

"That doesn't sound like much," said Josh.

"Yes, it's relatively cheap. But keep in mind with that equipment, we can only collect the ore, crush, and grind it. But then we must set up a plant that uses various heat and chemical processes to extract the silver. And that's where we'll face a few challenges because we need water and electricity. The latter we can produce with wind and solar, but the outlay will be significant. The water we can't produce. So, the only way will be to transport the ore to a reliable water source. I'd say we need about five to six million US and three to four months to start up."

"What paperwork do you have to file?"

"I have all the information I need. It'll take me a few hours to complete the application. The problem is the test results..."

"Unfortunately, you'll have to falsify them," said Rex.

Erwin nodded slowly. "I know, but I wish I didn't have to. I don't want to drag Thea into it. Is there any way to avoid filing false results?"

"We can wait twelve more weeks," said Thea, "but then you'll *have* to file a report or risk losing the claim."

"That doesn't solve the problem; it only postpones it," said Rex. He would not insult their intelligence by giving them a pep talk about it's-for-the-greater-good and the-end-justifies-the-means. They knew what was at stake.

After a bit of debate, they came up with a plan. They would rerun the tests but configure the machines to ignore REEs and only look for silver and accompanying metals such as copper, zinc, gold, etcetera. So the report would be truthful about the silver deposit but make no mention of REEs. A lie, no less, but much more difficult to prove than outright manipulation of the original results.

A little after midday, Rex asked if Erwin would mind

showing them the site. It was about two kilometers from the camp. They walked.

Kaiser was with Digger, patiently watching and waiting, while Digger examined every bush, tree, and grass stem he encountered on the way. Digger, who was used to being on a leash when outdoors and only ran free when in public parks where it was permitted, was enjoying the unlimited spaces he could explore on his African adventure.

Chapter Fifteen

KNOW YOUR NUMBER

Three months ago. United Nations headquarters, New York, USA

The thirty-four-year-old James Blake was at least forty pounds overweight. His short frame only made it more obvious. His curly dark hair was on the verge of being disheveled, and thick-lens, gold, wireframe glasses distorted his face. Very few people passing him on the street would've given him a second look. But if anyone did, it might have surprised them to learn that this unremarkable man was amiable, single, brilliant, and highly educated. He was a political officer in the US Foreign Service and soon on his way to his first overseas posting at the US embassy in Windhoek, Namibia.

The occasion was a cocktail party for international delegates attending a three-day conference about southern Africa's economic woes.

The young Canadian woman who approached Blake knew all about him. She worked at the Canadian embassy in Windhoek. She was part of the Canadian delegation attending the conference. She was also a spy—for China.

She told Blake her name was Sara Bishop. She didn't have to tell him she was beautiful; his vision was not *that* impaired. The mixture of a British father and a Chinese mother resulted in a smoldering exotic beauty. That she was a spy, she omitted. Blake didn't mention it either—she had her secrets to keep, and he had his. Nonetheless, they quickly found common ground when she told him she worked at the Canadian consulate in Windhoek.

In the espionage business, it is crucial to know your number. It's all about looks—on a scale of one to ten. Ten was drop-dead gorgeous. One was, well, ten times less fortunate than a ten. It was a subjective test, to be sure; after all, beauty is in the eye of the beholder. But if applied with brutal honesty, it could be the most effective defense mechanism against a honey trap—such as Sara Bishop.

James Blake knew he was a two. If he replaced his glasses with contacts, cut his hair, and lost thirty pounds, he could've been a three—perhaps. But Sara Bishop was an eight, leaning toward a nine. In other words, light-years out of his league.

I need information

Windhoek, Namibia

The Merriam-Webster Dictionary defines both espionage and spying as the secret gathering of information on others. But while secretly gathering information on others is part of it, it's also the art of deceit in a world of smoke and mirrors. A world where things are rarely as they seem to be.

Case in point. Three months ago, in New York at the cocktail party, James Blake knew Sara Bishop was a spy, but she didn't know he was a spy, neither did she know he knew she was a spy.

Sara was unsuspecting of James because she wasn't a trained spy. Working in a foreign embassy and having contact with the staff of other embassies, she saw as an ideal opportunity to use her good looks and allure to make good money. She had offered her services to the Chinese, and they jumped at the chance to get her on board mainly because she was smart, beautiful, didn't look Chinese, and she had mislaid her moral compass.

Her little scheme worked well; it was amazing how much information men will divulge to a beautiful woman after they had a few drinks. Things were going so well for so long that she never thought that her cover might have been blown.

As it were, unbeknown to her, a Chinese computer hacker, codenamed Flat Arrow, who worked for China's foremost military hacking outfit, Unit 61398, a subdivision of the People's Liberation Army (PLA), had defected to America eighteen months ago. Rex and his team had helped Flat Arrow and his family escape from China and took them to America, where he was employed by CRC's IT team. Flat Arrow brought with him the names of all the MSS spies operating against America and its allies across the globe. Among those names was the name of Sara Bishop. They decided not to arrest her but used her to feed false information to the Chinese.

Hence, that night in New York, Sara Bishop walked into a carefully laid trap. That James Blake had recently gone through a painful divorce was true. That he had a gambling addiction and had accumulated an obscene amount of debt were lies the CIA had fed to unsuspecting MSS agents.

Once they'd planted the false information, the CIA expected the MSS would use Sara Bishop to recruit James Blake as soon as he arrived in Windhoek.

But then the southern Africa economic workshop in New York came up before James moved to Windhoek. When the CIA learned Sara would attend the conference and the cocktail party, it was too good an opportunity to pass. So, they sent James to attend.

Sara earned ten thousand US dollars for James's "recruitment." The MSS Chief of Station in Windhoek was ecstatic. He paid James's twenty-five thousand-dollar "gambling debt" with a big smile. Having a Political Officer of the US Foreign Service on the MSS's payroll was a significant intelligence coup and would do wonders for his career. Moreover, wherever James Blake was transferred in the future, the MSS would have a spy working for them.

Sara was fifteen minutes late at Joe's Beerhouse. James made no mention of it. He was used to her shenanigans; it was her subtle way of letting him know she was in charge. In the lexicon of spies, she was his handler; that's what she believed. What made James a good spook was his unassuming mannerisms, almost slave-like demeanor, which created the false impression that he was a softy, a pushover.

"Hello, sexy." She grinned like the Cheshire cat when she kissed him on both cheeks.

James knew the game she played all too well and was happy to oblige. "Hey, cutie. How are you? I've missed you."

"So have I." She took the seat opposite him.

James made a show of taking his mobile phone out of his pocket, switching it off, and removing the battery before placing it on the table. Sara did the same. It was an insinuation that nothing would be recorded. Of course, it was a lie. Their relationship was a lie, everything was a lie, but it made Sara feel safe and in control.

James pointed at the glass of white wine in front of her. "I hope you don't mind; I've ordered your favorite—chardonnay. I trust it's still your favorite?"

"You're such a gentleman, James. Thanks." She took a sip. "Perfect. Now tell me, how are you doing? What have you been up to since we last met?"

"Well, for starters, I'm still gainfully employed by the US Foreign Service. But the most exciting thing that happened to me since we last saw each other is this lunch."

Sara laughed out loud. "Flattery will get you everywhere, James."

They enjoyed their food and wine for the next hour and talked about everything except why Sara wanted to see him.

When their coffees arrived, Sara got to the point. "Okay, here's what I need to know. A man by the name of Erwin Krige visited your embassy four times in the past ten days. A young woman accompanied him every time. I want to know everything about them, names, addresses, telephone numbers, family, etcetera. Nothing about them is unimportant. I also want to know who they met on every occasion and about what?"

James nodded impassively. "I'll see what I can do and get back to you ASAP."

"Thanks, James, you're a star." She drank the last of her coffee and said, "I wish I could spend more time with you,"—she winked seductively—"but I have to get back to the office."

"No worries. I must get back as well. Hopefully, we'll

catch up again soon when we have more time." James also winked, but it was nowhere near as alluring as hers.

Back at the embassy, James uploaded the recording of the meeting with Sara, which he had captured on his smartwatch, to the CIA server. Then he went to Laura Murray's office, his Chief of Station, and gave her a verbal report about the meeting. Then they discussed how to address the request for information that they knew came from Zhong Yang over at the Chinese embassy.

Because of the need-to-know principle, James and Laura were wholly unaware of the discovery of the world's biggest deposit of rare-earth elements in the Erongo Mountains less than 150 kilometers from where they were.

Chapter Sixteen

THE MOUNTAIN THAT COULD START A WAR

Erongo Mountains, Namibia

"There it is," said Erwin as the mountain came into view. It was not big, or high, or intimidating. If one has seen the Rocky Mountains, the Alps, the Himalayas, the Hindu Kush Mountains of Afghanistan, and many others like Rex and his team had, this didn't qualify for mountain status.

Until the mid-nineties, the United Kingdom and the United States defined hills as summits less than one thousand feet. They've since abandoned the definition. National Geographic says, *"Hills are easier to climb than mountains. They are less steep and not as high."* Not a very helpful definition either. Nevertheless, Erwin and Thea referred to it as a mountain, so they did the same.

This mountain stood out from the surrounding hills and rocks and outcroppings; it didn't look the same as the others. The vegetation on it was lusher. The rock faces looked different.

"I'm no geologist," said Catia, "but to me, it looks as if

this mountain was formed at a different time or in a different manner than the others in the area."

"You're right," said Thea. "Dad and I reckon it was formed maybe five to ten million years before the others in this area."

"And the plants seem to grow so much better on this mountain than the others," said Catia. "Why would that be?"

"Yeah, I always wondered about that," said Erwin. "Could never figure it out, but now we know—it's the REEs. Scientists have proven they can affect plant growth positively."

"Fascinating," said Catia.

It was surreal to think this nameless mountain in the middle of nowhere could trigger a war.

Erwin led the group over the mountain while he explained how he collected the samples and where he would set up the mining equipment.

It didn't take long for Josh to baptize the site, Mount Krige.

Everyone approved.

When they reached the summit, Erwin stopped and pointed to the north. "About five kilometers that way is another mountain very similar to this one in terms of size, age, and rock formations. I have the prospecting rights to it. My basic field tests showed it has silver. I think it could have it in the same quantities as this one. However, I doubt there would be REEs in the same amounts as here."

"Why do you say that?" asked Rex.

Erwin shrugged. "It's just a gut feeling, and it doesn't have the same lush overgrowth as this one."

"I see," said Rex slowly, preoccupied. He just had a lightbulb moment.

"The plan is to have a closer look just as soon as I get this show on the road," said Erwin.

Rex nodded. He was deep in thought. So much so that Digger must have sensed that his alpha needed his support. He nuzzled Rex's leg as if to say, "I'm here if you need my opinion."

It took a second or two before Rex noticed Digger's presence. He bent down and ruffled his ears. "Thanks, buddy; I'll let you know when I'm ready to talk about it." He turned to Erwin. "Can we have a look at that one tomorrow?"

"Sure, no problem. Also, I kept the samples; it should be easy for Thea to run tests on them and give us a better idea of what's there."

"Great."

They were back at the camp an hour later. Marissa and Catia went to work on the computers and mobile phones, scanning them for vulnerabilities and any signs that they'd been compromised. They were relieved to find no evidence of the latter but a lot of the former. It took them an hour to secure every device and install a chat application on the phones, which they could use to communicate securely with each other. They would secure Pieter's laptop and the internet router when they were back at Eldorado.

Mieke told them they were having a *braai* that evening. So, they were pacing themselves for another enormous meal, sipping slowly on the cold Windhoek Lagers and only nibbling on the *biltong* and *droëwors* while discussing the setup of the mine at Mount Krige.

The plan to start mining for silver as quickly as possible, they believed, would help keep the Chinese out of the picture while the US government negotiated a deal with the Namibian government.

"You won't be lying about the silver. So, I think it would make sense to let your workers know. It fits in with the narrative that you've discovered an economically viable silver deposit and want to mine it," said Rex.

"Yep, that makes sense," said Erwin.

"On that topic," said Josh, "how big is this silver deposit of yours here at Mount Krige? I mean, in terms of world production?"

"Insignificant," said Erwin.

"So, when this mine comes into full production, it won't crash the price of silver on the world market?"

Erwin and Thea laughed. "No, not at all," said Thea.

"How much silver is produced globally every year, and how much is needed?" asked Marissa.

"Currently, around eight hundred million ounces per year. The demand is a hundred million ounces more than that. So, silver is scarce now, and the prices are going up," Erwin replied. "But they will come down again in the next year."

"Who are the top silver producers in the world?" asked Rex.

Erwin held up three fingers. "Mexico, Peru, and China. In that order. Last year Mexico produced about a hundred and ninety million ounces, Peru about a hundred and thirty-five million, and China a little over a hundred and ten million ounces."

"Wait, hang on there," said Josh. "China is in the mix again, and we have shortages. And we all know the communists like to control things. So, what are the chances they're trying to get control of the market like they did with the REEs?"

"There's nothing that stops them from trying," said Erwin. "But there are silver deposits all over the world. It's nineteen times more abundant than gold. The estimated worldwide reserve is around five hundred and sixty thousand metric tons: that's about eighteen billion ounces. The market is growing as they find new uses, such as solar panels, water filtration devices, photographic and X-ray film, and medical instruments. About twenty-five percent of all silver goes into jewelry, thirty percent into coins and bars, and the rest in industrial uses. But as soon as the prices go up, silver mines that were shut down because it was uneconomical to mine will start production again. So, for them to get the monopoly on silver will be a fool's errand, I'd say."

Josh nodded. "So, how big is your deposit?"

"Between one-point-five and one-point-eight million ounces. Over ten years that would be about one hundred and fifty thousand ounces per year—insignificant in the overall scheme of things."

"Ah, okay, now I can relax," said Josh.

"My understanding is silver usually comes with other metals such as zinc, lead, copper, and such. Is that correct?" asked Rex.

"Yes, silver is often associated with quartz or, in tiny amounts, gold, lead, zinc, copper ores, or the sulfides of other metals. Usually, the ratio of silver is much less than the other metals. But sometimes silver, in its pure form, is present in volcanic rocks—such as these mountains where they're in placer deposits—like pockets of silver."

Rex nodded. "I'd also like to suggest you make the discovery public at the right time. Use the media if you can. Tell them it would earn Namibia millions in foreign currency, and it would create new jobs. In addition, you can mention that you've worked with the American embassy to find an investor who can put up the startup capital. In exchange, the investor will get exclusive rights to buy all the silver and byproducts produced."

"Good idea. It will help to explain our visits to the embassy," said Thea.

"Right," said Rex.

"So, who is this investor you're talking about?" asked Erwin.

"That still has to be decided. However, before one or more of them are engaged, it is necessary to let Dr. Liam Collins visit these sites to conduct an independent investigation. I'm told that you and Thea met him in a video conference a week ago. The idea is to bring him over soon if you agree."

"I see no problem with that. He's welcome to stay here with us if he doesn't mind the primitive accommodation," said Erwin and turned to see if Mieke agreed. She was nodding, but it was hesitant.

"I'll pass the message on," said Rex.

When the hills started making long shadows, Erwin invited everyone to join him and Mieke for one of their rituals—a sundowner on the hilltop on the west side of the camp. Mieke put a bottle of whiskey and shot glasses in a backpack, which Erwin shouldered.

Half an hour later, they stood in awed silence, watching, or rather, experiencing, the sun disappearing over the horizon, painting the western sky in stunning shades of amber and blue.

Catia articulated their thoughts when she raised her glass in a toast toward the setting sun. "I could look at this every day for the rest of my life and never tire of it. *Salute!*" The Italian word for cheers.

"Prost!" said the Namibians. The German word for cheers.

"Cheers!" said the three Americans.

Chapter Seventeen

SAMSON, THE PHILISTINES ARE HERE!

Langley, Virginia, USA | Erongo Mountains, Namibia

Before Laura Murray could report to her manager in Langley, the head of the African desk, she had to find the answers to the questions Sara asked James to get. Her manager would want that information before making any decisions. Getting Krige's details was quick and easy. So was getting Thea Naudé's and learning she was Krige's daughter. It was just as easy to find out that Krige and his daughter had all their meetings with the ambassador. But then things became complicated. Ambassador Edwards told Laura that she was not at liberty to divulge what was discussed in those meetings. "But I will contact the Director of the CIA and let you know what he says."

Laura waited in the anteroom outside the ambassador's office. Fifteen minutes later, Ambassador Edwards came out and told her she'd spoken to Director Lawrence. He had passed the matter on to the Deputy Director of Operations, Martin Richardson, who would phone her shortly.

Laura had barely made it to her desk when Martin Richardson's call came through. He asked her to repeat everything she told Ambassador Edwards. Then, when she had finished, he said, "Thanks, Laura, leave it with me. I'll get back to you within the next few hours with instructions. You can let your manager know about our conversation."

"Will do, sir."

Martin phoned John Brandt and asked him to come up to his office.

It was seven-fifteen p.m. in Namibia. Erwin had lit the *kameeldoring* fire just a few minutes before Rex's satellite phone started ringing. It was John Brandt.

"Let me guess," John started without preamble, "you're having or are about to have a barbecue."

"Wrong, we're about to have a *braai*; it's not the same as a barbecue."

"Oh. Okay. Whatever. Listen up, Samson, the Philistines are here."

"Huh. What are you talking about?"

"Ah, didn't pay attention in Sunday school, did you? I have you on speaker. I'm with Martin in his office. Christelle is with us."

"Christelle, Martin, has the Old Man been smoking that green stuff again?"

Martin laughed. "No, we took it off him. He's going through the withdrawal stages now."

By now, Rex and Digger were about a hundred meters away from the campfire. "Okay, I'm out of earshot of everyone; what's up?"

"The Chinese somehow discovered that Krige and his daughter have been to the US embassy in Windhoek four times in the past ten days, and now they want to know why," said John.

"Damn, I was afraid that would happen. How do you know this?"

Martin told him about James Blake and Sara Bishop.

"I see. So, I guess you're thinking of giving Blake some information to pass on to his handler?"

"Yep, and she'll pass it on to Zhong Yang, the MSS chief of station," said John. "So, we want to know if you have any ideas about what information Zhong Yang should get or not?"

"Okay, I'll talk to the others and call you back."

Erongo Mountains, Namibia

Everyone stopped talking and looked at Rex and Digger when they returned to the campfire.

Rex took a sip of his beer while organizing his thoughts. There was no gentle way to break the news. "That was our boss. The Chinese are asking questions. They know you've visited the embassy and want to know who you met and why."

A shocked silence descended. Erwin broke it. "How did they...?"

Rex shrugged. "As Josh said earlier, there's more than one way to find out."

"Or someone inside the embassy could've told them?" said Pieter.

"It's possible, but then I would've expected them to know more. They don't know who Thea is. They don't know who they've met or the reason for the meetings."

"How do they know who Erwin is, but not Thea?" asked Mieke.

"There could be many ways to come by that information," said Rex. "Something as simple as checking who a car is registered to. Or showing a picture around or having him followed or talking to the police..."

Mieke held her hand up. "Okay, I see what you mean."

Erwin had been staring at the fire quietly. Now he looked up at Rex. "How did your boss become aware of this? I'm pretty sure the Chinese ambassador didn't wander over to the US embassy to have a cup of tea with Ambassador Edwards and, while he was there, asked about us."

Rex had a decision to make—quickly. He and his team were playing the roles of fact-finders and advisors. Neither the Kriges nor the Naudés had given indications they didn't believe it. But Rex was sure they probably had some doubts. Nevertheless, did they need to know who he and his team were for the success of the mission?

"I agree with you, Erwin, it would probably not have happened that way, but my boss didn't tell me how they found out. However, he said he plans to feed some information to the Chinese, enough to give credence to the silver mine story. In the meantime, we must continue with the preparations for the start-up of the mine. He said he's happy with our plans."

Pieter started laughing. "You people are CIA, right?"

"We can't confirm or deny that," said Rex with a slight grin. The rest of the team kept poker faces.

"Okay, I can see, unless we hold your feet to that fire, we won't get more out of you," said Erwin, half smiling.

Rex nodded. "But, if you held my feet to the fire, I might have told you I heard a rumor that the CIA has a presence in Namibia and has assets that keep them informed."

Erwin was laughing and shaking his head. "Okay, thanks. I guess that's probably all we need to know for now."

"What do you need from us?" Mieke asked.

"Is there anything you want my boss to include or exclude in the information he sends to the Chinese?" asked Rex.

"When I was twelve, I promised my mother I would never use those words again," said Thea. "So, I've got nothing to say to them."

Erwin, Mieke, and Pieter had the same sentiments as Thea. Rex's teammates had nothing either. Rex asked to be excused for a few minutes to update his boss.

An hour later, Laura Murray received her instructions from Martin Richardson. She booked a meeting with James Blake for the next morning at ten.

At the fire's dying embers, the Namibians showed the Americans the star constellations of the southern hemisphere. Erwin showed them how to tell the time on the Southern Cross. They talked about Namibia and listened to the sounds of jackals, geckos, owls, and other denizens of the desert until the early morning hours.

Chapter Eighteen

TWOHILL AND PHILLIP'S CAVE

Erongo Mountains, Namibia

With Digger and Kaiser accompanying them on the excursion, the ten-seater minibus had no spare room. Pieter was the driver, and Erwin the guide. Mieke had packed a big cool bag with leftover food from the previous night's *braai* and two large, stainless-steel thermos flasks with coffee. She had filled another cool bag with bottles of water and beer kept cold with ice bricks. Their plan was to visit the second hill, make a trip to Phillip's Cave, and then go back to Eldorado for the weekend. They had a lot of work to do.

They arrived at the second hill at sunrise. As Erwin told Rex the day before, this mountain was about the same size as Mount Krige. The vegetation was not markedly different from the surrounding hills and mountains, as it was on Mount Krige. Nevertheless, the rock faces, types of rocks, and shapes made it different from the others. As with Mount Krige, it was apparent it had also been formed in a different epoch of earth's history than the surrounding outcroppings.

By the time Pieter had parked at the foot of the mountain, Josh had named it Twohill. "Sounds much classier than Hill Number Two, don't you think?"

Josh received applause for his originality.

Erwin led them around Twohill, pointing out interesting features and reiterating his thoughts that, in all likelihood, it would prove to hold silver but not rich deposits of REEs.

As they came down from the summit, Rex was walking next to Erwin. "You know, with the Chinese getting nosy, I think it's best not to wait until Mount Krige is in production before prospecting this one. I think we need to know if there are any surprises here as soon as possible."

"Agreed. I'll get it going first thing Monday morning." It was Friday; Erwin's employees never worked over weekends.

Rex had a second reason for wanting to know if Twohill had any REEs, but at this stage, it was only the foggiest of notions, so he made no mention of it. Starting on Monday was soon enough for him. As Erwin had told them around the campfire the night before, when they talked about the rhythm of life in the desert, "In these parts of the world, there's nothing worthwhile that can't wait a few days."

Before piling back into the minibus for the trip to Phillip's Cave, less than ten kilometers away, they had coffee, leftover *braaibrood*, and *boerewors*, which tasted delicious, even cold. Of course, it also thrilled Digger and Kaiser to again partake of last night's feast.

On the way to Phillip's Cave, Erwin explained that the many rock paintings in the Erongo Mountains proved humans inhabited this area thousands of years ago. Thanks to impermeable granite pans filled during the rainy season, the Erongo Mountains offered a reliable water supply to humans and animals alike during the dry winter months. During those months, the ancient humans lived in the caves and crevices and hunted the animals.

Phillip's Cave was a national monument, fifteen meters deep, thirty-five meters long, and seven meters high. Stone tools that were found there and the rock paintings of giraffes, rhinos, ostriches, springbuck, kudus, and six imprints of human hands date back to 3500 BC. The most famous painting was the White Elephant, into which a small red antelope had been drawn probably long after the original painting.

Getting instructions

US embassy, Windhoek, Namibia

James arrived at Laura's office at the scheduled time. She told him about the runaround she got the previous day, eventually leading to the telephone conversations with Martin Richardson and his instructions.

"So, what do you think is really going on here, Laura?"

"Well, as I told you, Martin Richardson said Krige discovered a commercially viable deposit of silver and wants to bring in an American investor."

"I see. And you believe that to be one hundred percent accurate?"

"Officially, yes. I am expected to listen to my superiors. So are you." Laura had an almost imperceptible grin.

"And unofficially?"

104

"I don't believe the information is exact. Something is missing or twisted."

"Uh-huh. They have trained us in the art of lying. So, we know a good lie is one that's mostly true. Here, all I can think of that can be lied about is what Krige discovered. Is it silver, or is it something else? Or maybe it's the quantity? Everything else, such as their personal details, can easily be verified."

"Well, the information you're supposed to give your 'girl-friend' is that it's a small but profitable silver deposit."

"And that's what's bothering me. If it's so small, why involve our director in it? Why Ambassador Edwards? Why not the attaché of Trade and Commerce?"

"It's obvious there's more to it than they think we need to know, James. Just make sure you convince that floozy that's the truth, lest the Chinese wonder about the same thing as us."

"Yes, boss. There's one thing that still troubles me, though; how did they know Erwin Krige's name but not his daughter's?"

"You know as well as I do, they could've found out in several ways, including asking someone. But, for now, the most important thing is to give them the information as soon as possible and hope they stop asking questions."

Twenty minutes later, James and Sara had made a dinner date for seven that evening at the Windhoek Hilton.

Chapter Nineteen

BACK AT ELDORADO

Khomas Hochland Mountains, Namibia

After visiting Phillip's cave, they returned to the Kriges' camp, packed their stuff, and returned to Eldorado. Erwin, Mieke, and Kaiser followed them in their own vehicle an hour later.

Thea and Erwin had to reconfigure the testing equipment to run new tests on the samples so that Erwin could use the results for his application. But before they could do that, they wanted to run tests on the few samples Erwin collected from Twohill months ago. Of course, they knew the samples were not representative of the entire hill. Still, it would give them an early indication of what to expect.

Mieke, Pieter, Rex, and Josh helped them with the preparations and testing.

In the meantime, Catia and Marissa worked to secure Pieter's laptop and the farm's internet connection the same as they did with the Kriges'. When they'd completed the initial security checks and updates, Catia phoned Greg Wade on her secured satellite phone.

Greg was the head of CRC's IT team on the Ranch. His team was a small but highly skilled group of IT specialists. Essentially, they were computer hackers, among the best in the business. With a few keystrokes, they could create havoc, blackout a city, take control of its traffic lights, enter government and corporate databases, access the bank records of any individual and organization, penetrate firewalls, break encryption, and much more.

"Catia, if a lion is about to have you for dinner, I'm not the guy who can help you," answered Greg.

Catia laughed. "Then Marissa and I'll have to take our chances and see if we can outrun the lion to the nearest tree."

"You know you don't have to be quicker than the lion; you only have to be quicker than Marissa?"

The bantering over, Catia and Marissa explained to Greg what steps they took to secure the Kriges' and Naudés' communications.

"Not too bad," said Greg. "Okay, give me remote access to their devices to check them and install the latest security patches. After that, I'll add all their devices to our e-watchdog's list to send me alerts if anyone tries to gain access. You okay with that?"

"Absolutely," said Marissa.

"Go for it," said Catia.

Two hours later, Greg told them everything was configured and secured.

With that out of the way, Catia and Marissa found Mieke and offered to help her prepare dinner. Erwin and the rest were preparing to run the first tests on the Twohill samples.

Just when dinner was ready, Erwin and the rest arrived at the main house.

"What's the verdict?" asked Mieke.

"There's silver, okay. But no REEs. Well, there is, but in negligible quantities. Definitely not worth mining. The silver yield seems to be on the same level as Mount Krige. But we can't be sure until we can test a much bigger sample size."

After a scrumptious dinner of game stew cooked in beer in a big cast-iron pot, freshly baked bread, and fresh salads grown on the farm, everyone agreed they had too many late nights over the last few days and headed for bed.

It can wait

Windhoek, Namibia

Sara Bishop's reply said she would be delighted to have dinner with James. He was not stupid enough to believe it. He didn't know how much she got paid for the information she gave her Chinese handler, but he was sure she wouldn't do it for free. She'd betray her own mother for money in a heartbeat.

As always, James played his role brilliantly—the subservient civil servant with a gambling problem, divorced and lonely, all too eager to please his vampish handler and be rewarded with a frolic between the sheets with her.

The lengthy text message from Snowmouse arrived on Zhong Yang's phone at 2:11 a.m. Saturday. He only saw it at eight-fifteen a.m., after he had breakfast. He didn't analyze the information. He had more important things to take care of than worry about a small-time geologist digging up a few ounces of silver somewhere in the desert. He reread the message and decided it could wait until Monday morning.

On Eldorado, everyone was up early on Saturday morning. After another of those meat-lovers breakfasts, they all helped Thea retest the samples from Mount Krige while Erwin filled out his application to the Ministry of Natural Resources and Energy.

By midafternoon it was all done; Erwin attached the test results to the application, put it all in an envelope, and gave it to Thea.

On Monday, the Naudés would go to Windhoek to lodge Erwin's application with the Ministry of Natural Resources and Energy. After that, there was nothing more for Rex and the team to do but wait for the application to be processed. In the meantime, Erwin would collect the samples from Twohill, and Thea would test them. They would also start preparing to kick off operations at Mount Krige as soon as the permit had been granted.

Over dinner that night, they spent most of the time talking about exciting places to visit in Namibia and worked out the details of a few trips Rex and his team could go on. They would accompany Pieter and Thea to Windhoek on Monday to explore Windhoek. Overnight at the Hilton, rent a vehicle the following day, and go on a ten-day tour of the Skeleton Coast and surrounding areas.

On their return from the Skeleton coast excursion, they would stay on Eldorado a few days before making a longer trip which would take them to the Etosha National Park in the northwest of Namibia and up to the border of Angola and from there to the east into the Caprivi on the border with Zambia and Botswana.

Being eternal optimists, they hoped everything would work out as planned. Still, the four Americans had been covert operations specialists for long enough to know things rarely turned out exactly as planned.

After dinner, Rex and the team assembled in the Daltons' chalet. Catia used her satellite phone and laptop to make a secured video call to John and Martin in Langley.

Martin started after the greetings. "James Blake met with his handler last night and passed on the information we gave him. Zhong Yang should have it by now. Let's hope that will be the end of Chinese curiosity."

Rex gave them an update of their activities of the past few days and told them about their plans to make a few sightseeing trips around the country while waiting for Erwin to collect samples from Twohill and for the mining permit to be issued.

"It seems to me it's a good time to send Dr. Collins over," said John. "His presence will confirm the story Blake told Zhong's spy last night."

"Agreed," said Rex. "Make the arrangements and let us know when to expect him."

The call ended a few minutes later. The four of them had a nightcap before going to bed.

On Sunday morning, Thea and Pieter took them in the minibus on a sightseeing tour of the farm. Thea was the driver and Pieter the guide.

He told them they didn't keep rhinos on the farm as it would be an open invitation to poachers working for international crime syndicates trading in prohibited wildlife products, including rhino horn. He had enough trouble with poachers, as it were. They hunted the game for the meat, which they sold directly to people in the city. Sometimes they supplied it to established meat processors and butchers who 'laundered' it through existing channels.

Pieter's workers spent their days patrolling the farm on horseback and quad bikes, looking for poachers and their snares. Some weeks they'd scare off as many as five prospective poachers and destroy up to fifty snares. But sometimes, they were too late. He showed them some photos of animals caught in the wire snares—it was at once nauseating, heartbreaking, and infuriating to see animals strangled or starved to death.

By lunchtime, they'd seen zebra, eland, springbok, kudu, oryx, steenbok, baboons, warthogs, even a few bat-ear foxes —more wildlife species than they'd be able to remember the names of the next day. Thea pulled up under a large *kameeldoring* tree. "One of our favorite picnic spots," she said.

"And if we're in luck, we might even get a visit from one of the most fascinating creatures on earth," added Pieter.

Of course, that immediately elicited questions about what it was, but it was obvious the Naudés had conspired to keep them guessing.

Fortunately, it didn't take long for their much-anticipated mystery guest to make a grand entry. Digger saw or sensed or smelled him first and growled softly to alert Rex as he got to his feet. Rex followed the direction of his gaze but saw nothing. "What is it, buddy?"

Digger growled louder but remained next to Rex, as he was trained to do. Everyone had gone quiet, trying to see what Digger was excited about.

And then there was a collective, almost choreographed,

gasp from the Americans as the strangest creature they'd ever laid eyes on walked into the clearing about ten meters away from them. It was a small animal about one hundred centimeters (forty inches) in length, weighing about ten kilograms (twenty-two pounds). Its body was covered in scales. It walked on its hind feet, using its long tail and front feet to balance—like a miniature dinosaur.

"A pangolin, or *Itermagô*, as the locals call it," said Pieter. "They've been roaming the earth for eighty million years. There are eight species in the world: four in Africa and four in Asia. The only species to be found in Namibia was the Temminck's Ground Pangolin (Smutsia temminckii). There are more of these shy little animals poached and kept in cages illegally than any other animal in Namibia. Pangolins feed mainly on termites and ants, which they 'lick' up with their very long, thin, round tongue. They also use their tongues to lick up water. They are totally harmless but are killed for their meat and scales to sell on the insatiable Chinese black market. The scales fetch over US$3,000 per kilogram.

"Wildlife conservationists consider the pangolin the most trafficked wild mammal in the world. Yes, it might look like a reptile, but it is a mammal. Twenty tons of pangolins and pangolin parts are being trafficked each year."

When they were back home later in the afternoon, Thea showed them her gemstone cutting and polishing factory. Of course, Catia and Marissa were ecstatic and required no encouragement to make a few serious dents in their credit cards to acquire some of the unique pieces of jewelry and gemstones.

Rex and Josh were wise enough not to voice their questions of when and where their wives intended to wear the pieces. Maybe in the future, when they were not constantly traveling around the world on covert black ops missions, they could go out to nice places where the ladies could parade their jewelry.

Chapter Twenty

IN THE IN-TRAY

Monday. Windhoek, Namibia

Monday morning shortly after stepping into his office, Zhong Yang summoned Tian Chao to his office.

He handed Tian a printed A4 sheet. "That's the information about the miner you wanted. The woman with him was his daughter. He's a bush-league miner who struck a jackpot of silver and wants to bring in an investor from America. The details are in that document."

"Thank you, sir. Much appreciated."

Zhong was in a hurry and happy to pass the ball back to Tian. "Please excuse me. I have to be at a meeting in a few minutes."

Tian went back to his office and studied the document while drinking a cup of tea. He had a different take on the matter than Zhong. His first question was, how big is the deposit? There was nothing about it in the document. His next question was why Krige and his daughter didn't see the attaché of trade and commerce? Why did they *have* to see the ambassador? — four times. Was the silver deposit so big they could only talk to the ambassador about it? Or was there some other explanation?

By the time Tian had concluded he had no choice but to investigate the matter further, Thea was at the offices of the Ministry of Natural Resources and Energy to file her dad's application.

The nametag of the clerk who served her said his name was Hago Amutenya. He had an air of haughtiness that didn't quite fit his position. It took him almost half an hour to complete a job that should have taken ten minutes. But as her dad always said, in Africa, time is savored, not rushed. To rush anyone, especially if at a disadvantage to that person, was not only rude but would almost certainly cause things to be delayed, if not completely brought to a halt. Thea was in no particular hurry, so she kept her quintessential sunny demeanor and made small talk while handing Mr. Amutenya the documents in the order he requested and answered his questions.

When Thea left, there were two people in the queue waiting to be served. But Mr. Amutenya did not fuss about them. He took his time to page through Thea's documents, put them into a neat pile, staple them together, and place them in the in-tray on his desk before he looked up at the next person in line and nodded.

A data entry clerk would come and pick the documents up to enter the information into the computer system. Mr. Amutenya didn't care that said data entry clerk had not cleared out the in-tray since last Wednesday. He would only care about it when there was no more space in the in-tray. Mr. Amutenya hated a messy desk.

Monday. Windhoek, Namibia | Beijing, China

Tian was in a quandary; he *had* to report to General Quan immediately, yet he knew the first thing Quan would ask was, "How big is the deposit?"

Quan was not a nice man. He was brought up to believe he was born to be a leader. He was used to giving orders and having them followed. He was a retired two-star general and a five-star jerk. His underlings and opponents alike feared him. Tian was no exception. Quan was successful at business because he had the power and resources of the PLA at his beck and call. It was easy to do business with that kind of backing; issues were dealt with in military-style —quickly, efficiently, and with overwhelming force.

Tian was damned if he phoned without knowing the answer to that question, and he was damned if he didn't phone soon. It was only late that night that he realized he couldn't postpone it any longer and decided the lesser of two evils was not knowing the answer, so he made the call.

"Keep it short, Tian. I'm busy," answered Quan without greeting.

"My apologies, General. I can call you at a more convenient time."

"You're wasting time. Speak."

Tian told him about Krige's silver mine and how it came to his attention.

"How big is the deposit?"

"I apologize, sir, I don't know. I thought I'd—"

"Tian, use your brains if you have any. What good is this information without knowing how much silver there is?"

"Yes, sir, that's what I—"

"Call me when you know."

The line went dead.

Tian sighed. "That wasn't so bad. I still have a job." He leaned back in his chair. Where to find that information? He got the impression Zhong wouldn't be too keen to risk compromising his source in the US embassy unless there was a compelling reason.

"Well, then I'll launch my own investigation," he mumbled.

Monday. Erongo Mountains, Namibia

Erwin's five employees didn't live in the camp; they lived with their families in Karibib and Usakos and commuted by minibus, driven by Nelis Goreseb, the work foreman, who lived in Usakos. They arrived at the campsite shortly before eight a.m. on Monday morning and gathered under the *kameeldoring* tree to talk about their assignments for the week as usual. But today, Erwin first wanted to share exciting news with them—the discovery of the silver and the plans to start mining Mount Krige as soon as the permit was granted. That brought big smiles to their faces; it meant long-term employment for them. He didn't tell them about the REEs.

Next, Erwin told them about the decision to prospect Twohill and the need to get the samples collected as quickly as possible. By midday, the prospecting equipment was in place at Twohill, and they started collecting samples shortly after lunch.

Chapter Twenty-One

A ROAD TRIP TO THE SKELETON COAST

Tuesday. En route to Swakopmund, Namibia

The day before, after submitting Erwin's application, Pieter and Thea had taken the Daltons and Farleys on an extended tour of Windhoek and dropped them off at the Hilton late afternoon.

Tuesday morning, they had breakfast at the hotel. It was nice, lots of choices, an abundance of food, well prepared, absolutely nothing anyone could complain about except for those who had Mieke Krige's breakfasts over the past few days. No breakfast would ever be the same.

After breakfast, they took a taxi to the nearest Avis Car Rental, rented a Toyota RAV 4 for ten days, and headed for Swakopmund on the west coast 352 kilometers away. Rex was the driver, Josh was in the front passenger seat, Catia and Marissa were in the backseat with Digger between them. It took Rex's brain a few minutes to adapt to driving on the left side of the road.

They took the B1 north and arrived in Okahandja, a

town with 24,000 inhabitants, known as the Garden Town of Namibia, seventy kilometers from Windhoek. The town was founded in 1800; the name means the place where two rivers become one in the Herero language. There, they took a slow drive around the town before taking the B2 west toward Swakopmund and the Skeleton Coast.

The further west they traveled, the sparser the vegetation became as they approached the outskirts of the Namib Desert. They drove through Karibib and Usakos, small century-plus-old towns of around 3,000 inhabitants in the Erongo Region, one of the 14 regions of Namibia. The capital of the region is Swakopmund, although the biggest town in the region is Walvis Bay.

The name "Skeleton Coast" was the title of John Henry Marsh's 1944 book chronicling the shipwreck of the Dunedin Star. Over the years, it became the official name for this part of the Atlantic coast of Namibia between the Kunene River on the border with Angola in the north and the Swakop River in the south, which during the heydays of the whaling industry was littered with whale and seal bones and the graveyard of more than a thousand shipwrecks.

The Bushmen of Namibia called the area "The Land God Made in Anger," the first Portuguese sailors to visit the area referred to it as "The Gates of Hell."

Erwin and Mieke Krige thought of it as the paragon of serenity on earth.

About twenty-four kilometers out of Usakos, they turned onto a gravel road that took them to the Spitzkoppe (German for pointed domes), which Erwin and Mieke told them so much about. It's a group of bald granite peaks, inselbergs, rising abruptly out of the floor of the Namib desert. Mieke had an awe-inspiring collection of photos she had taken and pictures she had painted of the views from the summits of these granite peaks over the years.

The highest peak is the Groot Spitzkop, 1,728 meters (5,669 ft) above sea level. A nearby minor peak, the Little Spitzkoppe, has an elevation of 1,584 meters (5,197 ft). Other outcroppings stretch out into a range known as the Pontok Mountains. Ancient rock paintings can be seen in the Spitzkoppe area.

The Groot Spitzkop is also known as the Matterhorn of Namibia because of its likeness in shape to the Matterhorn of the Alps, straddling the border between Switzerland and Italy. Legend has it that in 1904 one of the Schutztruppe scaled the Groot Spitzkop and made a fire on the summit. What he would've used to make the fire with no one knows; there is absolutely no natural fuel of any kind on the peak. He never returned, and his body was never recovered. The first documented conquests were made by teams of climbers in 1946, and for the next quarter of a century, the mountain remained a two to three-day struggle for climbers until 1971, when the peak was reached in four hours by a party led by J. W. Marchant from the University of Cape Town Mountain and Ski Club.

They spent almost two hours at the Spitzkoppe, and at three p.m., just when they were all in the car, ready to leave, Josh in the driver's seat, Rex's satellite phone rang. It was John Brandt. Rex put the phone on speaker.

"Morning, John, up bright and early, I see," said Rex. It was six a.m. in Arizona.

"Christelle and I've been up since dawn. We've already gone for a walk with Cupcake. I can't tell you how good it is to be back home. Enjoying your road trip?"

A chorus of yeses and a yelp from Digger answered John's question.

"Okay, here's the breaking news; Dr. Collins is all set to make the trip over to Windhoek on the CIA's private jet. He's scheduled to arrive tomorrow around midday your time. The ambassador has been briefed, and she has been in contact with Krige. Collins will be taken to the embassy on arrival. He will be introduced to the Kriges and will stay with them at their campsite for the duration of his visit."

"John, you can tell him he's in for the treat of a life-time," said Marissa.

"Yeah, it's like the Bahamas except for the desert, the food, the people, the beer, and the braai, oh and did I mention the food?" added Josh

John chuckled. "Sounds like you kids are enjoying your-selves over there."

"Let me put it this way," said Marissa. "Josh and I are volunteering to start CRC's African branch in Namibia for you."

"So are Rex and I," added Catia.

"Hey, hang on. You kids are not walking out on me, are you?"

When the mirth subsided, Rex said, "I take it Laura Murray has been briefed to be ready to send our Chinese friends a bit more information?"

"Yes, Martin did. She will give James Blake his instruc-tions as soon as Collins has left the embassy."

A few minutes later, the call ended, and they resumed their trip to Swakopmund.

Not long after, they were back on the B2. They saw a board with the name Arandis on it, and in the distance, to the north, they could make out a small town. "What's the story behind this place?" asked Josh.

Over the years, on many missions in many countries, Rex, with his undergraduate degree in history and Catia with her Ph.D. in history from the Sapienza University of Rome, had established themselves as the de facto history buffs of the group. Catia said, "Arandis is called the Uranium Capital of the World; it's only fifteen kilometers, about nine miles, from Rössing, the world's largest open-pit uranium mine, which Erwin told us about."

While she was talking, she did a quick search on Google, found a few pages with information, and continued, "The uranium was discovered in 1928, but mining only started in 1976. It's the world's fifth-largest uranium mine producing eight percent of global output. Namibia is the world's fourth-largest exporter of uranium.

"But," — she held her index finger up — "there's a bit of a worry about this mine. Rio Tinto owned sixty-nine percent of the mine until they sold it to the China National Uranium Corporation in November 2018. The Industrial Development Corporation of South Africa owns ten percent, the Namibian government three percent although they hold fifty-one percent of the voting rights, local individual shareholders have three percent."

"And the remaining fifteen percent?" asked Marissa.

"You won't believe it. Iran."

"What?"

"Yep, since 1976. But the Namibian government says they're not supplying Iran with uranium which could be used for nuclear weapons. According to them, Iran does not partake in the mine's management; their shareholding is entirely passive."

"Yeah, right," said Josh. "And Ali Khamenei would put his hand on the Quran and swear that they've never used a single atom of Namibia's uranium for anything but curing migraines, ingrown toenails, severe cases of flu, dysentery, and suchlike."

They were crying with laughter by the time Josh finished his rant.

Tuesday. Windhoek, Namibia

With the information provided by Zhong in hand, Tian called up Google maps to have a look at Krige's camp and Eldorado. Krige's campsite was visible, so was the Eldorado farmstead. He zoomed in, but the images became too grainy to get a good look at anything of interest. He logged into the MSS spy satellite systems, which had much higher resolutions, and got a closer look at the two places. He saw vehicles, farming, and mining equipment, but all of it only confirmed what he already knew; it was a small-scale operation. Eventually, when he logged out of the system, he felt like a dog chasing a car; he had caught up with it, only to realize there was nothing he could do with it.

It took him a while to realize the information from satellite images would not tell him how much silver was in Krige's mine. His best source of information was Simon Nuusiku, the Commissioner of Mining in charge of the Mines Directorate at the Ministry of Natural Resources and Energy.

Simon Nuusiku was as crooked as a dog's hind leg.

Nepotism was alive and well in Namibia just as much as in any other country, including quite a few first-world countries. Nuusiku's maternal uncle was the Minister of Natural Resources and Energy. He appointed Nuusiku as commissioner, where he oversaw the issuing of mining permits and had oversight of all mining activities in the country. It was a position that presented many business opportunities for an enterprising person such as Nuusiku. So, his uncle gave him the job, and they shared the profits. The profits, kept in Swiss bank accounts, were more than enough to guarantee a luxurious retirement for both.

The most lucrative deals came from the Chinese, many of whom were referred by his uncle. One such referral was General Quan's Sino-Africa Development Corporation. They paid Nuusiku an obscene amount of money as a retainer every year just to keep them informed about all mining activities in Namibia. That was on top of the bribes they paid for mining rights. Quan had similar arrangements with government officials all over Africa.

Tian assumed Krige had not applied for a mining permit for the new site yet, because, if he had, Nuusiku would've forwarded a copy of the documents to him without delay. It never crossed his mind that the application could be stuck in some conceited clerk's in-tray.

That left Tian with only one option; he had to get the information directly from Krige.

Chapter Twenty-Two

THE VIP

Wednesday. Windhoek, Namibia

About an hour into the trip to Windhoek to meet Dr. Collins, Erwin realized the reason for Mieke's uncharacteristic quietness was anxiety. "What's bugging you, my dear?"

"The American doctor. He's a VIP. What if he doesn't enjoy living natively like we do? He's a doctor, you know. He probably teaches at a university. He's not used to living under a tree in the desert like Bedouins."

"That would be his loss. Besides, the man's a geologist, Mieke. Geologists are outdoor kind of people."

"Yeah, but he's not doing that anymore. He's a bigshot in D.C. now."

Erwin chuckled. "Mieke, I can't believe it; you've gone la-di-da on me!"

Mieke started laughing. "I guess you're right; it *is* silly to worry about stuff like that."

Dr. Liam Collins was welcomed by a senior staff member of the American Embassy after he cleared customs at Hosea Kutako International Airport. Less than an hour later, he was introduced to Ambassador Edwards, who introduced him to his hosts, Erwin and Mieke Krige. Not even the ambassador knew he was CIA.

Twenty minutes in the car with Dr. Collins was enough to calm Mieke's nerves. She had nothing to worry about. Liam, he refused to be called anything else, might have been a VIP, but he was not pretentious.

Within half an hour after Erwin and Mieke had entered the American Embassy, Tian Chao received an alert on his email from the MSS's facial recognition system—Erwin Krige has been at the embassy again. He could ask Zhong to find out the details, but he knew he was probably not going to get more information than before. He thought it was better to stick to his plan to pay Simon Nuusiku to help him get the information directly from Krige.

He was, however, more than a little surprised when he got a phone call from Zhong to inform him that Krige was at the embassy again today. This time he not only met with the ambassador, but he also met with Dr. Liam Collins, the investor's geologist. Tian thought it was interesting, but it had nothing to do with the size of the silver deposit, which was the most pressing issue for him right now. It still bothered him, though, that the ambassador was still involved and not the attaché of trade and commerce. One reason for that could be the deposit was so big it required the ambassador's personal attention. Or it could be something else altogether.

I feel lucky tonight

Wednesday. Windhoek, Namibia

Simon Nuusiku didn't have a gambling problem, but he never declined an invitation to try his luck at the roulette tables if his clients funded the escapade—as Tian Chao did that Wednesday night. They were at the Avani Windhoek Hotel and Casino on Independence Ave in the Gustav Voigts Centre.

During the buffet dinner in the hotel's Dunes Restaurant, Tian took an envelope out of the inside pocket of his leather jacket and slipped it surreptitiously across to Nuusiku. He took it and not so surreptitiously looked at the contents and raised his eyebrows.

"Ah, just a little something you can throw on the roulette table later. If you wish," said Tian. There was a little over seven thousand Namibia dollars in the envelope, the equivalent of US$500. That was not the bribe; it was just to get Commissioner Nuusiku's attention.

The envelope disappeared into Nuusiku's jacket pocket. "Chao, my friend, you look a bit distracted. How can I help?"

Tian ordered another round of drinks for them before he leaned forward and, *sotto voce* explained what he needed.

Nuusiku listened without interrupting. When Tian finished, he asked, "When do you want this done?"

"Before the weekend."

"No problem."

"How much?"

"Mmm, let me see," Nuusiku mumbled softly, as if making calculations. He wasn't. He knew all too well Tian was under pressure to get the information. "Ten grand should cover it," he said after a while.

US dollars paid directly into the nominated Swiss bank accounts was the only acceptable denomination used in these kinds of transactions.

Tian didn't blink an eye. "Good. Here's what I want to know." He told Nuusiku.

Nuusiku nodded while fighting the urge to kick himself for not doubling the price.

Tian fiddled with his smartphone for a few minutes and showed the screen to Nuusiku. It was the receipt for the electronic transfer of US$5,000 into Nuusiku's Swiss account. The balance would be transferred upon completion of the job.

He grinned from ear to ear. "Thank you. What do you say we hit the roulette table?"

Tian smiled. "Why not? I feel lucky tonight."

Chapter Twenty-Three

NOT ENOUGH TIME

Thursday. Swakopmund, Namibia

The Daltons and Farleys had been enjoying themselves thoroughly. Swakopmund had 44,725 inhabitants. A city by Namibian standards, it is the fourth largest in the country, no less. It is believed that the name originated from the San words *xwaka* (rhinoceros) and *ob* (river), which the German settlers had pronounced *Swachaub*, which, over time, morphed into Swakop. The '*mund*' in the name is the German word for mouth, referring to the river mouth.

The city was founded in 1892 as the main harbor for German South West Africa. A 2008 New York Times article describes the town as having "the dislocating feel of a Baltic Sea resort set in the tropics."

A tour company described it thus: "A timeless historic German colonial-era town that is a favorite holiday destination for both locals and visitors... on the foggy Atlantic coast in the Namib Desert, it is a somewhat surreal and gracious hamlet set amidst sea and sand. With its palm-lined streets and seaside promenade, restaurants, and cafes, galleries, and museums, the town itself is laid-back and has its own charm. It has become an African adventure mecca due to the wide variety of adrenalin and adventure activities on offer in the surrounding desert."

Although the Naudés had offered them their beach house at Langstrand between Swakopmund and Walvis Bay, they preferred to stay at the Strand Hotel on the waterfront. Within the first few hours of their arrival, they knew they needed more than just the two days they'd allowed themselves to explore the place. They settled for a one-day excursion on Wednesday to see the prehistoric Welwitschia plants they'd heard so much about. People often use words such as living fossils, weird, peculiar, wonderful, strange, bizarre, and fascinating when describing these plants. They comprise only two leaves, a stem base, and roots. It's one of the few things on Earth that can truly claim to be one of a kind. They exist only in the Namib Desert and southwest Angola. On average, welwitschias live 500-600 years, although some larger specimens could be 2,000.

They climbed Dune 7, one of the tallest sand dunes in the world, towering at 1,256 feet (383 meters). Two meters taller than the Empire State building, without its tip. Four times higher than the Statue of Liberty and eighty-three meters above the Eiffel Tower.

On Thursday, Bateleur Helicopters took them on a one-and-a-half-hour scenic helicopter flight over the Namib-Naukluft National Park to the world-famous Sossusvlei, a salt and clay pan surrounded by high red dunes.

They spent the rest of the day visiting the city's three museums: the Swakopmund Museum, the Kristall Galerie

(Crystal gallery), and the Martin Luther (steam locomotive) museum.

The last trip of the day was a slow drive past the Chinese Satellite station north of Swakopmund. It is said the station is part of the Chinese Tracking, Telemetry, Command and Communications System. It is one of three overseas Chinese tracking stations—the other two are in Karachi, Pakistan, and Malindi, Kenya.

Rex and his team couldn't help but wonder what else the Chinese were tracking from this isolated place in the Namib Desert.

An inspector coming

Thursday. Erongo Mountains, Namibia

Simon Nuusiku got his backhander. The inspector, Leah Visser, who he'd ordered to inspect and question Erwin Krige got nothing. It was the same for the junior inspector-in-training who would accompany her. Commissioner Nuusiku believed, contrary to himself, their government salaries were ample compensation for the work they had to do. Visser and her protégé were wholly unaware that the commissioner had received a bribe rivaling their combined annual salaries for what they were told was a routine inspection of a mining site.

Leah Visser was a member of an ethnically mixed minority group known as Basters. The name Baster is derived from bastaard, the Dutch word for bastard or cross-breed. People often consider this term demeaning, but the

Basters have no negative connotation to the name. They are proud of the name—it asserts their ancestry and history—they say.

The Basters, also known as Rehobothers or Rehoboth Basters, are descended from a mix of Europeans and Africans. Since the mid-19th century, the Rehoboth Baster community has been concentrated in central Namibia, in and around the town of Rehoboth. Basters are closely related to the Afrikaners, Cape Colored, and Griqua peoples of South Africa, with whom they share a language and culture.

Visser gave Erwin a courtesy call on Thursday afternoon to let him know to expect her by ten a.m. Friday.

"The mandarins have outdone themselves," he said to Mieke and Liam. "Thea filed the application on Monday, and they'll be here for the inspection tomorrow. That's the final step in the process. Five days. Amazing. You should visit us more often, Liam."

Liam laughed. "Glad I could be of service."

Mieke smiled. *To think I was worried he would be a snob. Liam could've been Erwin's twin brother. Not identical, though.* The two of them got on like a house on fire. But then why not? They were rockhuggers, the geological equivalent of tree-huggers.

Liam didn't tell the Kriges that he worked for the CIA or that he was the senior advisor on strategic minerals to the President of the United States. However, Liam was honest about his role in the mission; he had to verify, with his own instruments and procedures, the accuracy of the size of the REEs deposit.

Erwin was not offended; if the roles were reversed, he would have done the same. He hired more workers and moved some of the equipment from Twohill back to Mount

Krige. Liam and his helpers had worked all of Thursday, from dawn to dusk, to collect samples and test them. His samples were not nearly enough to cover the entire Mount Krige, but all he wanted was several random tests to see how the results compared with those that Thea and the CIA lab reported.

Chapter Twenty-Four

PHONE REX

Friday. Erongo Mountains, Namibia

By early Friday morning, Liam was satisfied with the number of samples and ecstatic about the results. Every test he conducted confirmed the previous results were true. He compiled a report and sent it via secured email through his CIA encrypted satellite phone to Martin Richardson in Langley.

Operation Sierra, the mission to secure the richest deposit of REEs on earth for the USA, was a go.

Liam would repeat the process with Twohill, collect his own samples and conduct his own tests. The plan was to start after the weekend. So far, he'd enjoyed every moment of his visit. He wanted to use some of his time here to see more of this fascinating country and its warmhearted people.

To Erwin's surprise, Visser and her minion arrived half an hour earlier than scheduled. They were in a double-cab Isuzu 4x4 pickup with government license plates and the department's insignia on the sides. They pulled up in the space between Erwin's Toyota Landcruiser and Landrover. They got out and introduced themselves to Erwin, Mieke, and Liam.

Erwin put Visser's age somewhere in the mid-forties. She was of average height and skinny. She had neatly kept short dark hair and was dressed in a tan-colored office pantsuit with flat-heel shoes. Her companion, Joseph Hauwanga, was a tall Ovambo man in his early thirties, by Erwin's estimation. He had on dark pants, an open-neck dark-blue shirt, shiny black shoes, and a pair of oversized imitation Ray-ban Aviators. Probably acquired at one of the knock-off shops in Windhoek's Chinatown.

It immediately struck Erwin that Visser looked ill at ease. Her junior, on the other hand, looked jaded. Visser got straight to the point. "Mr. Krige, we've got only a few questions, it won't take long, and then we'd like to inspect the site."

"You're welcome, Ms. Visser. I have to say I really appreciate how quickly you have moved on this one. I'm glad you can also meet Dr. Collins, the geologist for the investor interested in this venture."

Visser had an uncomprehending look on her face. Erwin noticed but made nothing of it. Erwin smiled and pointed to the area under the *kameeldoring* tree. "Let's have a seat in our 'open-air lounge' and have something to drink while we talk."

After they were all seated, Mieke served coffee, tea, and a variety of home-baked cookies.

Visser picked up her briefcase and took out a notepad and a pen, closed the lid, and used it as a table on her lap. "Have you collected samples?"

It was Erwin's turn to look uncomprehending. He was

about to ask if she was joking but thought better of it. "Yes, I have."

"Have they been tested and by whom?"

Erwin was about to ask her what the purpose of collecting samples would be if they were not tested and tell her all the information was in his application but thought maybe this was just the inspector's way of checking that there were no discrepancies between the information in his application and what he was telling her. "My daughter, Thea Naudé, conducted the tests."

"What were the results?"

"Give me a second. I'll get you a copy." Erwin disappeared into the caravan and came back a minute later with the report and handed it to the inspector.

Visser looked at it for a long while and made a few calculations on the calculator on her smartphone. "Okay, so we're talking about a deposit of between one-point-five and one-point-eight million ounces?"

"Yes, that's correct."

"At current prices, that's around forty million US dollars?"

"Yes. That's the optimistic estimate."

"When are you planning to file your application for a mining permit?"

Erwin felt a tingle like an ice cube run down his spine. Mieke was staring at him in shock. Liam glanced at him fleetingly before averting his gaze toward the hills in the distance.

Erwin's mind was in overdrive. *So, if you don't know the application has been filed, how do you know about this mine? Who are you? Who do you work for?* "I am not sure," said Erwin with as much calmness as he could muster. "I'll have to check with my daughter. She handles all my administrative stuff."

"Thank you, Mr. Krige. Could we inspect the site now?"

"Sure. We can go in my vehicle."

When Mieke handed Erwin's hat to him, he leaned in and kissed her on the cheek and whispered, "Phone Rex."

She was on the phone minutes after Erwin and the others had left. Rex and company were in Walvis Bay, Namibia's main port. They were about to board a sailboat for a dolphin and seal watching cruise when Rex's satellite phone rang. Within fifteen minutes of taking Mieke's call, they'd canceled their trip and were on the way to the Krige's campsite in the Erongo Mountains, 180 kilometers away. With a speed limit of 120 kilometers per hour on every tarmac freeway, it was a ninety-minute drive.

Meanwhile, when they got to Mount Krige, Erwin drove at a snail's pace around the hill, explaining how he'd collected the samples and pointing out interesting geological features.

Visser asked what it was that made him think there could be silver at this site in the first place. Erwin launched into a long lecture about rocks and geology and geomorphological concepts that only elicited the occasional nodding or an "I see" from Visser.

They could've been genuine mine inspectors or imposters, Liam couldn't tell, but it was obvious they knew little about geology.

Erwin correctly assumed Liam had also realized there was a snake in the grass, which was why he had remained quiet.

On the way back to the campsite, as they drove past a twelve-meter farm shed surrounded by a ten-foot chain-link fence topped by rolls of concertina razor-wire, Erwin explained that it was where they stored their tools, equipment, and samples. Shortly after they had arrived back at the campsite, Visser thanked Erwin and Mieke for their time and hospitality and left.

As the department's vehicle drove away, Mieke looked at her watch. "Catia called about ten minutes ago; they're close by. But they didn't want to turn up while the inspector was still here. She also said they've asked Thea and Pieter to come over as well."

"Okay, you can let her know the coast is clear," said Erwin. He turned to Liam. "Do you know the Daltons and Farleys?"

"The Daltons yes, the Farleys no."

Friday. Erongo Mountains, Namibia

An hour later, they were in conclave under the *kameeldoring* tree; the Kriges, Naudés, Daltons, Farleys, and Liam Collins. Digger and Kaiser were happy to see each other. They took a quick trip around the camp before settling in the shade, each with a big bone to keep them busy while the members of their packs were meeting. When Rex saw how much Digger enjoyed the bone, he wondered if he'd let go of the bone if he was offered the kong filled with what Catia called Digger's gelato—peanut butter. Probably not.

After listening to the account of the inspector's visit, Rex said, "So, the application is probably stuck somewhere in the bureaucratic sewer, or some other misfortune befell it. Whatever happened to it, those mandarins who were here don't know you've filed it?"

"Yes, and we don't even know if she works for the department," said Erwin.

"It shouldn't be too difficult to check that. But it doesn't really matter. I think she was following someone's orders. And I'd bet dollars to doughnuts, her instructions came from the Chinese, directly or indirectly—"

"But how would the Chinese know about the mine...?" started Erwin, then stopped. "Ah, of course, the information your boss fed them a few days ago?"

"Right."

"The question is, what were they after?" asked Mieke.

"It sounds as if they only wanted to know how big the silver deposit is," said Pieter.

"I agree," said Liam. "She asked nothing else that was important. Or am I missing something?"

"I think you're right," said Erwin. "If the Chinese are behind this, my guess is they want to know if it's big enough for them to be interested."

"So, Rex, do you reckon we just leave it at that and see what happens?" Pieter wanted to know.

"No, we have to be proactive," said Rex. "But before we get to that, I want to know if she asked you what you did with the samples after the testing was completed?"

"No, she didn't," replied Erwin. "But I told her the samples were tested by Thea. I also told her we keep the samples in the shed with our tools and equipment."

"Okay, that's helpful. So, let's assume the Chinese are behind this. Now that they know how much silver there is, the best-case scenario is they might decide it's not worth pursuing, and they'll be out of your hair. However, I think it's also possible that there's enough silver to arouse PLA Incorporated's interest."

Noticing the inquisitive looks on their faces, Rex took a few minutes to explain to them about the PLA's sub rosa commercial division and their activities throughout Africa and other parts of the world.

"Okay, they might come after the mine," said Erwin. "But then they'll have to bribe or blackmail government officials to get me thrown off my claim."

"Yes. But we think they already have someone high up in the ministry in their pocket," said Josh. "That'd probably be the person who instructed the inspector to carry out this fake inspection."

Erwin nodded slowly.

Rex continued. "So, let's assume they want the mine. I'm sure they'd want to conduct their own tests on your samples or collect their own samples and test them."

"Either way, the cat will be out of the bag," whispered Erwin.

"Right."

"I could keep them busy in the courts for a while," said Erwin.

"I'm afraid if the government finds out about the REEs, they'll nationalize the mine in a heartbeat," said Catia.

Thea looked crestfallen. "I can't see a way out of this. Can you?"

Pieter, her parents, and Liam were nodding in agreement.

"I might have a plan," said Rex. "But for that, we need to know what's going on at Twohill. How many samples have you collected so far?"

"Yesterday afternoon, we had eighty-five bags. We should have more than a hundred by now," said Erwin.

"Good. I suggest we move them all to Thea's lab today and run tests on them over the weekend," said Rex.

"That should be easy enough. But what are you getting at?" asked Erwin.

"We need to know how many REEs we're dealing with."

"So, what happens if we find as many REEs at Twohill as at Mount Krige?" asked Mieke.

Liam smiled. "I'd say then the world's REEs crisis is over. The USA can have half and China the other, and Namibia could very well become one of the countries with the highest per capita income in the world."

"Well, in that case, let's hope and pray you'll find an abundance of them," said Mieke.

On the way to Eldorado, Marrissa made a conference call to John and Martin and gave them an update of the day's events.

By seven p.m., they were on the farm. The 110 bags from Twohill were secured in the storeroom next to Thea's lab.

Friday. Windhoek, Namibia

Tian had listened to the recording of the meeting between Krige and the department's inspector twice already. At first glance, he was happy that Krige seemed to be truthful about the size of the deposit. But something bothered him he couldn't lay his finger on. It was only when he listened to the recording for the third time when he realized—it was the size of the deposit. This was not exactly an earth-shattering discovery, yet it got the exclusive attention of the US ambassador. Forty million US dollars at current prices was an optimistic estimate, and that would be the turnover, not profit. If the mining costs were sixty percent of that, it left about eighteen million total. Spread that over ten years, and the picture was not so rosy at all. Even so, Quan's Sino-Africa Development Corporation might be interested.

He looked at Krige's quarterly reports filed with the Department of Natural Resources and Energy, which, thanks to Simon Nuusiku, he had unfettered access to. Krige had four mines in operation producing gemstones, copper, African blue sodalite, and marble. The fifth mine was the silver mine near Karibib. The sixth was a few kilometers north of there, but, according to the reports, no prospecting had been done as yet. By Tian's calculations, based on those reports, Erwin should've been generating good money from his other mines. "So, Mr. Krige, you have enough money to fund the silver mine operation yourself. Why do you need an investor, an American investor, no less?" he mumbled to himself.

He was more than just a little tense when he phoned Quan Zhelan.

"Are you going to waste my time again?" Quan answered.

"No, sir. I have the information about the silver mine."

"Spit it out."

Tian told him.

Quan went quiet.

Tian knew if he said anything in the silence, it would only invite Quan's chagrin. A few minutes later, Quan said, "If we're very optimistic, we're talking about forty million US dollars at current prices. Let's rather work with twenty-five million. The average cost to get it out of the ground and processed is about seventy-five percent. Six and a quarter million profit over the lifetime of the mine. Not worth the trouble. Let him keep his mine."

"Yes, sir. Sir, there's, however, one thing that troubles me. I'd appreciate your guidance on it."

"Speak."

"Why would the US ambassador be so interested in this?

It seems she's gone out of her way to find Krige an investor. The investor has even sent a geologist over, I presume to verify the results. But as you've noted, it's not a rich mine. I'm—"

"Why didn't you tell me this in the beginning?" barked Quan.

Tian made no reply. To remind Quan that he *had* been told was not a good idea—Quan was never at fault. Even if he were, it was a terrible idea for a subordinate to point it out.

"It's obvious there's something untoward going on there. Find out what it is and call me. Do I always have to spoon-feed you? Use your brains, man."

The line went dead.

Tian sighed. *The man's rudeness has no boundaries.*

He filed an application with the head of the MSS's electronic espionage unit in Beijing to open a case for the Krige matter. He made it clear that General Quan Zhelan supported the application and included a request for a comprehensive background check on not only Erwin Krige but also his wife, daughter, family, friends, and contacts, including Dr. Liam Collins. The request also covered electronic surveillance of their phones and internet activities. If there was something Krige was trying to hide, it was only a matter of time before Tian would know what it was.

Within an hour, Tian received confirmation from Beijing that his application had been received and a case officer had been assigned.

Chapter Twenty-Five

DIGGER LIKED THE PLAN

Saturday. Khomas Hochland Mountains, Namibia

After an early breakfast, they all helped Erwin and Thea prepare the samples, set up the lab equipment, and run the tests. Liam would run his tests independently from Thea's.

By late afternoon, they had their answer; Erwin was right; Twohill had the same amounts of silver as Mount Krige but almost no REEs. Liam's independent tests confirmed it.

They were discussing the results when Rex got a call from Greg.

"Still enjoying Namibia?" said Greg when Rex answered.

"Very much so, Greg. It's a fascinating place and amazing people. I can only highly recommend it," said Rex as he and Digger walked away from the group toward the lookout point.

"Hmm, I'll wait for you and the team to get back in one piece and show me the photos before I make bookings."

"What's up?" said Rex when he was out of earshot of the others.

"Our e-watchdog alerted us that your Namibian friends' Chinese admirers have been trying to access their phones and computers remotely. They started sniffing around about three hours ago, but so far, our security measures have kept them out. I reported it to John, and he thought you'd want to know about it."

"John's right. I definitely want to know. Who are the perps?"

"It's our old friends, Unit 61398, this time out of the Shanghai office."

In a nondescript twelve-story building on Datong Road in Shanghai's Pudong District toiled two thousand of the world's foremost computer hackers known as Unit 61398, the cyber warfare unit of the PLA. This building was one of many locations across China from where the virtual warriors waged cyberwar. The Chinese government, of course, vehemently denied their existence, yet the state-owned China Telecom had provided the unit with special fiber optic communication infrastructures—in the name of national defense.

Rex took a deep breath and let it out slowly, noisily. This was not good news. He and his team, which included Greg's team, knew all about Unit 61398; they'd encountered them frequently over the past few years on missions against China. They were China's special forces in cyberspace, and across the globe, there were few who could rival them. Greg's team was part of the few who could, not in size but in ingenuity.

A senior FBI security analyst once explained China's cyber onslaught against the US to Rex. "There are few people who can wrap their heads around the scale of

China's cyber-espionage program. There're not tens of thousands involved; it's hundreds of thousands. Every single day, they're penetrating or attempting to penetrate the computer networks and databases of private enterprises, government, financial, law enforcement, and military institutions to steal information and technology. The FBI opens a new case of intellectual property theft against China every ten hours."

"Okay," said Rex at length, "I want you to get Flat Arrow to help you find out who in Windhoek they're talking to?" said Rex. "I suspect it's not Zhong Yang, the Chief of Station; he's a declared. It must be someone else who's undeclared."

"He's already working on that."

"Great. Okay, keep watching them, and keep me posted."

"Will do."

Rex sat down on a bench overlooking the river. The vague idea he had about Twohill since Erwin told him about it had turned into a plan now.

Digger had sidled up and nuzzled him as if to say, "Let's talk about it, buddy."

Rex scratched Digger's ears and back while gathering his thoughts.

Digger stared at Rex with a dog-smile on his face as if to say, "Ready when you are."

"You won't believe it, but it's the Chinese again. It seems our plan to pull the wool over their eyes has bombed out."

Digger was a good listener. He whined softly. Rex interpreted that to mean, "What happened?" Or maybe Digger wanted Rex to continue scratching his back and ears.

"They've been trying to access our friends' phones and

computers. That means they're thinking our friends are hiding something from them."

Digger yapped.

"Yeah, I have a plan, but there's a lot to do. We'll have to move quickly."

Digger barked once.

"No, I haven't told them yet."

Digger turned and looked at the group sitting in the open-air dining room as if to say, "Well, what're you waiting for? Let's tell them." It was quite possible that Digger only wanted to get back there because that's where the *biltong* and other treats were.

"But I haven't told you about it yet."

Digger growled softly.

"Ah, of course, you already know. I keep forgetting you can read my mind."

Digger ignored him and started walking toward the others.

Rex followed. Obviously, Digger liked the plan.

Chapter Twenty-Six

THIS WAS NEVER ABOUT SILVER

Saturday. Shanghai, China / Windhoek, Namibia

Despite his irritation about being roused from a sound sleep at eleven p.m., General Peng Lan, commander of Unit 61398, answered the phone with as much politeness as he could muster. He knew Jia Jun would not be calling this time of night unless it was important. She had proved herself to be highly perceptive and an assiduous case officer. When Peng got the request for information from Tian Chao endorsed by General Quan Zhelan, he had no hesitation in giving her the job and instructed her to report directly to him. General Quan, although retired, had a fearsome reputation. Peng had no desire to do anything that would invite the general's wrath.

Peng was proud of his unit's performance. Over the past decade, they'd breached the computer networks of at least 141 organizations across twenty industries worldwide and systematically stole hundreds of terabytes of data from them. In the US alone, they'd been stealing intellectual property and trade secrets to the tune of US$600 billion per year. Worldwide, that figure would approach one trillion.

To name but a few of their major hacking achievements the past few years: From 2014 to 2015, they were responsible for the infamous Anthem data breach, the biggest single compromise of healthcare data in history—the complete health records of 112 million people in the USA.

In 2015, the same unit's cadres penetrated the United States Office of Personnel Management (OPM) and stole the personnel records of eighteen million people—everybody who has worked for, tried to work for, or was working for the United States government.

Equifax is an American multinational consumer credit reporting agency, one of the three largest consumer credit reporting agencies in the world. They collect and aggregate information on over eight hundred million individual consumers and more than eighty-eight million businesses worldwide. Between May and July 2017, Unit 61398's cybertroops breached Equifax's firewalls and stole the personal and financial data of 147 million people.

Peng listened patiently to Jia's report. As he expected, she'd done a sterling job. After all the years in the twilight world of cyber espionage, it still surprised him how easy it was to collect people's personal information from open sources. In the lexicon of intelligence communities, it was known as OSINT, Open Source Intelligence, the collection and analysis of information gathered from public sources such as Facebook, Twitter, LinkedIn, YouTube, Instagram, Pinterest, and others.

In the modern world, everyone lives out loud, telling the world what they have done, are doing right now, going to do next, and prove it all with photos and videos and posts.

Online followers and likes had become more important than friends of the flesh-and-blood kind.

More than 370 years ago, the French philosopher, René Descartes, said: "I think; therefore, I am." If he had lived today, he would probably have said, "I Tweet; therefore, I am."

The Naudés were active on all social media to promote their eco-tourism and hunting business. The Kriges not so much; they only had Facebook pages to keep in touch with family and friends. Using the information harvested from social media, Jia Jun and her team expanded their research and hacked into government databases and soon knew everything the Namibian government knew about the Kriges and Naudés. From there, it was a small step to find their financial information kept by the banks and insurance companies.

"But there's an anomaly with the Namibians," she told Peng. "We couldn't access any of their phones or computers. They've got US military-grade security measures on their internet-connected devices, yet all other information about them was easy to get."

"Interesting," murmured Peng.

"But the most exciting news is about Dr. Collins, the American. He has no social media account of any kind. That was the first sign he's probably working for a government organization. It was in the OPM database where my search algorithms came across the name William Edward Collins, a senior geologist at the United States Geological Survey. It took us a few more hours scouring our other databases to discover that William Edward Collins is also known as Dr. Liam Collins, the man who is currently in Namibia in the company of the Kriges and Naudés. He's the chief advisor to the President of the United States on geological matters and strategic minerals."

Fifteen minutes later, General Peng was talking to Tian on the phone. By the time the call ended, Tian had also received a comprehensive report on his computer in Windhoek.

"So, Mr. Krige, I was right all along," he muttered. "This was never about silver."

He stood, opened his window, returned to his chair, took a pack of Marlboros and a lighter from the top drawer, retrieved a cigarette, and despite the no-smoking policy, lit it, and took a long pull as he leaned back.

"Krige, what's at that mine of yours that's so important the President of the United States had to send his chief geological advisor to have a look? That's why the American ambassador is so interested in you."

He pulled up the list of thirty-five critical minerals published by the US government in 2018. Minerals which the US military, national infrastructure, and economy depended on. He glanced over the list a few times but real- ized it was futile to speculate—it could be one or many of them.

He lit another Marlboro and started talking to himself again. "It's obvious you found something of great impor- tance to the USA. And it's equally obvious you've been trying to lead us down the garden path with your story about the silver. Why else would you be getting help from their security experts to keep your phones and computers safe from prying eyes?"

Tian was at another impasse, to phone General Quan or not? But, after a few minutes of contemplation, he decided he didn't feel ready for another round of verbal abuse from the general for not having an answer to the obvious question.

Chapter Twenty-Seven

DIGGER IS A GENIUS

Saturday. Khomas Hochland Mountains, Namibia

Understandably the atmosphere around the *kameeldoring* fire that night was decidedly more subdued than the first time the Daltons and Farleys experienced a *braai* in the outdoor dining area.

"I'm afraid that call was not good news," said Rex. "The Chinese are obviously not satisfied with the answers given to the inspector yesterday; they've been trying to access your phones and computers for the past few hours."

"Did they get into any of them?" Erwin asked.

"They haven't got a prayer that would get them past Catia's and Marissa's security measures," said Rex. "Nevertheless, it's inescapable, something has triggered their curiosity, and if they keep on sniffing around, they'll find out what we've been trying to hide."

"So, the crux of the situation is," said Josh, "Plan A, which was to treat them like mushrooms—that is to keep them in the dark and feed them manure—has not survived?"

"Yep, that's the size of it," said Rex. "But Plan B is already in the making. We'll just have to work out the details."

Catia smiled. "In other words, we don't have a plan. From here on, we'll be flying by the seat of our pants?"

"Yep," replied Rex.

"Great, I was getting worried this mission was going to be boring," said Marissa.

Rex had John's standing permission to brief Erwin and company fully about Operation Sierra when he thought it was necessary.

He deemed it necessary now.

So, he told them Liam was the president's senior advisor on geological matters and who the rest of them were, who they worked for, and the orders of the President of the United States to ensure the Chinese didn't get their hands on Mount Krige.

None of them looked surprised by the revelation—that was what they'd been suspecting for some time already.

"So, now that you know a bit more about us and the operation, let's talk about what to expect from the Chinese. Anything goes; nothing is unimportant. No idea or question is stupid. If you were in their shoes, what would you do to get the information you need?"

There was a long silence before Liam said, "Well, I'd want to know everything about everyone who's involved in this. I'd be looking for personal information with which I can bribe and blackmail."

"You can bet your boots on that," said Josh. "They play dirty, and they're good at it. Their cyberwarfare teams will at this very moment be digging into your private lives, and before long, they'll know everything about you, from the day you were born."

Erwin smiled. "If skeletons are what they're looking for, they're going to be disappointed. While none of us are candidates for sainthood, we're probably the four most boring people on the planet as far as scandals go."

Catia laughed. "And there I was, thinking you're such interesting people."

When the humor of the moment was gone, Josh said, "One of the first things I'd do if I was in their shoes would be to put the tabs on you and anyone you associate with. Both physical and electronic surveillance. They probably don't know about us," Josh pointed to himself and the rest of the team. "But it's only a matter of time before they do."

"Maybe it's best if the four of you distance yourselves from us—" started Pieter, but Rex interjected.

"No. We're in it together. We stay together, and we work together to stop them—or we die trying." He took a deep breath and said, "Okay, ignore the 'or we die trying' bit."

"When they don't make any headway with our private lives, they'll probably employ heavy-handed tactics," said Erwin.

Rex nodded. "Yep, that's in character for them. They never need encouragement to get forceful when they don't get their way. We should all be watching our sixes from now on."

"Maybe we should get the police involved?" said Mieke.

"Too early," said Rex.

"I'm sure they still don't know what it is we've discovered. If I were them, I'd want to collect my own samples or at the very least test the existing samples," said Erwin. "But if they do, the ruse is over. Right?"

"Unless we misdirect them," Rex said.

Erwin stared at him, and so did the others, waiting for an explanation.

"You stop all prospecting activities at Twohill. We take the Twohill samples and put them in the shed at Mount Krige. The real samples from Mount Krige we hide somewhere."

The uncomprehending look on Erwin's face had made way for one of cognition. "In other words, the only samples they can get their hands on will be from Twohill?"

"Right."

"Okay, but how do you think they will go about getting the samples?" asked Liam.

"We can expect they'll be using any method from another fake inspection to violence and anything in between."

"I take it this is what you and Digger discussed earlier?" said Josh.

"Yep. He reckons it can work. At least for a while."

"Why is that?" asked Marissa.

"Because this scheme I'm proposing will work only until they discover they've been fooled."

"And then things will become hairy?" said Erwin.

"Precisely," said Rex. "There'll be a lot of ill-tempered Chinese around these parts. But hopefully, this will keep them in the dark long enough for the US to negotiate a deal with the Namibian government."

They continued the discussions over dinner and late into the night until it was time for Rex and his team to have a video conference with John and Martin.

Just before they said goodnight to their hosts, Mieke said, "Josh, I take it you misspoke when you asked Rex earlier if he'd discussed the plan with Digger?"

Josh, Marissa, and Catia started laughing. Rex looked impassive.

"Mieke, it's a long story. The best person to tell you about it is Rex, but the short answer is no, I didn't misspeak. He always discusses his plans with Digger. I can't comment about Digger's contributions, but I can tell you the plans the two of them make are nightmarish and usually work out fine."

Mieke looked at Rex, incredulous. "Is this true?"

Rex shrugged. "What can I say? Digger is a genius."

Digger had a big dog-smile and a tail that was wagging incessantly—he knew he was the center of attention.

Chapter Twenty-Eight

THE REST OF THE PLAN

Sunday. International video conference

Shortly after midnight, Rex and the team were gathered in the Farleys' chalet, where Rex explained the rest of his plan. When Rex was done, they gathered at the kitchen table around Marissa's laptop for a secured three-way video conference with Martin and Howard Lawrence in Langley and John and Christelle on the Ranch in Arizona.

After the greetings, Rex told them about the Twohill test results. "But the only verified information we have is the Chinese have been trying to get access to the phones and computers of our friends here, and the suspicion that they're behind the so-called inspection at Mount Krige on Friday," said Rex. "As you can see, our biggest limitation is a lack of information. Greg and his team have to find out who is behind this, everyone in the chain from here to China and back, including what's happening inside the Ministry of Natural Resources and Energy. We need to know who instructed the inspector. What happened to

Erwin's application? We suspect there's a can of worms waiting to be opened at the ministry."

"Okay, I'll let Greg know," said John. "He'll welcome a bit of action."

"Next, although we're not sure *what* the Chinese know, we know something got their hackles up; that's why they're trawling for information," said Rex. "One thing we think they might soon be after, if not already, are the samples so that they can analyze them for themselves. Therefore, we suggest that the Twohill and Mount Krige samples are swapped, and the Mount Krige samples disappear."

A big smile had broken across John's face. "Now there's an idea that's got potential. What do you think, Martin?"

Martin was quiet for a while, then started nodding slowly, almost imperceptibly, and then a smile broke across his face. "I can't think of a better plan to buy us the time we need."

Howard added his support for the idea, too.

For the next hour and a half, they fleshed out the details of the strategy to throw the Chinese off-kilter and keep it up while they get everything ready to make a play for the acquisition of Mount Krige. There were quite a few things to consider and prepare for. The team needed more surveillance and communications equipment. Martin would get it couriered to Windhoek in the diplomatic bag immediately.

Diplomatic bags or diplomatic pouches, as they are also called, are not necessarily a bag or pouch; they could be a cardboard box, a briefcase, a duffel bag, a large suitcase, a crate, or even a shipping container. Diplomatic bags are used by countries' diplomatic missions to carry official correspondence or other items between their embassies or consulates and their home governments. As long as the containers are marked as such, they have diplomatic immunity from search or seizure, as stipulated in article 27 of the 1961 Vienna Convention on Diplomatic Relations. The containers are often escorted by a diplomatic courier who has diplomatic immunity from arrest and detention.

Rex suggested it was time to meet Laura Murray, the Chief of Station, and James Blake. Martin agreed and undertook to arrange the introductions.

They also agreed that it might be a good idea to send Liam back home soon. Not that there was a problem with him being there, but because it would help to feed the narrative that Mount Krige was a small-scale silver mine and nothing more.

"I'd like to suggest we start thinking about how we're going to get private enterprise involved," said Rex.

Howard nodded. "Agreed. The thought had crossed my mind. Any ideas?"

"I thought a consortium of high-tech companies could be formed. Companies that are at present dependent on China's supply of REEs or products requiring them. A guy like Elon Musk might be one of them."

"Excellent idea," said Howard.

Finally, they prepared a report which Howard would present to the president.

Chapter Twenty-Nine

HAMMER AND TONGS

Sunday. International telephone call

As much as Tian loathed talking to General Quan only to be verbally abused, he knew it would be much worse if the general were to find out he hadn't been informed about Collins's real identity soon.

Tian decided to try a different tactic; he would lead with the information about Dr. Collins. It was a good plan except for his lousy timing. It was eight a.m. Sunday in Beijing. It was General Quan's day off. He had planned to sleep late, eat and drink a lot, and do no work at all.

When Tian's call came through, Quan's outburst gave new meaning to the word ill-tempered. Tian held the phone a few inches from his ear and breathed as softly as possible, trying feebly to throw in an apology now and then but eventually gave up and shut up until Quan ran out of boorish language.

"So, what's going on at that mine. What are they trying to hide from us?"

"I don't know yet, sir, but I—"

That was enough to send Quan into another frenzy. Tian sat back and listened quietly to Quan's invective. When he stopped, Tian told him about Collins and sat back, listening to another round of condemnation for not saying so in the beginning.

"What are you going to do to find out what they're hiding?"

"Sir, I am planning to steal the samples so we can run our own tests."

"Do it!" shouted Quan. "Do whatever it takes. If necessary, pay Krige and his daughter a visit."

Hammer and tongs, thought Tian—Quan's typical modus operandi.

"Yes, sir. I'll start on it immediately."

Planting the samples

Sunday. Khomas Hochland and Erongo Mountains, Namibia

The Kriges and Naudés were raised in a Christian milieu; Sunday was traditionally a day of rest and recuperation. However, this Sunday, the biblical principle of the sheep in the pit took precedence.

After breakfast, they labeled the Twohill samples and loaded them onto the back of the Kriges' Toyota Landcruiser. Josh, Marissa, and Liam would follow the Kriges in their rental back to the campsite in the Erongo Mountains. Rex, Catia, and Digger remained on Eldorado.

When the Krige party had left, Catia, with the assistance of Greg, helped Thea and Pieter to wipe all data related to the tests from the lab computers and their laptops.

While Catia was busy helping the Naudés, Martin introduced Rex, Laura Murray, and James Blake to each other via secured video conference and briefed them about Operation Sierra.

Laura and James were excited. James's role as Sara Bishop's deceiver was the most adventurous part of his job as an undeclared agent. Laura's job was collecting and analyzing information from open sources, building relationships with representatives of other countries and Namibian government officials. Being part of a real cloak-and-dagger CIA operation was a welcome departure from an otherwise monotonous job. Their first task was to find out who in the Ministry of Natural Resources and Energy sent the inspector to Krige's mine and to follow the trail of suspected corruption wherever it led.

Erwin and company were back at the campsite shortly before midday. They stacked the Twohill samples in the Mount Krige shed and tagged four of the bags with small GPS tracking devices. The 10x10x5.8mm gadgets weighed just 2.5 grams—the world's smallest GPS tracking devices. They had a battery life of 5 days.

"It's only because of the use of REEs that it was possible to miniaturize these little trackers," said Marissa. "The irony is there's a ninety percent chance the REEs in them came from China."

"Irony indeed," said Erwin. "Do the trackers have a self-destruct feature? If they don't, they'll be discovered during the testing."

"It would be nice if they could self-destruct," said Josh.

"Unfortunately, they don't; Rex and I'll have to remove them after they've reached their destination."

After placing the samples in the shed, they returned to the camp, where Marissa assembled her mini-drones. She and Catia each brought two of these drones with them from America. Each drone had four batteries, which could be recharged within fifteen minutes.

Mini-drones, known as Personal Reconnaissance Systems (PRS), have been in use by US military forces since 2014. The drones Catia and Marissa had were mini-helicopters and measured a little over sixteen centimeters in length and a little more than two-and-a-half centimeters in width. They weighed less than thirty-three grams without batteries. The three onboard cameras: one looking forward, one looking straight down, and one pointing downward at forty-five degrees, had night vision and thermal imaging capabilities. They were also equipped with long-wave infrared and day video sensors that transmitted video streams or high-resolution still images to their base station within a range of up to five kilometers. The drones could reach speeds of up to forty-six kilometers per hour and stay in the air for half an hour on a single charge.

After assembling and checking everything, Marissa launched one drone and steered it to Mount Krige, two kilometers away from the camp. She retrieved it after a while, launched the second drone, and repeated the process. Josh, Erwin, Mieke, and Liam were looking over her shoulder at her laptop screen and were amazed at the clarity of the images that came back from the drones' cameras.

Marissa tested the drones again a few hours later when it was dark to confirm the night vision equipment was functioning properly.

Chapter Thirty

WE'RE A STEP OR TWO AHEAD

Sunday. White House, Washington, D.C., USA

The president had invited Howard and Martin to have breakfast with him in the Executive Residence at eight a.m. so that they could brief him before the meeting scheduled for nine-thirty a.m. in the Oval Office.

Up till now, the president had been hoping against hope an agreement with the Namibian government for the mining of the REEs could be negotiated through private business channels. But listening to Howard and Martin over breakfast, his hopes were a little dashed but still alive. It was, however, abundantly clear it was time for contingency planning.

At 9:25 a.m., the secret service agent on guard outside the door told the president that the attendees for the meeting had arrived.

The group comprising the Director of National Intelligence (DNI) Jen Whitmer, the Secretary of State, James Hilton, and the Chair of the Joint Chiefs of Staff, Admiral

Bruce Wyatt, was seated in the Oval Office. The president had briefed the group about the discovery in Namibia the day after Howard had told him about it a few weeks ago.

After thanking everyone for coming on such short notice and giving up time with their families, the president got to the point. "The situation in Namibia needs our attention. Howard and Martin will bring us up to speed with the latest developments."

"The Chinese somehow learned about Krige's visits to the US embassy in Windhoek and have become nosy about the mine," said Martin. He told them about the fake inspection and the attempts to access the Kriges' and Naudés' phones and computers.

"As you can see, it's not a crisis yet," said Howard when Martin finished, "but it's obvious we have to start preparing for a rapid escalation of the situation."

Everyone agreed.

Howard nodded for Martin to continue. "Here's what we've done so far to buy us some time." He told them about the plan to swap the samples. "That should keep them at bay until they eventually find out they've been taken for a ride."

"How much time do you think we have?" asked Jen Whitmer, the DNI.

"Without knowing what the Chinese already know and suspect, it's difficult to predict what they'd do, but if our plan to lead them astray with the swapping of the samples works out, we'll probably have a month or two. If the plan doesn't work, it could be a matter of a week or two before the doors close for us."

"Howard, please step us through the various scenarios we might face," said the president.

"Mr. President, as far as we know, the Namibian government is unaware of the discovery. They'd have the records of Erwin Krige's mining activities, but none of them contained any information about the REEs. However, we have little doubt that when they find out, they'll not hesitate to nationalize the mine in the interest of national security."

"In other words, it all depends on who can get the ear of the Namibian government first?" said the president.

"Yes, sir," said Martin. "We don't know what the Chinese know, but we're reasonably sure they don't know about the REEs."

"Okay," said the president, "let's assume *that* part of your plan works; tell us how the rest plays out?"

"Sir, the moment they take the bait, the Secretary of State should announce a visit to a few African countries, including Namibia. At about the same time, the Chair of the Joint Chiefs of Staff should announce a major maritime exercise simulating a wartime operation in the South Atlantic off the southwest coast of Africa to take control of and safeguard the Cape Sea Route around the southern tip of Africa."

A protracted silence followed. What Howard proposed was consequential; it was enterprising and possibly the only way Operation Sierra could succeed, but it was also almost like a declaration of war with China.

The president studied the faces of James Hilton and Admiral Bruce Wyatt to gauge their reactions but learned nothing, so he asked. "James, Bruce, what are your thoughts?"

"Mr. President, I like the idea of putting a bit of persuasive and deterrent power behind the negotiations. I'll need a few days to draw up a plan," said Admiral Wyatt.

The president's gaze shifted to James Hilton. "Same here, Mr. President. I like the idea of having my military big brother close by when tangling with the Chinese. Besides, I've long been a proponent of the strategic value of the Cape Sea Route. I'll start work on a plan right away."

The president turned to Howard. "I want you and Martin to work out a plan of how we're going to get private enterprise involved in the bid for that mine."

"Will do, sir," said Howard. He and Martin had already talked about it since Rex brought it up.

The meeting continued for another forty minutes as they discussed more scenarios and solutions.

In conclusion, the president said, "Let's have a look at those plans by the end of the week. At the moment, we're a step or two ahead of the Chinese; let's keep it that way."

Chapter Thirty-One

VALUABLE INFORMATION

Monday. Windhoek, Namibia

Since the video conference with Martin and Rex the day before, Laura and James had put their thinking caps on. With the first coffee of the day in hand, they were in Laura's office by 7:30 a.m. Monday morning.

"Let's have a look at the Ministry of Natural Resources and Energy's org chart first," said Laura as she brought the organizational structure chart up on her computer's second screen.

At the top of the chart was the name of the minister, Jackson Kaura, and his mugshot. Below him was the director of the department, and below the director, there were four commissioners, one for each subdepartment or directorate, as they called it. For now, Laura and James were most interested in the Commissioner of Mining, Simon Nuusiku, the man in charge of the Mines Directorate. His was the directorate that dealt with applications for prospecting and mining permits. The mine inspectors also sorted under him.

"Aha, look at this," said Laura, hovering the mouse pointer over the four blocks below Nuusiku's name. "There are four senior inspectors reporting directly to Commissioner Nuusiku—Leah Visser is one of them."

"Hmm, interesting," said James. "Does this mean, Nuusiku could be the one who instructed Visser to carry out the inspection?"

"It's quite possible. At the very least, Nuusiku would know about it."

"If so, it means Nuusiku must've received instructions from higher up or directly from the Chinese, right?"

Laura leaned back in her chair and took a long sip of her coffee while staring at the screen. "I think you're right," she said after a while. "We need to dig right here." She selected the boxes representing Nuusiku and his inspectors.

"Okay, let's get our senior analyst to start digging," said James.

"Agreed. You brief Jeff while I see what I can find out about Minister Kaura; he's one of the few ministers I haven't met."

A few minutes later, James was briefing Jeff, the lead analyst at the embassy, to scour the records internal and external, the latter including OSINT, Open Source Intelligence databases, for every bit of information about Simon Nuusiku, Leah Visser, and Joseph Hauwanga.

James was barely back at his desk when the analyst called. "James, I've come across a bit of information I thought you might want to know immediately. Minister Jackson Kaura is married to Simon Nuusiku's aunt on his mother's side."

"So, the minister is his maternal uncle?"

"Yep."

"Thanks, Jeff. That's a good piece of information. Can you do me a favor and get me everything about Leah Visser first? Telephone number, home address, family members, and such?"

"Will do."

A few minutes later, James was back in Laura's office and told her about Nuusiku's and Kaura's family ties.

"That doesn't mean they're corrupt," said Laura. "Sometimes ordinary people have relatives in high places."

"But it's worth investigating?"

"Absolutely. Okay, let Jeff collect as much as he can get and hand it over to Rex Dalton."

"That's the plan."

"By the way, what's your first impression of him?" asked Laura.

"Rex Dalton?"

"Yes."

"Difficult to say from one impersonal video conference. Notwithstanding, I don't need another meeting to convince me it's only if you have a death wish that you'd want to cross swords with that guy."

Laura nodded. "I got the same feeling."

By midday, Jeff had all the information he could get about Simon Nuusiku, Leah Visser, and Joseph Hauwanga, which was not much more than what could be gleaned from Google and social media searches plus telephone numbers and email addresses collected from government websites.

To James, it didn't look like much, but Rex assured him it was valuable information.

The coordinates of the shed

Monday. Windhoek, Namibia

Since the telephone call with the intemperate Quan in the early morning hours on Sunday, Tian had been trying to get hold of Andreas Nakanyala, the man he thought of as a sewage worker—the one who did the dirty work. Tian was livid when Nakanyala finally returned his calls at one-thirty p.m. on Monday.

Nakanyala was a devious and ruthless operator in the shadow world of organized crime in southern Africa, including Namibia. He wanted people to believe that he had been a ferocious freedom fighter—a kind of Rambo of Namibia's war of independence. In his version of his fabled military career, he omitted the fact that he was only eighteen when the war ended more than thirty years ago. The few months he served among SWAPO's cadres, he was a bully with an AK-47 who went around intimidating defenseless people to vote for SWAPO.

Since then, he had tried his hand at honest jobs but found it unfulfilling. It was only when he ventured into the underworld of livestock theft, drug smuggling, prostitution, and poaching that he found purpose in life and eventually came to the attention of the Chinese triads. These days he fancied himself as the commander of a mercenary force.

Since the sixties, there had hardly been a coup or attempted coup in Africa where mercenaries were not involved. For decades they helped to prop up dictators in power or overthrow others, depending on who paid the most.

The Chinese triads in Africa often use mercenaries to do

their dirty work. So did Tian Chao and MSS agents across Africa. Mercenaries had no political affiliations, they were cheap, but most of all, they were deniable and dispensable.

However, what Nakanyala thought of as his private army was in reality not a group of trained soldiers; they were a group of lawbreakers, many of them ex-convicts operating in various illegal ventures such as drug smuggling, money laundering, human trafficking, prostitution, illicit trading in ivory, rhino horn, pangolin, and illegal lumbering of timber in Namibia, Angola, South Africa, Zimbabwe, and Zambia. Nakanyala's gang of outlaws was one of Sino-Africa Development Corporation's major suppliers of contraband.

"What's up?" said Nakanyala in a brusque, self-righteous tone without preamble when Tian answered.

Were it not that Nakanyala was his biggest supplier of illicit wildlife merchandise, Tian would've told him to perform an anatomically impossible sexual act on himself. But he kept his calm. "I want a meeting. It's urgent."

"The warehouse. One hour."

The line went dead.

Wonderful. If it's not enough to have an insolent boss, I also have to put up with an idiot who thinks there's a solar eclipse every time he takes a crap.

The warehouse, Windhoek's Chinatown, is in the Northern Industrial Area, not too far from Katutura, across the street from the Solid Waste Management Division. Windhoek's Chinatown differs from Chinatowns in other countries. In Windhoek, it's not an area where all the Chinese live and do their business; this one is a giant ware-house of small shops where many of the Chinese store owners sell designer-name knockoffs and fake products, thus making their contribution to the illicit US$2 trillion global counterfeit markets covering virtually every industry sector, including food, beverages, apparel, accessories, footwear, pharmaceuticals, cosmetics, electronics, auto parts, and toys, even currency.

One hour later, Tian and Nakanyala were in a back room of one of the Chinatown shops. The owner was one of Tian's informants who kept him up-to-date with the gossip and rumors in the Chinese community. Within half an hour, they'd agreed on the price. Tian gave Nakanyala the coordinates of the shed at Mount Krige and told him where to deliver the samples.

Chapter Thirty-Two

LIVING FROM PAYCHECK TO PAYCHECK

Tuesday. Khomas Hochland Mountains, Namibia | The Ranch, Arizona, USA

Rex's satellite phone alerted him about an email at six a.m. A few seconds later, before he could check the email, his phone rang. It was Greg.

It was nine p.m. Monday on The Ranch in Arizona. "Morning, Rex, nothing like sunrise on a farm in Africa, I presume?"

Rex laughed. "Greg, you have to be here to know what I'm talking about."

"Is that an invitation? Rehka is sitting next to me; she's been pestering me to join you and the team over there."

Rehka Gyan was the daughter of Rex's friend from Bilaspur, India. She had a master's degree in computer sciences and exceptional skills in programming and online research. Since she had met Greg Wade and worked with him and his team on several missions, her knowledge and abilities had gone from strength to strength, and so had their feelings for each other. The two of them were engaged.

"Depending on what our Chinese friends are up to, that's a distinct possibility," said Rex.

"You just let us know when we should start packing."

"Okay. Now, I am sure you didn't disturb our sun-worshipping to talk about your vacation plans?"

"Right. The team is still collecting information about your targets. The first tranche is related to Leah Visser, the inspector, and the junior, Joseph Hauwanga. Rehka did the research. It's in the email she sent a minute or so ago."

"Got it, but you phoned before I could read it. Give me the summary."

Rehka took over. "Hi Rex, it's good to hear your voice. How's Catia?" Catia, Marissa, and Rehka were the female equivalent of the Three Musketeers.

"Hey, Rehka, I'm right here. Marissa and I are having the time of our lives. Wish you were here—"

Rex interrupted. "Okay, ladies, business first."

Rehka laughed. "Yes, boss. Okay, first, the apprentice inspector, Joseph Hauwanga, is just that, an apprentice. He lives with his parents, has no savings or debt, quite a few girlfriends, no vices, and no criminal record. He's a boring kind of guy."

"Leah Visser is forty-five years old. She's a widow. Her husband was a devoted alcoholic who drank himself to death about two years ago, leaving behind her and their three children, a ten-year-old boy and twelve-year-old identical twin girls. She and the children live in a two-bedroom hovel in Katutura. I found that strange. She earns what is regarded in Namibia as an above-average salary of sixteen thousand dollars per month. That's about one thousand one hundred and fifty US dollars. Katutura is not a nice place to live and raise children. On her salary, she should be able to afford much better accommodation in Khomasdal, a low-income but decent suburb of Windhoek, closer to her work, better schools, and a better neighborhood than Katutura. Like her understudy, she has no criminal record or vices. And there's no love interest—there hasn't been one since the passing of her husband.

"So, I had a look at her bank statements for the past twelve months and found, every month, like clockwork, on the same day as her salary arrived in her account, there was a cash withdrawal of seven thousand Namibian dollars, leaving her with nine thousand dollars, that's about six hundred and fifty US, to support her family. She has no car. She has a pay-as-you-go cellphone and an internet data account that goes with it. She has no other source of income. She has no savings. What's left of her salary after the cash withdrawal goes toward rent, food, clothes, medicine, and such."

"In other words," said Catia, "she lives from paycheck to paycheck?"

"Exactly."

"What do you suppose the cash withdrawal is for?" asked Rex.

"Well, she could be a good Samaritan taking care of extended family or friends. Or she's paying off some unofficial debt."

"To the detriment of her own children? I doubt that. How long has she been working at the Ministry?" asked Rex.

"She started there five years ago as a general office worker. A factotum, cleaning the office, making coffee and tea, and carrying documents around. Then she became one of the three secretaries of the Commissioner of Mining,

Simon Nuusiku. She was in that role for three months before she was promoted to the position of inspector, two months after her husband died."

"What are her qualifications?" asked Rex.

"She has a one-year diploma in secretarial and administrative studies from the Triumphant College in Windhoek. Which, of course, is another anomaly. She was overqualified for the office gofer job, perfectly qualified for the secretarial job, but entirely unqualified for her current job."

"Good work, Rehka. Anything else?"

"No. But I'll keep working on her case. I just thought you might want to know what I've learned so far."

"I've got a feeling this information is going to be crucial to our mission here. I am going to take Digger for a walk so you and Catia can have a yarn. Have a good one, Rehka. *Auf Wiedersehen,* Greg."

Chapter Thirty-Three

SAYING GOODBYE TO LIAM

Tuesday. Windhoek, Namibia

At about ten a.m., Erwin, Mieke, and Liam, dragging his ever-present companion, the large rolling briefcase behind him, arrived at the US embassy. It's possible that the security guard checking the briefcase noticed it was empty, or maybe she didn't—she made no mention of it.

The three had a short meeting with Ambassador Edwards, after which the Kriges took Liam to the airport for his flight back to America. On the way to the airport, Liam transferred the contents of his briefcase, which the ambassador gave him during the meeting, to a backpack supplied by Mieke.

Less than an hour after they'd left the embassy, James texted Sara. "Drinks after work at the Wine Bar, Garten Street? My shout."

The reply came a few minutes later. "You've made my day! 5:30, ok?"

Of course, I've made your day. You're about to get paid by the

Chinese for the privilege of drinking with me on the American taxpayers' tab. James thought but typed, "5:30 is perfect."

The moment the fun starts

Tuesday. Erongo Mountains, Namibia

Josh and Marissa had remained at the campsite with Kaiser to keep an eye on things when the Kriges took Liam to Windhoek for his flight back home. On Monday, Erwin had reassigned Nelis Goreseb and his team to one of his mines near the Spitzkoppe until the mining permit for Mount Krige had been approved.

Since planting the samples on Sunday, Martin had ordered the two sites to be placed under the surveillance of a CIA keyhole spy satellite. Back in Langley, analysts were monitoring the activities at the sites.

On satellite images with a one-meter resolution, each pixel on the image covers one square meter on the ground. The satellites that Google Maps use have a fifty-centimeter resolution. The best commercial satellites have a twenty-five-centimeter resolution. Generally, spy satellites have a five-centimeter resolution making it possible to see people but not make out their faces. The CIA keyhole-class spy satellite looking down at Erwin Krige's mines had a one-centimeter resolution, not enough to see eye color or freckles, as in the movies, but enough to recognize faces.

At eleven-thirty a.m., Marissa's satellite phone dinged. It was an alert from the watchers in Langley. She woke her laptop from sleep mode. When the screen came alive, she said to Josh, "Looks like we have visitors."

"Where?"

"Mount Krige. Have a look."

Josh looked over her shoulder at the screen. It was a white Toyota Hilux pickup, driving slowly by the storage shed at Mount Krige. That was not an uncommon occurrence, per se. These vast stretches of land in the Erongo Mountains belonged to the Damara people, who were herders of cattle, goats, and sheep. They believed in communal ownership of land—God had given the land to everyone to share—therefore, there was no need for fences.

There was a mesh of two-track dirt roads all over the place. But the white Toyota raised suspicion because the man in the passenger seat was hanging out the window taking photos with his cellphone.

"This would have to be the reconnaissance team," said Josh. "And my guess is the only thing in that shed they're interested in is the samples. Do you think you could get one of your drones over there so we can get a few photos of their faces and the license plates of the vehicle?"

"Yep. Give me a minute."

A few minutes later, the drone was circling about four hundred feet above the truck, streaming high-resolution footage back to Marissa's laptop.

When the truck had left, Josh contacted Rex and told him about the visitors while Marissa sent the footage from the drones to Catia's laptop, which she immediately passed on to Laura Murray in Windhoek.

The Kriges arrived back at the camp about three hours later. Josh and Marissa told them about the scouts, and Erwin handed the backpack to Josh, "With the compliments of the ambassador."

"Thanks," said Josh and unpacked the contents while explaining to Erwin and Mieke what each item was.

It was about the same time when Laura phoned Rex. "Okay, the vehicle is registered to Andreas Nakanyala. According to my police contact, Nakanyala's name frequently pops up in conversations about organized crime activities across Namibia and neighboring countries. But so far, they have not caught him in the act. Apparently, he commands a band of ex-convicts and deviant youngsters to do his dirty work." She also told him about Nakanyala's self-aggrandizing war stories.

"Thanks, Laura. Please get me whatever information you can about this Andreas Nakanyala."

"Will do," she said.

Rex called Josh. "Hey, Farley, put down that Windhoek Lager, and get yourself a mug of strong black coffee so you can sober up. Trouble is heading your way."

"You know, Dalton, before I met you, I had lots of friends and couldn't even spell the word trouble. Now all I have is trouble and no friends. What kind of mess did you get yourself into this time?"

"Well, it turns out Namibia has its very own Rambo. And he might be heading your way."

"He's welcome as long as he understands this is a nuclear-free zone. That bow with the nuclear-tipped arrows stays at home."

Rex told him what Laura learned from her sources about the visitors to Mount Krige earlier. "So, I think you're right; those guys were the scouts. They'll be back, and they might bring some of their buddies along."

"Okay, we'll stick to the plan. If they turn up here, we'll make ourselves scarce and let them take what they want. If they decide to pay us a visit here at the camp, we might have to resort to kinetic action."

"Do you have the weapons for it?"

"We could start a war over here. Two nine-millimeter Heckler and Koch P30s, two point-two-two Berettas, a twelve-gauge pump-action Mossberg, and two .308 Musgrave hunting rifles with Schmidt and Bender night vision telescopes. Ammunition-wise, we'd be able to sustain the war for as long as it takes to fire off one and a half thousand rounds. Oh, and don't forget, we also have Kaiser; he'll guard this camp with his life."

"Okay, sounds like you'll be able to take care of yourselves."

"We'll call you the moment the fun starts."

Chapter Thirty-Four

THAT'S IT?

Tuesday. Windhoek, Namibia

The wine bar at Windmill Hill, 3 Garten Street, Auspannplatz, Windhoek, proclaimed to be Namibia's first and most popular wine bar. They also boasted about their restaurant and specialist wine shop, which, according to them, stocked the capital's largest collection of wines under one roof.

James arrived ten minutes early, and Sara, as always, ten minutes late. They went through their established feigned routine of excitement to see each other, including the French-style kisses on both cheeks.

A few minutes later, their wine had been served. They took a few sips and made small talk.

When there was a lull in the conversation, Sara asked, "What's the poop?"

"I'm afraid it's not much, but you asked me to get you everything about Krige and his silver mine. And, of course, I'm always looking for an excuse to be with you."

Sara screwed on one of her well-practiced I've-been-flattered smiles. It only reached her lips. "You're such a darling, James."

"I do my best. Okay, the poop is, the silver mine is too small for the investor. His geologist, Dr. Collins, told the ambassador so during a meeting this morning before he returned to the States."

"That's it?"

"Yep."

James was not surprised when Sara downed the rest of her wine in a few gulps while trying her best to hide her disappointment. He knew it was not about the uselessness of the information; it was about the pittance Zhong Yang would pay her for it. If only she knew she'd been fed false information, she would've been able to twist Zhong Yang's arm for a substantial payment. As it was, she didn't know and decided to keep Zhong happy by passing the information on free of charge.

Sara looked at her watch and said, "Sorry to love you and leave you, but I have another date with a few friends. I couldn't wiggle out of it. Let's catch up again soon."

"Yes, let's do that," said James, trying his best to also look disappointed.

We'll soon know the truth

Tuesday. Erongo Mountains, Namibia | Windhoek, Namibia

By nine p.m., when the information from Sara reached Zhong, four of Nakanyala's best poachers were in the bar at the Klippenberg Country Club in Karibib, having a few beers to build up courage and *esprit de corps* before the raid on Erwin Krige's shed.

Tian got a text message from Zhong ten minutes later. He wanted to believe it was the end of the saga and General Quan would be off his back. But he'd have to wait until the samples had been analyzed before he could close the case.

By eleven-thirty p.m., the four reprobates were lively and brave. It was time for action.

At the Krige campsite, Josh and Erwin had assigned themselves to sentry duty, six-hour shifts on the hilltop west of the camp from where they had a view of the shed at Mount Krige almost two kilometers away. The night vision telescopes on the hunting rifles were not made for that distance, but it was good enough to pick up any artificial lights such as those of an approaching vehicle.

It was almost midnight. Josh was on duty when Nakanyala's thugs turned up in two single-cab Toyota Hilux pickup trucks. The double-cab Toyota Hilux used for the scouting trip earlier in the day was nowhere to be seen. The vehicles had only their parking lights on and were creeping along the two-track dirt road toward the shed.

Josh phoned Marissa first and told her to get a drone in the air. Then he phoned Erwin and immediately after that

Rex. Marissa's drone was up in the air and on the way to the shed within minutes. The video feed from the drone displayed on her laptop screen, which she was sharing remotely with Catia's laptop on Eldorado.

The first truck pulled up at the gate. The man in the passenger seat got out and attached the cable of the winch mounted on the front bumper to the gate and signaled for the driver to reverse. By now, the entire area was illuminated by the glow of the solar-powered security lights. The gate got ripped off its hinges and dragged out of the way.

The two pickups proceeded to the shed. A large bolt cutter made short work of the lock on the double door. The marauders went to work immediately. The 110 bags of samples were loaded onto one truck. They then loaded the second truck with any other loot they thought of value— hand tools, a generator, mechanized augers, and several jerry cans of gasoline.

Fifteen minutes after the front gate had been removed, the two trucks were heading back the way they came. Wisely, they didn't extend their plundering to the Krige campsite—that would have ended very badly for them.

Marissa's drones had captured extensive footage of the faces of the criminals and the license plates of both vehicles. She brought the drones back to base and activated the GPS trackers hidden in the samples. They had a battery life of five days and used the local cellular network to broadcast their location every few minutes.

When four red dots came alive on Marissa's screen, she patched the data stream through to Josh's and Rex's satellite phones and Greg's computer in Arizona. Then she and Josh grabbed their bags, said goodbye to the Kriges, and followed the GPS signals in their rented SUV. But to their surprise, the vehicle with the samples didn't turn east on the

B2 toward Windhoek as they'd expected; instead, it turned west and headed for the coast. On Eldorado, Rex, Catia, and Digger got into Pieter's Range Rover and took the C28, the gravel road, to Swakopmund.

Not long after, Tian received a text message from Nakanyala. "ETA about 90 mins." Tian smiled. *We'll soon know what you've been hiding, Mr. Krige.*

Chapter Thirty-Five

OR OPERATION SIERRA WOULD GO PEAR-SHAPED

Wednesday. Walvis Bay, Namibia

The Farleys were about ten minutes behind the truck with the samples. Greg, who was keeping an eye on the satellite feed, told them that the second truck was heading east on the B2, probably going to Windhoek. "Great, two fewer thugs to worry about on the other end," said Josh.

Two hours later, Josh and Marissa pulled into a deserted parking lot between factories and warehouses in the wharf area on Ben Amathila Avenue in Walvis Bay. On the Ranch in Arizona, Greg and his team had also been following the truck's progress, and when it came to a stop at the front gate of Container Universe's premises, the team went to work. The only sound in the Cyber Room was the clacking coming from keyboards. John touched Christelle's hand and motioned for her to follow him.

Outside the room, he said to her, "Let's go to the Ops Room. The propeller heads, as Rex calls them, are a strange breed; they quickly get their noses out of joint when they're disturbed while working on these hacking jobs."

Christelle smiled and hooked her arm into John's.

Before long, Marissa had one of her drones circling at three hundred feet above the storage facility. She had to make several adjustments, and by the time she could focus on the video streaming in from the drone, the truck was parked in front of a storage container, and two men were unloading the polyethylene-lined canvas bags. She made a few adjustments on the control panel on her screen and patched the data feed from the cameras through to CRC'S Ops Room, and established an audio link so that they could talk to John and Christelle.

By one forty-five a.m., Rex, Catia, and Digger joined the Farleys. Greg and his team of hackers had penetrated the computer system of Container Universe and collected every customer's details, including their digital access codes for the front gate and their storage units. Not only that, they had also gained access to the facility's entire security system —the cyber equivalent of a *coup d'état*. Two of his team were working on getting access to the computer systems of the power supply company—just in case it became necessary to flip the power switches on the site at some stage.

Twenty minutes later, the truck had been relieved of the samples and left. The five were in the rental SUV, planning how they were going to get into the compound.

Digger was sitting between Rex and Catia on the backseat, letting out a soft whine now and then as he detected the familiar smell coming from the bodies of his human pack before they'd go into action—adrenaline.

But Digger's pack had a bit of a problem. Container Universe allowed its clients twenty-four-seven access to the premises. Clients only needed to know their unique six-digit access code for the front gate and the eight digits of the locks on their containers. CCTV cameras were covering every bit of the premises, basking in the light of industrial-strength security lights. There were two armed guards on duty. They were in a cubicle commanding the front gate. They were taking turns to walk the premises once every half hour. But none of that, including the guards and the ten-foot chain-link fence topped off with rolls of razor-wire, caused their collective headache; it was the two big German Shepherds roaming the premises.

"Where were the dogs when they unloaded the samples?" asked Rex.

"Let's have a look at the footage," said Marissa. "I missed the beginning of the video while I was busy getting the drone in place and adjusting the cameras."

She brought the stored video footage up on the screen and rewound it to the start. Zooming in, they saw one guard coming out of the office when the truck stopped at the front gate. He held his hand up to the driver, signaling for him to wait. Then he took something out of his shirt pocket, brought it to his mouth, and a few seconds later, the two dogs appeared next to him. He leashed them and waved to the driver to proceed through the gate.

"That must have been a dog whistle," said Catia. "It makes a high-pitched sound that only dogs can hear."

"Marissa, go back and zoom in on that guard's face, please," said Josh. She did it. As the face came into focus, it was unmistakable; the features were Asian. "Ten to one, he's Chinese," said Josh. "Let's have a look at the second guard."

Marissa scrolled until she found a clip where the second guard was out on his rounds. "Another Asian," said Rex.

"A quayside Chinese storage yard," said Josh. "Am I the

only one who senses something unsavory awaits us on the other side of that fence?"

"I won't bet against you," said Rex. Catia and Marissa agreed.

Despite having access codes for the front gate and the container with the samples, thanks to Greg and his hackers, they couldn't go in that way—the guards would remember their faces and log the details of their vehicle. They had to get in and out without the guards knowing. Were it not for the dogs, they would've been able to do it with Greg's help. Desperate as they were to get inside, they'd never contemplate harming the dogs. They had no tranquilizers they could use. But they had to get those trackers back, or Operation Sierra would go pear-shaped.

The guards were armed with sidearms, but the video images were not clear enough to identify the make and model, presumably Chinese. Josh and Marissa were armed with the Kriges' Heckler & Koch P30s. Rex and Catia had the Naudés' Glock 17s. But unless their lives were in danger, they'd do everything to avoid using them.

Chapter Thirty-Six

TOWARD THE SNARLING GERMAN SHEPHERDS

Wednesday. Walvis Bay, Namibia

Just when they ran out of fresh ideas of how to get onsite unnoticed, Rex started laughing.

"Here it comes," said Josh. "The last time I heard that giggle, he decided it was a great idea to jump out of an airplane in perfect flying condition in the middle of the night and land on the back of a moving boat in the middle of the Mediterranean Sea."

"A ship," said Rex.

"What?"

"It was a ship, not a boat. And we used parachutes to get onto it."

"You always get hung up on irrelevant little technical details."

"Such as the parachutes?"

"Precisely."

Rex put his arm around Digger and said, "Buddy, you're of Dutch descent. Those guys are of German ancestry.

Back in your original homelands, you're neighbors. You all speak a Germanic language. What are the chances you could wander over and have a friendly chat with the Germans while we do our thing?"

Digger yelped excitedly.

"Thanks, buddy. I knew you'd be keen to help. I reckon if you start off by telling them that all is forgiven for their invasion of Holland during World War Two, you might win them over quickly."

Digger was invigorated, yapping and whining. As if to say, "What are you waiting for? Let's get over there and do it."

"Okay, just keep your pants on for a while longer. I need to organize a few things with Greg before we go."

In the car, it was possible to hear a pin drop. Rex's companions were staring at him as if he was a few sandwiches short of a picnic. In CRC's Ops Room, Christelle looked at John in disbelieve. John shrugged and muted the microphone. "My dear, when it comes to those two, I learned long ago to just let them get on with it. Somehow they always make it work."

Christelle was shaking her head. "This I'll only believe when I see it."

In the car, Josh spoke first. "Let me see if I understand this correctly, Don Quixote. Your plan is to send Digger over there to befriend those German Shepherds and persuade them to look the other way while we cut a hole in the fence to get into the territory they're supposed to protect?"

"Precisely. Except if Greg will open the pedestrian gate at the back for us, we don't have to cut the fence."

"I see. And exactly how many times have you and your buddy done something like this?"

"Never."

"I thought so."

"If you have a better idea, tell us about it."

Josh said nothing.

"I thought so," said Rex.

Digger whined softly.

Catia looked at Digger. "What does that mean?"

His reply was to lick her in the face before she could get her hands up to stop him.

Catia laughed.

Rex turned his attention to Greg. "Okay, we're going to send Digger in to have a chat with his German relatives—"

"What?"

Rex explained what he had in mind.

Greg's only response was an incredulous, "I see."

Rex told Greg what he wanted, and Greg assured him he and his team would make it happen when he wanted it to happen.

Rex rigged Digger up with his tactical harness equipped with a video camera the size of a pencil eraser on the top of his head, between his ears, and practically invisible. Everything Digger would see would also be visible to Rex. Mini earphones were fitted in Digger's ears, completely hidden, and a mini microphone, not much bigger than a pinhead, was fitted on the harness between his front legs. All of it was wirelessly connected to an iPad mini, which Rex had strapped to his forearm.

He pushed his nose against Digger's wet nose and ruffled his ears. "Who's a clever boy?"

Digger yelped softly and licked Rex in the face, wagging his tail in excitement.

Next, Rex and Josh pulled ski masks over their faces, activated their molar mics, grabbed their small backpacks, and disappeared into the shadows with Digger scouting ahead. Marissa had two drones up following their husbands' and Digger's progress on her laptop. Catia was the mission controller. She followed the three on her laptop and stayed in contact with Rex and Josh through their molar mics. Everything she saw on her screen was also seen by the people in the Ops and Cyber rooms on the Ranch.

The Molar Mic is the latest communications technology for covert operators. The device consists of a mouthpiece equipped with a waterproof microphone, custom-built to fit the teeth of the operator. The mouthpiece translates incoming audio into vibrations on the teeth that travel through the bones in the jaw and skull to the inner ear, which convert them into sounds.

When the pedestrian gate in the fence at the back of the facility came into view, Rex called Digger back. He and Josh took a knee behind a low wall and waited for Digger to join them. They heard other dogs barking in the distance. Obviously, there were more businesses that used guard dogs to watch over their properties at night. Maybe the dogs had scented the intruders, but the Germans were quiet and out of sight. The human nose has about six million olfactive receptors. Dogs like Digger and those German Shepherds have three hundred million; they could smell a target from more than three hundred meters away. There are documented cases where dogs sniffed out methamphetamine hidden in the gas tanks of cars.

Rex said to Greg, "Time to do your magic on those cameras."

"Done," said Greg two seconds later.

If the guards happened to be watching the monitors the moment Greg took control of their CCTV cameras and started replaying footage recorded two hours ago, they would've noticed only a momentary blip on the screens. Whether or not they saw it, none of them came out of the guardhouse to investigate.

The premises were so well lit it would've been impossible for Digger, let alone Rex and Josh, to cross the thirty meters to the fence without being noticed by those cameras.

Digger materialized out of the dark next to Rex. He put his wet nose against Rex's. "Clever boy. Now, see that gate?" he pointed at the pedestrian gate. "Josh and I want to enter there."

Digger whined softly, and as if they were sent, the German Shepherds appeared at the fence about fifty meters to the left of said gate. They had their noses in the air. Fortunately, the slight sea breeze came from behind them. Contrary to popular belief, dogs' eyesight is not much better than that of humans. Rex pointed at the Germans and said, "Go tell them we say hi, and we mean them no harm."

Digger looked at Rex for a long moment, during which Rex felt his heart drop to the floor, as he thought Digger had no clue what to do now. He pointed to the dogs again. "Don't worry, buddy. I'm sure they'd like you."

The next moment Digger turned and started strolling, almost casually, unafraid, toward the snarling German Shepherds.

Chapter Thirty-Seven

HOW TO WIN FRIENDS AND INFLUENCE DOGS

Wednesday. Walvis Bay, Namibia

Rex and Josh were watching Digger through their monoculars and didn't realize that they'd stopped breathing. They had no way of knowing that the same had happened to Catia and Marissa in the RAV 4, a block away, and everyone at CRC headquarters, thousands of miles away. They were unaware that Greg had, on orders from John, patched Martin in on the video and audio feeds, who was in his office in Langley more than an hour ago. Martin was breathing while chewing his nails and mumbling softly to himself. "This won't work. It's crazy. It just can't... work."

The Germans' growls became louder and more frequent as Digger closed the distance. The hair on their necks and backs stood on end. Their lips were curled, displaying their enormous fangs. Yet Digger seemed cool as a cucumber and kept on walking toward them unhesitatingly. He showed no signs of aggression or fear. His demeanor was as if he was saying, "Hey guys, don't worry, I'm the new kid on the block and thought I'd drop by to introduce myself."

With bated breath, Rex and Josh watched Digger reach the fence. Josh whispered, "So far, so good, Digger. Now for the sweet-talk."

"They haven't barked so far," said Rex.

"Why not?"

"I think it's because Digger is not aggressive. Look at him; his hair is not raised, he's wagging his tail, and his tongue is hanging out. He's telling them he's coming in peace."

The Germans' tails looked like protruding broomsticks as they cautiously sniffed Digger through the chain-link fence from nose to tail and back again. Throughout it all, he didn't move; only his tail remained in slow motion. The thirty seconds it took for the Germans to check Digger out felt like thirty minutes. The biggest of the two, clearly the alpha, started wagging his tail. His underling followed suit seconds later. And like mist before the sun, the tension disappeared as the three with tails wagging in excitement started sniffing each other's faces while making what sounded to Rex as soft and happy whining noises.

"I'll be damned," said Josh. "Digger must have read Dale Carnegie's *'How to Win Friends and Influence Dogs.'*"

Rex had to fight the urge to erupt in raucous laughter. He regained composure, tapped the microphone icon on the iPad mini strapped to his left forearm, and said to Digger, "Okay, buddy, Josh and I are going to show ourselves now, and then we're going to start walking toward the gate. Tell your new friends we're coming in peace."

Digger's only reply was a soft yelp, which Rex took for a "Yes."

Catia said, "Coast is clear. You have twenty minutes before the guard makes the next round."

He and Josh rose slowly from their hiding place and started toward the pedestrian gate at a normal pace—deliberate, but not too slow and not too fast. The Germans stopped "talking" to Digger and looked at Rex and Josh. Through his molar mic connected to Digger's microphone, Rex heard the low growls. He knew if they stopped and paid the dogs any attention, they would see it as a threat and make a big palaver of it. He whispered to Josh through the molar mic, "Don't look at them, just keep on walking."

"Copy that."

When they were about ten paces from the gate, Catia's voice sounded in Rex's head. "Digger and his new friends are also heading for the gate." He threw a quick glance to his left. Touched the mic button on the iPad. "Digger, what are you doing, buddy? You're supposed to keep them away."

Digger made no reply. Not a yelp, nor a growl, not even a whine.

Rex and Josh reached the gate at the same time as the dogs. To their surprise, the Germans looked happy to see them, no aggression. In fact, it looked as if they were extremely keen to get through the gate.

Fifteen thousand kilometers away, Greg pushed a button on his keyboard, and the electronic lock on the pedestrian gate in front of them made a rather loud clicking sound as it unlocked. Rex pulled the gate open and had to jump out of the way as the two excited German Shepherds rushed past him to give their newfound friend the canine version of a welcome hug. They didn't even so much as glance at either of the humans.

After a few seconds of dog hugging, Digger glanced at

Rex, turned, and started jogging away toward the neighboring buildings with the Germans short on his heels.

Rex and Josh were gawking at the disappearing dogs.

"Bloody hell," said Josh. "Have you ever seen anything like that? It's as if Digger told them about a canine strip joint with gorgeous girls and cheap drinks just around the corner."

Rex chuckled softly at the image of Digger and his friends having a drink in a strip club.

"Now I've seen everything," said Christelle into her microphone, unaware everyone could hear her. "There's nothing Digger could do that could ever surprise me again."

In Langley, Martin poured himself a stiff shot of bourbon, raised his glass, and said, "To the cleverest damn dog on the planet."

Three minutes later, Rex and Josh stood inside the storage container where the samples were offloaded. In the beams of their tactical flashlights and the scanners on their satellite phones, they quickly found the bags holding the GPS trackers and removed them.

Rex looked at his watch when they were done. "We have ten minutes. Let's have a look around. As you said earlier, there's probably more than just stolen rock samples here."

Josh was right.

There were six forty-foot containers interlinked by internal doors. The contents reminded them of a house of horrors. Stacks upon stacks of rhino horn, elephant tusks, pangolin skins with scales still attached, lion and cheetah skins, parts of every protected species in Namibia.

They took a chance and switched the lights on so that they could make video recordings and take photos.

They were not nearly done when Catia warned them they were out of time and had to get out.

"I wonder if Martin could get another spy satellite to keep an eye on this place?" said Josh. "I think we've only seen the tip of the iceberg here."

Rex nodded. They were still talking about it when John's voice came over their molar mics. "Good idea, boys. Martin says he'll have a satellite assigned within the hour. Now get your asses out of there."

On the way to the gate, Rex said into Digger's earphones. "Come, buddy. It's time to go."

When they arrived at the gate, Digger and his German friends were waiting for them. Rex opened the gate and let them all in. He kneeled next to Digger and scratched his back. "Who is a clever dog?" Digger yelped softly. "You did it, buddy. I'm sorry I ever doubted you. Okay, time to say goodbye to your friends. We have to go now."

Digger turned to the Germans, rubbed noses with them, and then walked out through the gate while they sat there with what Rex would swear were sad faces as their newfound friend left.

It was four thirty-five a.m. when Josh closed the gate, and the three of them went back to their vehicles where Catia and Marissa were waiting.

Chapter Thirty-Eight

SEND CONNOR AND SAM

Wednesday. En route to the Krige campsite

Shortly after five a.m., Rex and company stopped at the twenty-four-hour Oceanview Shell Service Station in Swakopmund, where they used the bathrooms and bought takeaway coffees before heading to the Kriges' campsite.

On the way, Catia and Marissa had set up an audio conference between their vehicles, the CRC's Ops Room, and Martin's office in Langley. Digger, the hero of the mission, didn't take part; he was in the back, entirely focused on getting the *biltong* treats out of the kong.

Although the retrieval of the GPS trackers might keep the Chinese out of their hair for a while, they had a lot more to do to make Operation Sierra a success. Who was behind the theft of the samples? How did the Ministry of Natural Resources and Energy fit into the picture? Who owned the illegal wildlife products in that storage facility? Was there a connection? Was there more contraband stored on Container Universe's premises? They had little doubt there were Chinese masterminds behind all of it, but they needed names and faces and addresses.

"Though we should not get sidetracked, it's highly likely whoever is behind the stealing of the samples is also aware of what's in those storage units, if not the owner of it," said Rex.

"Agreed," said John. "What do you have in mind?"

"Send Connor and Sam to help with surveillance tasks. We're soon going to have more leads to follow than the four of us can handle. Also, Greg and his team should delve into the affairs of not only Container Universe but also every one of their customers. Start with the unit we visited tonight."

"On it," said Greg.

"Okay, I'll dispatch Connor Burns and Sam Price as soon as we finish the call," said John.

"I'll organize a ride for them on a CIA jet," said Martin.

Burns and Price were CRC surveillance specialists who assisted Rex and his team during an operation in Taiwan a few months before to prevent the assassination of prominent politicians by a PLA hit squad.

As agreed the night before, Erwin, Mieke, and Kaiser took an early morning walk and 'discovered' the break-in at the shed. Erwin immediately phoned the Karibib police, who arrived half an hour later.

The police inspector walked around the premises and the shed, shaking his head while his junior took photos and made notes. Apparently, the inspector didn't find it strange that the thieves took the samples. Maybe the polyethylene-lined canvas bags were worth something. When they were back at the police vehicle, he said to Erwin, "I hope you have insurance, Mr. Krige. I think there's little chance we'll ever get anything back or track down the criminals. Obviously, they've done this sort of thing before."

Erwin did his best to look disappointed. "Oh well, I guess there's little more I can do then. If you can give me the case number so I can provide it to my insurers, that would be great."

It would be better to behead the snake

Wednesday. Erongo Mountains, Namibia

Rex and company arrived at the campsite shortly after seven-thirty a.m., a quarter of an hour after the police had left. Mieke called them for breakfast under the *kameeldoring* tree the moment they got out of the RAV 4.

Over breakfast, Rex and the others told the Kriges and the Naudés, the latter had arrived an hour earlier, about Digger's antics and the discovery of the illicit goods in the storage units. Catia showed them the photos and videos.

It shocked them.

Pieter's face was distorted with rage when he spoke. "Scum. This would by far be the biggest haul of illegal wildlife products Namibia has ever seen."

"How much could it be worth?" asked Josh.

"Between fifty and a hundred million US on the Asian black markets."

"*What?* Are you serious?"

"Well, make your own calculations. Sixty-five thousand

US dollars per kilo for the rhino horn. Around one thousand eight hundred per kilo for the ivory. Over three thousand per kilo for pangolin scales. The lion and cheetah skins would fetch thousands each. The rest of the stuff won't be going cheap either."

"Unbelievable," said Marissa.

"They're growing rich by stealing Namibia's natural heritage," said Mieke. "They use poor Namibians to do their dirty work but give them less than ten percent of the profit."

"What's the government doing to stop this mayhem?" asked Catia.

"In 2017, the government increased the penalties for anyone caught in possession of rhino horn, elephant ivory, pangolin scales, or other controlled wildlife parts dramatically," said Erwin. "Fines of up to fifteen million Namibian dollars, that's about one million US, or up to fifteen years in jail, or both.

"Those caught trying to buy or sell these parts, either locally or for export, are facing fines of up to twenty-five million Namibian or jail sentences of up to twenty-five years, or both."

"We thought those penalties would deter the poachers; they didn't," said Pieter. "Africa's white rhinos have been wiped out. Black rhinos are rare and slow breeding animals. Poachers have driven them to the verge of extinction in Namibia. Elephant poaching in the northeastern parts has risen dramatically in the past few years, as has pangolin trafficking across the country."

"The government launched Operation Blue Rhino in 2018 to combat illegal wildlife trade in Namibia," said Thea. "It's a joint venture between NAMPOL, the Namibian Police Force, and MET, the Intelligence Investigation Unit of the Ministry of Environment and Tourism. Blue Rhino also works with the Namibian military, Save the Rhino Trust, and their colleagues in Botswana and Zambia. According to the media, Blue Rhino has had a lot of success thus far, but looking at those images you showed us, I'd say they'd better review their success record. It's not as successful as they'd like to believe."

"It just occurred to me," said Erwin, "whoever is behind the theft of the samples is ten to one involved in this horror as well?"

Rex nodded. "Yep, that's our take on it, too. And until we get evidence to the contrary, we can assume the main player is PLA Incorporated, for this is how they operate all over the world."

"I think we should get in touch with Blue Rhino," said Pieter. "Let them take the bastards down."

Rex shook his head. "I'd like to hold off on that. If the authorities get involved, they'll just send in a SWAT team or suchlike and confiscate the products. There's little to no chance they'll get their hands on the people behind this. We want to know who they are. All of them. From top to bottom."

Pieter looked a little dejected but started nodding his head after a while. "I guess you're right. It would be better to behead the snake while we're at it."

Thea and her parents agreed.

"My understanding is that various United States government agencies, development banks, foundations, and influential individuals support Namibia's wildlife conservation efforts, is that correct?" said Rex.

Pieter nodded. "Yes, that's true."

"Any from China that you know of?"

Pieter made a circle with his thumb and index finger.

Shortly after nine thirty a.m., Catia and Marissa got text messages from the Langley analysts monitoring the activities at the Container Universe site in Walvis Bay.

A Toyota pickup had arrived at the storage unit where the samples were stored, and two men were loading the bags onto the back of the vehicle.

They opened their laptops and logged into the satellite application, with everyone looking over their shoulders.

It took the men about fifteen minutes to load the bags onto the back of the pickup and drive out the front gate. Catia told the analysts to keep the satellite cameras on the pickup. By now, the satellite had a glimpse at the license plate.

About twenty minutes later, the pickup pulled into the loading bay at Namgeochem in Walvis Bay's light industrial area, and the men started unloading the cargo.

Greg and John were in conference with them while following the satellite footage on the big screens in the Ops and Cyber rooms on the Ranch. Within minutes, Greg told them that Namgeochem also had labs and offices in Windhoek and Lüderitz and who the shareholders and directors were.

It took his team half an hour to gain access to Namgeochem's computer networks and only a few minutes to find out that the client who requested the testing of the samples was Sino-Africa Development Corporation.

"Okay, Greg...," Rex started, but Greg interrupted.

"The data queries are already running. Watch this space."

"Great."

This was the first time the Kriges and Naudés saw the

technology Rex and his team had access to and how well it operated over the satellite links, enabling them to communicate with people halfway around the world as if they were sitting next to them. Whether or not one was a novice, it was impressive.

"The test results can be expected in two to five days," said Thea. "And unless my or their equipment is faulty, we already know what the results will be."

"Hopefully, that will keep the Chinese out of our way for a while," said John.

Before saying goodbye, John told Rex that Connor Burns and Sam Price were en route to D.C. from where they would be traveling to Windhoek on a CIA private jet. They'd be in Windhoek within the next eighteen hours.

Chapter Thirty-Nine

THEIR FIRST TARGET

Wednesday. En route to Windhoek, Namibia

When the conference call ended, Catia made reservations for them at the Windhoek Hilton. Connor and Sam already had reservations there. By two p.m., they were on the way to Windhoek and were talking to Rehka about Leah Visser, their first target.

True to her promise, Rehka had made an in-depth study of Leah's private life as chronicled in her emails, Facebook posts, text messages, and WhatsApp chats. And she had collected lots of photos of Leah and her children.

Rehka already told them Leah had no car. From her home in Katutura to her work in the city was five kilometers, a one-hour walk. Windhoek was the only city in Namibia with public transport. The problem was, it was so unreliable it might as well not have existed. Therefore, she walked the distance twice a day, five days a week. Tuesdays and Fridays, on the way home, she stopped at a supermarket to do grocery shopping.

Leah Visser was an honest, church-going, Christian widow struggling to make ends meet. Her priorities in life were her faith and her children. She worked hard, and with three children to raise, there was no time or money for anything else.

"Rehka, do you have bank statements going back to the time before she was an inspector?" asked Rex.

"Yes. I have statements for the past three years."

"Check them. What cash withdrawals are there before she became an inspector?"

A minute later, Rehka said, "There are small amounts not the same every time and at irregular intervals. The big cash withdrawal every month started the first month after she took the inspector job."

"Thanks, Rehka. Now I want you to dig into the life of Simon Nuusiku."

"Will do."

They ended the call, and Rex explained to his team that he had a gut feeling the cash she withdrew from her account every month went into the pocket of whoever appointed her as Inspector, probably Nuusiku. "Protection money," said Rex.

"So, how do we get to her?" asked Marissa.

"We don't have the time to build a relationship with her. I suggest we do surveillance on her for a day or two and see if we can find a way to arrange a meeting."

The next morning at seven a.m., Rex and Josh had positioned themselves in different locations along the route that Leah took from her home to work every day. As she passed their positions, the one who had followed her up to that point would drop back, and the other would follow. Even if Leah had countersurveillance training, it would've been all but impossible to detect her tail. Catia and Marissa followed the procession in the RAV 4, making sure they stayed about one kilometer behind Leah. Marissa had a drone up at about four hundred feet above Leah's head, recording everything all the way to her work.

When Leah disappeared through the front door of the office building where she worked, they found themselves a coffee shop that served breakfast over which they discussed what they'd learned about Leah during her hike to work.

They decided Friday afternoon would be the best time to approach Leah. That way, they had the weekend to brief her. Well, that was if Rex's gut feeling that she was a victim of a corrupt boss happened to be correct.

They finished their coffees, got into the RAV 4, and went back to the hotel to meet Connor and Sam, who had checked in half an hour ago.

How to get through customs

Thursday. Windhoek, Namibia

The pair of CRC surveillance experts were the same age, thirty-one. Connor was tall and black. Sam was short, white, and blond. They were bosom friends. If ever there were poster boys for ordinary-looking, it was Connor Burns and Sam Price. Unremarkable and nondescript. Nevertheless, those unmemorable features were their biggest asset. They could be anybody from the homeless man begging on the streets to the business executive with a briefcase, dressed in a fancy suit, and anyone in between, including some female roles. And over the years, on countless CRC surveillance operations, they'd indeed acted in all those roles —they were accomplished actors.

Rex had asked for them because they were the best he'd ever worked with.

Rex and the others agreed; Sam was the funniest of the two because of the emotionless monotone in which he spoke, no matter what the situation.

He had them screaming with laughter when he recounted, in much detail, their encounter with the border control agents at the airport.

Apparently, it started when the agent who stamped their passports wanted to know what the purpose of their visit was. Connor, the designated spokesperson, because he was black, just like the agent, said, "Tha birds, baby. Tha birds." From that moment on, according to Sam, the agent's hitherto impassive demeanor had become one of irritability, and the atmosphere in the arrival hall had changed. It was as if every border control agent had taken a sudden interest in them. Those who were not asking questions were glowering at them.

The second to last agent they encountered performed what Sam described as something akin to a full-body search, including cavities, on all their luggage except on the two metal suitcases marked fragile. That was the dominion of the last agent.

"What is fragile in there?" the last agent, apparently the expert on metal suitcases marked fragile, wanted to know.

Sam was at a loss to explain why, after the disastrous encounter with the passport lady, Connor was still their spokesperson. Nonetheless, he still was and answered, "Bro, let me see. This one here," he pointed to the one closest to him, "the first item is a Nikon Z 7 II Mirrorless. Bro, you ain't seen nothing like that. Not even in your dreams."

The agent was stunned.

Evidently, Connor then opened the suitcase, took the camera out, and launched into a lecture about the technical and not-so-technical features of the Nikon Z 7 II Mirrorless. "Ten fps for seventy-seven frames at a time. Can you imagine? Accurate eye and animal detection AF with wide-area AF option for stills and videos. Amazing stuff. Look at this; dual card slots for Cf express, XQD, and UHS-II SD cards. Let me tell you, bro, with this baby, I can inspect the inside of the eyelids of a bird a hundred yards away."

According to Sam, when Connor replaced the camera and reached for the Zeiss binoculars, the agent threw his hands up in surrender, rolled his eyes, and said, "Welcome to Namibia. Enjoy your stay."

Although it was hilarious the way Sam told it, the performance at the airport was staged. There is a misconception among the uninformed that spies fear attention. It was that misunderstanding they exploited by drawing so much attention to themselves that no one would ever think they could be spies.

After they'd briefed the newcomers in the Daltons' hotel room, Rex and Josh went out to rent an extra vehicle, a ten-seater Toyota Quantum minibus like the one Pieter had.

That afternoon the six of them were following Leah from work to home.

Chapter Forty

YOU UNDERSTAND THE RISKS?

Friday. Windhoek, Namibia

They followed Leah one more time on Friday morning before going back to the hotel for breakfast and a planning session in the Daltons' room. It was Marissa who came up with the idea about Leah's wallet. All four of them were competent pickpockets, but Marissa was the master.

Leah had a small leather wallet, which she carried in the right-side pocket of her pantsuit jacket. They knew this because Josh's bodycam recorded her taking the wallet out of that pocket when she paid for milk and bread at the convenience store on the way home the night before.

Marissa's plan was simple and workable. On the way to the supermarket that afternoon, she would "accidentally" bump into Leah and swipe her wallet. She would continue in the opposite direction from Leah and pass the wallet to Catia and Rex as she passed them.

Rex, Catia, and Digger would follow Leah to the supermarket, and when she had to pay for the groceries and discover her wallet was missing, they'd come to her rescue, pay for everything, and give her a ride home.

Shortly after five p.m., Josh alerted them through the molar mics that Leah had exited the building where she worked. Everyone was in place along the route. The supermarket was about one kilometer from her house.

The planned rendezvous between Leah and Marissa would happen in a quiet side street, about one and a half kilometers from the supermarket. It was one of the few shortcuts she took every day to and from work.

Rex, Catia, and Digger were about fifty meters behind Leah. She was about one hundred meters from the planned collision point when things went south.

Digger noticed them first. He didn't like them and alerted Rex with a growl. Rex and Catia heard it and saw the four black men filling the sidewalk coming their way. The word trouble might as well have been flashing on their foreheads like neon lights. Rex guessed they were between twenty and twenty-five years of age.

A few paces farther, he realized Leah was their target. Her handbag was hanging from a strap over her left shoulder. He pulled the quick release on Digger's leash. He stayed right next to Rex.

"We have to get closer," Rex told Catia and increased his pace.

When Leah was about five paces away from the thugs, they split two to the left and two to the right, forcing her to pass between them.

Rex, Catia, and Digger were now about ten paces behind Leah, closing in fast. The gangsters were focused on Leah.

The one closest on her right dropped his shoulder and rammed her toward his mate on her left side, where she carried her handbag. However, the bump was a bit too energetic; Leah's momentum almost threw him off his feet. Before he could regain his balance, Digger hit him in the center of his chest. The impact of sixty-six pounds traveling through the air at forty miles per hour lifted him clean off his feet. His head and heels hit the sidewalk at the same time. He was going to wake up with the mother of all headaches.

The one who shouldered Leah met with the same fate when Rex's left boot connected with the side of his head. Except he was unconscious before his head reached the sidewalk.

The tall one on the left pulled a knife and took a step in Catia's direction. Big mistake. Digger saw it. The man was bent over, brandishing the knife as he stepped slowly toward Catia, wholly unaware of the misfortune heading his way from behind. He screamed at the top of his lungs moments after Digger's jaws locked around the hand holding the knife. Those jaws could exert pressure in the order of two hundred and fifty pounds per square inch. The knife-wielding assailant was making so much noise no one heard when the bones in his hand cracked.

The fourth one was waving a knife at Rex. But then he saw the big black dog take down his friend, who also had a knife, and he heard the screams. That's when he decided, probably for health reasons, not to hang around any longer. Besides, his friend's screaming was unsettling.

The whole affair was over in seconds. Leah didn't know what happened after she got shouldered. She saw the blood and heard the moans from the guy with the forearm soaked in blood but couldn't bring herself to do anything other than stand there in shocked silence, unable to scream or make a sound.

Catia stepped up and put her arm around the shaking woman to comfort her.

"Must... call... police...," whispered Leah in a shaky voice.

"Please don't," begged Catia. "We did nothing wrong. They attacked us without provocation. We acted in self-defense. These scumbags won't go to the police, and they won't bother you again."

Digger had sidled up to Leah, nuzzling her gently while making soft, comforting noises.

Before Leah could respond, Josh and Marissa pulled up across the street in the minibus. "Get in!" shouted Josh. "There might be more of them. Let's get out of here."

They left the hoodlums where they were and piled into the minibus. Rex and Catia were quietly thanking God that there was no one else in the street when it all happened. Leah was sitting between Rex and Catia. Digger was on the seat behind them.

Leah was shaking like a leaf in a stiff breeze. She tried to speak but stuttered so much she couldn't get a full sentence out. Catia put an arm around her and said, "Take deep breaths. Don't talk. Just breathe."

Josh drove to within half a kilometer of the supermarket and pulled into a parking space.

Although not executed exactly as they'd planned it, the outcome was exactly what they wanted—a meeting with Leah.

Catia and Marissa had calmed Leah down and could now introduce themselves. Leah's voice was still shaky when she told them who she was and thanked them for coming to her rescue.

"Where were you going when those men attacked you?" asked Catia.

"Grocery shopping and then home. It's close by; I'll be okay now. Thank you again. I don't know what would've happened to me if you weren't there."

"Please, let us take you to the shop and then home."

"That's very kind of you, but you've already gone to a lot of trouble to help me. I'll be okay now."

"C'mon, Leah, you're not okay. It's no trouble at all. It's the least we can do for someone in distress."

After a little more back-and-forth, Leah agreed.

Catia and Marissa accompanied her into the shop while Rex, Josh, and Digger waited at a coffee shop at the entrance to the supermarket.

Catia and Marissa knew Leah was struggling to make ends meet. But having the knowledge was not the same as experiencing it. For the two of them, who couldn't remember when the last time was when they had to think twice when buying food, it was a heart-rending experience to see how frugal Leah had to be to make ends meet. When the shopping trolley was loaded with the items on her list, there was not a single luxury item among them. Not even a sweet treat for the children. The bulk of the contents comprised rice, pasta, maize meal, dried beans, meat stock, and soup bones with almost no meat on them, coffee, tea, and sugar.

Before heading for the checkout, she double-checked the items in the trolley against her handwritten list, added the prices up on her phone's calculator, counted the money in her wallet, and went to the cashier.

Ironically, Catia and Marissa, without knowing they were having the same thoughts, were fighting the urge to barge in and pay for the goods. Which was precisely what they would've done if their original plan eventuated. Now they were grateful it didn't.

Meanwhile, Rex and Josh had been discussing what would be the best strategy to get Leah to listen to them. She was still in shock, but it was obvious she trusted them. Notwithstanding, her trust could quickly vanish if they didn't play their cards right.

"We have from now until we drop her off at home to make our move," said Josh.

Rex was deep in thought and didn't reply.

"Rex." There was no reply. "Earth calling Rex Dalton. Anybody home?" Josh waved his hand in front of Rex's eyes.

"Huh. Sorry. Did you say something?"

"What are you thinking?"

"I think we should be honest with her. When they come out of the shop, let's invite her to have coffee with us and tell her why we're here."

"You understand the risk?"

"I do, but I think we should take it."

Chapter Forty-One

FOR A GOOD CAUSE

Friday. Windhoek, Namibia

Rex spotted Catia and Marissa when they came out of the supermarket to wait for Leah. He promptly went and told them what he had in mind. There was no time to discuss his plan. He had to be back in his seat in the coffee shop before Leah came out.

Leah protested when Marissa suggested they have coffee and cake before going home. But she had no chance against the persuasive powers of the two. Especially when Catia hooked her arm into Leah's and steered her toward the coffee shop.

She declined the offer of cake with her coffee but gave in when Marissa said, "Don't tell me you're going to watch us have cake and not regret it? Tell you what, let's surprise your children with a piece of cake when you get home. What do you say?"

Leah had tears in her eyes. "They'd enjoy that very much. But... I... I can't..."

Catia laid her hand on Leah's forearm. "It's our treat, Leah. Tell me what you'd like to have and what your children would like."

She wiped the tears from her eyes and said, "Why are you people doing this? I've never met strangers that are so kind. I'm a Christian, I understand the principle of loving your neighbor, but... this... why... you don't even know me."

Rex knew this was the moment; he had to use it or lose it. "Leah, we've got something of great importance to discuss with you. But before I continue, I'd like to give you some assurances. One, we're also Christians. Two, you can trust us. Three, we mean you no harm. Four, whether or not you talk to us, you have our word; nothing will happen to you. Five, we will not stop you if you want to leave. But I beg you to please hear me out first."

Leah's eyes had narrowed as she looked around the table at everyone. She might have been looking for signs of deceit, but she wouldn't find any. Finally, her gaze returned to Rex, "Okay, I'll listen to you," she said in a near-inaudible voice.

"We suspect that someone at work is using you to do their dirty work—"

"What's this alleged dirty work I am supposedly doing?" she snarled.

"We believe you're not aware it's happening—"

"You're right. I'm not."

"We believe you're an honest person, but some unscrupulous person at work is taking advantage of you. That's why we want to talk to you."

"This is creepy. I suggest you get to the point, or I'll be leaving."

"That's totally understandable, Leah," said Catia. "After your experience earlier, I'm so sorry we're putting you through this, but it's critical that you hear what Rex has to say."

Leah didn't make a reply; she just stared at Rex. But before Rex could continue, it was as if a light went up in her eyes. "Hang on, how do you know about my work? Who are you people?"

Rex saw things were rapidly heading in the wrong direction. He had to get her attention. "I will get to that soon. In the meantime, don't worry; we're not with the police or any Namibian government agency. But answer just this one question."

She nodded hesitantly.

"Every month for the past twenty-two months since you've been appointed as an inspector at the Ministry of Natural Resources and Energy, you've withdrawn seven thousand dollars in cash from your account on the same day you receive your salary. Is that correct?"

Her face was paper-white as she nodded almost imperceptibly. "Yes."

"And you're paying this money to Simon Nuusiku, right?"

She started crying.

"He's blackmailing you, right?"

"Who are you?"

"In a moment, Leah. I'm truly sorry to put you through this, but we *have* to know. What does he have on you?"

She shook her head. "How do you know all this stuff about me? Have you been following me? You've set up this whole thing, haven't you?"

"I'll tell you soon how we know all the stuff about you. Yes, we followed you yesterday morning and afternoon from home to work and back, and the same today. But I swear to

God we had nothing to do with the four men who wanted to rob you."

"Yes, the money goes to Commissioner Nuusiku." Rex's honesty must have won her over. She sighed. "If he finds out I've talked to anyone about it, I'm done for. I'll lose my job. My children and I will be on the streets. I'll never get another job in Windhoek or anywhere else. We'll be doomed."

"No, Leah, that will *not* happen. Trust me, you and your children will be taken care of."

"Do I have a choice?"

"Absolutely. Our word still stands. If you want to walk away, we won't stop you. All that we ask is that you listen to everything we have to say before you decide."

"Fair enough. Okay, I'll tell you about Nuusiku, but first, I have to get home and make sure the children are okay and feed them. After that, we can go wherever you want and finish the conversation as long as it's not at my house."

"I've got an idea," said Marissa. "Let's pick your children up and go to our hotel. The children can watch movies in our room while we continue the discussion in the Daltons' room. We'll order room service for everyone. How does that sound?"

Leah almost had a smile on her face. "You *have* thought of everything, haven't you?"

Marissa laughed and put her hands up. "Yes, but for a good cause."

Chapter Forty-Two

THEY TOOK THE BAIT

Friday. White House, Washington, D.C., USA

The president welcomed everyone and asked Martin to bring them up to speed with the latest out of Namibia.

"They took the bait," said Martin. "They stole the samples from the shed at Mount Krige. A few of the bags were tagged with tracking devices, so our agents could follow the signals. The bags were transported to a storage facility on the docks in Walvis Bay. Our agents visited the facility and found not only the bags containing the samples but also what seems to be the biggest stash of prohibited wildlife products in Namibia's history. Parts of every protected species in Namibia such as rhino horn, elephant tusks, pangolin scales, and more." Martin showed them a PowerPoint with a few of the photos taken by Rex and Josh.

"Do you know the value?" asked the president.

"Between fifty and a hundred million on the black market, sir."

"US dollars?"

"Yes, sir."

"It's mindboggling."

A shocked silence had descended in the Oval Office.

DNI Jen Whitmer broke the quiet after a while. "I take it we're going to hand the information over to the Namibian authorities and let them handle it?"

Howard was shaking his head. "We don't want to do that right now, Jen. We believe there's a connection between the people who stole the samples and the owners of the illicit goods in those storage units. Although we suspect PLA Incorporated has a finger in this pie, we need to know the names."

"Okay. That makes sense," said the DNI.

"Hopefully, we've thrown the Chinese off the track and will keep them off long enough to get our ducks in a row," said the president. "So, let's hear what you've been working on since our last meeting."

Howard was first. "Mr. President, our plan is to keep them in ignorance for as long as possible while we continue to gather information about the key players in Namibia and elsewhere. But, as we've said before, even if it works, it won't last. There are too many people who know about this. Eventually, they're going to figure out we're involved."

They would've been appalled to know the Chinese became suspicious the moment they'd discovered Dr. Liam Collins was the president's chief advisor on strategic minerals and geological matters.

Next was James Hilton, the Secretary of State. "Mr. President, I've prepared a statement that we can release at the right time, announcing that we've been working on a new strategy for investment and aid in African countries. The details cannot be revealed yet because the Secretary of State wants to first visit the countries we want to engage with to discuss the details. Nevertheless, it can be revealed that the strategy would aim to reward those countries who will take part in programs to eradicate corruption in their countries.

"Furthermore, Mr. President, at the same time, we should announce that I'm planning a visit to southwestern Africa, which is South Africa, Namibia, Botswana, and Angola, to kick off the initiative.

"I'm working with Ambassador Edwards in Windhoek to formulate a strategy of how to approach the high-ranking officials and politicians and President of Namibia when the time comes to negotiate about the rare-earth elements."

The president nodded and looked at the Chair of the Joint Chiefs of Staff, Admiral Bruce Wyatt.

"Mr. President, we're preparing to send a carrier task group, which would include a battalion of marines on a naval exercise to simulate wartime protection of the sea route around the Cape. During this exercise, we'll have warships and submarines patrolling the southwest coast of Africa, especially around Walvis Bay and Cape Town. We're planning to invite the Botswana military, one of our long-standing allies in the region, to take part in the operation.

"James and I thought it might be a good idea to make this announcement about the naval exercise just a few days after his."

The president smiled. "I like your ideas. Let's finalize them by Wednesday next week and decide when to start making those announcements."

Chapter Forty-Three

THE RECRUIT

Friday. Windhoek, Namibia

On the way to Leah's house in Katutura, she began apologizing in advance about her humble dwelling. "It's old, small, and dilapidated," she said. But Catia and the rest quickly put her at ease when they told her about some places they'd seen in their lives.

As can be expected, the children were surprised when the four strangers and a big black dog walked into the house but shocked when their mother told them what had happened along the way to the supermarket earlier and how the strangers from America had saved her from the gangsters. Nevertheless, their emotions soon turned to excitement when they heard Marissa's proposal.

Really? The Hilton? Room service? Movies?

"Is there pizza on the menu?" the boy, Luke, wanted to know.

"There sure is," said Catia with a big smile. "I'm Italian; I won't stay anywhere that doesn't have pizza on the menu."

"Let's go!"

While Leah was taking a shower and changing out of her work clothes into casual wear, Rex and Digger amused the children who had discovered the vicious-looking big black dog was actually very friendly. He enjoyed their back-scratching and petting.

Rex placed a piece of *biltong* on the bridge of Digger's nose and told him to look after it for him. Digger's eyes looked as if they were about to pop out of their sockets as he tried to see the *biltong*. But the moment Rex turned his back, Digger tossed it into the air and caught it in his mouth on the way down. When Rex turned back, Digger quickly turned his head—he didn't want to look Rex in the eyes.

The children were screaming with laughter.

They were still laughing when Leah appeared in the lounge, ready to go.

Josh drove them to the hotel where they first settled the children in the Farleys' room, showed them how to get to the paid movie channels, and ordered pizzas and soft drinks for them. The Daltons' room was across the hallway from the Farleys'.

Before they left the children, Rex asked Digger, "What do you want to do? Watch TV with them or have dinner with the adults?"

Digger yawned, turned, and walked to the TV, found himself a comfortable spot, and dropped to the floor.

Rex got the message.

"Can dogs understand what they see on TV?" Luke asked.

Rex smiled. "I don't know for sure. Most people will say, of course not. But many dog owners will tell you how much their dogs like Animal Planet and National Geographic. I've heard some dogs even like to watch tennis."

"What kind of movies does Digger like?"

"I've asked him, but he doesn't want to tell me. Maybe he'll tell you. Ask him when I'm not here, then you can tell me."

The little boy was beaming. "I'll ask him. But perhaps I should ask him if I'm allowed to tell you?"

Rex chuckled. "Good idea. We don't want to upset him."

A faint smile was playing on Catia's face as she watched Rex interacting with the boy. *And he's worried he won't be a good dad.*

"All I know is Digger doesn't like sirens, you know, like ambulances, police cars, fire trucks, and those. It always wakes him up."

After Leah's little pep talk, the children assured her they intended to behave, would not make a mess in the room, and wouldn't dream of doing anything that would embarrass their mother.

In the Dalton's room, Catia placed everyone's dinner order. Marissa had used her satellite phone to set up a three-way audio conference with John and Christelle in the CRC Ops Room and Martin in his office in Langley, so that they could listen to the conversation that was about to take place. Leah was wholly unaware that people from the other side of the globe were listening.

"Okay, Leah," Rex restarted the conversation that had been paused at the coffee shop, "you were going to tell us about your boss, Simon Nuusiku. After that, we'll tell you about us and why we're here. Is that still okay with you?"

"Yes, it is. But I want you to know the only reason I'm

telling you is that I trust you, and you promised nothing would happen to me."

It was quite obvious she was in a much better state of mind than a few hours ago. "We will not break our promise," said Rex.

Leah took a sip of her wine, then took a deep breath. "I was working as a secretary when my husband passed away. We both worked at the ministry. He had a heart attack at forty-two, after which he suffered from severe depression. He started drinking and didn't stop until he was dead. He lost his job because of his drinking, but that only drove him to more drinking. By the time he died, two months after he was fired, we had no money left. The life insurance we had got canceled months before, we couldn't afford the premiums. We were already living in the house in Katutura which you saw. To make a long story short, when Ben died, we were already in dire straits, and it only became worse.

"I earned a measly salary as a secretary, not nearly enough to support the children and myself. I have no family who can support me. Ben's only living family is his elderly mother, who's suffering from dementia, and his brother, whom we haven't seen in more than ten years.

"Nuusiku took pity on me. Well, that's what I thought it was. Pity. I didn't have money to pay for the funeral. Nuusiku offered to lend me the money, interest-free. When I told him I couldn't take it because I couldn't repay him, he made it a gift. I took it.

"In the weeks following Ben's death, once a week, Nuusiku would hand me an envelope with money for groceries. And every week, I wondered how much longer I could rely on his generosity. Was it not for that money, we would've starved. Nuusiku knew how desperate I was.

"About a month after the funeral, Nuusiku called me in

and offered me the job as an inspector. I couldn't believe it. But, with the wisdom of hindsight, what I should've done was decline the offer because I'm not qualified. I should've known he had led me into a trap. Maybe I did, but I was so desperate I wouldn't allow myself to admit it. Instead, I accepted his offer on the spot even after I heard the condition."

"Let me guess," said Rex. "You had to pay him seven thousand dollars a month in cash?"

Leah nodded.

"How do you get the money to him?" asked Josh.

"In an unmarked envelope which I leave under the blotter on his desk." She took a deep breath. "I know what I'm doing is criminal. They'll put me in jail for this. Even so, the choice is simple; shut up, pay up, and hope no one discovers it or face starvation."

"The thing is Leah, we discovered it, so can someone else," said Josh. "But if they do, it would not be through any of us."

Leah nodded. "I understand that, and that's the reason I've decided to talk to you. I'm hoping you can help me get out of this nightmare..."

"We will do everything we can," said Marissa.

"Thanks, that's all I can hope for."

"One last topic," said Rex. "Tell us about your duties as inspector."

"My job title says I'm an inspector. But I'm an inspector in name only. I am the most junior, inexperienced, and unqualified inspector in the directorate. I am just a glorified secretary for the other inspectors and Nuusiku. But I guess you already know all of that?"

"Sort of," said Rex. "Do you ever go out on inspections?"

"Yes. But those are few and far between. Since starting the job, I've been out on inspections only four times. The last one was last week Friday at a site in the Erongo Mountains close to Karibib. On every inspection, Nuusiku's administrative assistant, Joseph Hauwanga, accompanies me. He knows even less about geology and mines than I do."

"So, given that neither of you has the knowledge to conduct a proper inspection, what exactly is it you do when you go there?" asked Rex.

Leah smiled wryly. "Nuusiku gives me a list of questions to cover. I collect the answers and try my best not to look stupid. Joseph drives the vehicle, pretends to be a junior inspector, and keeps his mouth shut. And, I guess, report everything to Nuusiku. I suspect Joseph records everything on his mobile phone at each inspection."

"Do you know if Nuusiku has similar deals with other staff at the ministry?" asked Marissa.

"Nothing that I'm aware of. But I wouldn't be surprised if he does."

"Be that as it may, we've already established Nuusiku is corrupt," said Rex.

"So am I."

"Leah, I think everyone around this table will agree; you've got extenuating circumstances. But let's leave it at that for now. What about the director and the minister?"

"Again, nothing that I know of. The director is held in high regard by everyone. The minister is a different story. He's Nuusiku's uncle. I guess you know that?"

Rex nodded.

"Anyway, there are lots of rumors about the minister's infidelity. Lots of sexual harassment allegations floating around. And I've also heard about underhanded deals with the Chinese and Russians. But, as I said, those are all rumors."

"Well, where there's smoke, there's usually fire," said Josh.

"Now, as promised, it's your turn," said Leah.

For the next half hour, Rex and the others told her truths, half-truths, outright lies, and omitted much. They told her they were working for an organization that had been contracted by the CIA. That was true. That they were contracted to investigate the corruption going on in the Ministry of Natural Resources and Energy was a lie. They completely skipped the part about how they'd discovered that she was a fake inspector and made no mention of Erwin Krige, neither of his silver mine nor of rare-earth elements. When they told her they'd received information about the large cash withdrawals from her bank account every month, they didn't reveal the source of their information. She didn't ask. In fact, Leah asked few questions, and when she did, it wasn't probing. Her only concern was what would happen to the children.

Rex called a ten-minute break so that they could use the bathroom, check on the children, and he could get instructions from John and Martin.

"What do you expect from me?" Leah asked when they resumed.

"We want you to help us take down Nuusiku and every corrupt official in the ministry," said Rex.

"I can't. I'll go down with them. I will go to jail, and the government will take my children. Please." She started crying.

"That will not happen, Leah," said Catia. "We promised you nothing will happen to you. We intend to keep our promise."

"And if I don't want to?"

"Then it's the end of our conversation," said Rex. "We take you and the children home, and you will never hear from us again."

Leah was quiet for a while. "But that means I'm back where I was when I met you, living in fear of the day someone discovers what I've been doing."

"Right," said Rex. "But they won't hear it from us."

"So, if I work with you, I have nothing to lose?"

"Right," said Rex. "And much to gain."

"Does that mean I'll be a spy?"

Rex smiled. "Spies betray their country to its enemies. Patriots defend their country against its enemies, foreign and domestic, the latter includes corrupt officials."

Leah nodded slowly. "Okay, I will work with you."

An hour later, Rex called it a night. Leah was emotionally exhausted. The children had fallen asleep in front of the TV halfway through the second movie without finishing the pizza. Leah's briefing would continue Saturday and Sunday.

Rex and Josh dropped the Visser family off at their home shortly after eleven-thirty p.m.

Chapter Forty-Four

COUNTING HIS CHICKENS

Friday. Beijing, China

While Rex and company were busy recruiting Leah Visser, General Quan Zhelan was in his study, busy with one of his favorite pastimes, profit projections. Counting his chickens, so to speak.

According to Interpol, the trafficking of wild animals and their products is the third largest illegal business in the world—after drugs and counterfeit goods. Quan Zhelan's Sino-Africa Development Corporation was involved in all those plus illicit arms trafficking and illicit gemstones such as Africa's blood diamonds. There was serious money going around in those industries; US$360 billion per year in the drug trade, US$250 billion per year in counterfeit goods, and US$25 billion in the illicit wildlife trade. No one really knew how many billion were floating around in illegal arms trafficking or gems.

With five division managers controlling a vast global network of collaborators, mostly criminals who were only a few steps ahead of law enforcement, Quan had to run a tight ship, and he did. Division managers were expected to provide detailed and unambiguous reports every week by no later than midday Friday Beijing time. Quan hated to receive bad news late.

His managers were held accountable for everything and everyone under their control. Their one and only KPI (key performance indicator) was how much profit they had turned. And since they were operating in the most profitable industries on the planet where the profits were at least ten times the costs, Quan tolerated no excuses. Nonperformance meant termination of employment if the malingerer were lucky; sometimes, it was worse.

He was looking at the stock lists provided by Tian Chao for the Namibian wildlife venture. When it came to rhino horn, there was no other illicit product as lucrative, not even drugs. The poacher gets US$3,000 USD per kilogram the end-user pays US$65,000 per kilogram. The unrealized profits represented by the products sitting idly in secret storage facilities across the country were a pain in the neck for Quan. He wanted the money in the bank, not warehouses full of high-value but unsold products. But the problem was getting the products from storage to the end user undetected. In the drug trade, a ten percent loss of product confiscated by law enforcement was industry standard. In the wildlife trade, it was fifteen percent. For the smugglers of illegal goods, it was always a toss-up between small shipments frequently or big ones infrequently.

The stockpiles sitting in the warehouses across Namibia were worth more than US$230 million. It was by Quan's direct orders that those products would only be shipped out in small quantities in modified shipping containers with hidden compartments for contraband while the rest was filled with perishables such as frozen fish, meat, and suchlike. So far, the plan had worked; US$50 million worth of products had been shipped over the past six months without losing any to law enforcement agencies. The frustration was the money was dripping in instead of flooding in.

That Sino-Africa Development Corporation's felonious wildlife activities operated by ruthless crime syndicates and corrupt officials threatened the lives of people who worked legitimately in the industry and affected the economic development of some of the world's poorest countries didn't bother Quan in the least.

Neither did it bother him that the illegal wildlife trade had been linked to the emergence and spread of new infectious diseases in humans passed on to them from animals. Such as the bowl of bat soup, or was it the medium-rare barbecued pangolin meat at the Wuhan wet market carrying the deadly Severe Acute Respiratory Syndrome CoronaVirus 2 (SARS-CoV-2), which caused the COVID-19 pandemic. It was even possible that the virus was harvested from some exotic species and enhanced in the Wuhan Virology lab from where it escaped.

There was a time when the industry consisted of hundreds of small operators trying to do their own thing independently. Quan was busy unifying them all under his domination. A few independents who tried to hold out on him were found very dead, the suffering they endured before death very visible was a clear message—Quan's was a take-it-or-die rather than a take-it-or-leave-it proposition.

Before closing the report, Quan's thoughts returned to Erwin Krige's silver mine and the mystery of Dr. Liam Collins.

Gentlemen in black suits

Friday. Windhoek, Namibia

Back at their hotel, the four and Digger gathered in the Daltons' room and were joined by John, Christelle, and Greg from CRC headquarters, and Martin from his office at CIA headquarters in Langley.

"Good work, team," said John when they were all connected.

"Agreed," Martin chimed in.

"Okay, now that we have Leah on our side," said Rex, "I suggest we work our way up the ladder, Commissioner Nuusiku, Director Kaire Angula, Minister Jackson Kaura."

"My team is already working on all three of them," said Greg. "I can tell you Director Angula seems to be a good guy, honest, reputable, and friendly. Nuusiku and uncle Kaura are crooked as fishhooks. Uncle Kaura is a skirt-chaser and sexual harasser. Nuusiku seems to be the one with the knack for business."

"Probably why his uncle gave him the job," said Martin.

"Probably," said Greg. "Kaura is rich, he's corrupt, and he likes to travel—international."

"Any tax haven and secret banking destinations?" asked Rex.

"Yep. Switzerland, Cayman Islands, and Austria." Greg smiled. "Rex, and before you tell me to do it, we're already doing it."

"Huh?" That was Martin.

"Looking for offshore accounts owned by Namibia's Minister of Natural Resources and Energy," said Greg.

"Go for it," said Martin. "Let me know if you need any help."

Most people don't know secret bank accounts are not so secret when gentlemen in black suits, dark glasses, and black briefcases from countries such as the USA and UK came knocking. On those occasions, those banks will bend or completely forget their advertised secrecy rules. But then those dark-clad gentlemen were not to come on fishing expeditions; they had to bring concrete evidence of wrong-doing, i.e., terrorism, drugs, illicit weapons, government corruption, and such, before they'd get the information, or an agreement to freeze the funds of evil-doers.

Chapter Forty-Five

BRIEFING LEAH

Saturday. Windhoek, Namibia

On Saturday morning, when they went to collect the Vissers, Connor Burns and Sam Price had joined Rex's team. Their first stop was for breakfast at a Wimpy restaurant in Maerua Mall. After breakfast, Catia and Marissa bought bottled water, soft drinks, and snacks before heading to the Daan Viljoen game reserve in the Khomas Hochland mountains twenty-four kilometers west from Windhoek on the C28, the same route that would take them to Eldorado.

The forty square kilometers conservation area was home to a wide variety of plant and animal species, including mountain zebras, giraffes, kudus, klipspringers, blue wildebeest, springbok, and more than two hundred bird species.

Digger was welcome but had to be on a leash at all times.

There were several hiking trails varying from three to thirty-two kilometers where visitors could get a good view of the animals.

Catia, Marissa, Connor, and Sam took the children on a nine-kilometer hike while Rex and Josh continued Leah's debriefing.

Digger wasn't impressed when Rex told him, "Buddy, I'm truly sorry, but you're not allowed to go on the hike." He protested loudly with a sad howl as he watched the group leaving. The kong filled with *biltong* consoled him only a little.

Four hours later, when the hikers returned, Leah had told Rex and Josh everything about her work, the people she worked with, the office rules and routines. She had also told them everything she knew and every bit of gossip she'd ever heard about her boss, Simon Nuusiku, Director Kaire Angula, and Minister Jackson Kaura. What she told them about those three corroborated the information Greg gave them the night before.

The seven hikers were excited but tired, thirsty, and ravenously hungry. The stress of the past twenty-four hours had taken its toll on Leah—she was emotionally drained. They decided to call it a day and agreed to continue tomorrow.

On the way to drop Leah and her family off, it became clear that Catia and Marissa had conspired with the children when Marissa started giving Josh directions but refused to tell him where they were going. It turned out to be a KFC with a drive-through. They ordered the Family Feast, handed it to Leah, and told her she didn't have to cook dinner. Leah's protests about spoiling her and the children fell on deaf ears.

Sunday. Windhoek, Namibia

Sunday morning Rex and company arrived at Leah's home shortly after 10:00 a.m. to pick her and the children up for a picnic at Gross Barmen, a historic settlement and recreational hot-spring spa on the Swakop River twenty-five kilometers south-west of Okahandja. The water of the hot spring comes from a depth of 2,500 meters and has a temperature of 65 °C (149 °F) when it reaches the surface where it is cooled down to around 40 °C (104 °F) for the thermal bath.

While the four childcarers and their charges were enjoying the heated pools and the parks, Rex and Josh stepped Leah through what was expected of her when she returned to work the next day.

Digger could accompany the children as long as he stayed on a leash and was not allowed in the swimming pool. He wasn't too happy about that—he liked to swim. Luke didn't agree with management. "Can't they see how angry Digger is?" he told Catia.

She'd laughed and said, "I don't think they can. But Digger will be okay; he doesn't stay angry for long. Tell you what, let's try to get back in his good books." She took a handful of *biltong* out of a bag in her backpack. "Take this, stand before him, and tell him to sit. Tell him we're sorry he can't swim with us. Then hold your hand with the *biltong* out like this. If he takes it and starts wagging his tail, it means he's no longer angry with us."

Catia watched as he did exactly as she told him. When Digger started wagging his tail, Luke put his arms around Digger and hugged him. The little boy was on Cloud Nine.

Over the last two days, Leah's emotional condition had changed for the better. Partly because Rex and the team had shown they could be trusted, and they would not use and discard her like a wet-wipe.

Rex used his satellite phone to establish a secured connection to Greg from his laptop. Then he took a small box, about the size of a pack of cigarettes, out of his backpack. It contained a phone cable and an array of adapters, which he used to connect Leah's phone to his laptop. Once the connection was established, Greg went to work and upgraded the operating system on Leah's phone first before he installed security patches and a few special applications.

Leah didn't have a string of formal qualifications, but she was smart. Nevertheless, everyone in the team understood she was an untrained, unwitting, innocent civilian whom they dragged into a dangerous covert operation with potential international repercussions. Therefore, it was decided, in order to keep her out of danger, that her participation would be limited to just one simple task—to keep her modified cellphone switched on and in the same pocket where she always kept it when at work.

When her phone was ready, Rex went online and bought unlimited airtime and data for her phone for the next thirty days. Then he and Josh explained to her, in non-technical terms, what had been done to her phone and how it was going to help them collect information about their targets.

"Let's talk about tomorrow," said Rex when he was satisfied that she understood what was expected of her.

"I'm nervous," she said.

"Of course, you are; it's because you're human. But *what* makes you nervous?"

"They can catch me."

"Doing what?

She paused, looked at Rex, then at Josh. "I can't think of anything specific right now but..."

"Neither can I. What about you, Josh?"

"Nope. Not a thing," said Josh.

"Leah, the thing is you're going to work tomorrow, as always. Your colleagues will be at work, as always. You're going to do the same work, as always. You're going to talk to each other, have meetings, have phone calls, lunch, etcetera, as always. Your cellphone is going to be in the same pocket as always. You'll do nothing different from what you always do. Why would they catch you if you're doing what you always do?"

Leah shrugged. "Okay, I understand my fear is irrational. I'll work on it."

That was as much as Rex and Josh could expect from her.

Chapter Forty-Six

AS ALWAYS

Monday. Windhoek, Namibia

When Leah walked to work on Monday morning as she always did, despite Rex and Josh's reassurances that everything was going to be exactly the same as any other workday, she just couldn't stop herself from worrying. She didn't recognize Connor or Sam when she passed them. Although, even if she were calm, it was unlikely she would've recognized Connor in his business suit, sunglasses, and briefcase or Sam in a tracksuit and hoodie jogging past her. They were chameleons. They could blend into a concrete wall if necessary.

Leah arrived at the office in a state of tension, but as she kept on repeating Rex's mantra, "*Everything is the same as always, nothing has changed,*" she noticed no one was staring at her, no one asked weird questions, everyone acted as they always did. And her mobile phone was in the left pocket of her pantsuit jacket, as always.

By the time she and the other inspectors sat down in a

semicircle in front of Nuusiku's desk for their weekly meeting as always, she'd almost forgotten about her cellphone in her left jacket pocket.

What was not the same as always was totally invisible to everyone in the room, including Leah.

The Israeli cyber-arms firm, NSO Group, are the original developers of the Pegasus spyware that can be covertly installed on mobile phones and other devices. It is named after the mythical winged divine horse, one of the most recognized creatures in Greek mythology. IT gurus described it as a Trojan horse that can be sent 'flying through the air' to infect phones and mobile communications devices such as laptops and tablet PCs. And unless the phone is examined by an expert with special software, it's impossible to detect the spyware.

The version at work on Leah's cellphone was the CRC version of Pegasus—enhanced by Greg and his team.

Within minutes after she entered Nuusiku's office, Greg confirmed to Rex and the team that Nuusiku was now connected to them with his phone and laptop. From that moment on, Greg's team would be Nuusiku's constant though invisible companion reading his text messages, tracking his calls, collecting his passwords, tracking his location, accessing his phone's microphone and camera, and harvesting information from the apps on his phone.

Thanks to the Pegasus spyware on Leah's phone, within minutes after she'd arrived at her desk and logged onto her computer, Greg's team had access to it and were cloning the hard drive. She didn't know it was happening. Rex and Josh didn't go into that much detail on Sunday.

Greg's priority was to get the details about the mines that Leah had inspected. Rex believed everything was not kosher with the granting of the permits for those mines.

Chapter Forty-Seven

HIGHLY UNLIKELY

Tuesday. Windhoek, Namibia

Unbeknown to anyone but the data entry clerk, Nuusiku, Tian, and Greg's team, Erwin's application for the mining permit at Mount Krige had found its way from the out-tray of Hago Amutenya into Nuusiku's inbox late on Monday afternoon. Nuusiku found it in his inbox early on Tuesday morning, printed the application, and had it delivered by courier to Tian at the Chinese embassy.

As Tian skimmed through the application with much disinterest, he was satisfied that the information agreed with what Krige told Leah during the inspection.

He was still paging through the lengthy document when his computer dinged. A new email had arrived. He brought the screen to life; it was the test results from Namgeochem Labs in Walvis Bay. He flipped quickly through the preamble to the summary of the analysis. He didn't know whether to be disappointed or relieved; the results were the same as on the printout that Krige gave to Visser, which was the same as in his permit application.

Maybe I can now close this case and spend my time on something worthwhile? But then, why does Dr. Collins's visit still bother me?

He opened the window, lit a Marlboro, and started talking to himself quietly. "Surely Collins must have known the size of the silver deposit. Krige must have told him. Yes, Collins could've come over to verify it for himself, but why would the US be interested in silver? It's not a scarce and strategic metal."

And then a lightbulb lit up in his brain. He looked at Krige's permit application again. The submission date—four days before the inspection. He listened to the recording of the inspection again.

"When are you planning to file your application for a mining permit?" Visser had asked Krige.

"I am not sure. I'll have to check with my daughter. She handles all my administrative stuff." Krige had replied.

That last part was true; her name and signature were on the application as his representative. "But you want me to believe four days after submitting the application, your daughter hasn't told you about it?" Tian grinned. "Highly unlikely."

Tian sighed deeply. He had to report to Quan. He decided to try a different tactic; he wrote an email to the bad-mannered general telling him about the test results and about his suspicions. He kept it short.

An hour later, when Tian phoned Quan, he fully expected the general to tell him he didn't have time to read emails but was pleasantly surprised when Quan said, "Got your email, Tian. I agree with your take on it. They're hiding something. I suspect they've meddled with the samples to throw us off."

"Yes, sir. I think so, too."

"I want you to get Nuusiku to send an inspector out to tell Krige that the department wants to run their own independent tests on the samples. Of course, Krige will have to tell the inspector that the samples have been stolen. And that will open the door for the Ministry to send in a team to collect new samples."

"Understood, sir. I will get onto it right away."

Greg's team had access to Nuusiku's laptop at work and saw the application arrive in his inbox, but was unaware that it had been delivered to Tian. However, when Nuusiku received a call on his mobile phone at eleven-thirty a.m. from a man who spoke English with a Chinese accent inviting him for lunch at Nyama Restaurant in Jan Jonker Road, at the Windhoek Showgrounds, they were listening to the call.

Under their mattresses

Tuesday. Windhoek, Namibia

Since gaining access to Nuusiku's phone the day before, Greg's team had been listening and recording Nuusiku's conversations. His conversations on his government phone were boring, and on his private phone, they were not much better either. His work phone had only government-approved apps on it. The applications on his private phone were a different story.

Nuusiku kept all his passwords on his private phone on LastPass, a password manager that stores encrypted passwords online. It was a very handy tool, infinitely more secure than writing passwords in a notebook or a piece of paper as long as one remembered the LastPass password and not save it in a text file on one's phone, as Nuusiku did. Once inside LastPass, Greg's team copied all the credentials to all the applications on his phone.

One of the applications Nuusiku used was Signal, a messaging app similar to WhatsApp, iMessage, Facebook Messenger etcetera, but one that's geared toward privacy and security rather than cute emoji stickers. Its security measures were so good even Edward Snowden recommended it, and supporters of the Black Lives Matter movement used it to keep their messages hidden from the police.

Scrolling through the message history, they came across the recording made by Nuusiku's assistant, Joseph Hauwanga, during Leah's inspection of Mount Krige. Nuusiku had attached the recording to a Signal message to 'TC,' which they would soon learn was Tian Chao ostensibly a junior attaché of trade and commerce working in the Chinese embassy but in fact an undeclared MSS agent. Nuusiku's message to TC read: "The recording you asked for. Mission complete."

They also had a look at Nuusiku's bank accounts. He had savings and checking accounts and credit cards at First National Bank and Standard Bank. He had substantial overdraft facilities at both banks but was not using them at the moment. His credit card balances were also not alarmingly high, and it seemed he serviced them on time every month. He was paying a mortgage and installments on a Mercedes-Benz GLA 220D. In short, if Greg and his team didn't know the man was crooked, they would've concluded Simon Nuusiku was in the high-income bracket, living a good life but not above his means.

As it were, they knew different, and it didn't take them long to find what they were looking for; proof of Nuusiku's underhanded dealings, a Swiss bank account. The access codes were stored in LastPass. The balance was a few US dollars shy of two and a half million. Not a bad nest egg for the five years he had been working as a director at the Ministry of Natural Resources and Energy. Checking a few of the most recent transactions, they found a deposit of US$5,000 made into Nuusiku's Swiss account three days before Leah's inspection of Mount Krige and another US$5,000 shortly after the message on Signal to TC. The origin of the deposits was not immediately evident from the bank statements, but there was little doubt it would lead to a Chinese entity.

On the same day, the last deposit arrived in Nuusiku's account; US$ 6,000 was transferred from his account to a numbered Swiss account.

"Not keeping all his eggs in one basket?" wondered Greg.

"Or uncle Jackson Kaura's share of the ten thousand dollar booty," said Catia.

"We found no records of cash deposits made into any of his accounts. I'm wondering where he's hiding it," said Rehka.

"I'd look for it under their mattresses," said Josh.

Chapter Forty-Eight

OVER LUNCH

Tuesday. Windhoek, Namibia

Tian Chao arrived ten minutes early for the lunch appointment with Simon Nuusiku at Nyama Restaurant. Shortly after he was seated, a loud, tall, African American man in a dark business suit, white shirt, and red tie accompanied by a quiet, short, blond, white guy dressed in jeans and t-shirt entered and took a table not far away from his. Tian tried to ignore them, but the black guy was so noisy, forward, and audacious, it was all but impossible. Fortunately, when Nuusiku arrived, Tian had someone else to listen to rather than the American harassing the female waiting staff or regaling his taciturn companion with tales about the wild animals he'd encountered the last few days.

Tian and Nuusiku ordered drinks. The Nyama was a rodízio Brazilian-style steakhouse restaurant where, for a fixed price, customers were served with small portions of food several times throughout the meal until they signaled that they had enough.

When their drinks were served, and the first tranche of food was on their plates, Nuusiku leaned a little forward, closer to Tian. "I take it you've got something urgent to discuss, my friend?"

"Indeed," said Tian. "We suspect Krige has been lying to you about the results of the tests at that silver mine near Karibib."

"Why do you think that?"

"You remember that geologist, Dr. Liam Collins, who was there when Leah Visser inspected the site?"

"Yes."

"Well, we made a few inquiries and discovered although Collins is a geologist, he is also the senior advisor about geological matters to the President of the United States. Were you aware of that?"

"No! Not at all. Where did you hear that?"

"I'm not at liberty to reveal my source. But trust me, it's true."

"Okay, be that as it may. What would the President of the United States want with a small silver mine in Namibia?"

"Exactly what we've been asking ourselves as well. Krige's story is that Collins had been sent over here by a potential investor to conduct independent tests and advise his client. We were happy with that story until we learned that Collins's client is the President of the United States."

Nuusiku was annoyed. "Right under our noses. Okay, what do you want me to do?"

"I want you to send an inspector to confiscate the samples and bring them back to Windhoek for independent testing."

"Okay. And if Krige doesn't want to hand over the samples voluntarily, it'll be proof he's trying to hide something. I'll make sure he gets the message; he hands over the samples, or he can forget about the permit."

"Excellent." Tian didn't think it was necessary to let Nuusiku know Krige didn't have samples to hand over, even if he wanted to.

"Okay. How urgent is this?"

"Very. How much?"

"Five thousand."

"Okay, but I want it done tomorrow."

"Deal."

A few minutes later, Tian showed Nuusiku the electronic receipt for the US$2,500 transferred into his Swiss account. As always, the balance would be transferred upon completion of the job.

Nuusiku was happy. And so was Tian. However, had they known the true identities and mission of the annoying African American and his quiet friend two tables away, they would've been horrified.

Within minutes after Nuusiku had joined Tian at the table, Connor and Sam had received confirmation from Greg that the Pegasus trojan horse had installed itself on Tian Chao's smartphone. All they had to do was to take photos and videos of the meeting.

Before the lunch was over, Rex's team knew who Tian was and where he worked. The two friends didn't eavesdrop on the conversation between Tian and Nuusiku. That was the job of Rex and his team, in the Daltons' hotel room where John, Christelle, and Greg on the Ranch in Arizona, and Martin and Howard in the latter's office in Langley, had been patched into the conversation which was streaming to their speakers from Nuusiku's private cellphone.

When Nuusiku arrived back in his office, he called Leah in. Rex and company were holding their breaths, hoping and praying Leah's nerves wouldn't get the better of her. She had no reason to be nervous because Rex never gave her the big picture; hence, she didn't know that she and Erwin Krige were the kingpins in a brooding international storm. Nevertheless, people's anxieties were often irrational.

But she surprised them; her voice was even and calm. "You wanted to see me, sir?"

"Yes, have a seat. I have an urgent assignment for you," said Nuusiku.

"An inspection, sir?"

"No. Just a site visit. I want you to go back to Mr. Krige's site near Karibib and ask him to hand over the samples he collected. I'll give you a letter signed by me to take with you."

"Yes, sir. Anything else?"

"No. That's it. Show him the letter and ask him to hand over the samples."

"Yes, sir. When do you want me to do this?"

"Tomorrow."

Nuusiku dictated the letter to Leah; she went back to her desk, typed and printed it, and took it to him for his signature.

Chapter Forty-Nine

OPERATION SIERRA IN TROUBLE

Tuesday. Video conference

It was unnecessary to spell it out; everyone knew Operation Sierra was in trouble.

"How did they find out about Collins?" asked Howard when the video call was live.

"Doesn't matter," said John. "We can figure that out later. Right now, we need to focus on how to prevent the whole operation from going belly up."

Everyone was nodding.

John's eyes came to rest on Rex. "Initial thoughts?"

"Nuusiku will send an inspector out; whether or not it's Leah doesn't matter. Erwin will tell the inspector the samples were stolen. When Nuusiku hears that, he'll send in a team to collect new samples."

"We can't allow that to happen," said Martin.

"But how can we stop them?" asked Howard.

"We throw them another bone—" said Rex.

"Huh?" said John.

"We move the Mount Krige samples to the Twohill shed and let Tian know about them," said Rex.

John finally broke the pensive silence that followed Rex's suggestion. "O-k-a-y. What can go wrong?"

"They might decide to collect their own samples, at both sites—"

"But Krige might keep them busy in the courts for a while," said Howard.

"That's a possibility. Even if he does, we don't have as much time as we hoped for," said John. "The president's advisory council will have to move their agenda forward."

"Yep," said Rex. "Within days after Tian gets those samples, the Chinese will be storming into the minister's office to get him to nationalize the mine and give China the exclusive mining rights. Admittedly, Erwin could slow them down with legal action, but I suspect it won't be for long. Even so, it won't be long before they discover they've been duped, and they will descend upon Mount Krige."

"In other words, the Secretary of State should start making overtures about a visit to Namibia," said Howard.

"Exactly," said Rex.

"Okay, Martin and I will be heading to the White House the moment we're done here."

"Good, while you and Martin are busy with the president, Rex and his team will brief James and Laura," said John.

Martin nodded. "I'll give them a heads-up."

Half an hour later, Josh and Marissa were in the rental SUV on the way to the Krige campsite to brief Erwin and Mieke about the impending visit by Leah Visser.

Not long after the Farleys were gone, there was a knock on the Daltons' door. It was Laura Murray and James Blake.

Chapter Fifty

PLAY FOR TIME

Wednesday. Khomas Hochland Mountains, Namibia

Josh and Marissa had left the Krige campsite at the crack of dawn to inform Thea and Pieter of the latest developments.

"Dammit, I was really hoping the Chinese would take the bait," said Pieter. "Let's hope they'll take it this time."

"We'll know before the end of the day. When Leah gets back to Windhoek, Nuusiku will know, and shortly after that, Tian Chao. And then we hope to find out who Tian reports to."

"How will you know that?" asked Thea.

Josh looked at Marissa. She nodded. He told them all about the Pegasus trojan horse software.

Pieter and Thea were staring at him open-mouthed. They knew Josh was the jokesmith of Rex's team, and this must have sounded very much like a tall story.

They looked at Marissa for a sign. "Josh is serious; the technology has existed for quite a few years already."

Pieter was shaking his head. "Please remind me to never upset you guys."

Josh chuckled. "Pieter, don't upset us."

"So, we now know Tian was probably behind the theft of the samples," said Thea. "But he doesn't know about the other samples. How are you going to make him aware of them?"

"We planted misinformation with a Chinese spy," said Marissa. "The information should reach Tian within the next few hours. We're hoping he'll forget about Mount Krige when he hears about Twohill. He'll almost certainly try to get his hands on the samples, either through Nuusiku or his cronies who stole the others."

"So, in the worst-case scenario, Tian could still insist on collecting samples from Mount Krige despite the 'good news' we've sent him about Twohill," said Josh.

"But dad could stall them in the courts?" said Thea.

"Correct," said Josh. "We have to play for time."

Over a cup of coffee

Wednesday. Windhoek, Namibia

At nine forty-five a.m. James sent a text message to Sara. "Slowtown Coffee Roasters. Maerua Mall. 10:30 a.m. You don't want to miss it."

Her reply was instantaneous. "I'm excited! See you soon."

James arrived ten minutes early at Maerua Mall, the third-largest shopping mall in Namibia and the most popular in Windhoek. There were quite a few tables open in the coffee shop. He found an empty table toward the back of the room and told the server he was waiting for someone; he'd order when the person arrived.

True to form, Sara arrived ten minutes late. She kissed James on both cheeks, forced a smile which never reached her eyes, and took a seat opposite him.

Shortly after she was seated, an old couple with a big black dog displaying a service dog sticker on his harness entered. The man was slightly bent over, walking with the aid of a cane. The woman had one arm hooked into her companion's arm and the leash of their big black dog in the other. They sat down at a table a few meters away from theirs. James heard them talk in what he thought was Italian but couldn't understand a word of it. He ignored them and turned his attention to Sara.

"The usual?" he asked.

"Thanks, that'd be nice."

James waved the server over and ordered a cappuccino for Sara, a double espresso for himself, and two *brötchens*. Elongated, with an indent and various colors defined by dough type and flour dusting, filled with cheese and cold cuts, it's called a *brötchen* in Namibia and a bread roll elsewhere.

They made small talk until their orders arrived before James leaned forward. "Sara, this morning when I got to the office, I happened across a piece of information about Erwin Krige's mine, which I thought you might want to hear."

Sara's grin stretched from ear to ear. This meant money in her pocket. "I'm listening." She didn't even notice that James hadn't gone through the usual ritual of switching off his mobile phone, removing the battery, and expecting her to do the same.

Just then, she heard the Italian couple placing their order in broken English.

"I came in on the tail end of the story. I don't have all the details, but here is what I overheard. Krige indeed discovered a sizable deposit of silver in the Erongo Mountains near Karibib. He filed an application for a mining permit with the Ministry of Natural Resources and Energy. Now hang onto your skirt. Remember the investor's geologist, Dr. Liam Collins, I told you about last Wednesday? Well, he's the senior advisor to the President of the United States on all matters related to strategic minerals."

"Wow!" Sara's eyes were aglitter, like shiny dollar signs.

"Wait, there's more. Krige has the prospecting rights to another site about five kilometers north of the site where he discovered the silver. It seems he had made a major discovery of some strategic importance there. I couldn't find out what it is, but it must be of significance for the President of the United States to send his senior geologist to investigate."

Sara was shaking with excitement. "In other words, the whole thing about looking for an investor in the silver mine was a smokescreen to hide the big discovery at this second site?"

"Right. And that's why Krige hasn't filed for a mining permit for that site as yet. He wants to keep it under wraps until the US government can get involved."

Sara could not stop smiling. Surely, in terms of dollars, this must have been the most valuable piece of intel she'd ever received from James Blake. "Thanks, this is excellent information. I feel like celebrating. What do you say about dinner tonight? You pick the place; I'll pick up the tab."

James smiled. "I'll be counting the hours."

About fifteen minutes after James and Sara had left the coffee shop, the Italian couple with the service dog also left.

What James knew but Sara didn't was that the Italian couple had 'latched' onto Sara's mobile phone and installed Greg Wade's customized version of the iniquitous Pegasus spyware on it.

By midday, Greg and his team knew Sara had negotiated the tidy sum of US$15,000 for the information she had at hand. They also knew Zhong Yang had paid US$3,000 in advance into her offshore account in the Cayman Islands. The balance would follow if he was satisfied that the information was indeed as crucial as she alleged.

It took Zhong less than five minutes to assess the information and pay the balance into the same account and send her the receipt.

Fifteen minutes later, Tian was in Zhong's office. Rex and the team were listening to the conversation between them through Tian's phone.

Chapter Fifty-One

NO FURTHER INSTRUCTIONS

Wednesday. Erongo Mountains, Namibia

At eleven fifteen a.m. Leah Visser and Joseph Hauwanga pulled up at the Krige campsite. Leah was noticeably ill at ease, more so than on her previous visit. Erwin and Mieke knew why Leah was uneasy and tried their best to soothe her. After all, she was innocent—the victim of a ruthless racketeer.

Reading the letter from Director Nuusiku, Erwin had a hard time not laughing. According to Director Nuusiku, the demand to hand over the samples was under a ministerial directive that permits would only be issued after independent verification of samples.

"Ms. Visser, I wish I could comply with this request. Believe me, I would if I could. The problem is a bunch of criminals raided my shed last Tuesday night. I've been prospecting and mining in these parts for more than thirty years. It's the first time something like this has happened. I can understand why they took the equipment and the petrol and such, but the samples? What could they do with those? There was probably less than one gram of silver in them."

Leah was temporarily at a loss for words. Clearly, this was not a scenario she'd expected. "Oh, I see. Well, I guess then there's not much more we can do. I'll let the director know. Thank you for your time, Mr. and Mrs. Krige."

"I'm so sorry, Ms. Visser, but if you told me yesterday when you called that you wanted the samples, I could've saved you the trip. You're welcome to drive past the shed to have a look at the damage the vandals have caused."

"Thank you, we'll do that."

"Have a safe trip," said Erwin.

Greg's team at CRC headquarters and Rex and Catia in Windhoek were listening to the conversation at the campsite and followed Leah's return to the office. She reported to Nuusiku immediately and showed him the photos of the ransacked shed. Hauwanga must have handed him the recording after Leah had left his office because Nuusiku forwarded the audio file via Signal to Tian shortly after and asked for further instructions.

Tian replied, "Thanks. No further instructions for now. Balance to be transferred momentarily."

Nuusiku must have been very pleased. He got paid even though he didn't deliver the samples.

The watchers took note when, five minutes later, Nuusiku received an electronic receipt for the US$2,500 on his Signal app and immediately transferred sixty percent of it to the numbered Swiss account as before.

Midafternoon the Farleys were en route to Windhoek and the Naudés en route to the Krige campsite with the Mount Krige samples in the back of their Range Rover.

The dossier

Wednesday. Windhoek, Namibia

It was late. Tian couldn't sleep; his mind was working overtime. The revelation about Liam Collins convinced him that the information coming from Zhong's spy was trustworthy. The question uppermost in his mind was, what did Krige discover? He could kick himself for not paying attention to the other site. He had studied the satellite images of the second site and saw there was a shed, the same as on the other site. *Damn, Nakanyala could've raided that site as well.*

Tian reached for his cellphone to text Nakanyala. He hesitated; another raid was probably not such a good idea. *I'll work through Nuusiku first.*

He used his cellphone to email Quan, telling him about the new information and his plan. He didn't expect a reply from the general; he was a busy man.

Tian was unaware that a copy of his email arrived at CRC headquarters at the same time as it landed in the general's inbox. Greg immediately assigned Sun Yan, codenamed Flat Arrow, to find out who was the recipient of the email.

Yan, the former Unit 61398 hacker, had an intimate understanding of the MSS's and PLA's computer systems and their vulnerabilities. After all, he had created some of those himself before he'd defected to America. It was a breeze for him to determine that the recipient was General Quan Zhelan, ex-PLA, the CEO of Sino-Africa Development Corporation. The same organization that'd requested the tests from Namgeochem in Walvis Bay.

Yan's next task was to hack into Sino-Africa Development Corporation's servers.

Ever since discovering the dark side of Simon Nuusiku, Greg's team had been building a dossier about the bad actors. The shot in the arm for them came when Leah returned to work on Monday, and her phone infected Nuusiku's. That led to the uncovering of Tian Chao and the compromising of his phone, which led them to General Quan Zhelan, one of the big fish in the pond. Another big fish, top of their list, was Minister Jackson Kaura.

One of Greg's team had been dedicated to investigating the customers of Container Universe. He already knew there were six customers, companies that didn't exist, false addresses, and fake contacts. Container Universe apparently cared little as long as they were paid on time; no questions were asked.

"I reckon if the police raid that place, they're going to find a lot more contraband and counterfeit merchandise than what we've seen so far," said Josh.

Chapter Fifty-Two

OFF TIAN'S RADAR

Thursday. Windhoek, Namibia

At six a.m., Tian sent a text message to Nuusiku, "Breakfast at the Country Club 7:30. Urgent."

Nuusiku accepted within minutes; when Tian had urgent matters, he never quibbled about the price.

Over breakfast, Tian told Nuusiku about Krige's other site. "Do you think the story about his samples being stolen is true?" It was a rhetorical question. "Of course not; the man has been lying to you from day one, hasn't he?"

Nuusiku nodded. He was enraged—exactly what Tian wanted. He only needed a little nudge now to send him into a frenzy.

"So, Simon, are you going to allow Krige to continue making a fool out of you?"

Nuusiku hissed through pursed lips. "This time, I'm going there myself, and I'm going to teach Mr. Krige not to mess with me."

"I'm not sure that you'll find the samples on-site," said Tian. "It's quite possible they're with his daughter on their farm, Eldorado. She tested the other samples. I think she would've tested these samples as well."

"We'll know tomorrow morning. What do you want me to do about the first site? Are you still interested in that one?"

"No. Not at the moment. I think he just used that site to mislead us while he works out a deal with the damn Americans."

From Namibia to America, members of Operation Sierra were high-fiving. Mount Krige was off Tian's radar for now.

By the end of the breakfast, Tian had agreed to a fee of US$20,000 and subtly guided Nuusiku to conclude that the only appropriate action was to confiscate the samples from the second site and cancel Erwin Krige's prospecting permit for that site.

Greg and his team duly noted the US$10,000 deposit coming from a bank in Hong Kong into Nuusiku's Swiss account.

Strengthen the secretary's arm

Thursday. Video Conference

By eight-thirty a.m., Tian and Nuusiku were on their way to their respective offices, and the Operation Sierra team was in conclave.

"We gave the Kriges a heads-up about Nuusiku's planned visit," said Rex. "Connor and Sam have been assigned to Tian Chao's surveillance. The rest of us will head over to the Kriges later today to prepare them for Nuusiku's visit tomorrow."

"Okay," said John, "let's stare into the crystal ball and see how things might develop over the next few days. Over to you, Rex."

"Well, Nuusiku and company will turn up at the Kriges' place tomorrow and demand that the samples be handed over. Erwin will protest and threaten them with court action but stop short of preventing them from taking the samples. The samples will go to a lab, and the results will be available a few days later, let's say early next week. And then China will jump in and do everything imaginable to secure Twohill for themselves."

"Krige might slow them down through the courts," said Howard, "but that will depend on whether or not the government decides to nationalize the site. And, of course, the Chinese government will pull out all the stops to persuade them to do it."

Martin nodded. "Yep, owning almost sixty percent of Namibia's foreign debt puts them in a powerful position, doesn't it?"

"Right," said John. "Our strategy must be to slow that process down. To keep the Chinese off that site for as long as possible. Because all hell is going to break loose the moment they discover Twohill has no REEs."

"You can bet on that," said Howard. "Ideally, by the time they discover that the agreement for Mount Krige will be in place."

"That agreement has to be negotiated by the Secretary

of State, but I'm afraid he won't have the same leverage as the Chinese," said Howard.

"In that regard," said Rex, "the dossier about the corrupt actors we're working on might strengthen the secretary's arm when he sits down at the negotiation table."

Breaking news

Thursday. Windhoek, Namibia

By midday, the Namibian, Namibian Sun, and Republikein, the three biggest newspapers in the country, as well as the Namibian Broadcasting Corporation's TV and radio stations, broke the news.

US Announces New Aid Strategy For Africa

According to the US Secretary of State, James Hilton, they've been working on a new strategy for investment and aid in African countries. Secretary Hilton mentioned that the strategy would aim to reward those countries that will implement programs to eradicate corruption in their countries. The secretary continued to say, "We're planning to first launch the initiative in the countries of south-western Africa. Therefore, I've asked our ambassadors in South Africa, Namibia, Botswana, and Angola to help facilitate meetings between myself and their heads of state."

Of course, the ambassadors of every country that had

a presence in the countries of southwestern Africa, including China, took notice and passed the information on to their governments.

Both Tian and Nuusiku saw the news, but it didn't occur to them it could be connected to Erwin Krige's mines.

Chapter Fifty-Three

SHOWDOWN AT TWOHILL

Friday. Erongo Mountains, Namibia

Rex and his team arrived early on Thursday afternoon. They brought Erwin and Mieke up to speed with the latest developments before all of them took a walk to Twohill to check out the terrain. That night Catia and Marissa showed the Kriges how the molar mics worked and configured their mobile phones to act as recording devices at the push of a button.

When Nuusiku and his entourage arrived at ten a.m., there was no sign of the Daltons and Farleys. Their rental SUV was locked away in the large shed two hundred meters away from the campsite. Marissa and Josh were hiding in the hill from where they had a good view over the camp. Marissa had one of her drones in the air, and Josh was looking at the visitors through the .308 Musgrave's Schmidt and Bender telescope.

Rex, Catia, and Digger were in a similar strategic position hidden on Twohill overlooking the shed. Catia would launch a drone as soon as the group started moving toward their position. Rex had Erwin's second hunting rifle, the same make, model, and telescope as Josh's.

They were all praying they would not be forced to use those rifles. However, if Nuusiku or any of his cronies were stupid enough to endanger the lives of Erwin or Mieke, Rex and Josh wouldn't hesitate to send them off to meet their maker.

Digger was rigged with his tactical harness, lying flat on his stomach between Rex and Catia, just waiting for Rex to tell him what to do.

The six were in communication with each other through the invisible molar mics. It took Erwin and Mieke a little while the night before to get used to the weird sensations created by the devices in their mouths.

Nuusiku's entourage comprised Leah, Hauwanga, and a huge, mean-looking black guy. Hauwanga was the driver of their double-cab Toyota Landcruiser. All four of them got out of the vehicle, and the first thing Josh noted was the AK-47s hanging off the shoulders of Hauwanga and the big guy. They stayed with the vehicle while Nuusiku and Leah approached Erwin and Mieke, waiting under the *kameeldoring* tree.

Marissa's drone was circling one hundred and fifty meters above, recording everything below on video.

Josh whispered softly to everyone, "Don't worry about the guys with the AKs. I've got them covered. They're obviously here for intimidation purposes; I can see they don't really know how to use those weapons."

Erwin and Mieke played the game. Nuusiku was obviously not in a good mood. But Erwin and Mieke were welcoming, gracious, cooperative, and subservient. Nuusiku didn't have a single reason to throw his weight around. But he had US$20,000 riding on this job. He brushed away their civility in a brusque manner.

"I didn't come here to socialize, Mr. Krige," he said when Erwin invited them for coffee and refreshments.

Erwin kept a smile on his face, and so did Mieke. "Apologies if I offended you, Mr. Nuusiku..."

"Commissioner Nuusiku."

"Apologies, commissioner. May I ask what's the purpose of your visit?"

"I'll ask the questions, and you answer them. Understood?"

"Yes, sir." Mieke stood next to Erwin, and he could hear her taking slow deep breaths to calm the rising anger. She was a peace-loving person—up to a point, and Nuusiku was getting dangerously close to that point.

"I've received a report that you have a site north of here, not far away. Why didn't you file a report about it?"

"There must be a mistake, commissioner. I filed my report on time. I have a copy of it on my computer. My next report is not due for another six weeks."

Nuusiku probably expected to have instigated enough repulsion in the Kriges to elicit an aggressive response, but they remained unfazed. He seemed a little flustered. "I know that. But you've collected samples, and you didn't report it."

Erwin could've asked him how he knew about the samples but refrained. His mission was to keep the temperature of the conversation below boiling point. "Yes, I have been collecting samples. I'm not finished yet, I've collected less than fifty percent of what I need, and I haven't tested any of them. As far as I understand the regulations, I only have to report once I've collected all my samples and tested them."

"Where are the samples?"

"In a shed on the site."

"Who is Dr. Liam Collins?"

Erwin was a little surprised when Nuusiku brought that up. Again, he could've asked how Nuusiku knew about Collins but didn't. "He's a geologist from America. He came over to have a look at the silver mine on behalf of an investor, but it wasn't big enough for the investor."

"You're lying!"

"About what?"

"About Collins. He works for the American government and is the president's senior advisor on geological matters."

"Wow! Really? That's news to me. We had no idea we were in the presence of such an important man. He never told us."

"So, are you saying when Collins was here, you never showed him this second site?"

"No, sir, I didn't say that. We went there, but there's not much to see, and as I said, I haven't tested the samples yet. Dr. Collins was interested in the other site."

"Mr. Krige, I think you've got some underhanded scheme going with the Americans."

Erwin shrugged. "We're all entitled to our own thoughts, commissioner."

"You're wasting my time, Krige. Take us to the site."

Throughout the entire conversation, Leah had been standing a few meters away from her boss, ashen-faced and silent.

They arrived at Twohill and parked in front of the gate in the security fence surrounding the shed. Everyone except Leah got out of the vehicles.

Catia's drone was circling one hundred and fifty meters above, recording everything below on video.

"Where are the samples?"

"Inside."

"I'm confiscating them."

"With all due respect, Commissioner Nuusiku, I don't think you've got the authority to do that. Those samples are my property."

"Listen carefully, Mr. Krige. I *am* the authority. *I* decide who gets a permit and who does not. *I* decide who keeps their permits and who does not. I am taking the samples with me, and I'm shutting this operation down. I'm withdrawing your permit for this mine. And if you're not careful, I'll cancel all your permits before the end of the day. Now, unlock that gate and the door to the shed."

"Again, with all due respect, sir, you're overstepping the boundaries of your authority. You need a court order. I suggest you leave now."

Nuusiku nodded at Hauwanga and the big guy who were standing a few meters away.

About eighty meters away, Rex's finger was resting on the trigger; the big guy would enter the afterlife only a second ahead of Hauwanga.

They took a few steps forward, but thank God they didn't unshoulder their weapons.

Erwin knew it was time to bring the temperature down and quickly. He put his hands up halfway as if in surrender and stepped toward the gate. "For the record, Commissioner Nuusiku, what you and your men are doing is illegal. But seeing you're the man with the firepower, I'm won't argue with you. Take the samples and be on your way, but know one thing, you haven't heard the last from me."

"Mr. Krige, you're missing the point. This site has now reverted to the Ministry of Natural Resources and Energy. You have twenty-four hours to remove your shed and property from here. After that, you'll be trespassing. If you ever set foot here again, I'll have you arrested, and I will cancel all of your remaining mining permits. Understood?"

"I understand what you're saying, commissioner, but I promise you I'll have my day in court with you and the minister."

"Are you threatening me, Mr. Krige?"

"No, sir, it's a promise."

Nuusiku laughed. "You're welcome, but maybe you should know not even the courts can stop the minister."

"We'll see about that."

Erwin unlocked the gate and the shed and stepped aside so they could load the bags. Throughout it all, Leah remained in the vehicle, unspeaking and white as a linen sheet.

Erwin tried his best to hide his smile as Nuusiku and company drove away with the samples.

Not long after their departure, Rex got a message from Greg. It was a copy of the text message Nuusiku had sent to Tian.

"Samples confiscated. Site shut down. Where to deliver samples?"

Tian replied, "Excellent! Namgeochem, Northern Industrial Area."

Soon after, a message arrived on Rex's phone. It was a copy of the deposit of the remaining UD$10,000 into Nuusiku's Swiss account and the record of transferring sixty percent thereof to the numbered account.

Back at the camp under the *kameeldoring* tree with a Windhoek Lager in hand, Josh said, "Erwin, if this mining thing doesn't work out for you, there's always Hollywood. I'm sure they'll fall over their feet to have an actor of your caliber in their movies."

Erwin chuckled. "I'll keep that in mind, Josh. Hollywood makes movies in these parts now and then. Maybe I don't even have to go to California."

"I'll be his agent," said Mieke.

Later that afternoon, on their way back to Windhoek, they decided it was time to pull Leah out of the ministry. She'd done her bit in the forthcoming downfall of Simon Nuusiku and his uncle, the minister.

Catia sent a text message to Leah. "How about a picnic at the botanic gardens tomorrow? We can pick you and the children up at 9:00 a.m."

Leah replied, "That would be nice. Thank you."

Chapter Fifty-Four

PLANNING A RESIGNATION

Saturday. Windhoek, Namibia

The National Botanic Garden of Namibia is a twelve-hectare property almost in the city center.

Unlike other botanical gardens around the world, the larger part of this garden has not been landscaped; thus, visitors can see highland savannah plants in their natural environment. In the developed sections of the gardens, there are several special displays where visitors can see plants from other parts of the country, such as the Desert House display of the Namib Desert or the Kunene Region. There are several self-guided walking trails from where visitors can see the densest population of the Windhoek Aloe, which is the symbol of the city of Windhoek, a quiver tree forest, and a variety of mammals, birds, reptiles, and insects.

When they arrived at Leah's house to pick her and the children up, the children's excitement was noticeable, especially Luke's when he saw Digger. However, Leah was all but chewing her nails.

They would not tell her they were there the day before and knew exactly what had happened. It was for her own protection to know as little as possible.

Catia had the best rapport with Leah. She took her for a walk and got her talking about it. She told Catia what had happened the day before. Given how jittery she was, Catia was somewhat surprised at how well Leah remembered every tiny detail of what happened.

"What Nuusiku did was illegal, not to mention barbaric to threaten two innocent old people with guns," she said. "His men were going to shoot... them." She started crying.

Catia had to suppress a smile as she put her arm around Leah. She was sure Erwin and Mieke would've objected strenuously to being called old. She was tempted to tell Leah that the two gunmen would've been dead before they could've pointed their rifles.

"If Mr. Krige goes through with his threat of legal action, I'm going to end up in court, and although I've done nothing wrong, Nuusiku will find a way to throw me under the bus. Starting with forcing me to lie under oath. I'm convinced that was the only reason he took me along. I've been thinking of reporting this to the director, but I don't know if I can trust him or, for that matter, anyone."

"Let's go back to the others. We've got something important to discuss with you. Connor and Sam can take the children for a walk while we talk."

When Catia and Leah returned to the group, Digger must've sensed Leah's distress and immediately sidled up to her. When he 'heard' about the plan to go with the children on a walk, he had a hard decision to make. Rex saw

Digger's dilemma and said, "Don't worry, buddy, we'll look after her. She'll be okay. You can go with them."

The proud look on Luke's face when Rex gave him Digger's leash was something to behold.

When they were gone, Catia recounted what Leah told her. Rex, Josh, and Marissa kept straight faces as they listened.

"Well, Leah, you've been of great help to us to unearth the corruption at the ministry," said Rex. "We'll take it from here. We'd like you to hand in your resignation on Monday."

Leah was startled. She was shaking her head. "I can't resign. Nuusiku will never accept it. He knows if I'm not under his thumb at all times, I might talk about his misdeeds. And, after what I saw yesterday, I am scared to death of that man. He might have me killed or harm my children. Besides, how am I supposed to support my family if I'm not employed?" She started crying again.

Catia moved closer and put her arm around her. "Don't worry about any of that Leah, we're going to help you."

"How?"

"Let's start with your new job," said Marissa. "We've discussed your case with our boss. He pulled some strings, and the American embassy here in Windhoek has a secretarial position available which they'd like to offer you."

"What? How...?"

Marissa smiled. "It's not a fake position, Leah. If you decide to take it, you'll be doing a real job, one that you're qualified for. Oh, the salary is about fifty percent more than you're getting at the ministry now. And you keep all of it."

"I... I don't know what to say. It sounds too good to be true. But the problem is Nuusiku, he won't let me go."

"Don't worry about him. We'll take care of him. He won't lay a finger on you," said Catia.

"How can you be so sure about that?"

"You'll have to trust us with that," said Rex.

Leah wiped the tears away. "I have trusted you so far. In any case, what options do I have? If I stay, Nuusiku will certainly ruin me. If I go, he will *try* to ruin me, and you *might* stop him. I'd rather take my chances with you than with him."

"Wise decision, Leah," said Josh.

"Okay, how do you want me to do it?"

"We'll help you formulate your letter of resignation," said Catia. "On Monday, when you get to the office, you type it up, print it, sign it, and give it to Nuusiku personally, and also email a signed copy to him and yourself at your private email address."

"Do you have any idea how he's going to react when he gets my resignation? He's going to fly off the handle. I'm afraid of what he might do."

"Leah, I am sure he's not going to physically assault you in the office."

"No, he probably won't, but he's going to make a big scene, that's for sure."

"When you get to the office, first pack all your belongings before typing the resignation. If Nuusiku so much as raises his voice at you, walk out of his office, take your belongings, and walk out of the building. Remember, through your phone, we'll be listening to everything that's being said, and we'll be waiting for you outside," said Rex.

His words had a pacifying effect on her.

"Oh, I forgot something very important," said Marissa. "With your salary package comes a monthly car allowance and scholarships for your children from now until they've graduated from university."

The tears were streaming freely down Leah's face when she whispered, "And I thought miracles didn't happen anymore. At least not to me."

By the time the children returned from their walk Leah was in a much better emotional state. Digger confirmed it when he checked on her first before sitting down next to his young friend, Luke.

They dropped the Visser family off at their home in Katutura shortly before one p.m. after a sumptuous lunch at the popular family restaurant, Mountain Eagles Spur in the Maerua Lifestyle Centre, on Centaurus Street.

Chapter Fifty-Five

HER CHILDREN

Monday. Windhoek, Namibia

Despite Rex's and the others' reassurances, Leah was tense when she arrived at work on Monday morning. Nevertheless, she did exactly as they instructed her. Her belongings were a coffee mug, a framed photo of her children, a box of tissues, and a cheap ballpoint pen. After putting those in her bag, she called the draft letter of resignation up on her phone, typed it in a Word document on her computer, printed, signed, and scanned it. Then she took the original and went to Nuusiku's office.

Rex, Catia, and Digger were at a coffee shop across the street from the office. Josh and Marissa were a block away in the minibus. Connor and Sam were watching Tian Chao.

What happened next was unexpected. Leah walked into Nuusiku's office, greeted him, and handed him the letter.

"What's this?"

"My letter of resignation, commissioner."

A long silence followed. Rex and the rest who were

listening were worried that they'd lost connection to Leah's and Nuusiku's phones.

"So, you're not happy here anymore," said Nuusiku in a calm voice.

"Yes, sir."

"Is there anything I can do to change your mind?"

"No, sir."

"How about taking a week or so off? You might feel different if you had a good rest."

"Thank you, sir, but I'd rather work out my notice period and go."

"Did you get a better offer from somewhere?"

"I'd rather not discuss that, sir."

"Leah, I can see you're stressed about something. Do you want to talk about it?"

"No, sir."

"You're making a big mistake. Why don't we keep this between the two of us for a few days so you can have time to reconsider everything carefully."

"My mind is made up, sir. No amount of time is going to change it."

"Well, I haven't made up my mind yet. I'll need a few days to decide whether or not I'll accept your resignation."

"Sir, I don't think you can—"

"Refuse to accept your resignation?"

"Yes, sir."

"Sometimes, there are special circumstances. Such as yours, Leah. I'll let you know what I've decided."

"Sir, I don't want to be disrespectful, but—"

"Don't worry, Leah, I'm sure we'll come to an amicable arrangement. In the meantime, not a word to anyone, okay?"

"Sir, I'll be emailing you my resignation when I get to my desk. My notice period starts today."

"We'll talk about that in a day or two."

Leah left Nuusiku's office, not sure what to think. He didn't threaten her as she fully expected he would've. She had no reason to walk out as she thought she would've. However, one thing she was sure of was she couldn't trust the creep. When she got back to her desk, she emailed the scanned resignation to her private email and to Nuusiku.

Apparently, Catia and Marissa felt the same as Leah. "That miscreant is up to something," Catia said when Josh and Marissa had joined them at the coffee shop. "He was too smooth, not normal behavior for an egomaniac."

"I feel the same," said Marissa. "But what can he do? It's not as if he can go to the police and tell them there's this woman who's been paying him bribes every month, please arrest her. What can he hold over her head?"

"Her children," said Rex.

Catia drew a sharp breath. "If that scumbag gets within a mile of those children, he's a dead man."

"And it will not be a bullet through the head," said Marissa. "He'll be painted with honey and tied to one of those big anthills on Eldorado."

To anyone who didn't know Catia and Marissa, those might have sounded like idle threats; Rex and Josh knew differently. If Nuusiku were to avoid a sudden and most likely fatal decline in his health, he'd stay far away from the children.

Chapter Fifty-Six

MORE BREAKING NEWS

Tuesday. Windhoek, Namibia / Pentagon, Arlington, Virginia, USA

In Namibia, the people woke up to another breaking news story from America. This time it was an announcement from the Pentagon by the Chair of the Joint Chiefs of Staff, Admiral Bruce Wyatt.

A carrier task group consisting of two aircraft carriers and several warships, including a battalion of US Marines, were en route to conduct exercises off the southwest coast of Africa to simulate protection of the sea route around the Cape during wartime.

"During this exercise, we'll have warships and submarines operating along the southwest coast of Africa," said Admiral Wyatt. "One of our longstanding allies in the region, Botswana, will take part in the operation."

The admiral went on to say that during the operation, one of the aircraft carriers would be patrolling off the coast of Namibia, close to Walvis Bay. The second carrier was going to patrol the waters around the southern tip of Africa near Cape Town, South Africa.

Tian Chao and Simon Nuusiku followed the news with much disinterest.

Naturally, the military leaders in China took a bit more interest in the announcement. After a few hours of deliberation, they were in agreement and advised their president that it was nothing more than the Americans 'voicing' their concerns about China's rapidly expanding influence in Africa and the fact that they were worried China would establish a naval base in Walvis Bay from where they'd be able to control the Cape Sea Route.

China already had a naval base in Djibouti in the Horn of Africa from where they could control the Suez Canal.

"We'll divert satellites to watch them and send a few of our ships to monitor their operations," the commander of PLAN (People's Liberation Army Navy) told the president.

Auf wiedersehen

Tuesday. Geneva, Switzerland

After the completion of the latest transactions in Simon Nuusiku's Swiss account, Greg and his team had collected enough information for the CIA's Chief of Station in Bern, Switzerland, to pay a visit to Herr Uto Adler, CEO of the family-owned Adler Bancaire Privée, a boutique private bank in Zurich. Consequently, Howard Lawrence had phoned Herr Adler and informed him that the CIA had an urgent need to talk about the accounts of two of the bank's clients. The CIA had dealt with Herr Adler in the past. Howard, with his diplomatic background, made his demand sound like a polite request. It was lost on Herr Adler, by nature an impassive man; nevertheless, he agreed to see the CIA envoys.

Carter Rogers, the CIA's Chief of Station in Bern, and Laura Murray, the CIA's Chief of Station in Windhoek, arrived at Adler Bancaire Privée seven minutes early; the Swiss were nothing if not punctual.

Whether it was deliberate or oversight on Howard's part, they would never know, but Carter and Laura were wholly unprepared for the personality of Herr Adler. He was old, bald, bespectacled, borderline anorexic, refused to speak anything but German and was apparently incapable of smiling. He gave new meaning to the word impersonal.

Fortunately, Carter and Laura were both fluent in German.

"Good morning, Herr Adler," said Carter when he and Laura were led into Adler's office. The furniture and occupant made the room resemble an ossuary more than an office.

Adler nodded. It was possible that his lips had moved, but neither Carter nor Laura saw it. "I'm Carter Rogers. This is my colleague from Windhoek, Namibia, Laura Murray. I believe Director Lawrence spoke to you about our visit?"

"Yes. Take a seat."

He was capable of speaking. They did as instructed. There was definitely not going to be an offer for coffee, tea, or water.

"Where's the signed letter from Director Lawrence?"

Carter handed Adler the letter. He studied it, made a

noise that sounded a bit like a growl, and said, "Client name and proof of wrongdoing?"

Carter handed him a stack of documents, and he studied them for no less than ten minutes, during which the only sound in the room was their breathing.

Finally, Adler looked up and said, "Your request?"

"Every bit of data from the day those accounts were opened up till today. We want you to keep operating the accounts until we tell you to freeze them. And, of course, your clients will not be informed of our visit."

Adler stared at his desk for a while, as if he was considering agreeing or not. Eventually, he said, "Anything else?"

"No, that's all for now," said Carter.

"Request approved."

It was not as if Adler could refuse their request, but he could've made it much more difficult if he had refused to act without a court order. But then, the five billion the CIA had on deposit with his bank might have been transferred to another bank. "Thank you, much appreciated."

Adler nodded imperceptibly. *"Auf wiedersehen."*

Over coffee and pastries at a nearby coffee shop, Carter and Laura were speculating if Adler were indeed human. With the advances in artificial intelligence these days, there was a chance, however slight it might have been, that the guy was a cyborg (a being with both organic and bio-mechatronic body parts). Notwithstanding, Carter and Laura had everything they came for—proof that Simon Nuusiku was the owner of one account, and the numbered account to which he always transferred sixty percent of the booty belonged to his uncle, Minister Jackson Kaura.

Chapter Fifty-Seven

SOMETIMES A MAN'S PRICE IS NOT MONEY

Wednesday. Windhoek, Namibia

It was almost midday when Tian received a call from the senior analyst at Namgeochem asking if he could come over to the lab. Tian was excited. If the results were not out of the ordinary, the analyst would've just emailed the report.

Half an hour later, Tian was sitting in front of the analyst's desk, reading the report. When he finished, he looked at the woman, whose nameplate said her name was Julie Narimab. But he detected no trace of insincerity. He blinked a few times and read the report again.

"This is a joke, right?"

"No, Mr. Tian. What you see there is true. I couldn't believe it either. I ran the analysis twice, the results are the same."

"Who else knows about this?"

"Only me, sir. I conducted the tests on my own without help from anyone, just as you requested."

"Now, listen carefully, Julie. Transfer the report onto this memory stick. Then I want you to change your report."

"Sir, I... that's... I can't..."

"Julie, listen to me. You'll do exactly as I tell you. Turn your screen so that I can see what you're doing."

Julie turned her screen sideways.

"Now, remove everything about the rare-earth elements from this report and from your computers. Everything. Delete it. Wipe it out. No one must ever be able to retrieve that information. And that includes you. Leave only the information about the silver deposit and other minerals, but absolutely nothing of the rare-earth must remain. Understood?"

"Yes, sir. But I must protest. It's highly irregular."

"I'm the client, I'm paying, and you *will* do as you're told."

Julie's hands were trembling as she did exactly as ordered.

When she was done, Tian said, "Do I need to remind you how important it is that you forget you've conducted this test?"

"No, sir."

"Good, because if you ever talk to anyone about it, I'll pay you a visit, and believe me, you will not like it. Are we clear?"

"Yes, sir."

"Where are the samples?"

"In the storeroom next to the lab."

"I'll come and pick them up within the hour."

"Remember, not a word to anyone."

"Yes, sir."

Rex and his team were listening to the conversation

between Tian and Julie, so were John and the others on the Ranch and Martin in Langley.

They also listened as Tian spoke to Julie when he returned later with a pickup truck to remove the samples. What they couldn't hear was when he injected her with a lethal overdose of ketamine, threw her body in the back of the pickup, and covered it with the bags of samples. The GPS tracker on his phone showed him driving out to the municipal rubbish dump.

————————

Back in his office, Tian chain-smoked three cigarettes before sending the report to Quan. He smoked another while drinking tea before phoning the deranged general.

"Tian, how do you know this report is accurate?"

"I don't, sir. All I can vouch for is that those are the test results of the samples which Nuusiku claimed he took from Krige's site."

"How many people, other than you, know about the results?"

"Nobody, sir."

"What about the person who conducted the tests?"

"Julie Narimab. She's dead, sir."

"Great. Dead people don't talk."

"Yes, sir. That's why I terminated her."

"Who else knows?"

"Nobody that I know of, sir."

"Think, Tian. The purpose of your head is not only to keep your ears apart; it's supposed to house a brain as well. Do you not think Krige knows what's going on? Why do you think Collins visited the place? They know about this, Tian. That's why the American president sent his chief geologist."

"Yes, sir. Of course, you're right. I didn't think of that. What do you want me to do?"

"We need to negotiate a deal for that mine immediately."

"Sir, Krige threatened with legal action. He will slow us down."

"Tian, everyone has a price. Find out what's his price."

"Yes, sir."

"He's got a wife and daughter, right?"

"Yes, sir."

"Sometimes a man's price is not money..."

"Yes, sir."

When the call ended, Tian sent a text message to Nuusiku. "Avani 6:00 p.m. URGENT."

Nuusiku accepted a few minutes later.

Rex and his team and the usual crowd from the Ranch and Langley were listening to the conversation. When the call between Quan and Tian ended, they had a video conference to discuss what they'd heard.

The cold-blooded murder of Julie Narimab had put them in a somber mood. None of them had ever met her. They knew nothing about her, not even what she looked like or her age or whether she was married or had children or family. The heartless killing was a clear indication of things to come. The sad thing was they couldn't risk letting the police know about the murder—not yet. They could only hope that the body would be discovered soon and her next of kin informed.

They won't get a single ounce of it

Wednesday. Windhoek, Namibia

Although they were at Avani Hotel and Casino, there was going to be no dinner and no gambling tonight.

"Simon, do you have any idea what Erwin Krige has been trying to hide from you?"

Nuusiku shook his head. "What?" He took a sip of his beer.

"The biggest rare-earth deposit on the planet," said Tian. "The reserves are enough to supply the global demand for the next century and beyond."

Rex and company were listening to the conversation through Tian's phone, which was producing better quality sound than Nuusiku's, probably because Tian's phone was on the table between them and Nuusiku's in his pocket.

"How big is the deposit?"

"Between two and three hundred million tons. At current prices, it's worth between three hundred and twenty and four hundred and eighty billion US dollars."

Nuusiku whistled softly. "Unbelievable. Three... Hundred... Million... tons." He emphasized each word. "No wonder the Americans are interested."

"And I take it I can trust you to help me so that they won't get a single ounce of it?"

"Absolutely."

"Okay, great," said Tian. "Now the first thing is Krige's permit has to be canceled, and he has to be kicked off the site."

"You've listened to the recording of the meeting with

him on Friday; he's going to start legal proceedings if we try to do that," said Nuusiku.

"Yes, I heard that. But I'm sure you'll be able to come up with an excuse to cancel his permit. Make up something. Breaking of regulations. A labor dispute. Accuse him of racism. Sexism. Harassment. Discrimination. Anything."

Nuusiku was grinning. "I'm sure we can think of something."

"I've also done a bit of research on Krige. His great-grandfather arrived in Namibia in 1885, a year after Germany colonized your country. His name was Heinrich Krige; he was one of the German Schutztruppe, those who perpetrated the Herero and Nama Genocide. Krige's grandfather was Karsten Krige. He took part in the First World War when Germany lost all its colonies, including Namibia. During the Second World War, the South African government interned Krige's father, Oscar Krige, and his grandfather, Karsten, because they were Nazi sympathizers. Krige himself and his father fought against your people during Namibia's War of Independence. I'm sure you can use some of that information to drum up something against him."

"Where did you get this information?"

Tian lied because he didn't want to tell Nuusiku about China's hacker army, Unit 61398. "One of my assistants did it for me. I'm not sure where she got it from, probably from some archive. It doesn't really matter how accurate it is, does it? Just leak the allegations to the press and let Krige try to explain it away once they've sensationalized it."

"Excellent idea," said Nuusiku. "I'll discuss it with my uncle. We could also nationalize the mine."

"Don't, because then you'll have to reveal what was discovered. We want a permit for that mine in the name of the Sino-Africa Development Corporation before we let the world know what was discovered."

"I see," said Nuusiku.

"If you use the information about Krige's history correctly, there's going to be a lot of pressure on him to get out of the way."

"I'll talk to my uncle and get back to you."

"The sooner you can do it, the better. I take it you understand that none of this can be discussed with anyone but your uncle and myself?"

"Yes. I understand."

"Good. Now, how much is this going to cost us?"

"I'll have to talk to my uncle."

"Okay. I'd like to hear from you before the end of the week."

"I'll try my best," said Nuusiku.

Although Nuusiku had decided not to tell Tian about Leah's resignation, he decided he had to take care of her first. Then, he'd talk to uncle Jackson to figure out a way to intimidate Krige. He phoned a man who he addressed as Fritz and arranged a meeting at a clothing shop in China-town at one p.m. the next day.

The members of Operation Sierra were relieved—Tian and Nuusiku were hypnotized by the 'big find' at Twohill. Mount Krige seemed to have slipped completely from their minds. Exactly what Rex intended when he'd leaked the false information about the 'discovery' at Twohill to Sara Bishop.

Chapter Fifty-Eight

MURPHY'S LAWS

Thursday. Windhoek, Namibia

Rex and his team were equipped with the latest and greatest in espionage technology. Without it, they would've still been scratching their heads, trying to figure out what was going on. However, Murphy's Laws held true also for technology —it was great until it stopped working—usually at the most inconvenient time. As it did that afternoon when Connor and Sam were in Chinatown.

Connor was browsing for clothes in the same shop where Nuusiku met with the man who he called Fritz on the phone earlier. Sam was in another shop about three doors away. They were in communication with each other through their molar mics.

Conner had to do two things; one, get within Bluetooth range, less than ten meters, to breach Frtiz's phone to install the Pegasus software; two, get pictures of him. Connor didn't panic when he noticed his phone would not play ball; his bodycam operated independently from his phone, so he made sure he got clear shots of his target. He assumed the conversation between the targets would be relayed to Rex and his team through Nuusiku's phone. In the meantime, he restarted his phone but to no avail. Through his molar mic, he told Sam about the technology failure. But by the time Sam got to the shop, the meeting was over, and Fritz left. Connor followed him at a distance and got a few shots of his white Toyota Hiace van and its license plate when he drove out of the parking lot.

In the Quantum minibus, in the same parking lot, Rex and the rest were pulling their hair out in frustration. It was not just Connor's phone that failed; it was the entire system, which meant the Pegasus software on Nuusiku's phone was also inoperative at the time. They had no clue what had been discussed at the meeting. Greg and his team were working frantically to restart the servers and get the system up again, which they did, but way too late.

Rex told Sam and Connor to take a taxi back to the hotel while they followed Fritz's vehicle. It was risky. To follow a target vehicle without being noticed required at least three different vehicles. They couldn't use the drones; they were too slow and limited in range to keep up with a vehicle traveling at sixty kilometers per hour. The roads became less busy as Fritz headed south out of the city toward Rehoboth. Josh had to drop back further. After a few kilometers, they gave up and returned to the hotel.

Even so, they were not entirely empty-handed. They now knew Fritz was the big guy with Nuusiku at Twohill on Friday. They had the number on the license plate of his Hiace van, and they had his cellphone number, which they captured when Nuusiku had phoned him earlier in the day. Greg's team could track down his mobile phone's GPS signal.

Not long after Rex and the others were back at the hotel, Greg's team had hacked into Telecom Namibia's network and learned that the phone number belonged to one Justin Kamwanya. Fritz could've been a nickname or codename. It didn't matter; they had a location for him. He was on a homestead also known as a smallholding or small farm about ten hectares in size twenty kilometers outside Windhoek on the B1 main road to Rehoboth. The satellite images showed a big farmhouse and several outbuildings.

Nevertheless, they were left guessing what the meeting between Nuusiku and Fritz was about. Nuusiku had set up the meeting shortly after meeting with Tian. This Fritz character seemed to be a kind of enforcer for Nuusiku. This led them to the conclusion that the meeting had something to do with putting pressure on Erwin to let go of Twohill without making a scene.

But Rex disagreed. "I got the impression Nuusiku wanted to discuss that with his uncle first."

"You could be right," said Josh. "Then this could be about Leah."

"I wouldn't put it beyond that scumbag to harm a defenseless, innocent widow with children," said Marissa.

It was imperative to get the Pegasus app on Fritz's phone so they could keep an eye on him.

Looking forward to *your* contributions

Thursday. Windhoek, Namibia

It was eleven-thirty p.m. A cloudless, moonlit sky made it easy for Rex, Josh, and Digger to approach the house on Justin Kamwanya's farmstead without using flashlights. They were lying low next to a garden shed about a hundred and fifty meters from the house.

Catia and Marissa were about two kilometers away in the SUV at a rest stop next to the main road. As always on missions of this nature, Catia was the mission controller, and Marissa piloted the drones. With the drones' night vision and thermal imaging capabilities, they determined there were four humans, no dogs, two cows, five goats, and several chickens on the property. The horizontal and unmoving thermal images of the humans meant they were asleep.

Rex had rigged Digger up with his tactical harness. The mini video camera on the top of his head, between his ears, mini earphones fitted in his ears, and mini microphone on the harness between his front legs were all activated and wirelessly connected to an iPad mini, which Rex had strapped to his forearm. The moonlight made it unnecessary for Digger to wear night-vision goggles. He also had Rex's satellite phone strapped to the top of his harness on his back.

Digger whined softly. He was excited. Rex ruffled his ears and pressed his nose against Digger's. "Who's a clever boy?"

Digger yelped softly and licked Rex in the face.

"Okay, buddy, scout and hide." Rex pointed to the house.

Digger crawled forward, and within seconds, he'd disappeared among the shadows of the garden plants.

Catia checked the location of the GPS signal coming from Kamwanya's phone and Digger's position. "He's close now," she said to Rex and Josh through the molar mics. "Just a few more paces."

When Digger was next to the house, outside the bedroom window where, according to Catia's screen, Kamwanya's phone was next to two sleeping humans, she said, "Digger's in place."

Rex said, "Okay, buddy, stop and hide."

Digger let out a faint growl and lay down between a few shrubs next to the wall. He was about five meters away from the target phone.

Rex said, "Good boy. Stay."

Rex thumped the switch on the loop around his neck and said, "Okay, Greg, you're on."

"Great. Give me seven minutes."

Greg was out by forty-five seconds. It took him six minutes and fifteen seconds to install Pegasus on Justin Kamwanya's mobile phone.

"Welcome to Operation Sierra, Mr. Kamwanya," said Greg. "We're looking forward to *your* contributions to our noble cause."

Everyone who could hear Greg was smiling or laughing. CRC's IT guru was known for his dry sense of humor.

Ninety minutes later, the Daltons and Farleys were back in their hotel rooms, getting ready to go to bed.

Digger had a handful of his new favorite treat, *biltong*, and was already in canine dreamland.

Chapter Fifty-Nine

I'VE GOT BIG PLANS FOR HIM

Friday. Windhoek, Namibia

At eight-fifteen a.m., Nuusiku sent a text message to Kamwanya. "It MUST be done today. Acknowledge receipt."

Kamwanya replied, "Message received. Will report when done."

What's this about? Was the question on everyone's lips.

A minute later, Kamwanya made a call to a person in his phone's address book, Henry Shaanika.

"Henry, it's Fritz. Listen, I want you to get hold of Benjamin and come to my place immediately. We've got a big job that has to be done today."

"What is it? How much?"

"Get over here, and I'll tell you."

An hour later, Rex and the rest got their question answered as they listened to Kamwanya, aka Fritz, telling Henry and Benjamin about their mission and the money and the plan.

It was a quarter to midday when Rex and the team got an alert that Kamwanya was on the move.

Rex, Catia, Digger, Josh, and Marissa were in the Quantum minibus. Catia was driving. Sam and Connor followed in the SUV.

Marissa dropped Rex, Josh, and Digger off in front of Leah's house. They quickly entered through the backdoor after Rex had picked the lock and set themselves up inside to give Kamwanya and his comrades a warm welcome. The street was deserted, people were at work, and children were in school. There were a few dogs that started barking when they'd arrived but stopped when Rex, Josh, and Digger were inside the house.

Marissa and Catia proceeded to the children's school two kilometers away. They would wait for the children in front of the school when they came out at one p.m.

Sam and Connor were a block away from Leah's house. Sam had a drone up waiting for Fritz and his men to arrive, which happened at a little after twelve-forty.

Sam kept Rex and Josh inside the house posted with their progress.

Fritz was driving the white Toyota Hiace van and parked it two blocks away from Leah's house. Before they got out of the van, he gave his final instructions. "The children should be arriving from school by about one-thirty. You two take one of the girls each. I'll take the boy. Remember, quickly and quietly. Questions?"

There were none.

"Okay, Henry, you go first. Open the backdoor with the crowbar. Benjamin will join you five minutes later, and I'll be there five minutes after him. If you run into any trouble, phone me."

One by one, they arrived and entered the house from

the back. The only trouble they ran into was when they entered the house, but then things happened so quickly none of them had a chance to raise the alarm. The same fate befell all three of them. As they stepped through the backdoor, it was as if they were struck by lightning—the effect of 50,000 volts from a taser gun. Then everything went dark—the effect of the lorazepam injections they received. Even Fritz, who was built like a heavyweight wrestler, went down like a sack of potatoes a split second after the taser's darts lodged in his back.

By one p.m., when the school bell rang, Fritz, Henry, and Benjamin were unconscious, their hands and feet were ziptied, mouths were gagged with duct tape, and heads were covered with pillowcases, all of which they'd brought along to use on the children.

Poetic justice, thought Rex.

They were going to be in dreamland for at least two hours and wake up with the grandfather of headaches.

"Okay, our charges are secured," reported Rex over the molar mics. "Connor, we have the keys for the Hiace. You and Sam can come by to pick them up."

Two minutes later, Connor and Sam pulled up in front of the house, and Rex handed the keys to Connor. Five minutes later, Connor parked the van in front of the house and helped carry the unconscious men, rolled inside blankets, out and put them in the back of the van.

Sam had stayed behind in the SUV, keeping overwatch with the drone.

Thus far, not a single soul had appeared in the street. Maybe there were people in the houses, and maybe they saw the activities at Leah's house. Nevertheless, none had shown themselves, and none had phoned the police. Maybe it was a neighborhood where people respected each other's privacy and minded their own business. Or maybe it was a neighborhood where these sorts of things happened all the time, and people knew it was best to keep their noses out of other people's affairs.

With the three prisoners secured in the back of the van, Josh got behind the wheel, and he and Connor headed out to Pieter's farm, which was adjacent to Eldorado. The old farmhouse where Pieter had grown up was kept in good repair. Sometimes they used it as a guesthouse when there were too many visitors on Eldorado. The Naudés had left the keys for them under the pot plant next to the front door and had stocked the shelves and fridge with food.

When the children came through the front gate at the school with a stream of other children a few minutes after the bell rang, they immediately saw Catia and Marissa and ran toward them—expecting bad news about their mother. But Catia and Marissa were prepared for it and quickly put their minds at ease. "Don't worry, your mom's okay," said Marissa. "She has to work late tonight and asked if we could pick you up from school. We're taking you with us to the hotel, and your mom will join us later." The only part that wasn't true was that Leah had any knowledge of what was happening—she didn't.

Catia reported, "Our charges secured. On our way now."

"Great. See you soon," said Rex. After Josh and Connor left with the captives, Sam picked Rex and Digger up and drove them to the hotel.

At one-thirty-five p.m., Rex used Fritz's phone to send a text message to Nuusiku. "Got them. No issues. Await further instructions."

Nuusiku replied, "Excellent. Will send further instructions tomorrow morning."

Sam and Digger were charged with looking after the children while Rex, Catia, and Marissa were in a video conference with John and the rest back in America, trying to preempt what Nuusiku's plans were. Of course, he intended to use the children as leverage against Leah. The question was when and how.

Rex asked Josh to question Fritz the moment he came around to find out where they were supposed to take the children and what they were going to do with them. It took Josh less than half an hour after Fritz regained consciousness to get the answers he wanted.

At first, Fritz refused to speak. When he eventually did, it was in a language neither of them understood but presumed to be the Ovambo language. But it could've been any of the other indigenous languages.

However, Josh could be very persuasive without being violent, although, if required, he could be ferocious.

"Buddy, would you mind fetching my electric drill from my backpack, please?" said Josh to Connor.

"You reckon drilling holes in his kneecaps will make this guy speak English?"

"I never had a prisoner who didn't," said Josh. "Most of them learned English with only one hole in the knee. The most holes I ever had to drill were three."

Connor said, "I don't know. This guy looks like one tough sonofabitch. I think he might break your record." He turned to Fritz. "What do you reckon? Should I put some money on it?"

He got no answer from Fritz, left the room, and returned a minute later with a cordless electric hand drill. "Here you go. Fully charged. I've got ten bucks that say he's going to smash your record."

"A fool and his money are easily parted. You're on," said

Josh as he took the drill from Connor and pushed the start button.

The high-pitched sound from the drill was the proverbial straw that broke the camel's back. Fritz asked in perfect English what it was they wanted to know.

Connor was livid. He grabbed the drill from Josh and walked toward Fritz, hissing, "Yellow belly! You cost me ten bucks."

Fritz started begging them, in English, to please ask him some questions.

Josh did. But he and Connor were disappointed. They thought they'd put up a world-class performance, and all Fritz could tell them was he worked for Nuusiku. They were supposed to kidnap the children and take them out to his smallholding and wait for Nuusiku to give them further instructions. He was supposed to follow Leah when she left work and let Nuusiku know when she was close to home so that he could arrive there before she could phone the police. He also told them that his helpers, Henry and Benjamin, were just that, helpers. They were ex-convicts who made a living from petty crime and poaching.

Rex and the others were listening to the interrogation. All they could do was to keep a close watch on Nuusiku until he made his move.

Greg's team was monitoring Nuusiku's and Leah's phones for any conversations between them, but half an hour before closing time, Leah was still unaware of what had happened.

"Then Nuusiku must have a plan to grab her on the way home," said Marissa.

"Or maybe he plans to visit her at home tonight," said Catia.

"Okay. It's Friday. She'll be going to the supermarket to

do her weekly shopping before going home," said Rex. "Marissa, I want you to stay with the children. Sam, Catia, Digger, and I will follow her from the office to the supermarket to make sure she gets there safely. Inside the supermarket, Catia will make contact and tell her what's going on and ask her to work with us. While Catia is talking to Leah, Digger and I'll get a taxi to drop us off at her house. We'll wait for her to return and for Nuusiku to show up."

"I'll do it, but I'm not crazy about the idea of missing out on the opportunity to choke the life out of that miscreant," said Marissa.

"Same here," said Catia.

Rex smiled. "Ladies, you can't kill him—I've got big plans for him."

"Yeah, well then you better keep him away from us. What if he decides to bring a few ruffians with him?" said Catia.

"You and Sam will be in the neighborhood keeping overwatch with the drones. If he brings along company that Digger and I can't handle, I'll get Leah out of the house, and you'll have to pick us up."

Chapter Sixty

THE WEEKEND TO TALK

Windhoek, Namibia

When Leah left the office shortly after five pm., Catia's drone was hovering four hundred meters above. Sam followed her on foot. Rex, Catia, and Digger were in the SUV about half a kilometer ahead. They were in communication through their molar mics.

The trip to the shop was uneventful, and they were sure that no one was following her.

Leah got herself a shopping cart, took her shopping list out, and headed for the shelves. She was in the rice and pasta alley when a tall, blonde woman dressed in black jeans and a beige-colored blouse with large hornbill glasses carrying a basket approached her. "Excuse me, could you tell me in which aisle I can get chutney?"

Leah's eyes widened as she recognized the woman. "Catia! What are you doing here?"

"Shh, keep it down. I have to talk to you. It's urgent."

Leah nodded slightly. "I'll show you where to get the chutney." They continued slowly along the aisles while talking in soft tones. Naturally, Leah was shocked when Catia told her what was going on, but she settled down quickly when Catia assured her the children were safe and unaware of what had happened.

She was calm when she walked home, knowing Catia and Sam were watching her back, and Rex and Digger were at home waiting for her. She experienced an indescribable feeling of relief as she realized this had been her last day at the Ministry of Natural Resources and Energy. Simon Nuusiku's hourglass had run empty. And if everything worked out as her American friends envisaged, she and the children had a new and bright future ahead of them when this was over.

As Catia had promised, Rex and Digger were there when she arrived home. Rex helped her unpack the bags while he explained in more detail what had happened earlier in the day and what the plan was.

Rex used Fritz's cellphone to send a message to Nuusiku. "She's about fifteen minutes away from home."

Nuusiku replied with a thumbs-up emoticon.

Fifteen minutes later, the commissioner pulled up in front of Leah's house in his three-liter Jeep Grand Cherokee. He was alone.

When Leah opened the front door for him, she looked forlorn; her hair was disheveled, and her makeup was smudged.

"My children!" she cried. "They're not here! I have to phone the police."

Nuusiku stepped into the house. "Sit down, shut up, and listen to me."

"My children!"

"Stop screaming, woman. I won't tell you again to sit down and shut up."

Leah slumped into one of the plastic kitchen chairs and sniffed. "Do you have something to do with this?"

Rex was impressed—Leah was a brilliant actor.

"We'll get to the children in a moment. First, I want to tell you how disappointed I am about your resignation. You're disloyal and ungrateful. I helped you when your husband died. I've looked after you and cared for you all this time. And this is how you repay me? This is how you show gratitude?"

"You might think you're a good Samaritan; I don't," said Leah in a shaky voice. "You're a criminal. You're corrupt. You've used me to enrich yourself. You've used me to carry out phony mine inspections. And God knows how many others you're abusing in the same way."

"Shut up, woman! You don't know what you're talking about. And you clearly don't understand what's about to happen to your children. You'll never see them again. Your beautiful girls are just the right age to decorate the harem of a rich Arab somewhere in the Middle East. And your son is just the right age to please men with a proclivity for young boys."

"You're an animal!"

"You're not going anywhere. You will stay with the ministry, and you will keep on working for me. And just so we're clear, if you tell anyone about our arrangement, I'll see to it you're the one going to jail. Think carefully about that, and about your children. Understood?"

Nuusiku was wholly unaware that Rex and Digger had entered the room and were standing about one meter behind him.

Leah didn't answer.

"Do. You. Understand?"

Leah made no reply.

"Answer me!"

One of Digger's pet peeves was people offending and threatening the members of his pack. He barked. Nuusiku spun around, saw the big black dog, the bared teeth, and the black-clad man with a black balaclava pointing a taser gun at his upper torso.

His hands raised slowly in surrender. A wet spot started spreading slowly down the front of his pants as his bladder forsook him.

The probes from the taser gun lodged in his chest. His chest muscles started spasming, and then the rest of his body seized up. When the needle plunged into his neck, he didn't feel it.

Rex reported to Catia and Sam over the molar mic. "Target down. You can come over now."

Five minutes later, Rex and Sam shoved Nuusiku's comatose body, wrapped in a blanket, unceremoniously into the cargo section of his own vehicle. His hands and feet were ziptied. His mouth was covered with duct tape. His head was covered with a pillowcase.

Sam and Rex loaded the bags with clothing and toiletries Leah had packed for herself and the children into the SUV. Sam took Leah to the hotel. He and Leah would stay with the children. Rex, Catia, and Digger in Nuusiku's vehicle with him in the back followed Sam and Leah to the hotel, where Marissa joined them before they headed out to Pieter's farm.

According to Greg's team, Mrs. Nuusiku was in Walvis Bay for the weekend to visit their son and his wife and their three-year-old granddaughter. She'd only return on Monday afternoon.

Rex and the team had the weekend to talk to Commissioner Simon Nuusiku.

Chapter Sixty-One

THE CONFESSOR

Friday. Khomas Hochland Mountains, Namibia

Catia and Marissa felt Nuusiku's most atrocious transgression was how he treated Leah. Not to mention trying to abduct her children and threatening to sell them as sex slaves. Therefore, they opined, as women, they had a God-given obligation to stand up for Leah. They insisted on interrogating Nuusiku.

Rex and Josh tried their best to dissuade their wives, but they were unmovable. In the end, the men relented and made a compromise—they would be present while their wives questioned the man just to make sure they didn't kill him.

Digger didn't have to ask to be part of the questioning; he was a skillful interrogator and would assist the ladies of his pack in making Nuusiku talk.

John, Christelle, and Greg in the CRC Ops room were dialed into the video and audio stream coming to them via satellite from the farmhouse lounge in the Khomas

Hochland Mountains of Namibia. Martin was connected from his office in Langley.

Catia and Marissa, and their husbands were having coffee and some of Thea's homemade raisin rusks when Nuusiku began to show signs of regaining consciousness. His hands and feet were strapped with duct tape to an upright plastic chair with armrests. A large plastic sheet covered the floor. His head was still covered with the pillowcase, and his mouth was still wrapped with duct tape. He moaned and groaned. Probably because of the stupendous headache.

They ignored him and continued their discussion about corruption in government and perverts that blackmailed widows and abducted children.

As Nuusiku became more aware, he made such a racket it irritated them. Marissa nodded to Catia. They approached Nuusiku, poured a big bucket of cold water over him to wake him up and get rid of the urine stench, then they sprayed him generously with air freshener before ripping the pillowcase off his head and the duct tape off his face as violently as possible—all without saying a word.

Nuusiku's high-pitched screaming, when some of his beard, hair, and skin was ripped off, quickly turned to a tsunami of expletives. To air his feelings, he used one of the indigenous languages, probably Ovambo, his mother tongue, but also German and Afrikaans, and to a lesser extent English because English is not nearly as rich in profanities as the Germanic languages. He promised them the most painful punishment imaginable as soon as he was free, which he expected to happen soon because he was an important man—people would be looking for him.

But Catia and Marissa ignored him. They'd returned to

their coffee and rusks and their conversation, turning their backs on him.

Nuusiku thought of himself as a man of authority, fearsome. Entitled to talk more than he listened. Being ignored like this drove him to distraction.

However, Digger was not as calm as Catia and Marissa. Clearly, he knew this guy in the chair was threatening two of his most favorite humans, and he wouldn't stand for that. The hair on his back stood on edge. He growled softly as he walked slowly toward Nuusiku.

When Nuusiku became aware of Digger, his eyes shot wide, and his mouth snapped shut mid-sentence.

Digger stopped, sat down, and stared at him. His tongue lolled out, the corners of his lips slightly drawn back and curled up—the canine version of a smile, as if to say, "Go ahead, scumbag, make my day."

But the women were so engaged in conversation they seemed to not even notice the silence that erupted.

After a while, Nuusiku must have thought Digger wouldn't come closer and launched into a diatribe about women's place in society—at home, raising kids, cooking and cleaning, and pleasing their husbands. Definitely not detaining important government officials. Especially not the nephew of the Minister of Natural Resources and Energy.

Digger started growling.

Then Nuusiku made another mistake. He lied. "I did nothing wrong... I've only been kind to her. I took care of her! She would've been..."

He was the only one in the room who didn't know Digger could sense and smell when humans lied. Digger was on his feet. He barked and jumped forward.

"Stop him!" yelled Nuusiku.

No one reacted.

Digger barked again. He was now within striking distance of Nuusiku's face.

"Please! I beg you. Please stop him!"

Slowly, Catia raised her hand in a stop motion.

Digger sat down and stared at the man in the chair, moaning softly. Obviously not happy that he couldn't have his way with this lowlife.

"I'll tell you everything. Please, just take the dog away."

Catia and Marissa stared at Nuusiku with raised eyebrows.

"The dog first," said Nuusiku.

Catia and Marissa made to turn their backs on him again.

And Digger growled right on cue.

The reality of his situation must have finally dawned on him. He was clever enough to know the plastic cover on the floor was there for one reason only—so that his blood wouldn't stain the wooden floor. And that his captors didn't hide their faces meant they were planning on killing him; otherwise, they wouldn't let him see their faces.

"I'll talk!"

"Jeez, I don't know if we're interested in what you have to say," said Marissa. "We're paid to kill you and dissolve your carcass in drain cleaner."

"We've got a bit of time," said Catia, making a scene of looking at her watch. "I am mildly interested to hear what the vermin has to say. What do you think?"

After a while, Marissa nodded. "O-k-a-y. But if he lies, I hand him over to Digger."

"Agreed," said Catia.

Digger growled again on cue.

Nuusiku didn't wait for Digger to back off or permission to talk from the ladies. He bared his soul as though he were on his deathbed, making his final confession to his priest, begging for absolution before entering purgatory.

He started with Leah and told them everything. He was the sorriest man in Africa about his thoughtless act when he had the children abducted. He gave them the address where they'd be able to find them. He still had no idea how spectacularly his kidnapping operation had failed. He alleged he wasn't serious when he told Leah he was going to sell the children into bondage. He just wanted to keep them for the weekend so that he could scare Leah into compliance.

He was unaware that he came to within a hairbreadth of sustaining serious injuries when he talked about Leah and what he did to her. Was it not for Catia's and Marissa's solemn undertaking to their husbands not to harm the man, he would've ended up in a bad way.

Nuusiku told them there were two more workers in the department with whom he had the same deal as with Leah. He kept the cash in a safe at home. He apologized for not being able to remember the exact amount, but he'd collected in the order of half a million Namibian dollars over the past three years. He'd kept about two hundred thousand. The rest went to uncle Jackson. He elaborated about the deal with his uncle, who got sixty percent of the booty from all deals. He didn't withhold any of the information about their Swiss bank accounts, the details of which were on his phone and laptop if the ladies were interested in having a look.

"Not interested," said Marissa. "We get paid to kill you, not for reading your laptop."

Before he launched into his relationship with the Chinese, he asked for a cigarette. His request was met with a low growl from Digger and blank stares from the women.

He got the same response when he asked for water after

telling them about the discovery of the richest rare-earth deposit on the planet near Karibib. He told them that Tian Chao wanted China to get control over the proceeds of the mine.

Thus far, on each of the topics covered by Nuusiku, Rex and the team had enough prior knowledge to verify that he was truthful. And they were not entirely surprised that he was so brutally honest and self-incriminating. Faced with death, people tended to be truthful, hoping to receive absolution.

The veracity of the information about his complicity in the illicit wildlife trade was not so easy to verify, because they had little prior information. But Nuusiku didn't know what they knew or not. Presumably, he was as honest as he was with everything before. Besides, if he lied, Digger would've let them know.

Nuusiku said his relationship was primarily with Tian Chao, who was connected to the Sino-Africa Development Corporation. They had a large network of poachers and criminals throughout Namibia and neighboring countries who supplied them with products. He didn't know who they were. Even Tian dealt with them through third parties. Nevertheless, he knew one of the third parties was a man known as Andreas Nakanyala. Apparently, Nakanyala had a bit of a reputation as a violent man with a mercenary force of unscrupulous men.

Nuusiku explained that his role in the wildlife operation was to supply the "export permits." He and uncle Jackson got twenty percent. The merchandise was stored in warehouses and storage facilities across Namibia, from where it was moved to the storage facilities of Container Universe in Walvis Bay. From there, it was shipped out of the country on board the vessels of dishonest shipping captains. He had the names and details of the captains, their crews, and their ships. All the information was on his laptop.

By the time Nuusiku finished his confession, he was a defeated man, sobbing painfully. Arrogance had cost him everything and left him with nothing.

On the ranch in the CRC Ops room, Christelle was shaking her head. "John, if I didn't see this, I wouldn't believe it. Digger on his own made this guy talk in what, ten minutes? And not only that, he kept him talking, and he kept him honest right to the end."

"Mindboggling, is it not?" said John.

"Indeed," said Martin from his office in Langley. "I've never seen anyone have a change of heart quite like that. The day Digger dies, he deserves a star on the CIA's Memorial Wall."

Marissa placed the pillowcase over Nuusiku's head and checked that his restraints were still intact. They left him in the chair and ordered Digger to watch him.

Nuusiku sobbed in silence, unmoving.

Catia had set up a video conference on her laptop in the kitchen with John and the team on the Ranch and Martin in his office in Langley.

During the discussions about how they could use Nuusiku and the information he'd provided, Rex had lapsed into silence. John noticed the telltale change in Rex's demeanor. After sixteen years, he knew Rex better than anyone else. He had seen that mannerism on many missions —Rex had a plan. Actually, it was more than a plan; it was a look into the future. Not that Rex had a prophetic gift, but he had the ability to identify the pieces of the puzzle and figure out where and when they'd fit into the final picture long before anyone else could.

Although John could see Rex wasn't ready to talk about

the plan, it filled him with excitement. Soon, he and Digger were going to take time out and work through the plan. No one knew how they did it. Josh had decided long ago they spoke a unique language. Maybe they did, but neither of them ever talked about it. What was not a secret was that they had an excellent track record.

Chapter Sixty-Two

THE RECRUITMENT

Saturday. Khomas Hochland Mountains, Namibia

It was shortly past midnight when Rex and the team returned to Nuusiku. Through another bout of tears, he wanted to know if there were any prospects of clemency, seeing that he was so honest and showed so much remorse. And, of course, if they'd let him live, they could count on his full cooperation.

The four of them conferred for a few minutes in whispered tones.

Rex called Digger and told him to sit. He sat down and whined softly while looking at Rex and Nuusiku in turn.

"Yes, I know," said Rex loud enough for Nuusiku to hear.

Digger yelped.

"Not now. Maybe a bit later," said Rex.

Digger yelped again.

"Okay, okay, I promise."

Digger relaxed, and a dog-smile appeared on his face.

Rex whispered in his ear, and Digger licked him in the face.

"Just relax while I make the call, okay."

Digger yawned.

Rex turned to Nuusiku. "The dog says he'd like to rip your throat out for what you did to Leah and her children, and he's really incensed about all those protected animals you killed. But I've convinced him we should first take instructions from our client before he can have a go at you. The dog reckons our client is unlikely to change his mind, however as a reward for your honesty, I'll call him."

Nuusiku nodded enthusiastically. "Just keep that dog off me."

Rex took his mobile phone out, typed a string of numbers, and brought the phone to his ear. Nuusiku was too far away from Rex to see that the phone was switched off.

"Sorry to trouble you, general. Do you have a minute?"

...

"Yeah, all good. Yes, we have him here."

...

"Well, we were about to execute him when he started spilling his guts about all the other criminal activities he's been involved in. He told us all about his connections and coconspirators."

...

"Yeah, all of them, names, addresses, and everything. Yes, bribery, blackmail, kidnapping, drugs, poaching, illegal wildlife products, adultery, probably child molestation as well."

Nuusiku groaned and shook his head violently.

Rex gave him a withering look and continued. "This guy

is a scumbag, and his uncle, Minister Jackson Kaura, is the kingpin in this criminal enterprise."

...

"Yeah, he wants to make a deal. His cooperation for his life."

...

"Uh-huh."

...

"I agree. A bullet through the head is best."

...

"I don't think he can be trusted. I mean, how can one trust a lowlife who abducts children and exploits widows. Let me shoot him in the head and put him out of *our* misery."

...

"What! Are you serious?"

...

"Okay. Well, it's your money. If that's what you want. But if he tries to doublecross us, we're taking him up to the Zambezi River next week and using him for bait on our crocodile hunting trip.

...

"Uh-huh."

...

"Okay, I'll let him know."

...

"Will do."

Rex put the phone on the table and looked at Nuusiku.

"Turns out the general is a softy. He reckons we should give you a chance at redemption. I think he's making a *big* mistake."

Nuusiku nodded slowly. "You won't regret it. But after I've given my cooperation, what happens?"

"Well, if we're happy with your performance, I'll do you another favor and call the general again."

"Who is this general? Why does he want me dead?"

"I've never met him in person. He pays well, and as long as he pays on time, his name and his reasons are unimportant. As to what happens when you're not useful anymore, that's for the general to decide. If it was up to me, I'd shoot you in the head and throw you in a bathtub of drain cleaner. But the general might have different ideas."

"What does he want me to do?"

Rex explained what he wanted, and, as can be expected of a man on death row, he accepted the conditions without hesitation. Nuusiku loved life above all else. Even so, just to make sure he would not renege on his undertakings, Rex and Josh used one of their old tricks to keep him on the straight and narrow. They stuck two plastic beads the size of small peas, one in each armpit, and secured them with super-adhesive waterproof band-aids.

Josh explained. "Nuusiku, pay close attention; it concerns your health. Those devices under your arms have two functions. One, they're the most powerful microphones on the planet. So, we'll be listening to every sound you make and any sound made by anyone and anything within five meters of you. Two, they contain the most powerful explosives known to man. The bombs operate on biochemical batteries, which are charged by the chemicals emitted by your skin. In other words, they will never run out of battery. Now, here's the thing, there are two ways in which those little bombs can be triggered. One, remotely from any of our phones. To prevent that from happening, you only have to do exactly what we tell you to do. Two, when you or anyone else tries to remove them. If those bombs explode, you and anyone within two meters of you will be vaporized. No one up to ten meters will survive.

"Oh, and don't even think that we won't understand what you're saying in other languages. We have translators who'll be listening to every word. All it will take for us to push the button that'll vaporize you is one wrong word. Questions?"

Nuusiku was ashen-faced. Unable to speak, he only shook his head.

"Good. You'll be okay as long as you do nothing stupid."

Nuusiku nodded. After this, he was sedated, tied up, gagged, and hooded.

Fritz and his men were kept under sedation in different rooms in the outbuildings, where they would remain until Nuusiku had done his job.

It was a little after five o'clock Saturday morning when Rex parked Nuusiku's Jeep Grand Cherokee in the lockup garage at his house in Ludwigsdorf, one of the best suburbs in Windhoek. Nuusiku was in the back, still unconscious.

Sam was already waiting for them when they arrived.

Rex, Catia, and Digger went into the house while Sam kept guard outside. Catia established a video conference with the Ops Room on the Ranch and Martin in his office. Everything was recorded as Rex cleared out Nuusiku's safe, confiscating his passport, two hundred and fifteen thousand Namibian dollars in cash, fifty one-ounce gold coins known as Krugerrands, gold and silver jewelry, and a small metal box containing sixty gem-quality diamonds ranging in size from one to twenty carats, worth between two and five million US dollars. Rex also confiscated the two laptops. Everything went into a big grip bag they brought along.

They went back to the garage, where Rex removed all the restraints from Nuusiku's arms and legs before they left.

He would wake up in about ten minutes with a terrible headache, a vivid recollection of what had happened to him, but no idea where he was when it happened.

Sam took them to the hotel, where they picked up Leah and the children and took them to Pieter's farm. She and the children would stay on the farm until it was safe for them to return to Windhoek.

Chapter Sixty-Three

THE OPPORTUNITY OF OUR LIFETIMES

Saturday. Windhoek, Namibia

By anyone's standards, Simon Nuusiku was a devious, immoral, unethical, and dishonest man. His uncle, Jackson Kaura, was much worse.

Kaura was the fifth and youngest child of a dirt-poor peasant communal family close to Ondangwa, Ovamboland, in the north of Namibia, close to the border with Angola. His formal education was limited to graduating from senior high school at eighteen, after which he joined SWAPO in the war of independence. He was thirty-five when Namibia became independent. For his seventeen years of service as a freedom fighter or terrorist, depending on one's political view, he was rewarded with the position of Member of Parliament of the Ondangwa region.

Although Namibia was a parliamentary democracy, it was a one-party dominant state with SWAPO in power. Opposition parties were allowed but had no real chance of gaining power, as ethnicity plays a significant role in party affiliation and voting behavior. Some parties, such as SWAPO, were dominated by single ethnic groups; its government and administration were predominantly Ovambo, who made up fifty percent of the total population.

When Kaura took up his seat in parliament, he couldn't write a cheque for a hundred dollars which the bank would honor. Twenty years after entering politics, he was the Minister of Natural Resources and Energy. Five years after becoming minister, he was also a very rich man. The plebeian farm boy had morphed into a self-aggrandizing, power-hungry, gluttonous man who never let an opportunity pass to let people know just how much sway he held in Namibia. After all, he was in charge of mining, the mainstay of Namibia's economy, the largest contributor to the country's GDP. He liked to tell people Namibia was the fourth largest exporter of non-fuel minerals in Africa and the world's fifth-largest producer of uranium. Rich alluvial diamond deposits along the west coast made Namibia a primary source of gem-quality diamonds.

And he, Jackson Kaura, was in charge of it all.

He believed his N$940,000 annual salary was a pittance, definitely not fair compensation for a job as crucial as his. Hence, he entitled himself to supplement his government salary from other sources. In short, Kaura believed he was above the law. And thus far, no one had challenged him on that.

A perverted skirt chaser and a rumbustious man, he spent money like water, especially taxpayers' money. He was always accompanied by an entourage of assistants, including at least two superficially attractive but intellectually mediocre women who could have been concubines or pleasure wives or status symbols or all of the above.

It was shortly after ten on Saturday morning when

Nuusiku parked his Jeep Grand Cherokee in front of his uncle's house in Auasblick, one of the most affluent suburbs in Windhoek. As can be expected from Kaura, since his meteoric rise from rags to riches, the house, 1,831 square meters under roof, was an opulent affair on two hectares. It comprised five ensuite bedrooms, study, reception, swimming pool, servants' quarters, four garages, gym, and well-kept gardens, valued in excess of twenty million Namibian dollars. The average house price in Windhoek was one-point-four million Namibian dollars.

He met Nuusiku at the front door and steered him to the study. On the way, he barked orders to the servants to bring refreshments.

The painkillers Nuusiku took for his throbbing headache helped somewhat for the pain but did nothing for his nerves. The little lumps in his armpits were a constant reminder that he was in a life-or-death situation. He had to act normal or end up with a bullet in the head in a bath filled with drain cleaner or, worse, live bait for crocodiles or that monstrous black dog's dinner.

"Now, Simon," Kaura said when they'd made themselves comfortable in the easy chairs in the ostentatious study lined with shelves filled with a few thousand books, none of which Kaura had ever read, "what's so urgent on this Saturday morning that I had to give up my golf game?"

Nuusiku almost smiled—he had saved his uncle's golf buddies a great deal of frustration. Uncle Kaura's skill at the game was all but atrocious. He only got on the fairways when he crossed it to get to his ball, which almost always landed in the rough. His scorekeeping was like his professional and personal life, a total farce. He never counted the balls he lost nor the penalty shots he was supposed to take when he went out of bounds, or the times he hit fresh air.

His partners were well-aware of his cheating but wouldn't dare to challenge him on it.

"The opportunity of our lifetimes, Uncle Jackson," said Nuusiku with as much enthusiasm as he could muster, while being painfully aware that the assassin with the dark eyes was listening. His body was ravaged by cold shivers at the thought of that dog that could communicate with humans. For all he knew, the dog was probably also listening.

By now, Greg had taken remote control of Nuusiku's phone and was busy installing the Pegasus app on the Minister's phone.

Kaura leaned back in his easy chair and took a sip of his Single Malt Scotch. "Tell me about it."

For the best part of an hour, Nuusiku told his uncle about the discovery of the rare-earth deposit and the Chinese interest in it.

Kaura's brain was flashing dollar signs as Nuusiku stepped him through the numbers. This could make him rich beyond his wildest dreams—and powerful, as in presidentially powerful. His mind was racing with all the possibilities. With this kind of money behind him, the farm boy from Ondangwa would become president. A dream he'd been nurturing since Justus Aruseb became president. He despised the man. Kaura opined that Aruseb's first mortal sin was that he was a Damara. Damaras were inferior to Ovambos. Second, Aruseb's mind got poisoned during his Ph.D. studies in America. Western-style democracy was not what Namibia needed; the country would do much better with an autocratic leader such as himself.

"There's, however, one small problem," said Nuusiku.

Kaura raised his eyebrows.

"Erwin Krige, the man who made the discovery. He has

a legitimate prospecting permit. He threatened with legal action if I were to cancel his permit."

As instructed by the assassin with the big black dog, Nuusiku made no mention of Dr. Collins.

"Easy. We nationalize the mine," said Kaura.

Nuusiku shook his head. "The Chinese don't want us to do that. They don't want any publicity. They want the deal signed, sealed, and delivered by the time the media finds out. We could make up a reason to cancel his permit. I think the best and quickest way to get rid of him is if you talk to him."

"What leverage do we have over him?"

"I think we have more than enough to scare the daylights out of him," said Nuusiku and repeated verbatim the information about Krige's background and ancestors provided to him by Tian.

Kaura grinned. "Excellent, I see you've done your homework. If that doesn't convince him, we'll use heavy-handed tactics."

Nuusiku nodded. "Uh-huh."

"I'll get my secretary to summon him to a meeting next week. Now, let's talk about the Chinese," said Kaura. "What do they want out of this?"

"I'm sure they want the sole rights, but that's something you and General Quan Zhelan should negotiate."

Kaura took a sip of his whiskey. He had many high-ranking 'business associates'; they've all contributed to his personal wealth but none as much as the CEO of Sino-Africa Development Corporation, General Quan Zhelan. He owed the man a debt of gratitude.

As instructed by the assassin with the big black dog, Nuusiku continued, "I suggest you invite him over here, treat him like a king and squeeze a king's ransom out of him in exchange for the exclusive rights to that mine."

Kaura smiled. "Good idea."

"I suggest I let Tian know as soon as we've received the sum of one and a half million US in our Swiss bank accounts, General Quan can book his trip to Namibia."

"You're full of good ideas today, Simon. Do it."

In the family room on Pieter's farm, the Ranch in Arizona, and Martin's office in Langley, the members of Operation Sierra were smiling and high-fiving. Nuusiku had done his part to influence his uncle to do exactly what they wanted.

By eight o'clock that night, over dinner at the Hilton, Nuusiku delivered on the second part of his promise. Tian had agreed to part with one-point-five million US dollars for his uncle's undertaking to get rid of Erwin Krige, after which General Quan Zhelan would visit Namibia as the personal guest of Minister Jackson Kaura.

Two hours after the dinner at the Hilton ended, Josh and Connor dropped Fritz and his goons off at Fritz's house. Before they sedated him for the last time, Josh and Connor had a fatherly talk with him and his men. They understood all too well what would happen to them if they tried to run away. They were to stay put at Fritz's house until they were called upon by the police to testify against Nuusiku. It could be days, weeks, or maybe a month or two. If they ran away, the deal was off; they'd be tracked down and charged with kidnapping. Furthermore, if they contacted Nuusiku or talked to anyone about what had happened to them, the deal was off; they'd be charged with kidnapping.

When they came to Fritz's house an hour after being

dropped off, just like Nuusiku, they had terrible headaches, a vivid recollection of what had happened to them, but no idea where they were when it happened.

Chapter Sixty-Four

NO WINNERS, ONLY SURVIVORS

Sunday. Khomas Hochland Mountains, Namibia

Marissa had asked Erwin and Mieke to come over to Eldorado so that they could brief them all about the events of the past few days.

They arrived on Eldorado midmorning on Sunday. Sam and Connor stayed with Leah and the children. The Kriges arrived shortly after. Thea steered them to the outdoor entertainment area, where she served tea, coffee, and a variety of home-baked delicacies, including the Americans' favorite, *koeksisters*. For lunch, Pieter told them they were going to make *potjiekos*, a stew cooked in a cast iron three-legged pot over an open fire.

Rex and the team brought their friends up to speed with everything that had happened since they last saw each other.

"So, Kaura is going to summon me to his office sometime this week?" said Erwin with a slight grin.

"Yep, he's going to try and intimidate you in all manner possible, including accusing you and your ancestors of racism and genocide of the Herero and Nama tribes," said Rex.

Erwin shrugged. "Not that I condone what my ancestors did or deny that I was born into privilege under the apartheid system, but those times ended thirty years ago. All we can do is apologize, make amends, and do everything in our power to make sure that it doesn't happen again."

Rex nodded. "I agree. It is as Shakespeare said, 'What's past is prologue.' But I suspect Kaura has never read Shakespeare."

"Probably not," said Erwin. "So, how do you want me to handle this? Should I even agree to see him? He's got no authority to summon me to his office like that."

"We want you to play along," said Rex. "That doesn't mean walk in and surrender. You'll have to put up a convincing protest. But in the end, you'll allow him to 'intimidate' you enough to give up. In other words, don't make it too easy for him lest it raises suspicion."

For the next two hours, until lunch was ready, they discussed all possible scenarios that might develop during the ministerial meeting and how Erwin should handle each.

"We need only a little more time to get our backups in place," said Rex when they were done play-acting.

"Backups?" asked Mieke.

"Yes," said Catia. "Bringing the US Secretary of State over for a meet and greet with your president and the arrival of the US Navy carrier task force for their exercises."

There was a long silence as the Kriges and Naudés were gaping at their American friends in near-disbelief.

Pieter was the first to regain composure. "So, that's

what's behind the planned American naval wargames reported in the news?"

Rex nodded.

"I pray God will forbid that it escalates into war," whispered Mieke.

"We believe the show of force will keep the Chinese at bay," said Josh.

"What are the military experts predicting about the outcome of a war between America and China?" Thea's question was on everyone's mind.

"As your mother said, let's pray God will forbid it ever comes to that," said Rex. "In a conventional war without nuclear weapons, the losses on both sides would be of epic proportions. If nuclear weapons enter the equation, we're looking at a Biblical scenario—Armageddon. We have five thousand eight hundred nuclear warheads; they have three hundred and fifty. More than enough to wipe our planet from the solar system.

"Military experts analyze and model factors such as how close the conflict will be to mainland China. The further away from the mainland, the less China's chances of success. But keep in mind the analysis is three years old. America's military has grown in that time, but the Chinese military has grown more than ours. Less than ten years ago, America would've dominated the Chinese military in almost any scenario. Now some military strategists think the US may lose a conventional conflict.

"The US Air Force has about three thousand seven hundred warplanes in service. China has about one thousand two hundred. We have about one-point-four-million service personnel, China has one-point-nine-million. They have three hundred and fifty warships, and we have two hundred and forty-nine. We have twenty aircraft carriers, they have only three. We have roughly the same number of submarines as they. Fifty-two of our attack submarines are nuclear-powered; only seven of China's sixty-two attack submarines are nuclear-propelled.

"There'll be no winners, only survivors."

Chapter Sixty-Five

THE MINE IS YOURS, MINISTER

Wednesday. Windhoek, Namibia

Erwin could write the times he'd worn a suit and tie on the back of a postage stamp and have enough space left for his signature. As if what felt like being strangled by his tie was not enough to irritate him, the minister's security detail searched him for weapons and confiscated his cellphone, smartwatch, and briefcase, and then he was faced by a haughty secretary staring at him over lowered glasses as if the cat had dragged him in. All of it contributed generously to his indignation. Not to mention that he had arrived seven minutes early out of courtesy, yet the minister, although he had no other visitors, made him wait in the anteroom for nearly forty-five minutes. By quarter to eleven, when he finally entered the minister's extravagant office for his scheduled ten o'clock appointment, Erwin was more than just a little miffed.

Though Catia and Marissa had fitted him with a molar mic, it was just a backup in case Kaura's and Nuusiku's cellphones were out of order or not near enough to pick up what was being said. It turned out that both their phones were working properly, allowing Rex and the others to listen and record the meeting.

Simon Nuusiku stood when Erwin entered and nodded curtly. "Mr. Krige."

Erwin returned the gesture. "Commissioner Nuusiku."

Nuusiku said, "Minister, this is Mr. Erwin Krige. Mr. Krige, meet his Excellency Minister Kaura."

Erwin stepped forward to shake hands, but Kaura remained seated behind his desk and ignored Erwin's hand. He said nothing, just nodded slightly toward the two empty chairs in front of his desk.

Too high and mighty to be civilized.

Erwin and Nuusiku sat down in the chairs.

Like puppies undergoing obedience training.

Kaura opened a folder, made a big scene of cleaning his reading glasses, and started reading. Apart from a few guttural sounds, which could have been displays of disgust or maybe postnasal drip, he remained silent while paging through the folder for nearly five minutes, as if he had no idea what was in that folder.

Erwin was a peace-loving and patient man, but this man's impertinence was pushing him to the brink.

Finally, Kaura looked up at Erwin. "Mr. Krige, I've decided to cancel your prospecting license for site K108."

"May I ask why, Minister?" Erwin managed to look a little taken aback.

"You didn't file your regulatory reports for the past twelve months. Yet, you have conducted extensive prospecting and never reported it. That's a serious breach of contract."

"With all due respect, Minister, you must've been misinformed. I've filed all the required reports on time. I brought along copies of all documents pertaining to this mine. They're in the briefcase that your security detail took possession of. If I can access the briefcase, I'll give you the copies."

Kaura sighed loudly and motioned for Nuusiku to get the briefcase.

A minute later, Nuusiku was back with the briefcase. Erwin immediately saw the locks were broken and the contents removed. He shook his head and tried to look embarrassed, not an easy feat, given the amount of provocation he had already endured. "My sincerest apologies, Minister, I'm embarrassed. It seems, in my haste, I took the wrong briefcase this morning. The empty one with the broken locks. I don't know what I was thinking. I will deliver copies to your office within the next twenty-four hours."

Kaura was shaking his head. "No need. I've made my decision. Your permit is canceled."

"Minister, again, with all due respect, you don't have that kind of authority. I'm entitled to a fair hearing. At the very least, I should be allowed to present the documents in question."

"Not going to happen, Mr. Krige. That's final."

"Minister, if you don't allow me that basic right, I will have no choice but to seek relief in the courts."

"Mr. Krige, my patience is wearing thin. Go to court if you want to. But keep in mind if you do, the gloves are off. Not only will we put forward your flagrant disregard for the Ministry's rules and regulations, we'll also put forward the atrocities committed by you and your ancestors against the people of this country. You're the one who is going to look and smell bad, not the Ministry."

Erwin had been waiting for this. "Atrocities?"

"Krige, don't tell me you're unaware of the fact that

your great grandfather was one of the Schutztruppe who killed tens of thousands of this country's citizens. Or that you don't know your grandfather and father were Nazis. Are you going to deny that you fought for the apartheid regime of South Africa against the people of Namibia?"

"Minister, that's something I've been thinking about for many years. You know, in South Africa, at the end of the apartheid era, they had a Truth and Reconciliation Commission. They traveled through the entire country and listened to the testimony of thousands of victims and offenders. They revealed the truth, and they moved on from there. I'm of the opinion that Namibia should've had its own Truth and Reconciliation Commission. Don't you think, Minister, that it would have been nice if we could get it all out in the open, asking each other's forgiveness, draw a line in the sand and move on?"

"What are you getting at, Krige? Don't waste my time or the little patience I have left."

"Minister, what I'm getting at is that I admit my ancestors did wrong. Maybe not entirely as grossly as you portrayed, but if we go to court, we can present the evidence and ask the court to rule on those matters once and for all. And while we're at it, we should present all evidence of our country's history of the last two centuries. That way, SWAPO can come clean about the details of thousands of missing people, which they've been hiding for over thirty years. Perhaps they could show the loved ones of those who are missing where to find the bodies? Maybe they could also come clean on hundreds of charges of torture and rape leveled against them? Maybe they could put names to the unmarked graves found in the north of the country recently?"

"Enough!" roared Kaura. "I will not be lectured by you

about how this country should be governed. Neither about the history of this country to which you and your ilk were neither invited nor welcomed. Your permit is canceled. Commissioner, see Mr. Krige out."

Erwin repressed the smile that threatened to besiege his face. He stood and extended his hand to the Minister. It was ignored again.

"Oh, one more thing Krige, you've got twenty-four hours to remove your stuff from the site. After that, if you ever set foot on that site, you'll be arrested for trespassing on government property. Understood?"

Erwin was tempted to explain to the minister the Biblical principle of casting one's pearls before swine. Instead, he said, "My family name is worth more to me than a piece of rock in the desert. I'll remove my stuff. The mine is yours, Minister. I bid you and Commissioner Nuusiku a good day."

There was nothing more to say. He had accomplished his mission. He turned and headed for the door.

When the door closed behind Erwin, Kaura looked at his watch and said, "That's how you earn one and a half million US dollars in twenty minutes. Let Tian know General Quan can start packing for his trip to Namibia."

None of them saw the grin on Erwin Krige's face when he stepped out of the building.

As per the orders of the man with the big black dog, Nuusiku made no mention of Erwin Krige's other mines or the fact that he had issued the mining permit for site K110 (Mount Krige) to Erwin Krige first thing on Monday morning. Neither did he tell his uncle that on Monday morning, he had also ordered the HR department to immediately process Leah Visser's resignation, and to pay out her final salary, leave, and pro-rata bonus before the end of the day.

Chapter Sixty-Six

THINGS WOULD GO VERY BADLY FOR THEM

Wednesday. Oval Office, Washington, D.C.

Two and a half hours after Erwin left Minister Kaura's office in Windhoek, Howard Lawrence and Martin Richardson entered the Oval Office to brief the president and his advisors.

"Mr. President, the end game kicked off a few hours ago," started Howard after the president opened the meeting and deferred to him for an update. "Krige met with Minister Kaura. The latter told him his permit had been canceled forthwith. Krige played his role like a Hollywood pro. Minister Kaura stuck to his guns, and Krige eventually gave up his claim to the mine exactly as we planned. General Quan Zhelan will be on his way to Namibia shortly."

"In other words," said the president, "it's now only a matter of time before they know they'd been deceived?"

"Yes, sir. Within the next week or two."

"How far away is our carrier group from Walvis Bay?"

"Four days, sir," said Admiral Wyatt.

The president turned his gaze to the Secretary of State, "What's the situation on the diplomatic front, James?"

"Mr. President, Ambassador Edwards has obtained the schedules of not only the President of Namibia but also the presidents and senior ministers of South Africa and Botswana. She has paved the way for meetings with some of them on short notice. Namibia's President Justus Aruseb has expressed much interest in our new aid initiative and is keen to meet with me to discuss the opportunities."

"Good. It seems we've got all our ducks in a row on the military and diplomatic fronts. Now, what can we expect from the Chinese?"

"They're going to wake up with egg all over their faces, sir," said Howard. "They won't take kindly to the public humiliation."

"And to add insult to injury, around that same time, they'll also figure out why we've chosen this time for naval exercises in the region," said the DNI, Jen Whitmer.

"How long will it take them to bring in a force that could be a threat to ours?" asked the president.

"Our satellites have been tracking two of their battleships and one nuclear submarine from Djibouti in the Horn of Africa, which are on their way to Cape Town. Obviously, they're planning to spy on us during the wargames," said Admiral Wyatt. "So, they'll be present when we get there. But, they won't be much of a threat to us. For them to scrounge together a decent size fleet of battle craft and move them so far away from their homeland would take the better part of six weeks, maybe even longer. And even then, they'd be hard-pressed to pose a serious threat to us. Their navy and strike craft were built and equipped for war off the shores of mainland China. On the technological front, especially, they're not on the same level as us. So far away from their shores, they just don't have the blue water capability that we have. Not yet."

Few people fully comprehended the terrifying power of an operational carrier strike group, usually made up of about seven thousand five-hundred personnel, an aircraft carrier, at least one cruiser, a destroyer squadron of at least two destroyers or frigates, submarines, plus logistics ships and a supply ship. Add to this an air wing of eighty-five to ninety fixed-wing and rotary-wing aircraft. The fixed-wing strike fighters were primarily F/A-18E and F/A-18F Super Hornets and F/A-18A+ and F/A-18C Hornets. The firepower of one supercarrier on its own rivaled the military forces of entire nations. Since March 2016, the US Navy has had ten carrier strike groups. Two were taking part in this exercise dubbed Operation Southern Cross.

The Nimitz class aircraft carriers were named after World War II United States Pacific Fleet commander, Fleet Admiral Chester W. Nimitz, the last US Navy officer to hold the rank. The carriers were one thousand and ninety-two feet (three hundred and thirty-three meters) long with a full-load displacement of over 100,000 tons. They cost in excess of US$9.55 billion in 2019 dollars to build, were nuclear-powered, and could travel at thirty knots (thirty-five miles or fifty-six kilometers per hour) nonstop for twenty to twenty-five years.

Since the 1970s, Nimitz-class carriers have participated in Operation Eagle Claw in Iran, the Gulf War, and more recently in Iraq and Afghanistan.

"Let's hope and pray they don't do something stupid.

Like attacking us," said the president. "I'd prefer not to go down in history as the man who started World War Three."

"We believe, as soon as China discovers they've been hoodwinked, though they'll be raving mad, they'll also realize things would go very badly for them if they started a shootout with the Southern Cross armada," said Admiral Wyatt.

Chapter Sixty-Seven

HE'S IN CHARGE NOW

Friday. Erongo Mountains, Namibia

On the way back to their campsite after the meeting with Minister Kaura Wednesday, Erwin called Nelis Goreseb, his foreman, and asked him to bring all the laborers over to Twohill early the next morning so that they could remove all equipment and structures from the site.

They were there shortly after sunrise. By sunset on Thursday, the last truck left Twohill and headed for the shed at the Mount Krige site to drop off its load.

Friday, before midday, two Toyota Hiace vans with four black men and camping equipment arrived at Twohill. Apart from the CIA keyhole spy satellite assigned to monitor the site, Marissa had one of the mini drones hovering over the site as well.

A smile was playing on Erwin's face as he and the others watched the unfolding scene. The four men were dressed in black ballcaps, Ray-Ban sunglasses, black t-shirts, black jeans, and Caterpillar boots. They were armed with AK-56s, the Chinese-manufactured 7.62×39mm variant of the Soviet-designed AK-47. The men also packed Chinese 9-millimeter QSZ-92 pistols in hip holsters. To the untrained eye, they certainly would have looked formidable. But Rex, Josh, Marissa, and Catia were not fooled by appearances. True professionals possessed a quiet inner strength and seldom dressed to impress.

"The occupying force, I presume?" mumbled Erwin.

"Yep," said Josh. "Armed gangsters, not trained soldiers, by the looks of it."

Rex, Catia, and Marissa agreed.

They watched the listless men smoking, eating, and drinking beer while unpacking the vans and setting up camp with little enthusiasm as if on a go-slow. They selected the spot where Erwin's shed stood the day before for their campsite.

Two hours after their arrival, a helicopter displaying the insignia of the Ministry of Natural Resources and Energy landed at the site. Minister Kaura, Tian Chao, and Simon Nuusiku disembarked. They were all dressed in dark suits and white shirts and were wiping sweat from their faces with handkerchiefs within minutes after stepping out of the air-conditioned chopper into the scorching African sun.

They watched the minister and his minions mill around like sheep. There was not much to see other than four indo-lent men, a large, barren hill, and desert. Rex and company were hoping to eavesdrop on the conversations through the Pegasus infected cellphones of Kaura, Nuusiku, and Tian. But they'd left their phones in the chopper. All they could hear was the pilot and copilot talking to each other about their weekend plans.

Half an hour later, Kaura and company must have been tired of doing nothing, got back into the chopper, and left.

"What was that all about?" said Erwin as the helicopter disappeared in the distance.

"I think Kaura wanted to let you know he's in charge now," said Rex. "The second objective could've been to show Tian what a powerful and influential man he is."

"And don't forget taking a joyride in a helicopter at the taxpayer's expense," said Mieke.

"And that," said Rex.

Rex, Catia, and Digger left the Farleys behind with the Kriges and drove to Windhoek; they had an invitation from Ambassador Edwards.

Full credit for the operation

Friday. US Embassy, Windhoek, Namibia

The occasion was a cocktail party at the embassy to which Ambassador Edwards had invited not only President Aruseb but also the Minister of Environment, Forestry and Tourism (MEFT), the Minister of Safety and Security under whom the Namibian Police Force sorted, the Defence Minister, the Chief of the Defence Force, and the ambassadors of Botswana and South Africa to Namibia. The event was organized ostensibly to inform attendees about the new aid initiative by the American government and the Secretary of State's impending visit.

While mingling with her guests, Ambassador Edwards introduced Mr. Rex Dalton and his beautiful wife Catia, accompanied by a docile-looking big, black dog with a service dog notice on his harness to the Ministers of MEFT and Safety and Security.

Ambassador Edwards immediately got the ministers' attention when she told them, "The Daltons work for ICCWC, the International Consortium on Combating Wildlife Crime. I thought you might have common interests." She smiled as she withdrew from the group to mingle with the other guests.

The ICCWC was an umbrella establishment for five organizations collaborating to support wildlife law enforcement agencies. The ICCWC's partner agencies were the Convention on International Trade in Endangered Species (CITES), INTERPOL, the United Nations Office on Drugs and Crime (UNODC), the World Bank, and the World Customs Organization (WCO).

The ministers soon discovered that Ambassador Edwards was right; they certainly had common interests. When Mrs. Dalton and their wives wandered off to powder their noses, Mr. Dalton told them about a major wildlife crime syndicate operating in Namibia and neighboring countries. The Minister of Safety and Security was intensely interested in the information about the murder of Julie Narimab of Namgeochem.

By the end of the night, the ministers were enthused by the prospect of working with Mr. Dalton and his organization to bring the criminals to justice, especially so when they heard that the executive of ICCWC insisted that their organization's involvement in the operation be kept a secret. Mr. Dalton would be the only contact to ICCWC, and the Namibian law enforcement agencies would get full credit for the operation.

The party was also an opportunity for Ambassador

Edwards to extend an invitation on behalf of the Chair of
the Joint Chiefs of Staff, Admiral Bruce Wyatt, to the President of Namibia, the Defence Minister, and the Chief of
the Defence Force to visit one of the Nimitz aircraft carriers
taking part in the upcoming wargames. The invitation was
accepted with great enthusiasm by all three men.

Chapter Sixty-Eight

THE PAWPAW IS GOING TO HIT THE FAN

Saturday. Erongo Mountains, Namibia

Shortly after sunrise, Kaiser's raised hair and soft growls alerted the Kriges and Farleys that someone was approaching. Soon after, they heard vehicles, big ones, heading toward Twohill.

"Your new neighbors are right on time," said Josh.

Through the Pegasus app on Tian's phone, they'd been eavesdropping on his conversations the past few days and were well aware of the arrangements he had made to bring a geologist and a group of workers in to survey the site before General Quan's arrival.

Within minutes, Marissa had one of her drones up and over Twohill.

It was a convoy of six vehicles. Two heavy vehicles carrying mining equipment and supplies, two trucks carrying six-meter (twenty-foot) shipping containers, one of them a refrigeration unit, the other probably holding food supplies, and two buses carrying about fifty men.

Zooming the drone's camera in on the people revealed they were all of Asian descent. "Chinese more than likely," said Josh.

The convoy came to a halt at the site where Erwin's shed had stood before. The four guards onsite stood aside, watching the procession arrive.

The first person to put his feet on the ground was a middle-aged Chinese man with a bullhorn who started barking orders to the men in the buses. The man's voice sounded like the crack of a whip, reminding Erwin of his days in the army when the sergeant major's voice could move mountains and make troops tremble.

"Let's hope you get along well with the new neighbors," joked Josh.

Erwin grinned. "We'll do our best to be as neighborly as the Bible says we should be. But I suspect as soon as they find out they've struck silver and not rare-earths, they might lose interest in this locale and blame us for the mishap."

The men from the buses went to work, and by mid-morning, their campsite had been set up. They unloaded the mining equipment, took a half-hour lunch break, were divided into teams, and began the work they came to do. They marked the boundaries of the claim with red flags and No-Trespassing signs. They used ground-penetrating radar to "see" what was going on below the surface. A bulldozer ripped inspection trenches, and the laborers marked spots pointed out to them by the two geologists where they would be drilling and digging to collect samples. By sundown, the site had been prepared, and they stopped for the day.

"So, tomorrow, they'll start collecting samples," said Marissa.

Erwin nodded. "Yep, and by the end of the week, they should have enough samples to analyze and... then..."

"The pawpaw is going to hit the fan?" said Josh.

"Precisely," said Erwin.

"And then you won't be safe here anymore," said Marissa to Erwin and Mieke.

Mieke nodded contemplatively. "The thought crossed my mind. I think it's best if we stay with Thea and Pieter on Eldorado for the time being."

"Agreed," said Erwin. "Mieke and I have never liked crowded neighborhoods. Come Monday, we'll break up camp."

"Good idea," said Josh.

A journalist who was unafraid

Saturday. Windhoek, Namibia

Namibia had three television stations, thirteen newspapers, and twenty-five radio stations. The three TV stations belonged to the Namibian Broadcasting Corporation (NBC). In other words, there were enough media outlets in Namibia to carry a big story and rapidly spread it internationally.

The challenge was to get a journalist who was unafraid to expose corruption. Thirty or so years ago, generally speaking, journalism was an honorable profession, and the truth reigned supreme, well, more often than not. But that was long ago. Now, generally speaking, journalism was a partisan, cutthroat, political quagmire.

Namibia was no exception. The ruling party, SWAPO,

could make a dissenting journalist's life difficult, if not outright unbearable.

But Rex wanted an honest journalist with an international reputation. Someone who would not fold under pressure and enter into an adulterous relationship with the truth at the first sign of trouble.

Such a journalist was Derek Njoba, Ambassador Edwards had assured Rex. He was a highly respected free-lance journalist writing not only for the major news outlets in Namibia and African countries south of the equator but also for the New York Times and Washington Post. And occasionally for Time Magazine, The Economist, and National Geographic.

He was an unapologetic Christian, pro-democracy, politically independent, and brutally honest. During his storied career, he had caused the downfall of quite a few double-dealing officials and politicians. He pursued scandals with the same vigor that he pursued heartwarming stories of success and achievement. The corrupt hated him, the honest loved him. Even though Njoba had published glowing reports about America's involvement in southern Africa, he had not neglected to write scathing articles about their harmful actions or lack of action in the region.

He treated China's involvement in the region with the same fairness he treated everyone else—he commended what was commendable and condemned what was condemnable.

The ambassador called Derek Njoba personally to invite him to breakfast at the embassy on Saturday morning. Like any good journalist, Derek could smell a good story from a mile away, and the smell couldn't have been more distinct than getting a personal call from the ambassador to invite him for breakfast with her and two friends.

The ambassador introduced Rex, Catia, and Digger to Njoba upon arrival and led them to the embassy dining room. Njoba was a tall, almost skinny man in his late fifties. He had gray hair, wore silver-framed glasses, and was attired smart-casual, like the ambassador and her guests.

After giving their breakfast orders to the chef, Ambassador Edwards steered the conversation to the impending visit of the Secretary of State. "Derek, you must have been wondering why I invited you over for breakfast?"

Njoba smiled and nodded. "Indeed, Madame Ambassador, I can hardly contain my curiosity."

"I'll tell you as soon as you start calling me Megan."

"Megan, it is."

Edwards told him as much as she knew about the purpose of the Secretary of State's visit but made no mention of the rare-earth mine. She expressed the desire to have him write a series of articles to be published locally and abroad to explain the new aid initiative in a nonpartisan, nonpolitical manner and how it could benefit participating countries.

When Edwards finished, Njoba said, "I'm honored, Megan. I'm happy to accept the assignment." He looked at Rex and Catia, and turning his gaze back to Edwards, he said, "But why do I get the impression this breakfast was not only about the Secretary of State's visit?"

Edwards laughed. "Because it was not. In recent times agents of one of our security agencies happened across what seems to be a big, if not the biggest, illegal wildlife trade syndicate. Your Minister of Environment, Forestry and Tourism, and the Minister of Safety and Security have been informed, and our agents will be working closely with them to break up this ring of smugglers from here to China. But to make sure the criminals don't corrupt the investigations, we thought the best way to keep them all honest is if you inform the world about them."

Njoba smiled. "Megan, you can congratulate the analyst who prepared my background brief for you. That person must have noticed that the world authorities' lack of action and sometimes outright unwillingness to stop the pillaging of Africa's wildlife, timber, and mineral resources have been a major source of irritation for me. I would take great pleasure in exposing the wrongdoers involved in this."

Megan nodded. "Thanks, Derek, that's exactly what I hoped you'd say. I'll let Rex and Catia tell you what they have."

"Are you the agents Megan referred to?"

Rex didn't have a problem trusting Njoba. The man became successful because he was honest, and usually, honest people could be trusted. Besides, Digger had shown no signs that the man shouldn't be trusted.

"Yes, we are. We work for a private consulting company sub-contracting to the CIA."

Njoba's eyes shot wide for a fleeting moment. "How did you come across this?"

"At this stage, unfortunately, I'm not at liberty to tell you that."

"Mr. Dalton, it might make it difficult if not impossible to publish a believable story if there are obvious gaps in it."

"It's Rex. My father was Mr. Dalton. He was a teacher. Unfortunately, that's the nature of the beast; there are things I can share with you, and there are things I can't. However, I will give you as much as I am allowed to and enough hints and directions so that you can do your own investigations and get the answers."

"Okay, Rex. You may call me Derek. Let's go with your

suggestion and see how it works out. But unless I can verify every bit of information you give me, I'm not publishing."

"Deal," said Rex.

"I have one more question before you tell me what you're allowed to tell me. Am I right when I say this syndicate is connected to something much bigger than plundering our wildlife?"

"Yes, it is," said Rex without hesitation.

Njoba nodded. He had a smile on his face. He took out his paper notebook and pen and looked at Rex.

Chapter Sixty-Nine

WE MUST HAVE THAT MINE

Sunday. Beijing, China

General Quan and the President of China had known each other since their childhood. They were the same age, grew up in the same suburb in Beijing, and went to the same school. Calling them friends would have taken it a bit too far, but they were well acquainted. They saw each other regularly at social and formal events. However, over the past seven years, since the 12th National People's Congress near-unanimously elected him as President of the People's Republic of China with 2,952 votes for, one against, and three abstentions, Quan and the president have seen little of each other.

The Communist Party Congress (CPC) determined who led the 1.39 billion people of China. On paper, the CPC is the most powerful legislative body in China. But it was widely known that it would approve what it was told to approve. The CPC delegates elected the Central Committee of about two hundred members. The Central Committee, in turn, elected the twenty-four-member Politburo, and they selected the seven-member Politburo Standing Committee, China's top decision-making body.

Under the PRC's constitution, the president was supposed to be mostly a ceremonial office with limited power. But this president changed that. He managed to remove the term limits to his presidency, which was always two terms for his predecessors. He had also centralized much of the institutional power by taking personal charge of economic and social reforms, military restructuring and modernization, and the internet. He had elevated his status to the level of its founder, Chairman Mao Tse Tung. And with that came an increase in censorship, increase in mass surveillance, and dramatic deterioration in human rights.

It was no wonder political and academic observers across the world described the president as a dictator. But on this Sunday morning, as General Quan's chauffeur pulled up at the security gates in front of Zhongnanhai, none of those things bothered him. He was an ardent supporter of his old school friend. China was a big and complex society; it required a strong man as its leader—this president was such a man.

Zhongnanhai, literally translated as 'Central and Southern Seas,' was the former imperial garden in the Imperial City of Beijing next to the Forbidden City. It was the central headquarters for the Communist Party of China and the State Council, China's central government, and the Office of the President of the People's Republic of China.

Zhongnanhai was China's version of America's White House.

"It's been too long, Zhelan," said the president when he and Quan were seated in the comfortable chairs in the presidential study. "How long has it been since we had time to talk?"

"You're right, Mr. President, too long."

For the next ten minutes or so, they talked about their own wellbeing. The president's secretary served them tea and refreshments, and when she left, the president said, "So, Zhelan is it good or bad news you're bringing?"

Quan smiled. "Good news, Mr. President. Only good news."

The President leaned forward in anticipation.

"The discovery of a very large rare-earth deposit in Namibia, Mr. President."

"How big a deposit?"

"More than double the current world reserves, Mr. President." He continued and gave the president the details of the estimated yield.

The president stared at Quan, skepticism written all over his face. China's meteoric rise from a third-world country to the second-largest economy in the world was spectacular. It lasted for more than three decades, but lately, the tides had changed—against China.

During the previous American president's four years in the White House, the US-China trade war started and gained rapid momentum. The US imported $539.5bn in goods from China in 2018 and sold to China $120.3bn in return. The difference between those two numbers—$419.2bn—was the trade deficit and the reason for the US-China trade war and one of the major factors impacting negatively on China's economy. China had channeled vast sums of money into the election of a new president in America, hoping he would end the trade war. They got their wish—a new president in America. The problem was he didn't stop the trade war, not yet.

China's state-sponsored intellectual property theft, currency manipulation, and fentanyl production were also to blame for the growing antagonism among their trading partners.

And that was the state of affairs before COVID-19. For almost two years, China was able to avert the blame for causing the crippling global pandemic, but now the dam wall had sprung leaks, and it was becoming all but impossible to contain them. More and more voices across the globe were blaming China for the death and destruction caused by the virus and demanded restitution. In some parts of the world, people had taken to calling it the CCP (Chinese Communist Party) virus.

The global economic downturn that existed before the virus had only worsened during the pandemic. As countries were implementing austerity measures, China was rapidly losing its glitter as an investment haven. Its trading partners were withdrawing business from China, and the economy was operating at only eighty percent of capacity. The biggest challenge for manufacturing companies across China was demand, not supply.

However, this discovery in Namibia could help to stem the tide, even turn it around.

"You would not be lying to your old friend and president, would you?"

"I wouldn't dream of it, Mr. President. As far as we can determine, those numbers are correct, maybe even a bit conservative."

"Please tell me you've secured the rights to that mine, Zhelan."

"That's the reason for this meeting, Mr. President. I have an invitation from the Minister of Natural Resources and Energy to visit Namibia and negotiate a deal."

"And I take it the minister will want his palm greased?"

"Undoubtedly, Mr. President. My question is, how far I should go? What leverage is there that I can use?"

"Well, we already own sixty-nine percent of the Rössing uranium mine. We can offer them a similar deal. We also own sixty percent of their foreign debt. We could look at lowering interest rates, renegotiating the terms, and writing some of it off. There'll be more we can do, but I suggest you go over there and hear what he has in mind, and we take it from there."

Quan nodded. "I will start making arrangements for my trip as soon as this meeting is over, Mr. President."

"Do you know what it will mean if we can get control of that mine, Zhelan?"

"I think I have an idea, sir. We will remain in control of the world's electronics market, and as the rest of the world tries to save the planet from overheating, we'll be their sole supplier of microchips, semiconductors, lithium batteries, and other electronic goods to build their green economies. They'll have to come to us to build their computers and supply them with any product requiring rare-earths, including their guided missiles, fighter jets, night vision equipment, satellites, and such."

"Precisely. We will control the technology that runs their economies. And we'll prevent America and its allies from building sophisticated weaponry with which they could wage war against us. Yet, they could not stop us from building such weapons for ourselves."

"In other words, sir, Chairman Mao's Hundred Year Plan to make China the world leader by 2049 could be realized in the next five to ten years, almost twenty years ahead of schedule?"

"Exactly, and for that, if necessary, I'll sanction military intervention. Whatever it takes, we *must* have that mine, Zhelan."

"Understood, sir." He decided that it was unnecessary to tell the president about Dr. Liam Collins of the United States Geological Survey, the senior advisor on strategic minerals who had visited Namibia a few weeks prior. He deemed it unwarranted to bother the president with speculations that would only dampen his enthusiasm.

Quan made one last visit before he left China, a high-ranking Politburo member the CEO of China National Uranium Corporation, the company that owned a sixty-nine percent share of the Rössing uranium mine. If he could secure the REE mine in Namibia, he'd need to get a mining operation going as soon as possible. Fortunately, he and the CEO were old friends, and the president was a mutual friend.

Monday, Rex, Catia, and Digger spent a few hours briefing senior delegates of the Ministry of Environment, Forestry and Tourism (MEFT) and the Minister of Safety and Security about the discovery of the wildlife crime syndicate. However, they kept the specific details about the big names and exact locations of the loot out of the conversation, hinting that they were still trying to find those details. They worked out the details of how they'd cooperate in the future to bring the culprits to justice.

Josh and Marissa spent the day helping the Kriges and their workers to break up camp and move to Eldorado.

Chapter Seventy

WELCOME TO NAMIBIA COMRADES

Tuesday. Eros Airport, Windhoek, Namibia

Although China had more than four million millionaires and almost nine hundred billionaires, they had only about two hundred private aircraft. Private ownership of aircraft has been allowed only since 2003. For those allowed to have private aircraft, there was a warren of legal and administrative hoops to jump through to fly anywhere. Requests to undertake a flight had to be made in multiple places and filed days, even weeks in advance. Just hopping in one's plane and flying somewhere at a moment's notice was not possible.

But, as in many countries across the world, rules and regulations were often bent if not completely ignored for the rich and famous. China was no exception. General Quan Zhelan's Sino-Africa Development Corporation owned one of the two hundred private planes in China, a Dassault Falcon 8X with a range of 6,450 nautical miles, a cruise speed of 500 nautical miles per hour, and room for thirteen passengers. And General Quan was one of those to whom the rules didn't apply.

At a quarter past four Tuesday afternoon, when General Quan's private jet touched down at Eros Airport about five kilometers (three miles) south of Windhoek's central business district, Minister Kaura and his entourage were there to welcome him.

Eros was one of the busiest airports in Southern Africa, Namibia's tourism gateway handling in excess of 74,000 passengers and 17,600 aircraft movements per year.

Rex, Catia, and Digger were also at the airport but not part of the welcoming committee. They were in their SUV in the parking lot from where Catia had launched one of the mini-drones to get a good look at the occupants of the plane.

Thanks to the Pegasus spyware, Rex et al. were privy to the phone conversations of Kaura, Nuusiku, and Tian. They hoped to add General Quan to the list before long. They knew all the details of the plans Kaura had for the visit of his distinguished guest.

There was no one from the media when the general's plane came to a stop outside one of the hangars. On Kaura's and Quan's explicit orders, the visit had been kept under wraps.

Kaura and company were in three black SUVs with tinted windows positioned outside the hangar. Five men dressed in black and armed just like the security guards at the Twohill site formed a security perimeter. When Kaura was informed that General Quan would bring a contingent of bodyguards with him, he didn't want to be outdone by the general, so he ordered his aide to hire private security guards.

The airstairs were lowered, and a few minutes later, two

Chinese men in their early to mid-thirties appeared and descended the stairs. They were dressed in dark suits. They wore dark glasses, earpieces, and the bulges under their left arms were caused by their guns. The men were met at the bottom of the stairs by Tian Chao.

"Welcome to Namibia, comrades," said Tian in Mandarin.

The men mumbled something inaudible in reply. The Pegasus software didn't perform well in environments with lots of background noise. Catia understood more Mandarin than she spoke. Rex was fluent. He spoke the Beijing dialect of Mandarin known as Pekingese with the accent of a native.

"Everything is safe and secured," said Tian.

One of the men tapped his earpiece and said, "All clear."

A few minutes later, General Quan appeared in the doorway, followed by two more bodyguards clad and armed the same as their colleagues. The general was also dressed in formal attire, just like his men, sans the dark glasses, earpieces, and gun.

The contrast between Kaura's and Quan's security details could not have been starker. Kaura's men were, on average, twenty kilos (forty plus pounds) overweight. The demeanor and actions of Quan's men left no doubt; they were in shape, and they were professionals. Obviously, they'd received extensive training in protecting high-value targets. On the flip side, it was equally clear that Kaura's men were amateurs. The closest they ever came to protecting a high-value target was to patrol barbed-wire fences armed with batons and walkie-talkies.

Catia maneuvered the mini-drone while zooming in on the facial and body features of the general's retinue of guards from all possible angles. The footage was being live-streamed to the CIA's facial recognition systems in Langley. Soon, names and personal details would be assigned to each face.

When General Quan reached the bottom of the airstairs, the driver of Kaura's vehicle got out from behind the wheel and opened the door for the minister. He got out and approached the general.

Tian was on his boss's right, half a pace behind, as protocol dictated. He introduced the two dignitaries and took a step back.

He must have been surprised to see General Quan *was* indeed capable of smiling, even able to converse in a civilized manner.

When Kaura's convoy of black SUVs had left, the Daltons returned to their hotel.

Greg had configured Kaura's phone to connect to Quan's phone the moment it was within the Bluetooth range and installed the Pegasus app. Less than an hour after leaving the airport with Kaura, the app was installed on Quan's phone, and Rex got a text message from Greg.

Within two hours, they got word from Langley's facial recognition unit, Quan's bodyguards were all MSS agents. Background details were attached in a secured email.

Rex knew General Quan had an open-ended return date. They were going to visit Twohill and the warehouse in Walvis Bay, where Quan would inspect the illicit wildlife merchandise destined for China. One of the special treats Kaura had lined up for him was a hunting trip that many hunters around the world could only dream of—Africa's most sought-after trophy animals, the big five—lion, elephant, white rhinoceros, leopard, and buffalo. A package that would cost a hunter anywhere from US$186,000 to US$287,000 and more.

Quan wouldn't pay a cent.

And they would nudge out the details of an agreement to let China have the sole rights to the richest rare-earth elements deposit ever discovered.

Chapter Seventy-One

IN THEIR SECRET CAUCUS

Wednesday. Windhoek, Namibia

Quan had been briefed by a senior analyst about the African way of negotiation. "Directness is rudeness," the analyst told him. "Don't force the agenda; let your host set the tone and the pace." That was wise counsel. Quan tried his best to follow it.

Kaura wanted a bit of pleasure before business. Exotic food and drink were supplied in abundance, along with a few Asian hookers. Quan pretended to enjoy it all, including flirting with the *filles de joie*. He was taking great care not to affront his host. After all, China's economic future, the Chinese Communist Party's future, and his own future and reputation depended on this man's goodwill.

In the lull moments when he and Kaura took a break from the prodigality, he circumspectly tried to probe the minister to find out what he had in mind. But Kaura kept his cards close to his vest until midafternoon of the second day after Quan's arrival, when he spilled his guts about his president.

Kaura loathed President Justus Aruseb. The reasons were simple—racism and egotism. "He's a Damara—not of my people. My people make up more than fifty percent of Namibia's population. His make up less than six percent. The man's an idiot. He is a Christian, Lutheran, no less. Can you believe it? The Lutherans are German, the very people who colonized this country and exterminated tens of thousands of our people. But Aruseb wants to worship *their* god. He believes western-style democracy can work in Africa. The Americans brainwashed him when he studied in their country. He has to go. I'd be a much better president."

Quan nodded. "It sounds as if your president might have a few screws loose in his head. But is Aruseb going to have any say in whether or not we get a contract?"

"Not if I can help it. However, he might get in the way, and then he has to be removed. By any means necessary, *coup d'état,* scandal, assassination, whatever it takes to get rid of him."

Quan was nodding slowly, contemplatively. "Hopefully, that won't be necessary."

Rex and the team were on Pieter's farm in the study, listening to the conversation. John, Martin, and the others were listening from America.

Coup d'état, assassination, scandal—those were stomach-churning words.

"Damn," said Martin. "Those guys surely know how to complicate things."

"Maybe they do," said Rex. "But maybe they've just handed us the rope with which we're going to hang them."

"I'm all ears," said Martin.

"We give the Secretary of State a transcript of this recording to take with him when he meets with the President of Namibia. After showing it to the president, it might be the ideal time to talk about Mount Krige."

"Uh-huh, not a bad idea at all," said Martin. "I need to brief Howard, the president, and the Secretary of State about this."

"Okay," said John, "let's take a three-hour break, and when we come back, I'd like us to look into the crystal ball to see how this is going to play out."

Wednesday. Khomas Hochland, Namibia

Rex grabbed a bag of *biltong* and *droëwors* and two cold Windhoek Lagers, shoved them into his backpack, called Digger, and grabbed Catia's hand. "How about a sundowner on the hill?"

Since the first time she'd experienced it at the Kriges' campsite, sunset in the desert had become her favorite time of the day. She smiled. "Let's go."

Ever since partnering with Digger, Rex had been trying to analyze the relationship between them, but it remained a mystery to him. Catia thought it was an understandable, almost spiritual relationship. Marissa thought Rex, with his exceptional language prowess, had mastered the K-9 language. To Josh, it was easy; Rex and Digger read each other's minds. John didn't even try to explain it. He regarded Rex as his best agent ever and Digger the second best, although sometimes he thought Digger was the best. Those were the thoughts that brought a smile to Rex's face as he and the woman he loved and his best friend ascended the hill a kilometer west of the farmhouse.

Scientists knew that, on average, humans process more than 6,000 thoughts per day. They also knew that we often talked to ourselves. Nothing wrong with that, they'd say, but when their patients heard someone or something talking back, they'd be quick to reach for straitjackets and behavior control drugs.

Rex never discussed this with a shrink. It wasn't necessary; he knew he hadn't gone around the bend even though when he talked to Digger, it was as if there was someone in his head talking back.

Imagination? Quite possible. Telepathy? Not entirely out of the realm of possibilities. Whatever it was, it all started years ago in Afghanistan when he and Digger were forced into this partnership, and ever since, they'd relied on each other for their survival.

Rex shook his head. *All this psychoanalytical stuff can do a man's head in.*

Arriving at the summit, there was still about an hour left before the sun would be down. Digger sat in front of them eagerly awaiting his share of the *biltong* and *droëwors*. He also looked longingly at the beer cans in Rex's and Catia's hands, but Rex had explained it to him before. "Alcohol is toxic to dogs." Rex thought Digger was just checking if the rules had changed perchance. He waved his finger in a no-no motion. "Sorry buddy, you're still on the wagon."

Digger relaxed, and Catia laughed. "Looks like he understood what you said."

Rex grinned. "Of course he did; he's the Einstein of dogs."

Catia punched him in the arm playfully.

Rex took a swig of his beer and said to Digger. "Okay, buddy, you and I need to do a bit of crystal-ball gazing."

Digger looked excited and yelped softly, as if to say, "Ready when you are." Or maybe he was excited about the piece of *biltong* in Rex's hand.

"So, as you know, it's now only a matter of days before the Chinese discover we've pulled the wool over their eyes."

Digger whined softly.

"The thing is, how will they react?"

Digger whined again.

Rex laughed as he gave the *biltong* to Digger. "That's the understatement of the century, buddy. A little upset? You must be joking. They're going to be seriously pissed."

Digger licked his lips.

"Yeah, I know you don't want to use swearwords in front of Catia. Very gentleman-like of you."

When Catia realized Rex and Digger had allowed her as an observer into their caucus, she'd gone quiet lest she disturbed them. Though she couldn't help but smile at Digger's "gentleman-like" behavior.

"So, what do you reckon they will do when they find out?"

Digger let out a soft growl and licked his lips again.

Rex gave him another piece of *biltong*. "You're right. They'll want to take out their rage on Erwin and his family."

Digger yawned.

"I see, so you reckon Quan might also get his nose out of joint with Kaura and his nephew. What about Tian?"

Digger's eyes were fixed on the piece of *droëwors* in Rex's hand, which he was waving as he talked. He yelped.

"I agree with you, Tian will be blamed for the debacle, and he will almost certainly disappear."

Digger whined.

"Now, there's a brilliant idea! Recruit him."

Digger sighed. Catia thought he was getting frustrated because that *droëwors* would never land in his mouth. Rex clearly understood that differently. "Yeah, I know he's not going to be a pushover, but I can be very persuasive if necessary."

Digger groaned.

"Don't get your knickers in a knot. Of course, you've always helped me, and yes, you made Nuusiku talk without any help from me. But Tian is a trained MSS agent, former special forces operator. He's not going to piss in his pants at first sight of you." Rex broke the *droëwors* in half, gave one piece to Digger, and shoved the other into his own mouth.

Dusk was falling rapidly.

The full moon was rising in the east as they walked down the hill hand-in-hand in silence. Catia kept her own counsel. *So this is what happens at these mysterious caucuses. Rex doesn't speak K-9, and Digger speaks no human language. People use different techniques when they want to focus their brains on finding solutions to problems. Some want solitude. Some go for a walk. Some meditate. Some close their eyes. Some go for a run. Some listen to music. Some talk to other people. Rex talks to Digger... Right Digger?*

Digger stopped, raised his head, and howled at the moon.

A cold shiver ran down Catia's spine. *But I could be wrong.*

Chapter Seventy-Two

THE PAWPAW HAD HIT THE FAN

Thursday. Windhoek, Namibia

The workers at the Twohill site were told there was supposed to be a sizable silver deposit. No one mentioned anything about rare-earth minerals. Not even Dr. Liu, the geologist, knew anything about the expectations of finding massive deposits of rare-earths.

Dr. Liu had been analyzing the samples as they were delivered to his makeshift lab in the forty-foot shipping container onsite at Twohill.

By late Thursday afternoon Liu was happy that the samples he had received and processed were enough to make accurate forecasts about the yield of the entire mine. He generated his final report on screen and read through it one more time. Mr. Tian was right; there was silver. Not earthshaking quantities, but enough to make a good profit over the next ten to fifteen years. He called Mr. Tian and told him the report should be arriving in his email momentarily.

Reading the report, Tian's stomach churned and started begging for antacid tablets. By the end of the report, his stomach was in a full-scale rebellion. In a matter of minutes, his world had turned upside down and inside out. Site K108 had tons of silver, to be sure, and rare-earth elements— enough to fill a teacup, but only a small one.

Maybe there was a mistake. He called Dr. Liu.

"Did you analyze enough samples to be confident that the report is accurate?"

"Yes, sir, absolutely."

"Is your equipment working properly?"

"Yes, sir, without a doubt. It was calibrated and checked before coming on site. I've also checked it against bench-mark samples. It's definitely functioning properly."

"Doctor Liu, are you prepared to stake your reputation and your life on this report?"

"Sir, unless the samples have been tampered with between the time they were taken from the ground and my lab, I will stake my reputation and life on it."

Tian's end of the line was quiet.

"What were you expecting to find, Mr. Tian?"

"Rare-earth elements. Large deposits."

Now Liu was quiet for a long while. "I'm sorry I can't give you better news, sir."

Rex and the rest of the team eavesdropping knew the pawpaw had hit the fan.

Tian was a deeply troubled man, chewing antacid tablets as if they were candy.

How did this happen? In his mind, he ran through everything from the beginning, slowly. He opened the window in his office and lit the first of many cigarettes.

He thought about Nuusiku. Where did those samples that Nuusiku confiscated come from? Could it be that he seeded those samples? But why? He couldn't think of a single reason why Nuusiku would've double-crossed him.

The information about the samples from both sites came from Zhong Yang's spy in the US embassy. Come to think of it, every bit of information about Erwin Krige and Dr. Liam Collins had been provided by Zhong Yang's spy. The more he analyzed the facts, the more the names of Erwin Krige and Dr. Liam Collins flashed in front of his eyes. And the word uppermost in his mind was misdirection.

The samples stolen by Nakanyala's men from K110 (Mount Krige) were real, and so were the samples confiscated by Nuusiku from K108 (Twohill), except they'd been swapped around. Krige and the Americans had been feeding them false information through their fake spy. Playing him like a fiddle for weeks already.

It was galling to admit Krige and the Americans had outwitted them all.

Fury and fear descended. Fury for being made a fool of, fear for what General Quan was going to do to him.

What options did he have?

He could take the news to Quan. The problem was he was the one at the wheel when it happened. He would be charged with treason, criminal negligence, and many other charges. When one embarrassed the Party, they threw the book at you. They were going to disappear him. Probably send him to a labor camp or penal colony in Africa or elsewhere where he'd be starved and worked to death. Those who got a bullet in the back of the head were the lucky ones.

He could withhold the information from Quan, but he only had to contact Dr. Liu to find out about the results. No, if he decided to withhold it from Quan, he had to run and hide and hope he could stay hidden from the MSS for the rest of his life while constantly looking over his shoulder.

He could defect to America, but he couldn't think what value he could be to them. And the thought of what would happen to his family made him shiver. In China, the families of defectors received the punishment the defectors would've received if caught.

The last option was to try to salvage the whole thing before the weekend was over. For that, he had to get hold of Erwin Krige, choke the truth out of him, and kill him. He would've given his firstborn to have a team of Chinese special forces operators at his beck and call right now. As it were, he had no time, no firstborn, and no choices. It was Nakanyala and his bandits or nothing.

He gulped the last bit of tea in his cup, grabbed his cellphone, and headed for the toilet. And that's where he proved yet again that the maxim was true—men can't multitask. He dropped his cellphone in the urinal while trying to type a text message at the same time as relieving himself of all the tea he'd been drinking. But before he could retrieve the phone, the urinal flushed, and his cellphone drowned. He was, however, able to retrieve his Sim card intact.

Back in his office, he took a spare phone out of a box, inserted his Sim card, and texted Nakanyala for a critical meeting.

When Tian's phone died, a flickering red dot appeared on the electronic wall chart in the Comms Room on the Ranch in Arizona. It showed the last known GPS location of Tian Chao's cellphone before it went off the air.

Rex got a text message telling him the phone had gone offline.

An hour later, when Tian's phone had not come back

online, Rex and his team were more than a little worried. They knew Tian had received bad news from Dr. Liu; what they wanted to know urgently was what he planned to do about it. There could hardly have been a more inconvenient time for Tian's phone to go off the air.

Rex told them that Digger thought Quan would blame Tian for the debacle. "And he thinks Tian might just get it in his head to go after Erwin and his family," said Rex. "I agree with Digger."

"Well, if Digger says so, we better believe it," said Josh.

"Agreed," said Marissa.

Catia smiled and nodded.

Chapter Seventy-Three

SAFETY FIRST

Thursday. Khomas Hochland Mountains, Namibia

Tian's last known location was his office; more than an hour ago. Being incommunicado made it difficult to find out where he was and what he was up to. Rex had expected him to at least contact one of the other people they were monitoring through the Pegasus app, Nuusiku, Kaura, or Quan, but he didn't.

"What are his options?" asked Josh.

"Tell Quan and see what happens. Or don't tell Quan and run away," said Marissa.

"Or, as Digger said, he might go after Erwin and his family," said Catia. "We have to track him down and watch him."

"Agreed," said Rex. "But safety first."

Rex, Catia, and Digger took the SUV and drove the three kilometers from Pieter's farm to Eldorado. Erwin and Mieke had moved to Eldorado at the beginning of the week. They gathered in the family room, where Rex and

Catia told them that the cat was out of the bag. The Chinese would be on the warpath. The safety of the Kriges, Naudés, and Leah and her children was the highest priority, and it was decided it would be easier to protect everyone if they were all on Eldorado.

Mieke was wondering if they shouldn't call the police in. But Josh explained, "I don't think we'd get much understanding, let alone cooperation, if we turn up at the copshop and say, we've got this little problem. We've managed to upset this Chinese gentleman and his boss, a former general in the PLA. Oh, and we suspect we've embarrassed the Minister of Natural Resources and Energy. How we did it is a long story, but it all boils down to a mountain made of rare-earth minerals. We suspect the Chinese might want to kill us because we made them look like idiots, and it's entirely possible that China might right now be preparing to start World War Three because of that mountain. Could you please come and protect us?"

Mieke and the others were screaming with laughter by the time Josh finished. "Well, now that you've explained it like that..."

Two hours later, everyone was safely on Eldorado. The main dwelling had four bedrooms. Leah and the children occupied two. Erwin and Mieke were in their motorhome parked next to the house. The Daltons, Farleys, Sam, and Connor were spread across the two chalets closest to the house. Leah and the children were a bit wide-eyed when they arrived on Eldorado, but that disappeared quickly as everyone doted on them.

By midnight, Rex and his team had a security system in place. Martin had arranged for satellite coverage. Two mini-drones streaming infrared images to two laptops were loitering one kilometer above the farmstead. Between

Connor, Sam, Catia, and Marissa, they had eight mini-drones, enough to keep a round-the-clock watch.

The laser tripwires and mini-CCTV cameras Connor and Sam brought with them were deployed in strategic places and connected to the same laptops as the drones. A third laptop was dedicated to receiving data from the keyhole satellite. The laptops were set up in the study of the main house, which had become their Ops Room.

In the meantime, while all these activities were going on at Eldorado, unbeknown to Rex and the others, Tian had accompanied Nakanyala and a team of five armed men to the Kriges' campsite.

"Is this a bloody joke?" said Nakanyala when they arrived at the space where the Kriges camp was supposed to be.

Tian started swearing softly. This was definitely not a good day for him. He wouldn't admit it, but he had only himself to blame for not keeping an eye on Krige. "The son of a bitch knew I'd be coming for him. Let's go back to Windhoek. I know where the coward is hiding."

"Where?"

"Eldorado, the Kriges' family farm about fifty kilometers out of Windhoek on the C28. That's where his daughter and her husband live. We'll get all of them in one go, get the answers I want, and then kill them all."

"You want to go out there tonight?"

"No, we'll do it tomorrow night; we need more men."

Over breakfast the next morning, Rex laid down a few safety rules. "Okay, from now on, no one goes anywhere without escort, and everyone else knows where you're going and when you'll be back." He nodded at Catia.

"Besides the satellite, the drones, the CCTV cameras, and laser tripwires, we've also got our furry friends Digger,

Kaiser, Tom, and Jerry looking out for us. Anyone who thinks they'd be able to get past them must have rocks in their heads," she said. "We'll take turns to monitor the screens. I suggest two per shift, two hours on six off. Staring at surveillance screens can be a tedious job. Marissa and I will install apps on your phones that will enable us to use them like walkie-talkies."

For the rest of the day, everyone except the Kriges and Naudés stayed inside the house in case someone was watching the place.

Chapter Seventy-Four

THE SIGN WAS MISLEADING

Saturday. Khomas Hochland, Namibia

By nightfall on Friday, Nakanyala had assembled a ragtag force of thirty men, twenty-four of whom were barely out of puberty. But everyone had an AK-47. Some also had sidearms of Czech, Russian, and Chinese origin and two ancient Colt six-shooters—the type used to sign Indian treaties with. Other weapons included hunting knives and a variety of traditional African weapons such as spears called assegais, machetes called pangas, and bludgeons called knobkerries.

What the men lacked in combat skills and experience, they tried to make up with their rowdy display of courage and aggression—undoubtedly brought on by the cannabis, known as *dagga* in these parts of the world, they'd been smoking. Over thousands of years of warfare, from the Assassin sect of ancient Persia, ancient Indian warriors, American troops in Vietnam to the child soldiers in modern-day Africa, cannabis had been used to embolden soldiers engaging in conflict. Nakanyala thought he'd enhance the effect of the cannabis with a few cans of beer for each.

It was impossible for the CIA'S keyhole satellite to miss the convoy of seven vehicles heading west out of Windhoek on the C28 gravel road in the early morning hours on Saturday. That road, on the busiest of days, would see maybe twenty vehicles travel on it—seven vehicles in convoy at 1:30 a.m. was abnormal. In the light of the full moon on this cloudless night, the vehicles drove without their head-lights for the last few kilometers before the turnoff to Eldorado.

By the time they crossed over the cattle gate underneath the arch with the words 'Welcome To Eldorado' two kilome-ters from the homestead, the mini-drones had 'eyes' on them as well.

As far as Tian could establish, only the Naudés and Kriges and four families of farmworkers were on the farm. The dwellings of the workers were almost a kilometer away from the farmhouse, and although expected to be loyal to their employer, Tian assumed they were highly unlikely to try and stop thirty armed men who had no gripe with them at all.

Tian and Nakanyala had been studying Google maps of the farm during the day. They knew what the terrain looked like, and so did the men, well, some of them. Tian would've liked to have more time for onsite reconnaissance, but he didn't have that luxury. The size of the force and their fire-power had to compensate for any surprises they might encounter. After all, how much resistance can two men and two women put up against a platoon of motivated men armed with AK-47s?

Tian's instructions to Nakanyala and his men were

straightforward. Erwin Krige and as many of his family as possible had to be taken alive for questioning. After the questioning, whoever was still alive would be handed over to the men to kill at their leisure. But the big motivation was the money. Every man who survived the mission would get one thousand US dollars in cash, and anyone who delivered Erwin Krige to him alive would get a bonus of five thousand US dollars. For each of the other family members delivered to him alive, there was a two thousand US dollar reward.

A kilometer from the farmhouse, the convoy came to a halt; the men disembarked and formed three sections of ten each. The section leaders had hand-held two-way radios all tuned in on the same channel to communicate with Nakanyala and each other.

He told Tian in no uncertain terms that he was in charge of the operation, and to make sure Tian didn't interfere, he spoke only Ovambo to his men. The plan was for the men to surround the house. There was no rhyme or reason for this strategy except that Nakanyala thought it was a stroke of genius to attack from all directions at once. The worst part of this 'ingenious' strategy was that it effectively created a circular firing squad.

It was 2:00 a.m. when the men were ready, and Nakanyala gave the order to approach the house.

Tian and Nakanyala made many mistakes in their planning and the execution thereof. Drugging the young men was one of the major blunders. Another egregious mistake was to underestimate their adversaries. It was not only the six American special operators and the military dog they didn't know about; it was also the four certified professional hunters (PHs) working for Pieter, which they mistook for ordinary laborers whom they thought would not want to get in the middle of this conflict. The PHs knew the farm and the animals and nature like the backs of their hands. They could stalk wild animals and poachers undetected and get so close they could touch them while watching them. And they were crack shots who could shoot a rat through the eyes from a hundred meters.

Rex, Digger, Erwin, and two PHs were spread out on the south side of the house. Josh, Connor, Sam, and one of the PHs were on the east side. Pieter and the remaining PH were deployed in the attic of the barn from where they had a commanding view of the compound through the night vision Schmidt and Bender telescopes of their .308 Musgrave hunting rifles. Between the Naudés and Kriges and the PHs, they had enough firearms to equip everyone in the group, including the women, and sufficient munitions to start a small war and keep it going for a while.

They were in communication with each other via molar mics. Rex and Josh also had comms with Catia and Marissa. Pieter and the PHs had their hand-held two-way radios, which they used on the farm every day.

Digger was rigged up with his full tactical harness, night-vision camera, micro earphones, and microphone, all of it wirelessly connected to the iPad mini strapped to Rex's left forearm. He was flat on his stomach right next to Rex, eagerly awaiting instructions.

From their strategically selected hideouts on the high ground around the house through their night-vision telescopes, binoculars, and monoculars, Rex and the team were watching the mercenaries approaching the house.

Jake, one of the PHs in Rex's group, was flipping

between the channels on his two-way radio to see if he could find out on which channel the attackers operated. He found it a minute or two later.

A slight grin spread across Rex's face. "Jake, would you mind if I borrow your radio?"

"Of course not, sir," whispered Jake.

He whispered. "Jake, if you call me sir one more time, I'm telling Digger to bite you in the ass."

Jake laughed quietly as he handed the radio to Rex.

To anyone with basic military knowledge, even if the knowledge was obtained by watching war movies, it would have been clear Nakanyala's mercenaries could only be described as an armed gang of thugs with testosterone-induced egos and drug-befuddled brains.

Nevertheless, Rex and the team had no illusions; the bullets from their guns would kill just the same as bullets from guns in the hands of trained soldiers.

The three dogs, Kaiser, Tom, and Jerry, were with the women inside the house. Catia was the mission controller. Marissa was in control of the drones. The rest were staring at the thermal images of thirty-two men, including Tian and Nakanyala, leopard-crawling toward the Eldorado farmhouse, streamed to the laptop screens from the drones and keyhole satellite.

Rex whispered into the molar mic, "Steady guys, let them through and let them do their thing. Let's see what their intentions are."

The men were about twenty meters away from the house when Rex heard the command on the radio. "Stop and hide. Breaching team, move forward. The rest of you stay in position and be ready." A few moments later, all of them had stopped moving. Next, two men from each section crawled forward and met at the front door.

Rex retrieved a roll of duct tape from his backpack. When the men reached the front door, he pushed the talk button on Jakes's radio and taped it down. The channel on which the attackers were supposed to communicate was now effectively blocked.

What followed could, if not so tragic, be described as a comedy of errors. Unfortunately, there was nothing comical about it. Misguided young men, stoned out of their minds, still in the prime of their lives, were about to be killed and maimed because of Nakanyala's monumental stupidity.

When the six men reached the front door, they took up their positions—just like the SWAT teams in the movies do —two to the left, two to the right, and two in front of the door. Except this SWAT team had no battering ram or explosives—they would use their shoulders.

Nakanyala, standing two paces off to the left, nodded.

The two men stormed and hit the solid Oakwood door with their shoulders. The door didn't squeak. They stepped back and did it again. They did it twice more but succeeded only in proving Einstein's definition of insanity to be correct —doing the same thing over and over and expecting different results.

Why Nakanyala was bent on gaining entry through the most solid of all doors on the house and not through the windows or any of the other, less sturdy doors was unclear. Be that as it may, by now, he had lost his patience; he stepped up, pushed the human battering rams out of the way, unslung his AK-47, and emptied a full magazine into the hinges. He stepped up and kicked the door down. With that macho act, Nakanyala had set an example for his men to follow—a violent one, to be sure.

The six men rushed through the opening and started

shouting at the top of their lungs, "Police! Put your hands up! Freeze!" Just like the SWAT teams in the movies.

But then, one of them who must have missed those movies got so carried away he started firing short bursts at nothing in particular as he ran through the house. The rest of them took that as their cue and did the same as they ran through every room in the house, causing irreparable damage to the old wooden ceilings, stone walls, antique furniture, paintings, and such.

Nakanyala's roaring voice ordering them to stop got drowned out by the noise of the gunfire. In the tumult, two of them misidentified their comrades as the enemy and shot at them, killing two and wounding the remaining two by the time Nakanyala shoved his AK-47 into their faces and stopped them.

When the gunfire stopped, they couldn't hear the screaming of the wounded or the swearing of their leader. They could, however, see his lips moving and his AK-47 pointing at them. It was time to vamoose from his presence. They turned and scrambled for the front door. When the two of them came shoulder-to-shoulder through the front door, it was their turn to be mistaken for the enemy. They were cut down by a hailstorm of bullets from their jumpy comrades outside. Out of the six who stormed into the house, four were dead and two wounded—clearing a house SWAT-style was hazardous work.

But not every man spraying the front door with 7.62mm bullets from their AKs was able to keep them on target. Some of their bullets missed the house completely and slammed into their comrades on the opposite side of the house. Their comrades, on the receiving end, concluded they'd come under attack from the enemy and returned fire.

The leader of the third section, not to be outdone by his

comrades, shouted, "Fire!" At who or what he didn't say, but his men didn't need detailed instructions; they opened fire in the general direction of the house or thereabouts—where they were told the enemy would be.

Rex and everyone else, present and watching remotely, were stunned into silence as they watched Nakanyala's men succumb in their self-engineered holocaust.

It took about two minutes for Nakanyala to persuade his men to cease fire. "You idiots!" he shouted into the radio, unaware that only those within earshot could hear him and no one else. "The house is empty! They're not here! You morons! We're shooting at each other."

Nakanyala's orders were passed on by word of mouth when they discovered their radios didn't work. Five minutes later, they were all gathered on the lawn, looking at their handiwork in stunned silence—eight dead, twelve wounded, four of which would not make it to sunrise—two-thirds of Nakanyala's force out of commission.

Throughout it all, Tian had been hiding behind a tree about thirty meters from the front door. From the moment he had laid eyes on Nakanyala's mercenaries earlier that night, he had misgivings about their abilities, and the feeling had grown in leaps and bounds as the night progressed. But, despite witnessing the biggest fiasco of his life and despite his better judgment, he had hoped at least one of the Krige family would be alive. Nakanyala's announcement that the house was empty hit him between the eyes like a sledgehammer. His plan had failed.

Nakanyala's and Tian's second mistake, almost as hideous as the first, was not doing proper reconnaissance. If they'd kept a watch on Eldorado, they would've known that two ten-seater Toyota Quantum minibusses, carrying all the women, children, three dogs, and all their equipment, had traveled from Eldorado that night when Nakanyala's convoy was spotted by the CIA's keyhole satellite with their lights off to Pieter's farm three kilometers away.

Rex spoke into the molar mic to Pieter and Erwin. A few seconds later, the PH with Pieter flipped the main switch on the circuit board in the shed. The security lights lit the place up as if it was midday.

In fluent Ovambo, Erwin shouted, "Nakanyala, you and your men drop your weapons! Put your hands in the air if you want to stay alive!"

Including Nakanyala and Tian, twelve men were left standing. Tian was still hiding behind the tree. Nakanyala spun around in the direction of the voice and raised his AK-47. But he only got halfway when a .308 caliber bullet from Pieter's Musgrave made an ugly mess of his right shoulder and slammed him into the ground. The remaining men needed no further instructions—their weapons clattered as they hit the ground.

Connor's group appeared out of the shadows, herded the attackers away from their weapons, and ordered them to lie down on the ground, face down.

Tian sighed deeply as he realized he had been outmaneuvered again. Slowly, he sunk to the ground and slithered away like a snake.

They were busy cuffing the prisoners' hands behind their backs with zipties when Catia said to Rex, "Tian is trying to get away."

"Josh, take over here," said Rex into his molar mic. "Digger and I will go after him."

Rex didn't have to tell Digger to come with him. He was already a few meters ahead. "Buddy, just in case you didn't know," said Rex into the microphone connected to Digger's earphones, "this is the guy you and I talked about the other night. He's a former special forces operator. He's armed. I want him alive and unharmed, but I want you to promise me you'll be careful."

Digger made no reply. He threw Rex one look over his shoulder and put his nose to the ground.

Tian was not in shape anymore. He was in his mid-forties and overweight from desk jockeying for the past eight years. His body was tensed up, he was frightened; he was bone tired from lack of sleep and food, and his senses were dulled. Which was why he was unaware of the danger closing in from behind until he got smashed face-first into the ground. In his stupefied mind, the deep growl meant only one thing—he was about to be devoured by a lion. His primordial scream reverberated through the surrounding hills, and then a boot came down on his neck. Until now, Tian had believed in no god. But the deep voice coming from above speaking Mandarin with a Beijing intonation could only have belonged to the deity whose very existence he'd denied his whole life.

"Not so fast, Tian. Didn't your mother teach you it's bad manners to leave a party without thanking your hosts?"

Or was that the voice of General Quan? Nah, sounds nothing like him.

As his captor tied and gagged him, Tian couldn't help but think about the sign at the front gate that says Welcome To Eldorado. *It's misleading. This is not Eldorado. It's hell.*

Chapter Seventy-Five

TO RUN A FEW ERRANDS FOR ME

Saturday. Khomas Hochland Mountains, Namibia

Rex and Digger frogmarched Tian to one of the chalets about half a kilometer from where they'd caught up with him.

In the meantime, Catia, Marissa, Mieke, and Thea had arrived at the Eldorado farmhouse to help attend to the wounded. Knowing full well that Nakanyala and his men had come there for the sole purpose of killing everyone who was in the house, no one was overcome with feelings of Good Samaritanism toward the survivors. The Naudés especially so after seeing the damage caused to their property. It would probably run into hundreds of thousands of dollars to repair some of it. Much of the furniture, paintings, and such were antiques—irreplaceable. Notwithstanding their rage, they were not savages; they treated the wounded and captured with clinical efficacy and civility.

Leah and her children, as well as the wives and children

of the PHs, stayed behind on Pieter's farm with the three dogs. Josh had sent Connor, Sam, and two of the PHs over for protection.

In the meantime, Rex and Josh interviewed their prisoners.

Nakanyala was in the shed where Josh had tied him up in a standing position against the wall. That was to make sure the man was as uncomfortable as possible but not in danger of dying. Marissa had stopped the bleeding in his shoulder, bandaged it, and given him two codeine tablets for the pain.

From Nuusiku's confession a week before, Josh already knew Nakanyala was Tian's main supplier of illegal wildlife products. All he wanted now were the names and contact details of his poachers and the locations of their caches.

Nakanyala tried to play tough, telling Josh to take a hike and some other suggestions of what Josh should do to himself, indicating Nakanyala had a lot to learn about anatomy.

Josh was in no hurry. He reckoned half an hour, an hour at most, before the codeine would wear off and the pain in Nakanyala's shoulder would become unbearable.

Josh was wrong; Nakanyala's pain threshold was much lower than his tough façade suggested. Within twenty minutes, he was begging Josh for painkillers. The information Josh wanted was all on his cellphone and on his laptop in his Range Rover, which by now had been moved to the farmhouse. Josh took his time checking everything was on the cellphone and laptop, as Nakanyala said before giving him a shot of morphine.

On the way to the chalet, Tian Chao had enough time to take stock of his situation. It was very simple—his hour-glass was empty—this was no time for bravado. His options were: A short stay in a Chinese prison until he was shot in the back of the head or shipped off to a labor camp. He'd be dead within a year, two at the most, if he went to a camp. Or, he could ask for asylum in America if it were indeed the Americans behind all of this. But in exchange for what?

In the kitchen, Rex shoved Tian into a chair, duct-taped his legs to the legs of the chair and his hands behind his back, and removed the duct tape from his mouth. He took a chair next to the kitchen table, took the Glock 17 from its holster, and placed it on the table in front of him.

Digger knew the drill. He took his place on Tian's left, sat down, and stared at him with his tongue lolling out. His lips curled slightly upward at the corners. Rex called it the canine smile. To most people, though, it would have looked nothing like a friendly gesture.

"Listen carefully, Tian Chao," started Rex in Mandarin. "I am one of many people who'd like nothing better than to shoot you in the head tonight. And believe me, if you don't cooperate with me, I'll take great pleasure in doing exactly that."

Tian nodded slightly.

Rex continued. "You're an undeclared MSS agent masquerading as a junior attaché of trade and commerce. Your real boss is General Quan Zhelan, former PLA. You killed Julie Narimab of Namgeochem, an innocent young woman, a wife, and mother of two minor children. You bribed Simon Nuusiku and his uncle Minister Jackson Kaura. You're paying that lowlife Nakanyala to pillage the protected fauna and flora of this country.

"You've just been told by your geologist, Dr. Liu, that the mine you paid Nuusiku to take away from Erwin Krige has no rare-earths.

"You and Quan have been made fools of, Tian. And you know Quan is going to have you executed for that. Therefore, you hired Nakanyala and his child soldiers to come here and kill our friends, the Kriges and Naudés. You thought if you could get your hands on Krige, he could tell you what's going on—"

"Ok, I'm convinced, you know it all," Tian interjected. "I'll cooperate. But I want to make a deal. I suspect you work for the CIA or some other security agency in America. I defect. You protect me. I tell you everything I know."

Rex shook his head. "Tian, you're a bestial scumbag. Making a deal with a reprobate like you, a murderer, briber, liar, ecoterrorist? You must have shit for brains."

"So, why haven't you killed me yet?"

"Because you're going to run a few errands for me before I shoot you or hand you over to Quan or send you back to China. I haven't made up my mind which one it will be."

"Why would I want to do anything for you?"

"I don't know why you would, except that you might want to convince yourself that if you do a good job, I might change my mind about what to do with you. But I could be wrong."

Tian's head was hanging. "What do you want?" he whispered.

Chapter Seventy-Six

A DAY OF MEETINGS

Saturday. Windhoek, Namibia

It was 4:15 a.m. when Rex aroused an unimpressed yet gracious Ambassador Edwards from a deep sleep. He needed an urgent meeting with the Minister of Safety and Security under whom the Namibian Police Force sorted and the Minister of Environment, Forestry, and Tourism.

Three hours later, Rex, Catia, and Digger were in the SUV on the way to Windhoek to meet with the ministers and Inspector General of Police. At the same time, Tian was in his own vehicle on the way to the Twohill site.

It was 8:30 a.m. when the Daltons were welcomed at the Ministry of Safety and Security offices at Brendan Simbwaye Square Goethe Street, Windhoek.

They told the ministers and Inspector General about the farm attack. The assailants managed to kill eight and wound twelve of their own—without interference from the residents. However, in the aftermath of the attack, the leader was wounded by one of the residents, and four of the wounded had joined the ranks of the dead. There were also ten unscathed men tied up in the shed.

To the officials, it was immediately clear that the police had to take charge of the situation. Not only did they have to make arrests, take care of the bodies, and get the wounded treated, they had to do it while keeping it all under wraps for a week, maybe longer.

Rex didn't tell them about Tian. He also told them nothing about the rare-earth elements and the Chinese interest in them. That had to be handled at a different level of government.

After the meeting, Rex called Derek Njoba and asked him to meet for coffee at the Mugg & Bean in the Grove Mall.

Njoba was waiting for them when they arrived. The Mugg & Bean was a South African franchise operating throughout Africa and a few middle eastern countries. They specialized in African cuisine.

When their coffee and cake had been served, and Digger had been fed a few pieces of *biltong* and a tiny piece of cake when no one was watching, Rex started. "Derek, I told you last week we're not at liberty to share all information with you. But, we promised to give you enough information to help you uncover all the facts for yourself."

"Yep," said Njoba, "that's what you said."

"Good, so here we go." Rex nodded at Catia.

She took a sip of coffee and started. "If I had to investigate who are the major culprits in the destruction of the wildlife of Africa, specifically Namibia, I'd start with the Sino-Africa Development Corporation.

"A bit of Googling should reveal that their CEO is a former PLA general by the name of Quan Zhelan. What you would also find on the internet is that Tian Chao is a junior attaché of trade and commerce at the Chinese embassy here in Windhoek. But you won't find on the internet that he is, in reality, an MSS agent and Quan's lackey in southern Africa." She paused and took a sip of coffee.

"If you get the chance to interview Tian, you might want to ask him about his associates in Namibia. The first is Andreas Nakanyala, a psychopath who wants people to believe he is a commander of a fearsome mercenary force while in reality, they're a gang of teenagers with AK-47s, turned into drug addicts and poachers.

"The next associate is Simon Nuusiku, the Commissioner of Mining in charge of the Mines Directorate at the Ministry of Natural Resources and Energy."

Njoba was ashen-faced. "Simon Nuusiku, the nephew of the Minister of Natural Resources and Energy?"

Catia nodded.

"Is the minister involved?"

Catia nodded.

Rex said, "Okay, now I want you to switch off all recording devices, remove your cellphone's battery, and put away your notebook."

Njoba did as requested.

For the next hour, Rex and Catia gave him the details and backed them up with copies of the recordings they'd made of Nuusiku's and Tian's meetings, Nuusiku's, Nakanyala's, and Tian's confessions, and the various telephone calls between them.

Those recordings were collected illegally and therefore inadmissible in court, but that didn't make the contents less true.

When they left the Mugg & Bean, Njoba had information about the illicit activities of the Sino-Africa Development Corporation in Namibia and other southern African countries. Included in that information was the corruption going on in the Ministry of Natural Resources and Energy. He had a copy of the information taken from Nakanyala's laptop and mobile by Josh, which contained the names and contact details of his poachers and the locations of their caches. He also had the details of the warehouses at Container Universe on Ben Amathila Avenue in Walvis Bay, including the names and details of the captains, crews, and ships used by the smugglers to transport their loot to the black markets of the Far East and elsewhere.

However, about the discovery of the richest rare-earths deposit in history and the Chinese interest in it, Rex and Catia said not a word. Neither did they mention the farm attack on Eldorado in the early hours of the morning.

"Thanks for the coffee," said Njoba when they were outside the restaurant. "It seems I've got some serious investigation to do."

"Indeed," said Rex with a slight grin on his face.

Saturday. Erongo Mountains, Namibia

After Greg had 'upgraded' Tian's phone, Tian contacted the site manager at Twohill and ordered him to start breaking up camp and send his men back to their normal jobs. Tian arrived at Twohill an hour and a half later and went straight to Dr. Liu's field lab in the shipping container.

He was in a hurry, so he didn't have time to be polite. "Dr. Liu, start your computer and bring up the report you emailed me Thursday night."

Liu did as he was told.

"Now email it to me again and then print it out."

Liu complied.

Tian took a stack of papers out of his briefcase and put them next to the stack of papers printed by Liu. "Now, you're going to change the report on your computer to read exactly the same as the report I just gave you."

Liu started shaking his head and opened his mouth to protest, but then he saw the expression on Tian's face and promptly abandoned his objections.

It took him more than an hour to produce the false report. Tian suspected the report could've been generated by Erwin Krige and his daughter. He was right.

When Dr. Liu was done, Tian confiscated his laptop, and while he formatted the hard drive, he ordered Liu to reset all his equipment to their factory settings.

Liu again abided by the orders without objections.

When he was finished, Tian said, "Doctor, you have an hour to pack your belongings and equipment and be ready to move out. You're flying out to a remote site in South Sudan this afternoon. Apparently, they've found a major deposit of cobalt. I need you to check it out for me."

While Liu scurried around to pack his stuff, Tian watched him like a hawk. He didn't want Liu to talk to anyone before he left. Through Tian's cellphone, Greg had gained remote control of Liu's phone and installed a few nasty bugs on it. Among others, Liu could never receive a call from General Quan's phone on that phone.

When the truck with Dr. Liu and his equipment had left for the airport, Tian called General Quan. He told the general that the geological report produced by Dr. Liu corroborated the report produced by the late Julie Narimab of Namgeochem a few weeks ago. "In other words, general, it looks like we're in business. I'm emailing you two reports, one which shows only the silver deposit and no REEs and the true report containing the REEs information."

"Good thinking, Tian."

It was the first time Tian could recall when General Quan didn't respond with a condescending remark to anything he'd suggested.

The timing was perfect. Quan and Kaura just had an extravagant lunch which included a few bottles of wine. Quan had been anxiously awaiting the confirmation Tian had just supplied so that the negotiations could start. Ten minutes later, Quan and Kaura had settled in the easy chairs in the family room.

From Namibia and America, the members of Operation Sierra were listening intently to the audio streams coming from the phones of Quan and Kaura.

Saturday. Khomas Hochland, Namibia

Arriving back at Eldorado late afternoon, Rex and Catia had an opportunity to listen to the recording of the negotiations between Quan and Kaura a few hours before. The pact between the two master criminals was simple and utterly unscrupulous.

Kaura thought Quan was a genius when he produced the two geological reports. Kaura would instruct Nuusiku to issue a mining permit to a subsidiary company of the Sino-Africa Development Corporation first thing on Monday morning. This shadowy company, Afrinex Pty Ltd, one of many shell companies Quan had ready to use when necessary, would be fronted by two Namibian nationals and one

Chinese-Namibian. The lawyers only had to fill in their names.

The geological report showing the silver deposit, but no rare-earths, would be used for the application. Mining operations would start immediately, and a few months down the track, a major discovery would be made.

Kaura and Nuusiku would have a five-million-dollar payday upon issuance of the permit on Monday, and they'd get a three percent stake in the mine through an offshore company with heavily disguised registration and shareholding.

"Easy. Simple. Brilliant." That's how Quan described their deal.

Of course, Kaura concurred—after all, great minds think alike—and fools never differ.

Chapter Seventy-Seven

WE HAVE TO BRIEF THE PRESIDENT

Windhoek, Namibia

Sunday morning when his hangover from the previous night's debauchery had subsided, Quan phoned the Namibian manager of the China National Uranium Corporation at the Rössing uranium mine.

Within half an hour, Quan had a commitment from the manager to equip a contingent of workers from Rössing and send them to site K108 to set up temporary accommodation and start mining operations first thing on Monday morning.

Kaura had phoned Nuusiku and told him to prepare an application for a mining permit on behalf of Afrinex Pty Ltd, the subsidiary company of the Sino-Africa Development Corporation. He provided his nephew with the names of the three directors, all fictitious, and told him to use his imagination when he signed the application.

If Nuusiku had any doubts that Rex and his associates didn't know what he was doing every moment of the day, they were removed when he got a call from the tall blond one a few minutes after he ended the call with his uncle. The man instructed him to do exactly as his uncle told him to do. Those little lumps in his armpits were technological marvels.

Monday morning, by the time the first trucks and fifty miners arrived at site K108, Nuusiku had issued the required mining permit to Afrinex Pty Ltd.

When the five million US dollars hit Nuusiku's Swiss bank account, the minister and the general boarded a commandeered government helicopter which transported them to the Rössing mine where Quan had a two-hour meeting with the manager of the China National Uranium Corporation while Kaura did a surprise inspection of the mine.

By midday, they landed at a private lodge in the Etosha National Park, one of the largest national parks in Africa, for a five-day hunting safari. If the public and the media *had* to know, the explanation was simple; part of wildlife conservation was to keep the animal numbers in check. In other words, from time to time, it was necessary to selectively cull some of them.

Wednesday. Etosha National Park, Namibia

It was day three of the hunting safari, Wednesday evening; Quan had bagged three of the big five, a lion, elephant, and white rhinoceros so far. Over dinner and copious amounts of Cape Brandy, Quan had one more question about the REEs. "What if, after the big discovery, your president decides to declare it of national importance and wants to nationalize the mine?"

Kaura took a while to answer. His speech was a bit slurred. "Then you have to assassinate him and make sure I become president."

Now there was a long pause from Quan's side. "What will be in it for China if you're president?"

"Name it."

"A naval base in Walvis Bay."

"Deal."

"Okay, just explain; why wait until Aruseb interferes in our deal before getting rid of him? Why not preempt it?"

"I am ready to be president when you've rid Namibia of that dogpile, Aruseb."

If that conversation was not enough to cause the eaves-droppers from Namibia and America heartburn, Quan's telephone conversation with an anonymous but clearly important person in China did it.

The phones and connection between Quan and the person on the other end of the line were heavily encrypted. Even so, the Pegasus app didn't care; it didn't even try to break the encryption; it simply monitored Quan's phone's audio and streamed everything it heard to the CIA and CRC servers.

Despite the assurances that their communications were secured, they still didn't use each other's names or titles.

"You might want to sit down for this one," Quan said as soon as they were connected.

"I am seated."

"I've just been offered an opportunity which I believe is much, much bigger than the deal we made last week."

"I'm listening."

"A naval base."

There was a protracted silence. "In the main harbor?"

"Yes."

"Are you a hundred percent sure of this?"

"Absolutely."

"The price?"

"He wants us to put him in the top position."

They didn't have to say it; to have a fleet of Chinese warships deployed in Walvis Bay was a longstanding dream of the Chinese Navy. It would not only pose a serious challenge if not upend America's supremacy in the Atlantic altogether, but it would also give China control of the Cape Sea Route. This was definitely much bigger than the rare-earths. And getting rid of President Justus Aruseb was a small price for that kind of strategic advantage.

"Leave it with me. I'll make the necessary arrangements. Good job."

Rex and Catia were the only ones who understood Mandarin; the rest of the listeners had to rely on the machine translation, which lagged about ten to fifteen seconds behind the conversation and was only about seventy to eighty percent accurate. Even so, they got the gist of what was being said.

When the call ended, Martin said, "I'll get our voice identification team onto it right now. We need to know who was on the other end of that line."

"Tell them to start with the president of China," said Rex.

"You recognized his voice?" asked John.

"No, but who else in China has the power to order the assassination of the president of another country? Besides, according to Quan's personal file, he and the president are old school buddies."

"Uh-huh. Okay, I'll tell them to run that one first," said Martin.

Voice identification used what's called a sound spectrograph to create voice graphs of people's voices, analyzing over 100 physical and behavioral factors such as pronunciation, emphasis, speed, accents, and physical characteristics to produce a unique voiceprint for each individual. Voice graphs or voiceprints had been used as evidence in court cases, and there was a time when it was believed people's voiceprints were as unique as their fingerprints; however, that idea had been called into question by some speech scientists.

But this was not a court case; all they wanted was proof on a preponderance of evidence not beyond a reasonable doubt.

The NSA had millions of voiceprints in their databases. Was it not for Rex's intuition, it would've taken a long time to find a match. As it were, he saved them a lot of time. The result came back within minutes. The voice on the other end was a ninety-eight percent match for that of the President of China.

"Please excuse me," said Martin when he got the result. "I have to get hold of Howard; we have to brief the POTUS immediately and the Secretary of State."

As Martin left the conference, Rex's brain was already working on the next opportunity.

When John saw the faraway look on Rex's face, he knew what it meant. "Spit it out, Dalton."

Rex told them.

It was a Rex Dalton plan, to be sure—unconventional, audacious, crazy, and, above all, workable. After the usual debate about the craziness of his plan but no better alternative, it was approved.

Digger was fast asleep during the entire meeting. Rex didn't have to wake him to get his opinion; he had no doubt Digger would've approved. After all, he was probably going to see his German buddies at Container Universe again.

Rex called Derek Njoba and asked him to meet him and Catia in Walvis Bay the next day. Derek was excited and agreed without hesitation.

Chapter Seventy-Eight

NO STRIP CLUB TONIGHT

Thursday. Walvis Bay, Namibia

Rex and the team, including Sam and Connor, drove to Walvis Bay in their Toyota Quantum minibus early in the morning. Njoba arrived on a chartered flight arranged by Catia at Walvis Bay Airport, where they picked him up. It was the first time Njoba met the rest of Rex's team.

As they drove out to the Naudés beach house at Langstrand (the Afrikaans and German word for 'Long Beach') between Walvis Bay and Swakopmund, Njoba told them that Langstrand came into fame when Angelina Jolie and Brad Pitt stayed at Langstrand's Burning Shore Hotel during the end of her pregnancy with their daughter, Shiloh, in 2006.

They spent the day at the house planning their mission for that night. Rex and the team gave Njoba the final piece of this illegal wildlife trade puzzle when they told him about the impending visit by the partners in crime General Quan and Minister Kaura to the storage unit in the Walvis Bay harbor. They also told him what they found on their visit to the site a few weeks ago and showed him the footage they took then.

The plan was to go back in to bug the place and give Njoba the opportunity to collect his own evidence firsthand. The problem was they needed more time to do their thing than they had last time. They soon realized the only way to do it was to take control of the guardhouse.

That's when Josh looked at Njoba and said, "You wouldn't perchance know where we could get a few good-looking Chinese hookers?"

Marissa punched Josh in the arm as everyone exploded in laughter. Josh obviously didn't mean it like it sounded, but no amount of explaining and backtracking could make them 'unhear' it.

Njoba had a good sense of humor. "You're in luck; I do. Want me to hook you up?"

Josh was rarely at a loss for words, but this was one of those occasions. When the levity ended, Njoba told them he had published an article about prostitution in Namibia a few years ago. Prostitution was legal and highly prevalent across the country, particularly at border crossings, transport corridors, and, of course, Walvis Bay and Windhoek.

A 2018 World Bank study estimated there were about 11,000 prostitutes operating in Namibia. However, prostitution-related activities such as solicitation and running of a brothel were illegal. Most women worked independently because it was illegal to have pimps. They'd meet their clients on the streets or in bars. Many of those bars had a room on-premise for the prostitutes to use. In other words, it was a brothel in disguise. But there were also the upmarket sex workers whom one contacted via cell phone or the Internet.

It was one of the latter that Njoba contacted. She was the woman who gave him a lot of insight into the sex industry in the coastal towns of Walvis Bay and Swakopmund when he wrote his article.

The two Chinese guards on duty at Container Universe that night didn't have a chance. The two beautiful Chinese ladies that came running toward their guardhouse and screaming for help at eleven-thirty that night were clearly in distress. They were terrified and shaking. The ladies explained in Mandarin that they were invited by the captain of one of the ships at anchor for late-night drinks on board his ship. But when they got there, before they could reach the captain's cabin, they were stopped by three inebriated crew members who told them the captain got called away for urgent business and that he had left instructions that the two of them should entertain the crew until he got back.

There were ten crew members.

The ladies turned and ran.

The rowdy sailors who followed them were too drunk to catch up.

"Please protect us from those animals."

"Of course, we will."

By now, there couldn't have been any doubt in the minds of the guards that the ladies were working girls. Within minutes they'd stopped shaking, got rid of their faux mink coats, revealing plentiful curves and skin while sharing the whiskey they brought with them with their protectors and making no secret of exactly how grateful they were to their knights in shining armor.

Within half an hour, the guards were fast asleep. The drugs in their whiskey assured neither a bomb explosion nor a terrible nightmare would wake them for the next three to four hours.

Connor and Sam tied and gagged the guards. Njoba paid the ladies US$1,000 each in cash, and Sam dropped them off at their houses. From CRC'S comms room in Arizona, Greg's team kept the CCTV cameras happy by playing pre-recorded footage.

Rex had blown the dog whistle which had brought the two German Shepherds to the front gate, and before they could get aggressive about the intruders, they were met by their friend Digger.

Rex had to smile when Josh commented as they watched the joyful reunion of canine friends. "Sorry guys, but there'll be no strip club tonight."

The Germans didn't seem to mind as they disappeared with Digger among the containers for what Rex thought must be the royal tour of their domain.

They locked the front gate. A sign on the gate was saying there had been a chemical spill inside the facility, and it was closed until further notice. Hopefully, access would be restored by the next morning at 8:00 a.m.

Catia and Marissa were outside in the minibus, keeping overwatch with their drones.

Rex and Josh spent almost two hours bugging Sino-Africa Development Corporation's six-container storage unit with audio and video spy bugs and testing that they were working properly.

Meanwhile, Njoba took photos and videos and made an assessment of the number of items and their value. By 2:30 a.m., when they were finished, he was thoroughly enraged and deeply saddened.

Digger and his friends weren't happy to part ways again. But Rex thought they didn't look as miserable as last time when Digger had to say goodbye to them. Maybe he told them he'd be back. After all, Digger was no stranger to play-acting; he was, in fact, very good at it.

They were relieved when they were all back in the minibus on the way to Langstrand. There would be no evidence of their visit; no one had visited the place while they were busy inside, not even a drive-by.

The guards were going to wake up with phenomenal hangovers and memories that would stretch back only to the time of the arrival of the beautiful Chinese courtesans at their guardhouse.

Chapter Seventy-Nine

THEY SHOOK HANDS

Friday. Windhoek, Namibia

The first carrier task force of Operation Southern Cross had arrived at a location about 200 nautical miles off the coast of Namibia the previous Sunday, where it started preparing for maneuvers with the other carrier task force about 150 nautical miles off the southern coast of South Africa. The media mentioned it, but there was not much to show on TV. However, almost two weeks later, on this Friday morning, the residents of Walvis Bay woke up to behold what would probably be a once-in-a-lifetime event. A few miles outside the Port of Walvis Bay was the USS George Washington, a nuclear-powered aircraft carrier named after the first President of the United States. Surrounding the carrier was the task force's full complement of two cruisers, a destroyer squadron of two frigates, plus logistics and supply ships. The nuclear submarines were nowhere to be seen, but no one doubted they were there.

Seven hundred nautical miles to the south, off the coast

of Cape Agulhas, the southernmost tip of Africa and the beginning of the dividing line between the Atlantic- and Indian Ocean, the second carrier task force of Operation Southern Cross had also made its appearance.

By the time the images hit the TV screens around 6:00 a.m., the Secretary of State's Boeing had touched down at Hosea Kutako International Airport.

"It's as if the arrival of the US warships and their Secretary of State had been coordinated," one of the TV commentators said.

She had no way of knowing how true it was.

The Secretary of State was met at the airport by Ambassador Edwards and the secretary's Namibian counterpart, the Minister of International Relations and Cooperation.

They were transported in a motorcade surrounded by police and security personnel to the State House, the administrative capital of Namibia and official residence of the President of Namibia.

The State House is in Windhoek's Auasblick suburb. It was constructed between September 2002 to March 2008 by a North Korean company, Mansudae Overseas Projects, at a cost of N$400 million.

The site covers twenty-five hectares (sixty-two acres), surrounded by a steel fence. The administrative area of the complex comprises the Office of the President, the offices of cabinet members, and more than two hundred staff offices. There is a guest house and two apartments for visiting dignitaries from other countries. There are also garages, accommodation for security personnel, and two helipads.

Shortly after 8:30 a.m., the Secretary of State, James Hilton, and his entourage were welcomed by President

Aruseb and the Prime Minister in the entrance hall where there was a painting of the members of the first Namibian Cabinet, a wood carving showing women from all ethnic groups in the country, and a large painting by a North Korean artist of the Epupa Falls. The Epupa Falls is a series of large waterfalls created by the Cunene River on the border of Angola and Namibia.

Refreshments were served before Secretary Hilton and President Aruseb retreated to the latter's personal office to discuss matters of a sensitive nature, while the rest assembled in a conference room to talk about the new US aid initiative.

The Secretary of State was America's chief foreign affairs adviser, and his duties included, among others, acting as the President's representative to negotiate international agreements such as the agreement for the mining rights to Mount Krige. However, first, he had to warn President Justus Aruseb about the plot against his life by one of his ministers.

As was expected, the news was upsetting, though not entirely surprising.

"I know the man hates me with a passion. My biggest sin is I am not Ovambo. I'm a Christian and studied in America. But that's how democracy operates; people are allowed to dislike their leaders. But, voting an opponent out and assassinating him are very different things."

Hilton agreed. Thus far, President Aruseb had made a good impression on him. He could only hope the feeling was mutual.

"Most troubling is to learn it has been sanctioned by the President of China for the sole purpose of getting a naval base in Walvis Bay."

"Extremely troubling for us too, Mr. President. The only

reason they want the base is to spread their sphere of influence to the Atlantic Ocean and end our domination. We'll go to great lengths to prevent that from happening."

"If you're here to ask me not to let them have that base, you have my word; I'll never support it." The president smiled wryly. "As long as I live."

"That's comforting to know, Mr. President. It addresses one of our great concerns about China's rapidly expanding military."

"That brings me to the next point, Mr. Secretary. Handling the betrayal of Minister Kaura is a matter for my security detail, the NCIS (Namibia Central Intelligence Service), the police, and the Department of Justice. But handling the Chinese President is out of my and my country's league, and it's not exactly a matter the United Nations can deal with either."

Hilton suppressed a smile. This was the opportunity he'd been waiting for. "And that, Mr. President, brings me to the second reason for this meeting. Please bear with me; I have to tell you how we discovered this conspiracy to assassinate you."

Hilton was an experienced diplomat and negotiator. Sometimes one had to hide things when negotiating, keep the opponent guessing. And sometimes, it was crucial to be painfully honest—like now.

For the next forty-five minutes, Secretary of State Hilton told the President of Namibia everything about the richest rare-earth deposit ever found. A deposit so enormous it could provide the entire planet's rare-earth needs for a century or more. He told the president about China's plan to get their hands on it and how a team of Crisis Response Consultants had kept them chasing their own tails thus far.

He told the president why the American Navy had

chosen this time to conduct a major naval exercise in the region. And he told the president about Minister Kaura's and General Quan's involvement in the biggest illegal wildlife trade operation in the history of Namibia.

President Aruseb was shaking his head in disbelief. He was dumbstruck by everything that was going on in his country, of which he had not even an inkling. But he was probably not the only head of state in the world with that kind of problem.

Two hours later, the President of Namibia and the US Secretary of State shook hands on heads of agreement about the President's protection, the Port of Walvis Bay, mining site K110 near to Karibib, also known among a small group of people as Mount Krige.

It was 10:45 a.m. when President Aruseb asked his secretary to get the officials in charge of Operation Blue Rhino on the line.

Operation Blue Rhino

Friday. Windhoek, Namibia

Expecting the outcome of the meeting between President Aruseb and Secretary of State Hilton, Rex, Digger, and Njoba had flown by private charter to Windhoek a little after nine o'clock on Friday morning.

They were approaching Eros airport when Rex got a message from Martin that the managers of Operation Blue Rhino were waiting for them.

Established in 2018 to combat illegal wildlife trade in

Namibia, Operation Blue Rhino was a Nampol initiative that pooled resources from various departments and agencies, including the Namibian Defense Force.

The Blue Rhino Taskforce consisted of Nampol investigators and members of the MEFT IIU (Ministry of Environment, Forestry and Tourism's intelligence and investigation unit). The Taskforce was jointly managed by the head of the police's Protected Resources Unit and the head of the Ministry of Environment, Forestry and Tourism's intelligence and investigation unit.

Fighting wildlife crime was a relentless, 24/7 task. They had made more than 700 arrests since their inception. It was not only poachers they'd brought to justice; they'd arrested many kingpins, dealers, aiders, and abettors too. Among the criminals were foreigners, police officers, defense force personnel, and even a pastor. Nobody was above the law.

They knew there was a lot going on out there that they didn't know about, but what Njoba showed them was bewildering.

Rex had let Njoba do most of the talking because he had a good rapport with the members of the Blue Rhino Taskforce since the glowing articles he'd published about their work in the past.

Of course, they would've been keen to work with Njoba and his friend who worked for the ICCWC (International Consortium on Combating Wildlife Crime), even if they hadn't received personal instructions from President Aruseb to do so.

By late afternoon the Blue Rhino Taskforce had a plan in place and was rearing to go.

Friday. Etosha National Park, Namibia

Friday was Quan's last day in Etosha National Park. He had bagged his big five, the buffalo on Thursday and leopard he got on Friday. And of course, just for the fun of it, over the past five days, while they were at it, he also shot a variety of trophy antelopes, kudu, eland, and oryx. And just to show his bodyguards what a nice employer he was, he allowed them to each shoot two antelope of their choice. The meat was left for the scavengers; hyenas, jackals, vultures, and suchlike. The skins and horns would be treated, mounted, and shipped to them in a month's time.

That night they saw the news about the arrival of American naval forces for the wargames.

Chapter Eighty

GAME, SET, AND MATCH

Saturday. Walvis Bay, Namibia

Saturday morning, the helicopter picked Quan and Kaura up from the private lodge in Etosha and took them for a short visit to Twohill before heading west to Walvis Bay.

On approaching Walvis Bay, Quan was the first to spot the carrier task group outside the harbor and asked the pilots to fly in closer. Quan had visions of the warships of the People's Liberation Army's Navy (PLAN) in the harbor. *Who knows? Maybe they'd name the Chinese fleet to be stationed here after me.*

They arrived at Walvis Bay International Airport midday, where Nuusiku awaited them. He had arrived the day before to make the necessary arrangements for the arrival of his uncle and his distinguished guest, including their transportation from the airport to Container Universe.

The president had banned the purchase of new official vehicles for ministers for three years and channeled the savings into fighting COVID-19. But there was no ban on the use of existing vehicles. So, Nuusiku had arranged for the Minister's three official vehicles to be driven from Windhoek to Walvis Bay for the occasion. A small convoy of luxury vehicles, albeit three-year-old vehicles, awaited the minister when they landed.

Kaura was impressed and well-pleased by the arrangements made by his nephew in honor of him and his guest.

Still keeping General Quan's identity under wraps, they were picked up on the tarmac right next to the helicopter. Kaura and Quan were in a black Mercedes SUV with dark tinted windows. There were two police cars and four motorcycles with flashing blue lights escorting them. From the airport, they made a short detour around the harbor for General Quan's benefit before heading to Container Universe. Kaura, more so than Quan, was basking in the glory of the plebs on the streets, staring at them in awe.

Kaura had visions of being president.

At Container Universe, the gate was wide open, the police guards threw them a salute as their motorcade passed. Quan made a feeble attempt to return the salute. Kaura couldn't be bothered to respond in kind—he was too important to be polite.

Nuusiku, Tian, and two police officers were waiting when the procession pulled up in front of Sino-Africa Development Corporation's depot.

When the vehicles came to a stop, the bodyguards jumped out of their vehicles and opened the doors of the Mercedes for Kaura and Quan. The men barely nodded at Nuusiku and Tian or the police officers when they walked past them into the storeroom. Nuusiku and Tian followed and closed the door behind them. The guards remained outside.

Nuusiku and Tian were giving their bosses a tour of the

depot, stopping at each shelf explaining what they were looking at, where it came from, how much it was worth, and when it would be shipped out.

Rex and Josh had done an excellent job when they planted the surveillance bugs in the storeroom. The images were crystal clear. The ultrasensitive microphones even picked up the sound of the occupants' breathing.

About one kilometer away, Catia, Marissa, Sam, Connor, and Derek Njoba were in the Quantum minibus watching the feed from two drones and a variety of cameras inside the depot on their laptop screens. From America, John and the others were watching on big screens in the comms room on the Ranch. Martin and Howard were in the latter's office in Langley, watching with bated breath.

When Rex and Josh got the message from Catia, they stepped out from behind the shelves with Glock 17s in their hands. Rex's pointed at General Quan, Josh's at Minister Kaura.

Digger stood next to Rex. He had his trademark smile on his face, which, in this setting, was probably more of a smirk than a smile. And if Rex were asked what that smirk meant, he would've quoted from Clint Eastwood's Dirty Harry movies, "So you've gotta' ask yourself one question. 'Do I feel lucky?' Well, Do Ya, Punk?"

Kaura's jaw dropped. His eyes shot wide, followed by his hands flying up above his head as if reaching for the roof.

Quan's right hand reached for the sidearm in the holster on his right hip only to find emptiness there. He hadn't carried a gun in more than two decades. But old habits die hard.

"Hands above your head, General Quan."

He refused to obey the order.

Digger growled. He was practically begging Rex to let him take down this scumbag.

But Rex disappointed him. "Stay!"

Meanwhile, Josh had swiveled his Glock toward Nuusiku and Tian. "Step back. Away from them." They took three steps back from Quan and Kaura. "On your knees. Hands behind your heads." They did so without hesitation.

Quan started swearing in Mandarin, using choice words to issue threats to inflict pain, injury, damage, and death.

Rex didn't interrupt him. He had seen this movie before, many times. He knew how it ended. It was just a matter of time before the general would realize that his life of privilege was over. His sins had finally caught up with him.

All the while, Kaura stood frozen, hands in the air, unspeaking. Eventually, he was going to come to the same realization as Quan.

In the meantime, Digger was getting agitated with this man, hurling insults at his alpha. He was snarling and growling and yelping. But Rex told him to stay.

Had Quan known what was happening outside the storeroom, he would've dropped his swagger. The message Catia gave Rex and Josh was that the SWAT team of Blue Rhino operators was ready. Shortly after, the operators appeared from the neighboring units with guns leveled at Kaura's and Quan's guards. They were so surprised they didn't even attempt to reach for their guns. In silence, they placed their hands up in surrender. Using their weapons and hand signals while motioning for the prisoners to be quiet, the SWAT team quickly herded them away to the guardhouse at the front gate, where they were searched, cuffed, and loaded into the back of police vehicles.

In the CRC comms room on the Ranch, John let out a

breath he was unaware he'd been holding. So far, the events had followed the script of Rex's plan more or less to the letter.

Catia told Rex and Josh that the guards were secured.

Rex said in Mandarin, "Last warning, General. Hands on your head."

Quan told him to take a hike.

Rex nodded at Digger. "Buddy, please show the general what I want him to do."

Rex hadn't finished his sentence when Digger was in motion. He closed the gap between him and Quan in two bounds; by the third, he was airborne. He hit Quan in the chest, smashing the screaming general into the metal shelf behind him stacked with boxes filled with pangolin scales. Some boxes tumbled down and smashed into Quan's head, breaking open and spilling the scales all over him and the floor.

Quan was dazed. The back of his head was bleeding where the edge of the shelf had cut him. When he had wrestled himself from under the boxes and pangolin scales, his hands were on his head.

"Now, all of you get up and start walking to the door," said Rex.

Digger backed Rex's order up with a low growl.

The four men did as they were told. Kaura had not uttered a single word thus far, and judging by his ashen face and trembling body, he would not be speaking anytime soon.

Tian and Nuusiku seemed to be calm. They'd also not said anything, probably not because they were in shock but because they made a deal with the Blue Rhino management; they'd cooperate fully with the investigators, hoping to get shorter jail terms than their crime bosses.

Tian's deal also included not being deported back to China.

Quan had a small grin on his face. Obviously, he fully expected to have his bodyguards waiting to rescue him on the other side of the door.

As they approached the door, it opened as if by magic. Four dark-clad, ski-masked Blue Rhino SWAT members with assault rifles leveled at the four prisoners awaited them.

Quan and Kaura stopped in their tracks.

But Quan was a sore loser. He turned to face Tian. "Traitor!" he hissed in Mandarin. He took a deep breath, turned back to the SWAT officer in front of him, dropped his hands from his head, and extended them toward him to be cuffed. The officer relaxed, shouldered his rifle, and stepped forward to put the cuffs on. Quan launched forward, dropping his shoulder at the same time. He hit the officer in the solar plexus, got his hand on the officer's pistol, and pulled it free from its holster.

He managed to get three shots off in quick succession.

The first shot had gone through the officer's hip. The second bullet hit Tian between the eyes and sprayed his brain against the wall. The third shot, which General Quan Zhelan wanted to send through his own head, went wide when Digger landed on his back. The bullet went straight through Minister Jackson Kaura's shoulder and lodged in Simon Nuusiku's stomach. The gun fell from Quan's hand.

Rex walked over to Quan, who was facedown on the cement driveway with Digger's teeth in his neck. "Thanks, buddy; I'll take it from here."

Digger let go of Quan's neck and stood back. He let Rex know with a short yelp that he was following orders but under protest.

Rex pulled the general to his feet, looked him in the eyes, and said, "Game, set, and match, asshole."

Then he walked over to Kaura and Nuusiku. They were writhing, moaning, and groaning from the pain. "Kaura, you and your cronies have proven Darwin wrong. If his theory of survival of the fittest was correct, stupid people like you would not have been walking the earth now."

Rex stepped back and nodded at the SWAT team leader.

John Brandt smiled when he spoke into the microphone for everyone to hear, "Don't y'all just love it when a Rex and Digger plan comes together?"

Chapter Eighty-One

DO YOU RECOGNIZE THE PEOPLE?

Windhoek, Namibia

Kaura, Quan, and Nuusiku joined Nakanyala in custody in their own cells in an unknown location. Except for Quan, the next of kin and colleagues of the rest were informed that they'd all contracted a new and nasty mutation of the COVID-19 virus and were placed in quarantine. The bodyguards met with the same fate.

Article 11 of the Namibian Constitution stated that no person could be subject to arbitrary arrest or detention. However, it provided for special measures during a state of emergency or war. The president's constitutional lawyers assured him that a conspiracy by a foreign government to overthrow the government of Namibia was an act of war, more than enough reason to declare a state of emergency and arrest all the suspects and hold them without trial for the duration of the investigations.

The prisoners had no prospects of seeing the inside of a courtroom any time soon.

The mining activities at Twohill had been ramping up since the first work teams arrived on Monday. The geologist on-site had little to do, so he used the time to calibrate his equipment using the samples left by his predecessor Dr. Liu. He soon realized something was wrong; either his machines were faulty, although they were still working when he left Rössing, or someone had falsified the geological report his boss gave him.

He had a dilemma. He couldn't ignore it. He couldn't tell his boss until he was a hundred percent sure. He spent the rest of the week frantically collecting and testing new samples. The results were the same. A sizable quantity of silver but no mineable rare-earth elements.

Late afternoon on Saturday, not long after Kaura, Quan, and Nuusiku were arrested, the perplexed geologist got into his pickup truck and drove the 134 kilometers to Rössing to see his boss.

His boss immediately called General Quan but gave up after failing to make a connection after several attempts. He called his boss in China, who was a high-ranking Polit-buro member and friend of Quan and the President of China.

The Politburo member also made several attempts to get hold of General Quan before he decided on Sunday morning to inform the President of China.

The President of China gave his Chief of Staff instruc-tions to track General Quan Zhelan down. But by Monday morning, the Namibians woke up to a fresh off the press story published by the country's foremost journalist, Derek Njoba. It was about an operation executed by the Blue Rhino Taskforce, which exposed the biggest illegal wildlife crime syndicate in the history of Namibia.

That news reached the ears of the President of China a

few hours later, and then he knew why General Quan was unreachable.

The next day the ambassador of China was summoned to the State House for a meeting with President Aruseb.

President Aruseb didn't have a long message for the President of China. It was a handwritten note attached to an official envelope containing a USB drive with two audio files on it. One was the recording of the conversation between Kaura and Quan about the assassination of the president, and the other was a recording of the last telephone call between General Quan and the President of China. The note read:

Dear Mr. President,

Do you recognize the people speaking to each other in these recordings?

I do.

Yours truly.

Justus Aruseb

President of the Republic of Namibia

The second part of the meeting with the ambassador was also short and to the point. The ambassador was informed that Zhong Yang, the MSS's chief of station in Windhoek, had been declared persona non grata because of his espionage activities and given twelve hours to leave the country and stay away—in perpetuity.

No mention was made of Tian Chao or General Quan Zhelan or his bodyguards.

On receipt of the message from President Aruseb, the President of China immediately called his military advisors and propagandists in. From the former, he expected a plan for the invasion of Namibia. From the latter, he expected a believable excuse for the invasion. But the military advisors reminded the president about the American carrier task groups on maneuvers in the waters around southern Africa, thereby admitting how wrong they were when they told him the American navy wargames were nothing to worry about. Notwithstanding the president's discontent about his advisors' misjudgments, he believed them when they advised him that America's navy would destroy China's navy in a matter of hours in a conflict so far away from the mainland.

That's when the president knew China had been outmaneuvered.

The final nail in the coffin was the story published by the same journalist about the Namibian government's contract with a conglomerate of prominent high-tech companies from America for the funding and management of a silver mine with considerable deposits of rare-earth minerals in Karibib, a little town in the heart of Damaraland, west of Windhoek on the way to Swakopmund.

That's when the president knew that the writing was on the wall. China's monopoly of the world's rare-earth elements and the world's principal supplier of electronics technology would soon be over.

Two days after the meeting between President Aruseb and the Chinese ambassador, James Blake invited Sara Bishop for drinks with him and a friend after work. Sara was genuinely surprised to learn that James was friends with the counterintelligence officer at the Canadian embassy, whom she knew but feared. Counterintelligence officers' job was to catch spies, such as Sara Bishop. She was shocked to learn that her subservient 'boyfriend' had been 'cheating' on her since the first time they'd met. She was a wreck when she was arrested by the fearsome Canadian counterintelligence officer.

In the weeks that followed the 'isolation' of Kaura and the others, Njoba published a series of articles revealing shocking facts about not only the corruption in the Ministry of Natural Resources and Energy but also about China's role in it.

Rex handed the cash, jewelry, diamonds, and gold coins that he and Catia confiscated from Nuusiku's safe to Operation Blue Rhino's managers. The cash Nuusiku had squeezed out of his underlings over the past few years was returned to them, including Leah. But that was only forty percent of what was due to them. Kaura would cough up his share when his assets would be liquidated. Their Swiss bank accounts were frozen. The money would be repatriated to Namibia and forfeited to the state. There were many people who had to be compensated for the pain and suffering and damage to property caused by Sino-Africa Development Corporation's activities over the past few years, including the damage to the Naudés property.

Sino-Africa Development Corporation's jet was confiscated by Operation Blue Rhino. The two ships at anchor in the Port of Walvis Bay that were being loaded with illegal wildlife merchandise destined for the Asian black markets were confiscated, and the captains and their crews were arrested.

On Saturday afternoon, three weeks after the attack on Eldorado, Rex and his team and the Kriges, and Naudés turned up on the doorstep of Leah Visser's new four-bedroom home in Hochland Park, Windhoek, for a surprise housewarming party and for Rex and his team to say goodbye to Leah and the children as they were heading back to America on Monday evening.

When the idea of the surprise party was born, it was decided the women would be responsible for the presents for Leah and the girls; the men were responsible for the boy, Luke.

The girls got new school uniforms, dresses, shoes, cosmetic bags, and iPhones. Leah got the keys to a brand-new Toyota RAV 4, compliments of an anonymous donor whose name only Rex and his team knew and would never reveal, not even under torture unless Howard Lawrence and Martin Richardson gave them permission to do so. The CIA kept a slush fund to use for various licit and illicit purposes, including to reward people who helped them keep the American Homeland safe.

To say that the females of the Visser family were elated with their presents would have been an understatement, but it was the men's present to Luke who stole the limelight and everyone's hearts when Digger walked into the family room holding the loose end of a leash in his mouth with an eight-week-old version of Lassie the Collie of movie fame on the other end and dropped the leash into the boy's hand.

It was an indescribable moment. The boy was thunder-struck. He just sat there with the leash in his hand, staring at the puppy with a friendly face. When the tears started rolling down his cheeks, Laddie, as Luke would soon baptize him, walked forward and licked the tears from the boy's face.

Everyone was swallowing hard to get the lumps out of their throats as they watched the emotional scene playing out in front of them.

Epilogue

Sunday afternoon with the temperature hovering around thirty-nine degrees Celsius (a hundred and two Fahrenheit), they were all relaxing in and around the swimming pool on Eldorado.

Since they'd returned from their trip to the Caprivi a few days before, Rex had noticed that Digger was giving more attention to Thea than before but didn't make much of it.

When Catia and Marissa jumped into the pool, Digger followed. He loved playing in the water. A minute or so later, Thea waded into the water, and Digger went berserk. He was barking at a pitch that Rex immediately recognized as panic. Digger rushed toward Thea and tried to block her from going further into the water. Everyone stopped talking and looked at Digger and Thea. All except Rex was laughing at Digger's antics, thinking he was playing a game with her. Seconds later, Tom and Jerry appeared and started barking as well.

Then it struck Rex. He *knew* what Digger was going on

about. He was trying to protect Thea and her baby or babies. Rex had a dilemma; should he tell her what he was thinking? He said to her, "Do me a favor, get out of the pool, let's see what Digger does then."

She did.

Digger stopped barking immediately, got out of the water, and sat down next to Thea. She scratched his head and back. "So, Digger, what's your story? Why am I not allowed to swim?"

Digger made no reply. He just smiled at her.

She looked at Rex. "What do you think?"

He smiled, embarrassed.

Catia was watching. "What is it, Rex? Tell her what you're thinking."

"Nah, just a thought that crossed my mind. I think he was just playing."

Catia was wondering why Rex was lying and pushed the issue. "C'mon Rex Thea is like family, tell us."

Strange enough, Rex didn't look at Thea when he answered; he looked at Mieke and Erwin. "He was trying to protect your daughter and your grandchild or grand-children—"

Mieke and Erwin looked at their daughter just in time to see the glass of fruit juice slipping from her hand.

Pieter was on his feet and next to his wife before anyone could blink an eye. "Are you okay, Thea?"

She nodded slowly.

The next moment Mieke was next to her, then Catia and Marissa. Five minutes later, the ladies were on their way to the house. Some very sensitive pregnancy tests would produce a result from as early as eight days after conception and can be used any time of the day; it didn't have to be in the morning. And the results were available within three minutes.

Ten minutes later, the four jubilant ladies were back at the pool.

Rex had to explain how it was possible that Digger could know Thea was pregnant.

"Dogs have an amazing ability to sense a change in the world around them, and that includes changes in the body chemistry of the humans in their pack. Some dogs can detect when a person has cancer or is about to have an epileptic fit. They can be trained to detect low blood sugar, and low oxygen levels, high blood pressure, and high heart rates. They're particularly adept at detecting our emotions such as joy, sadness, and others. And as we've all just discovered, including me, when one of their pack is pregnant."

"The Afrikaans words for grandpa and grandma are *oupa* and *ouma*," said a beaming Mieke.

Nine months later, they would receive a series of family photos. Pieter and Thea holding their two-day-old twins, Hester and Daniel. *Oupa* Erwin and *Ouma* Mieke with smiles stretching from ear to ear, holding their grandchildren.

Fact and Fiction

To the best of my knowledge, Crisis Response Consultancy, CRC, does not exist, nor do they have headquarters on a ranch in Arizona or anywhere else.

I've tried my best to be factually correct and neutral about the history of Namibia, including the German occupation, the Nama and Herero wars and genocide, and the Border War (*Grensoorlog*), aka the War of Independence.

Visitors to Namibia will search in vain for the farm Eldorado in the Khomas Hochland Mountains west of Windhoek; it doesn't exist. They will, however, be able to find the town of Karibib and the Erongo Mountains, but they won't find Mount Krige or Twohill; they don't exist.

Visitors to Windhoek will find no Canadian embassy, only a consulate. They will also discover that Namibia has no Ministry of Natural Resources and Energy, but they have a Ministry of Mines and Energy.

They will find Chinatown and the many counterfeit knockoffs on sale there. The figures about the size of the global counterfeit markets quoted in this book are, to the best of my knowledge, correct. Maybe even a little understated.

I herewith offer my sincerest and unreserved apologies to the owners and managers of the following establishments for conducting unauthorized fictitious spy operations on their premises: Joe's Beerhouse, 160 Nelson Mandela Ave. Maerua Mall. Avani Windhoek Hotel and Casino on Independence Ave in the Gustav Voigts Centre. Mugg & Bean, The Grove Mall, Chasie Street. Nyama Restaurant. Klippenberg Country Club and Guest House in Karibib.

Windhoek has a Hilton Hotel but, as far as I can establish, have never been visited by any member of the Dalton or Farley families, or Digger, or Sam Price or Connor Burns or the Visser family.

I've done my best to be factually correct about the world's rare-earth dilemma and China's role in it. According to K.A. Gschneidner, Jr. of Iowa State University, China is the source of nearly all of the rare-earth elements utilized in commercial products. This unstable position does not speak well for the future of technology in the United States and around the globe.

The executive order issued by President Donald Trump about rare-earths described in the story is factually correct.

Some readers have asked me about the technology and gadgets used by Rex and his team on their missions. Yes, they are real. The satellite phones, drones, GPS trackers, molar mics, turning a cellphone into a walkie-talkie, surveillance bugs, all of it is true, and they are being used by special forces, black ops operators, and spies across the globe every day.

What about the Pegasus spyware? Yes, it's real. Pegasus

is a highly sophisticated form of spyware, originally developed for military use, that has been in circulation since at least 2016. It is considered one of the most advanced tools for hacking mobile phones and has reportedly been used to access the smartphones of at least 40 journalists in India, allowing for the extraction of sensitive data from these devices.

What about Digger's tactical vest? It's true. All of it. Just Google "special forces dogs tactical vests."

Is Digger really capable of doing all those things you describe in your stories? Yes, of course! He's a genius. On a serious note, though, yes, dogs can do what I'm describing and much more. But it's highly unlikely that one dog will be capable of doing all of it. Various breeds of dogs have capabilities unique to their breed. Some breeds are excellent sniffer dogs. Others are excellent guard dogs, others are excellent military dogs, or emotional support dogs, or just the best companion a human can hope to have. Digger has a combination of the skills of various breeds.

Can they read our minds? Probably not if you're not a dog lover. If you're a dog lover, though, you'd be convinced they can. The same with that smile on Digger's face. The answer depends on whether or not you're a dog lover.

How many words can they understand? Research by Dr. Stanley Coren, a psychologist and leading authority on canine behavior at the University of British Columbia, suggests that the typical dog can understand about 165 words, including a range of commands and signals. The most intelligent dogs—those in the top 20 percent—are capable of recognizing up to 250 words.

Dr. Coren notes that people are naturally interested in what their dogs are thinking, often trying to interpret the quirky, amusing, or puzzling things their pets do. He points out that dogs sometimes display surprising cleverness and inventiveness, reminding us that, while they may not be geniuses, they share more similarities with humans than we might expect.

As for whether a scenario like Digger tricking a group of German Shepherds could really happen, there is some basis in reality. Dr. Coren explains that dogs are able to intentionally mislead both other dogs and people during play to gain rewards, and they can be nearly as successful at deceiving humans as humans are at deceiving them.

Admittedly, I gave my imagination a bit of free rein in that scene.

Is it true that dogs can smell our emotions and medical conditions? Yes, absolutely. I recently met a lady with a support dog on the train, and she told me he was trained to detect when her blood oxygen levels dropped, or her heartbeat was too high. He was also trained to detect high sugar levels in people with diabetes and the onset of an epileptic seizure. Dogs can smell cancer and have occasionally proven they can detect it on a patient's breath long before the laboratory tests can detect it. Can they smell when a woman is pregnant, as you've described in the epilogue? Yes. It happened to our family doctor when she was pregnant. Now you know where I got the idea for that last scene. And I haven't even mentioned those amazing seeing-eye dogs.

Is it possible to tell the time from the position of the southern cross star constellation? Yes, it is. Just Google, "How to tell time on the southern cross."

About China's status as the second most powerful economic and military power in the world, there is no doubt. Neither can there be much doubt about China's expansionism into Africa and the rest of the world. The parts about China's activities in Africa, specifically Namibia in this case, and how they are perceived by the populace are, to the best of my knowledge, correct.

Many international security experts agree that China is the biggest threat to world peace and stability.

The details about the outcome of a war between the USA and China are, to the best of my knowledge, correct.

Is China sending prisoners to work overseas? It certainly seems to be the case.

Unit 61398 is real. They're a division of the People's Liberation Army (PLA). In May 2014, Zoe Li of CNN wrote an article titled, "What we know about the Chinese army's alleged cyber spying unit," in which she exposes the activities of Unit 61398. A simple Google search for Unit 61398 will provide many more pages about this group of nefarious, state-sponsored hackers.

DAS SÜDWESTERLIED

Hart wie Kameldornholz ist unser Land.
Hard as the wood of the camel thorn tree is our land.
Und trocken sind seine Riviere.
And dry are its rivers.
Die Klippen, sie sind von der Sonne verbrannt.
The rocks are scorched by the sun.
Und scheu sind im Busch die Tiere.
And the animals are hiding in the bush.
Refrain:
Und sollte man uns fragen:
And if someone asked us:
Was hält euch denn hier fest?
What is keeping you here?
Wir könnten nur sagen:

We could only say:
Wir lieben Südwest!
We love Southwest!

Doch unsre Liebe ist teuer bezahlt.
But our love came at a high price.
Trotz allem, wir lassen dich nicht.
Despite all, we won't leave you.
Weil unsere Sorgen überstrahlt.
For our sorrows are outshined.
Der Sonne hell leuchtendes Licht.
By the sun's glary light.
Refrain:
Und sollte man uns fragen:
And should we be asked:
Was hält euch denn hier fest?
What is keeping you here?
Wir könnten nur sagen:
We could only say:
Wir lieben Südwest!
We love Southwest!

Und kommst du selber in unser Land.
And when you come to our country yourself.
Und hast seine Weiten gesehen.
And have seen its vastness.
Und hat unsre Sonne ins Herz dir gebrannt.
And our sun has burned into your heart.
Dann kannst du nicht wieder gehen.
Then you won't be able to leave.
Refrain:
Und sollte man dich fragen:
And should someone ask you:

Was hält dich denn hier fest?
What is keeping you here?
Du könntest nur sagen:
You could only say:
Ich liebe Südwest!
I love Southwest!

Next in the Rex Dalton K9 Thrillers Series

vinci-books.com/remorseless

**A secret hidden for over sixteen years is about to be
exposed...**

When Rex's college sweetheart reaches out to him after years of
no contact, Rex has no idea that the trajectory of his life is about
to change forever. She reveals she's dying and his daughter has
been abducted by a trafficking ring. Vowing to rescue his daughter
before time runs out, Rex and his team uncover a web of
corruption that reaches far beyond their darkest fears, ensnaring
powerful figures across the globe.

Turn the page for a free preview...

Remorseless: Prologue

There was more than one hell. In her short life, Abbie had been through several, and she was about to go through another.

"You knew what she'd planned. You didn't tell me," hissed the man she only knew as TJ.

Theirs was a world of fake names and a strict prohibition against sharing personal information. Notwithstanding, before Chrissy had escaped, she and Abbie had exchanged real names and personal information.

Abbie's real name was Eva Hansen. She was nineteen, born and bred in Orlando, Florida. She ran away from her abusive parents at age fifteen. Her parents never reported her as missing; Child Welfare did, weeks after she'd disappeared. That was it. That's what the entire United States law enforcement system knew about Eva Hansen.

Chrissy's real name was Elizabeth (Beth) Clayton. She was sixteen.

"I've put *you* in charge of them. Your job is to supervise and control them. Watch them. Maintain discipline among them. Prevent them from escaping. You were supposed to report to me that she'd left. You helped her get away."

Abbie was shaking her head violently. "I didn't. . ."

"Shut up, bitch! She was in your room less than an hour ago. She told you where she's going."

Abbie bit her nails and stared at the floor.

"You're not their mother. You're their supervisor. Supervisors don't fraternize with subordinates. I'm going to teach you to remember that. Where is she?"

"I don't know. She didn't tell me!"

TJ took two steps and struck her in the face. "Okay, in that case, I'll beat it out of you. And you'll never lie to me again."

At five-foot-nine and only a hundred- and thirty pounds, Abbie was on the verge of being underweight for her height. Her unkempt blonde hair was natural. Although she was still beautiful, four years in this hellhole as a sex slave, a bad diet, the physical abuse, smoking, alcohol, and drugs were ruining her looks rapidly.

Her broken nose was bleeding profusely when she got back to her feet. She was dwarfed by the thirty-something six-foot-two, obese, beer-bellied bully in a stinking black wife-beater vest.

"I don't know anything! I was with a client. When I came back, she was gone."

"You're lying!" A punch in the gut threw her to the floor in a sobbing heap, breathless.

"She was in your room." A vicious kick to her side cracked two ribs.

She was delirious from pain when he ripped her mini skirt and scanty underwear off. Removing his belt, he said to Johnny, one of his henchmen, "Get the other bitches in here. It's time for an obedience lesson."

Nude from the waist down, her body was shaking with fear, and tears were streaming down her face as she whimpered softly. She had been the subject of such a lesson once before. The scars and welts were permanent reminders. That time it was for being disrespectful to TJ in front of the girls. Abbie had witnessed such lessons many times. She knew begging wouldn't help. Even if she told him everything right now, it wouldn't stop the beating. He had a lesson for the teenage girls.

Besides, TJ found erotic pleasure in inflicting pain. The more pain, the more satisfying for him. As Abbie heard the whistling sound of the metal-studded leather belt traveling through the air, she was terrified of the pain she knew would come. But overriding the fear of the pain was the fervent belief that Chrissy had indeed escaped the abode of the condemned. Which meant the police were on their way already. She only had to hold out until they arrived.

She gave up the information five minutes later. Her escape from hell came a minute later when TJ kicked her in the side of the head, which mercifully rendered her unconscious.

The police never came. Chrissy was back in perdition less than two hours later and was killed two days after that.

Remorseless: Chapter One

JANE DOE

It was an old couple out on an early morning walk with their dog that made the discovery. The dawn, pre-breakfast stroll was a daily ritual, even when it was a cold, bleak morning like this. On their route was a dog park where their little Jack Russell Terrier could run free. He had his favorite copse of small trees on the bank of the creek running through the park where he performed his daily toilette. This morning, as always, when they got to the park and unleashed him, he headed straight to his 'bathroom.' Usually, as soon as he was finished, he would let them know with a few short happy yaps and set off exploring while they performed the poop scoop regimen.

By nature, Jack Russells are happy, energetic dogs. Playful and noisy. But this morning, instead of the usual cheerfulness, his yapping signaled distress. The old couple hastened their pace. When they arrived on the bank of the brook, they drew a collective sharp breath as they laid eyes on the source of the little dog's anxiety.

Completely naked, her bruised and battered body lay in

the motionless pose of death, half in and half out of the water.

The 911 call made by the old gentleman from his cell-phone was logged at 7:12 A.M. The nearest police patrol car was two miles away and arrived on the scene at 7:17 A.M.

Within minutes of their arrival, the two patrol officers called in the experts.

Forensics, Homicide, and the Medical Examiner were onsite thirty minutes later. By now, the entire area had been cordoned off with crime scene tape. It was a formality for the ME to declare the life of the young Caucasian female to be extinct. Lieutenant Benson Harris of the LAPD's 77th Street division and the forensics team quickly established that death had almost certainly occurred somewhere else and the body dumped in this location.

An ambulance transported the body to the state morgue, where an autopsy was performed to establish identification and the cause and time of death.

The old couple and occupants of nearby houses were questioned by the police, but no one had heard or seen anything suspicious.

Twenty-four hours later, Lieutenant Harris arrived at the morgue to get an update from the coroner.

"I found no jewelry, no tattoos, no distinguishing marks to help with identification. She's around sixteen, about two years past puberty," he told Harris.

Grab your copy...
vinci-books.com/remorseless

Acknowledgments

During my research, I consulted hundreds of websites, articles, books, and newspapers and spoke to numerous people, too many to list here. However, I will be remiss if I don't mention three of my old school friends, Kobus van Wyk, Abram Blaauw, and Leon Kotze, who had gone to the trouble of reading the manuscript and provided valuable feedback. The same goes for my beta readers, your feedback are extremely important and highly appreciated.

Special thanks to Abram Blaauw for coming up with the title for the book.

I wish to extend my deepest gratitude and love to my wife, Esta, and our children, Hester and Susan, for their loving assistance in writing this book. My debt to them is immeasurable, as is my love.

Last but not least, thank you to my good friend Mitch Pender, a military dog trainer, for giving me the idea for this series and guiding me through the intricate and amazing capabilities and psychology of those majestic four-legged soldiers.

Mitch has a lifetime of experience and an exceptional depth of knowledge as a military dog handler and trainer.

About the Author

JC Ryan is a bestselling author known for crafting intricate espionage and archaeological thrillers, and conspiracy mysteries. His work has received high acclaim. With over thirty published novels, including the popular K9 Thrillers, the Rossler Foundation Mysteries, and Carter Devereux Mystery Thrillers, Ryan has developed a devoted following who celebrate his masterful blend of historical mysteries and contemporary adventure.

Readers praise Ryan's work for its exceptional research depth and how he skillfully weaves actual history into fictional narratives. His engaging plots, featuring multiple storylines, have earned him a reputation for creating "unputdownable" stories.

Ryan's diverse life experiences deeply inform his writing. After receiving a military degree, he served as an officer for seven years until a crippling back injury forced a career change. Undeterred, he returned to university to study law and ran his private practice for over fifteen years. His career path then led him to another country, where he worked as an IT project manager before finally pursuing his lifelong dream of becoming a writer in 2014.

When not writing, Ryan enjoys life with his college sweetheart, whom he's been married to since 1978. They are proud parents of two daughters and two sons-in-law and grandparents of two grandchildren.